MW01130196

# DEATH
## at 21 Brix

Best wishes—
Kathy Kaye

# DEATH

## at 21 Brix

### A Warehouse Winery Mystery

Kathy Kaye

Copyright © 2019 Kathy Kaye

ISBN: 978-1-07-340712-5

All rights reserved. No part of this book may be reproduced, stored, or transmitted by any means—whether auditory, graphic, mechanical, or electronic—without written permission of both publisher and author, except in the case of brief excerpts used in critical articles and reviews. Unauthorized reproduction of any part of this work is illegal and is punishable by law.

Because of the dynamic nature of the Internet, any web addresses or links contained in this book may have changed since publication and may no longer be valid. The views expressed in this work are solely those of the author and do not necessarily reflect the views of the publisher, and the publisher hereby disclaims any responsibility for them.

*Once again to Nancy Mohrman, and to friends and family—*
*wine drinkers all—who shared their enthusiasm and support.*

# Who's who in the story

## Woodinville Police Department

**Kally O'Keefe**: protagonist; cop by day, winemaker by night

**Police Chief Dale Foster**: Kally's boss

**Robert Riggs**: major crimes detective

**Rose "Bud" Milano**: policewoman and Kally's friend

**Arturio Rodriguez "A-Rod"**: policeman and Bud's fiancé

**Jon Nakamura**: King County (Seattle) medical examiner

## Woodinville wine people

**Kirk Remick**: dead winemaker

**Kendall Mahoney**: tasting-room assistant at Remick Cellars and Kirk's last paramour

**Mark Manning**: assistant winemaker for Remick Cellars

**Justine**: assistant to Kirk and Mark at Remick Cellars

**Denny Lane**: former assistant winemaker at Remick Cellars and Janie Remick's sometime paramour

**Seth and Leah**: part-time assistants at Kally's Wine Babe Cellars

**Jason**: intern at Remick Cellars, now at Wine Babe Cellars

**Paul Storey**: winemaker next door to Kirk Remick's winery. Sells "PS" wines

**Mindy Peters**: *Wine Hound* blogger in Woodinville

## *Kally's friends and family*

**Chris Winthrop**: millionaire, ex-Microsoft employee, owner of Vino Tours of Woodinville

**Sam Cutler**: attorney for Kally and Chris

**Janie Remick**: Kirk Remick's recent ex-wife

**Sarah "Somm" Parker**: sommelier at high-end Seattle restaurant

**Ellie Fishback**: ex-Seattle Seahawks cheerleader and tasting-room manager for Red Mountain Productions

**Zack Morris**: Kally's on-again, off-again love interest

**Phil O'Keefe**: Kally's brother, guitar player

**Becky "Becks" O'Keefe**: Kally's former sister-in-law

**Maureen O'Keefe**: Kally's mother

**Guillaume Tablet**: winemaker in southern France

## *People at Kirk Remick's wine event*

**Joshua Arnaugh**: Microsoft employee

**James Monroe**: Microsoft employee

**Jeffrey Banks "Surfer"**: Microsoft employee

**Samuel Lee**: Microsoft employee

**Noel Jacobsen**: Bellevue attorney

## *Tiger Creek recording studio*

**Travis Mason**: co-owner, former band-mate of Kally's brother, Phil

*Woodinville, Washington*
*Saturday*
*6:14 a.m.*

T he sound came out of the fog, a warning of sorts, with short, irritating *beeps* that were insistent and loud. And it was close. Very close.

She was on a boat. But where? And with whom?

Wait a minute.

*Why am I on a boat?*

Kally O'Keefe opened her eyes. She recognized a lamp only a foot away. And there was a clock there, too. She realized she was in her bedroom. And...

*Oh my God! It's my phone!*

Kally bolted upright and sat on the edge of the bed, the move repositioning Zack, her on-again, off-again...friend...sleeping next to her. She put her hand up to stop the pounding in her head as the previous evening came into focus.

She grabbed her phone. "This is Kally!"

"Wake up, Winestein!" It was her boss, Dale Foster, chief of the Woodinville Police Department. "Get over here! Immediately!"

"Why?" Kally barely voiced the word.

"A winemaker, Kirk Remick—you know him?—was found dead this morning in his winery."

"*What?*" She stood up quickly. Bad move. She crouched down, thinking it would ease the pain in her head.

"What did you say?" Kally asked him.

"Remick's helper—"

"Probably his assistant winemaker," Kally corrected him, standing upright again. She felt cold. She was naked.

"Whatever," Dale continued. "He went in this morning and found him. I need you here. "Nakamura"—the King County medical examiner—"is on his way. Meet me in front of the winery."

*Click.*

Kally stood there, stunned, the news—and the headache—more than she could comprehend. She grabbed a tee shirt and sweat pants, bumping into things as she maneuvered around obstacles in her small bedroom and tiptoed out of the room. She closed the door behind her and got dressed.

Walking into the kitchen, she poured herself a much needed glass of water. And made coffee for Zack. Kally took the glass to a chair in her living room and sat down. With her thumb and forefinger she put pressure on her forehead where the sledgehammer was hitting the hardest, and thought about Kirk.

He was a friend, and the pre-eminent "cult" winemaker in all of Woodinville, the town outside of Seattle known for its burgeoning wine scene, especially in what was referred to as the Warehouse District or "the hood." It was where winemakers young and old fashioned their trade.

Including herself, in her own winery, Wine Babe Cellars, her part-time gig.

Kirk Remick's winery was only two doors from her own. She and Zack had been at his harvest party the night before where Kirk poured generous portions of his highly prized wine. Thus the headache.

*This death will take a long time to settle in.*

Kally got up, put the glass on the kitchen counter and returned to her bedroom, slowly opening the door. She went to a dresser and pulled out underwear. Then she went to her closet, the door squeaking as it opened.

Zack stirred in bed. "Hey."

"Hey back," she whispered.

"What're you doing?" he said, turning over.

"I have to go," she said.

"Why?"

"That was Dale on the phone," she answered, louder now. "You are not going to believe who died."

"Who?"

"Kirk Remick."

"*What?*"

Kally quickly stripped off her sweats and tee shirt and put on underwear, her uniform and her belt, repositioning the holster and gun.

"That will be everyone's reaction." She moved to the bed and quickly kissed him.

"We were just there." Zack reached up to pull her close, but she pulled back.

"I know. There's coffee in the kitchen. I'll call you later."

"Okay." He sat up. "Well…what happened to him?"

"Don't know yet."

Kally grabbed her backpack containing notebooks, evidence bags, and more accoutrements for a crime scene. She glanced at her phone: 6:23 a.m. Then she touched the badge over her heart with two fingers, a gesture she did every morning in honor of her father, also a cop, who had died too young.

She took her car keys, gave Zack a quick kiss on the top of his head, and was gone.

# 2

Two television trucks turned left in front of her onto the road that led to the Warehouse District. Kally followed, driving slowly, as men, women, and dogs crossed in front of them. People lined both sides of the street as if waiting for a parade.

*At this time of the morning?*

A death in Woodinville is a big deal. And Kirk was well known.

Their procession stopped and Kally leaned out the window. Seeing a bottleneck ahead, she turned right in front of the first grouping of one-story warehouses, then left onto another street, and then left again into the alley behind her winery. And Kirk's.

At one time these warehouses had been used for light industry and storage, their intended purposes. Today they were repurposed as wineries, distilleries, breweries. You could lose an afternoon imbibing here. And many did.

She passed an ambulance and two King County SUVs blocking Kirk's open garage door. The lights were on inside and people milled around in there, too.

Kally pulled in next to her own winery and got out, remembering Dale's directive to meet in front. She unlocked the back door to her winery, flipped on lights, and strode through the cramped space, passing stainless-steel tanks holding Riesling and Pinot Gris. She walked by her cold room filled with barrels of red wine, then down the hallway to her tasting room. She unlocked the front door.

And stepped outside into a sea of people, cars, reporters...

Helicopters paused overhead, the noise deafening.

"There you are!" Dale came forward and grabbed her arm. "Come on!"

With much difficulty, he got her to the front of Kirk Remick Cellars where Arturio Rodriquez, the police department's own "A-Rod," managed the crowd. Yellow crime-scene tape squared off the front entrance. A-Rod got them inside and placed his hand on the glass door in a good-bye gesture.

Dale and Kally stood there in Kirk's tasting room, which was oddly quiet. And dark.

*How strange to be here with my boss.* Dale hadn't bothered to put on a uniform, and he needed a shave. He looked tired.

"Bud is coming," Dale said. Rose "Bud" Milano was the only other female cop on their small police force. "Nakamura is in back with the body."

He paused. "You knew him, obviously, the deceased."

The news of Kirk's death still hadn't sunk in, as a friend's death registers. "Yes. I knew him."

"From what I saw, this looks like an industrial accident," Dale said.

She didn't know that yet but found it hard to believe. Kirk didn't make mistakes in winemaking.

"I'm putting you in charge," he proclaimed. "You know this…this world that's so foreign to the rest of us."

"But—"

Dale put his hand up. "Don't worry. He'll cooperate," he explained, referring to Robert Riggs, the major crimes detective still on vacation. "He'll work with you."

She wasn't sure about that either. She felt her headache coming back.

"Go see Nakamura. Then come see me at the office."

With that, he turned and left.

Kally stood alone in the tasting room. Or so she thought. A figure came toward her, away from the wall. Her heartbeat ratcheted up. It was Justine, one of Kirk's assistants.

*How did I not see her?*

Kally put her hand to her chest. "You scared me! I didn't see you."

Justine didn't say anything. Kally thought she might be in shock. They had been classmates together at Seattle's Northwest Wine Academy. But this morning, Kally barely recognized her.

Justine came closer and burst into tears, and hugged her.

"I wish I hadn't..." she cried, barely getting the words out. "I can't..."

Then she hurried away, leaving Kally standing alone. Slowly, she moved through the tasting room and into the hallway that led to the production area in back, this area also barely lit. Nonetheless, she knew the frames on the walls held awards, pictures of celebrities with Kirk, and vineyard shots with rows clearly marked for Remick wines.

Kally walked on, her shoes clicking on the waxed floor. She heard muffled voices out of sight.

Did anyone have as many 95-point wines as Kirk? It would be difficult to come up with someone. Thoughts about him jumped around in her head, mixed in with a range of emotions. She was having a hard time concentrating on the task at hand.

The voices got louder. She stopped at the entry to the large garage-like setting where Kirk's wines were made. It was bathed in bright light. Beyond, outside, were the ambulance and the two SUVs she'd seen on her drive down the alley.

She walked on. Several half-ton, thigh-high white bins sat in the middle of the floor, used for both harvesting grapes and fermenting red varieties, each covered with a cloth sheet.

First impression: *He's still fermenting his reds.*

Second thought: *I just used present tense.*

Kally looked to her left, at a wall of barrels that had been taken out of his cold room for the "party effect" the previous night. The voices were coming from the other side of the barrels. She walked forward and turned the corner around them.

And then she saw him.

"Here she is!" Nakamura yelled, walking over to her. She'd met Jon Nakamura exactly once, and not that long ago, during a routine meet-and-greet in her initiation week.

Kally didn't answer. Instead she stared at Kirk, who was splayed over one of his large white bins, face down in the must, his legs thrust out behind him—

—*Dragged there?*—

One shoe was partially off. One hand was clenched in a fist.

He had on the same clothes he'd worn the night before: blue jeans and a blue striped shirt, fashionably untucked. Two CSI technicians moved around the bin taking photos. Mark Manning, Kirk's assistant winemaker, stood to the side leaning against a pole, arms crossed, staring at the floor, not acknowledging her.

*He looks positively distraught.*

Kally turned to Nakamura who now stood before her.

"We waited to move the body. But now that you're here…"

"Right." Kally gritted her teeth.

"Come over here," Nakamura added, walking with her to the bin. Nakamura signaled to his associates. "Let's move him to the floor."

Two men reached over and gently pulled Kirk's body off the bin and lay him on his back on a plastic sheet.

Manning remained where he was, motionless.

Kally could see that rigor mortis had begun. Kirk's arms and legs remained in the same position and both hands had formed fists. His eyes were open in a lifeless death stare. Grape skins hung on his dark curly hair. But even more startling was the purple tinge to the whites of his eyes, along with the portions of his face and hands exposed to the grape skins.

"This is not pretty," Kally said.

"It never is," Nakamura replied calmly.

Kally stepped gingerly around Kirk's body without looking at it and bent down to read the words written on blue painter's tape stuck to the front of bin number four, the bin he had rested on. She studied the notes, not sure they would tell her anything.

But she was the only one in the room aside from Manning who understood them: *Klipsun cab sauv*; *H* 10/20; *C/D* 10/20; *S* 10/20; and *P* 10/21.

It was winemaker shorthand for harvested, crushed/destemmed, saigneed—French for "bleeding off" some of the juice to make the rest of the lot concentrated and the bled-off juice rose—and pitched-in yeast. In this hot year, these late-ripening grapes had come in early. The yeast had been added only yesterday, which would explain why the must, the cap of floating grape skins, was still relatively hard. And why Kirk was resting on the cap and not in it.

"We've done everything we need to do here," Nakamura said. "The body will go downtown…"

—to the King County Medical Examiner's Office, she knew—

"…unless you have reason for holding off."

Kally noticed that the two crime-scene techs with cameras had moved to the other side of the room near Kirk's stainless-steel tanks.

"Before you go," Kally said, transitioning into police mode, "will you take a sample and have the crime lab do a panel on the juice?"

"What are you looking for?" Nakamura asked.

"Anything unrelated to grapes."

"Okay."

"And I want one of the techs to root around in the must." She pointed to the floating cap of grape skins. "To see if an object is in there."

"All right."

Nakamura called over another member of the CSI team and repeated her instructions. Over his shoulder, Kally saw Bud enter through the big garage door.

"Come with me," she said to the CSI employee. "There is something you can use."

Kally walked into Kirk's kitchen to get the punch-down tool, a stainless-steel implement with a disk on one end and a long handle on the other. Every winemaker used one. The disk had large holes in it to make it easier to push down the grape skins—done twice daily during fermentation—so that they stayed in contact with the juice.

She moved back to the bin and waited as one of the CSI people took the juice sample and another worked the punch-down tool through the thick must, not an easy task.

"Hi," Bud said, coming up to her.

"Hi."

"Tell me what to do."

"I will."

Kally addressed Nakamura again. "I was here last night. Kirk—the deceased—had a party."

"Oh?"

"But I left around eight thirty p.m. All the bins you see here... they weren't out during the party. They were in the cold room"—she pointed to her left—"and the barrels normally in there were placed around the room."

"And why is that?" Nakamura asked.

"For the winery 'look.' And so that nothing falls into the bins, like keys or drunk people. But the bins would have been brought out at the end of the night and the barrels put back in. If this helps at all."

"Not sure," Nakamura answered.

"I'm seeing that that job was only partially done since the barrels are still out," Kally added.

Nakamura nodded. "I'm estimating time of death at around twelve thirty a.m. based on rigor and lividity."

Kally knew that lividity was the internal pooling of blood at death that stains the skin and looks like bruising, since her cop classes weren't that long ago. But she wondered about bruising from lividity and staining from grape juice. Surely Nakamura would know the difference.

"I'll know more once I do the autopsy." Nakamura watched the CSI team again then said to her, "If there's nothing else, I'm going back to my office. The Woodinville office."

"Okay."

# 4

Kally led Bud to the other side of the room where the CSI techs had been snooping around Kirk's tanks. They stopped in front of a three-tiered cart that held winemaking items, with the most-used on top: gaskets; clamps; valves; fasteners; a long, glass wine thief to obtain wine from barrels.

"Look around here and behind the tanks and tell me if you find anything," Kally said.

"Okay. Anything in particular?" Bud asked.

"Nope. Just let me know if you see something." She wasn't sure why Dale had asked Bud to help her, since she could do this herself and Bud was busy with her own work. Probably because Riggs was out of town, difficult Riggs who would lead the investigation and infuriate everyone within two feet of himself. Plus, Bud had her wedding to plan. To A-Rod.

Kally touched Bud lightly on the arm. "I appreciate your help. But I could have done this myself."

"Dale is just following procedure," Bud answered. "Better me than Riggs, right?"

"No kidding. Come see me when you're done."

Kally walked back to the bin and approached Kirk's assistant winemaker Manning. She needed to console him somehow. But she also needed information from him. He had worked with Kirk for years, as a volunteer, as a part-time employee, and now as a full-time assistant winemaker.

This close to him now, he looked thinner than she remembered, like a rail. And he was tall, which exaggerated his thinness. Most winemakers gained weight during harvest with all the junk food and beer consumed.

But Manning looked like he'd dropped weight. She wondered if there was a reason why.

She looked up at him. "Hi, Mark."

He didn't answer or make eye contact. She noticed that the cotton sheet that covered bin four—to protect the grape must from fruit flies—was thrown in a heap on the floor.

"You've probably gone through this already, but can you tell me what you saw when you came in this morning?"

He nodded, finally looking at her. "I came in for the morning punch downs," he began in a monotone. He glanced at the CSI tech moving the punch-down tool in the must.

"How did you enter?" Kally asked.

"Through the back door."

"Was it open?"

"Yes. I thought I would be the first person here." He glanced at Kirk, who was being put in an extra-large body bag to account for rigor.

"Go on," she prodded, hearing the bag being zipped.

"I opened the garage door and went back outside to wait, you know, for the $CO_2$ to dissipate."

She nodded. Venting a room of $CO_2$ gas, a by-product of fermentation, was done for safety.

He continued: "I stood around, looked at my phone, checked e-mail, then after ten minutes I came back in."

"What did you do when you re-entered?"

"I turned on the lights and...then...I saw him. He was bent over the bin, just like you saw him."

"Hmm." She looked over at the white bin again.

"I don't think he went home," he added. "Those are his same clothes..."

"I know," Kally concurred. She had more questions, too many to organize coherently, so she just jumped in.

"What time did you come in this morning?"

"About six a.m.," Manning answered.

"What time did you leave last night?"

"Around twelve thirty a.m., I think." He shook his head. "Not sure."

"Was Kirk still here when you left?"

"Yes."

"Was anyone else here?"

"The interns."

"When did they leave?"

"Same time I did."

"What were they doing?"

"Cleaning up. Moving the bins out of the cold room."

"Speaking of bins, why is this sheet on the floor?" Kally asked.

Manning looked at it, then turned back to her. He shrugged. "I don't know. Maybe he was taking a sample."

"Don't you normally do that?" she asked.

"Yes."

An awkward silence enveloped them. Kally moved on.

"Was Kirk waiting for someone? Was he going to meet someone later?"

Manning shook his head. "I don't think so. But I don't know. You know...he was seeing someone new."

She nodded. "Why do you think he was still here?"

Manning dropped his arms then stuffed his hands in his pockets, thinking. "He was going over the logs for the fermenting wines. Sometimes he would stay late and get the next day's work organized... leave notes for the staff."

Manning stopped, then continued. "I said good-bye to him and said I'd be back around six a.m. He looked over at me, smiled, and said, 'See ya.' That was it."

Kally hesitated, searching for the right words. "Other than finding him, was there anything else you noticed this morning?"

He thought for a moment, then shook his head.

"Who has keys to the winery?" she asked.

Manning took his time answering. "There must be...ten or twelve of us."

"I'll need to talk to everyone."

He nodded. "Some people didn't return keys when they stopped working here."

"Like who?" she asked.

"Like Denny," Manning answered. Denny Lane, the former assistant winemaker, was ensconced at a hangar at Walla Walla Regional Airport. The airport, a former military base, was an incubator of sorts for beginning winemakers.

She made a mental note of what Manning had said, hesitating before asking the next question. "Do you know anyone who had a grudge against Kirk?"

For the first time, he smiled. "Yeah. Everyone!"

She smiled, too. "I know." Success was not something Kirk chased. Everything, seemingly, went his way: handsome as a model, 90-plus wine rankings, all the women he could handle…

—Actually that last point was a sore spot with Kally, since his ex-wife was a friend.

"This has been a huge shock. Is there someone you can be with?" she asked.

"Yeah, my brother."

"Do you want me to call him?"

"No. I'll go to his apartment."

The CSI team member who had worked the punch-down tool through the must approached them. Kally saw that he'd left the tool sticking straight up in the bin.

"I didn't find anything," he said to her. "We're gonna take off."

"Okay." She glanced again at the tool. "In the kitchen is a big plastic bowl," she said, to the tech. "Would you put the bottom of that tool"—she pointed at it—" in the bowl and take it back to the kitchen and put it in the sink? That way you're not dripping juice on the floor."

"All right," he said, and left.

Kally turned back to Manning who was watching another CSI tech place yellow crime-scene tape across the top of bin four while others lifted the body bag onto a gurney.

He turned to her. "How am I going to do a punch down on that bin?"

She glanced at it. *Could the juice even be used now, given everything?*

"You won't be able to. Just leave it for now."

"Okay."

"I'll need to talk to you again later," she said. "Will that be okay?"
He nodded.

"Before you go, can you get me a few things?"

"Sure."

"Those logs Kirk was looking at. I'll need copies."

"All right."

"And I'll need your wine club list, your sales receipts from last night, and the employee list. And a set of keys."

"Okay."

"What else needs to be done here today?" she asked.

"All the punch downs."

"Don't ask Justine to do them,"Kally said. "She's...um..."

"I know. I'll do them, later," Manning offered.

Two CSI techs rolled the gurney with the body bag past them and out the large garage door and into the ambulance. She and Manning stood there watching, not saying anything.

*You are leaving your winery for the last time, Kirk.*

The finality of it hit her hard as the men closed the ambulance doors, got in, and drove away.

She turned back to Manning. "Let's go to the office and get those things."

Kirk's office was off the main floor of his production area. Since his winery was bigger than hers, he had an actual office, not a closet like her own. Assistant winemaker Manning sat at Kirk's desk and worked on his computer while Kally stood in the doorway.

Kirk had made the place comfortable, not that winemakers spent much time in an office. Posters for Seattle rock bands hung on the walls—and were signed, she could see.

Picture frames lined the desktop, although she only saw the backs of them. A leather jacket was thrown over a chair in the corner. She saw keys, a coffee mug, a half-eaten candy bar, a wallet, and unopened mail on the desk. On a credenza behind the chair were folders and stacks of papers.

*A life in full swing.*

The office didn't need to be gone over in detail right now. She'd be back soon enough. But she would have to go to his condo. She stepped forward and took the keys off the desk. And his wallet. She opened it to ensure it was Kirk's and saw his driver's license.

She scanned the desk top again, looking for something. "Where is Kirk's phone?"

The copier started. Manning turned to look at her, hesitating. "I don't know. Maybe in his pocket?"

"Right." She made a mental note to ask Nakamura.

"I found something," Bud said, coming up behind her. "But I don't know what it is."

"Okay, I'll be there in a minute."

"And I checked outside. Didn't see anything."

"Great, thanks."

"I'll stand by the back door," Bud said, moving away. "Make sure no one enters."

"Good." Kally reached into her backpack for an evidence bag and dropped the wallet in. She turned back to Manning.

"What is the name of the woman Kirk was with last night?"

"Kendall. She works in the tasting room."

"Do you have her last name?"

Manning stopped, stumped.

"Never mind," Kally said.

"It'll be on the employee list," he said. "Give me your e-mail address."

Kally complied, taking in the office one more time.

"I just sent you the wine club list and the employee list," Manning said. "I've copied the wine logs. And here are the sales receipts." He handed them to her. The receipts were haphazardly paper-clipped together, the top slip upside down.

Manning rose and went to another office to get the copies, then returned and gave them to her.

"Thanks," she said. "Why don't you take a break…go home…see your brother…get some coffee"—*and consume a 4,000 calorie breakfast* is what she wanted to say—"and come back later. This has been a shock of a morning."

He seemed to think about that. "Yeah, I guess I will."

"I'm going to lock the door here," Kally said. "No one will be able to enter."

Manning nodded that he understood and then left, barely saying good-bye.

Kally put the pages under her arm and locked the office door behind her. Then she went to the front of the winery to ensure that that door was locked. A crowd hung around outside, but there were fewer people than earlier. A-Rod was still there, too. But Justine was nowhere to be seen.

She went back into the production area to see what Bud had found.

# 6

Bud stood outside, her back to the winery, hands resting on her belt. She looked left and right down the empty alley. After the morning's activity, the place was quiet, even with the large garage door open.

Kally took in the vastness of the wine production area, the hum of the HVAC system the only sound. She eyed Kirk's kitchen in the corner and thought about making coffee. But refrained.

Instead, she walked over to bin four. She looked past the yellow crime-scene tape to the cap of floating grape skins, now glistening under the fluorescent light. She thought the fermenting juice could still be used if it were sterile filtered. But many high-end winemakers didn't fine or filter, thinking those processes stripped too much from the wine's character.

And Kirk was one of them.

Knowing him as she did, he would have enjoyed this macabre moment, using wine a dead body had lain on. He would have named it after a song with the word "death" in it, slapped on a dark label, and sold it at a high price, perhaps naming it a reserve.

She turned away, Kirk's product the least of her worries. Instead, she walked around, looking at the floor for clues—for anything. She passed several tall tables that people had stood around during the party. There was nothing on the tables, nor under them. She wondered what Bud had seen.

Bud turned and Kally signaled her inside. "So what did you find?"

"Over here."

Kally followed and Bud crouched down near the three-tiered cart, then pointed under it. "There."

Kally crouched next to her and saw them immediately: three rubber gaskets. How had the CSI team missed them? Well...they were hard to see, gray on gray concrete.

"What are they?" Bud asked.

Kally took out her phone and took pictures of them. "They're used with valves and clamps that attach to tanks."

Kally reached up and took a clamp off the top shelf. "This is a clamp."

"Oh. Looks like half a handcuff," Bud replied.

Kally stared at it a moment. "I never thought of it that way!" She put the clamp back and looked further under the cart and spotted one more gasket. And took another picture.

*Was this where he had been standing? Had Kirk's hand brushed them somehow?*

Most winemakers were fastidious about cleanliness, wine being a food product and all. Leaving gaskets on the floor was a big no-no, contaminated as they now were.

"You knew him," Bud said, still crouched down.

"Yeah. It hasn't sunk in yet."

"It will be hard, then, this investigation," Bud added.

Kally didn't know that yet or what the next few weeks would hold. She hadn't thought beyond what she was presently doing.

She nodded at Bud, and without saying anything reached for evidence bags in her backpack. She put on sterile gloves and took out long tweezers, and picked up the gaskets one at a time, placing each in a separate bag. Then she assigned numbers to them and wrote corresponding numbers on the outside of each bag.

It was a long shot, but maybe there was DNA or fingerprints on one of them.

They stood up. "Anything else in here?"

"Not that I saw," Bud answered.

They walked into the alley.

"It's like a forest out here," Bud said, looking up at the empty stacks of white bins, which dwarfed them on both sides.

"Yep."

"Do you have these in your winery?"

"I do. They're full at the moment, inside."

They stood together where the ambulance had been. Kally looked to her right and saw her SUV and her back door. To her left was Paul Storey's winery, PS Wines, next to Kirk's.

"Anything out here?" Kally asked, walking around the bins and the back side of the building.

"Nope," Bud answered, following behind her. "Not a gum wrapper...cigarette butt...piece of paper...

Kally saw Kirk's trash can by the garage door. She walked up to it, took the lid off, and peered inside.

"Did you see anything in here?"

"No."

Kally rattled the can and heard something.

"Oh," Bud exclaimed.

Kally put on gloves again and reached in. She pulled out a lone beer bottle and put it in another evidence bag.

"Good job," Bud said, nodding her approval.

Then they stood there, not saying anything. Kally looked back through the garage door, taking in Kirk's quiet production area.

*This is going to take a while.*

K ally closed and locked the back door to the winery, then walked the short distance to her SUV. Dale would ask if they'd gone to the deceased's home and looked around. So that's where they were headed, Bud in her own vehicle.

As she exited the Warehouse District, Kally saw people still milling around, including three winemakers talking in a group. They had been at Kirk's party the night before and she would need to talk to them eventually. No doubt they would head back to work this morning, Kirk's death notwithstanding, this being crush and all when winemakers worked around the clock processing grapes.

*Right where I would be if not for this.*

She realized she needed to depend even more on Seth and Leah, her part-time winery employees, while she worked this case.

Kally drove onto the main road for the short trip to Kirk's condo, which gave her time to think about the man she still couldn't believe was gone. Most people in the Seattle region knew Kirk because he was a regular on the local weekly television show *Wine Star Northwest*. He was a natural in front of the camera, and he was generous with his knowledge, especially to new winemakers. He had mentored her, one of the few women in the industry, and others who followed.

Kirk had married Janie, his ex-wife, when she became pregnant with Emma, now five years old. So the marriage lasted five years, the divorce finalized just a few months ago. But Janie was not someone Kally thought Kirk would ever be with. Janie was close to his age, tended to be on the serious side, and was a brunette. Kirk gravitated toward younger blondes who adored him and got free wine.

She knew all this because she'd seen it unfold. Many times.

Kally pulled up behind Bud in Kirk's driveway. She hesitated before getting out, admitting to herself that she wasn't the best person to be handling the case, regardless of what Dale thought. She was too close to it because of her friendship with Kirk. But in order to get her work done, she would have to stop thinking of him as a living being and think of him instead in the worse possible terms: as a dead body.

A *suspiciously* dead body, in her opinion.

Kally grabbed her backpack and walked with Bud to the front door. She took out latex gloves and gave Bud a pair. Then she tried a few keys. Finally finding the one, she opened the door and they walked in.

"Hello?" Kally called out. Eerily quiet. There was something ominous about being in a dead person's space, but better during the day than at night, which creeped her out. For the first time, she was glad Bud was with her.

"Would anyone else be here?" Bud asked.

"That I don't know."

They walked up a few stairs to a landing. To the left was a living room and dining room, and a kitchen out of sight, she presumed, having not been here before. To the right was a hallway leading to what she thought were the bedrooms.

"Looks like he just moved in," Bud said, taking in the sparse furniture and framed pictures leaning against the wall.

Kally agreed and shifted her backpack to her other shoulder. A couch and one chair sat in the living room. A table with a lamp was situated by the couch. No coffee table. Cases of wine in white boxes, with Kirk's label on the front of each, were stacked against another wall. The dining room had no table, nor any chairs.

They walked through this area and into the kitchen. A coffee pot was there with coffee still in it, probably made the day before. Kally opened the refrigerator. There was a quart of whole milk on the right side of the top shelf. She looked at the expiration date: a week away. A line-up of different beers sat on the left, along with an unopened bottle of his own Chardonnay. Condiments filled shelves in the door. Other than a few take-out containers and a bag of apples in the crisper, that was it.

Bud opened cabinets above the oven where there were some canned goods. Mostly the shelves were empty. Kally looked in the sink. There were dirty dishes and utensils. She looked under the sink. There was dish soap and one box of large plastic garbage bags.

They moved on, saying nothing, the drill routine, to the bathroom. Bud remained in the hallway while Kally walked in and opened the medicine cabinet. Shaving equipment, a box of condoms, toothpaste, and a few empty pill containers sat inside. She picked up the pill containers, reading dates from six months ago. Prescriptions for antibiotics. She noted the physician's name at Kaiser Permanente, then took out a plastic bag and dropped the pill containers in.

*Nothing feminine here. Maybe he stayed with women at their places.*

"See something?" Bud asked.

"Not really."

They walked on, to the bedroom. A large queen-size bed, unmade, dominated the space. Underwear and tee shirts sat in a pile in a corner. A pair of jeans, discarded, the belt still in the belt loops, lay next to the pile. Kally picked the pants up gingerly and felt the pockets. No phone, only loose change. She let them fall back to the floor.

Bud walked around the perimeter of the room examining the floor and then looked under the bed. Kally stood next to a table by the side of the bed. A lamp, a glass of water, and wrappers from throat lozenges sat on it. She moved to a dresser and went through the drawers. She saw tee shirts, folded, and a few gold chains. And a pile of letters from his mother, she presumed, seeing the name: Barbara Remick, Chicago, IL. She took these out and flipped through them, focusing on the return address: Chicago, Chicago, Chicago.

Kally reached for another evidence bag and put them in.

She opened the closet door. Nothing of interest. A few long-sleeved striped shirts. And jeans. And a pair of dress pants and a black blazer. Not much clothing, really.

Kally looked down. Shoes lined the floor. But not many. A large duffle bag sat on a shelf above. She reached for it and brought it down onto the floor. And opened it.

Empty. She put it back.

"Nothing here," Bud said.

"Right."

They walked out of this room and into another bedroom.

Part of the problem in looking for something was not knowing what that something was. You're just looking for anything out of order, out of sync with the person you knew, if you knew the person, she remembered Dale telling her once. So far Kally had nothing.

The second bedroom held Kirk's makeshift office. Kally took in a desk, chair, laptop, and lamp. A large treadmill hugged one wall. More framed posters lined the floor of the room, not yet hung.

Bud went to a closet and opened the door, then moved around the room.

Kally thumbed through more envelopes on the desk, seeing bills, financial statements, and something from an attorney. Probably regarding the divorce.

*Had he made provisions for his winery and his 95-point library wines?*

Kally peered inside a coffee cup next to a laptop. A quarter full. *How much work did he do here and how much at the office?* She took the mail and added it to a new evidence bag.

Then she sat down in the chair and opened drawers.

She remembered something her late father had once said to her mother, and she had overheard it: There is always something you remember going through a person's personal effects or being the first person at a crime scene. Every cop has a story of what that is, the odd non sequitur that stays with them.

Except that there was nothing out of the ordinary here. The only thing that stayed with her were Kirk's closed fists.

Kally waved to Bud as she pulled out of Kirk's driveway and drove back to headquarters. She herself had someone else to see.

She took out her phone and made a most difficult call. It was answered on the second ring, but the person at the other end said nothing.

"Janie? It's Kally."

Still nothing.

"I'm coming to see you. Right now."

Kally heard a small voice answer. "Okay."

She retraced her earlier route, passing the turn for the warehouse wineries, and drove up a long, steep hill. After about a mile, she turned right into a neighborhood of one- and two-story homes and pulled into Janie Remick's driveway, her headache making its presence known again.

Steeling herself for the task, she exited the car and walked up the front steps.

Janie—eyes red, face puffy—opened the door. She motioned her in, then hugged Kally and began crying softly. Kally hugged her back. Over Janie's shoulder, she saw Kirk's daughter, Emma, sitting on the couch staring back at her.

Finally, Janie stood back. "I can't believe it."

"I know. How…did you find out?" Kally asked.

"Larry"—one of those three winemakers—"called to say he was sorry. I didn't know what he was talking about. It was awkward. He didn't realize I didn't know."

"Has anyone else been here or called?" Kally said, holding onto Janie's arm.

She shook her head. "But I knew I would hear from you."

Kally nodded.

"I have some coffee," Janie said.

*Magical words.*

Kally followed her to the kitchen and stood by as Janie got out two mugs and poured the coffee. She moved in slow motion, as would be expected.

Janie turned to her. "Anything in yours?"

Kally shook her head and reached for the mug, hoping that she had not appeared to be *grabbing* for it. Back in the living room, they settled in, Kally sitting next to Emma on the couch. She would have preferred talking to Janie without Emma there, but no one else was around to entertain her daughter. Regardless of who would be here or how many people stopped by to offer condolences, Kally had the distinct feeling that Janie and Emma were alone.

"Did you...see him?" Janie asked suddenly.

Kally glanced at Emma. "Yes." Then quickly: "The medical examiner is handling everything."

Janie nodded.

Kally cradled her coffee in her lap. "Can I ask you some questions?"

Janie nodded again.

"Did Kirk have any enemies that you know of?"

"You mean other than the people who were jealous of him?"

"Yes."

"I don't think so." Janie looked at her daughter. "He was likable. *Very* likable, as you know, with a certain set."

"Right." Kally's response was a cop-out that didn't tell Janie what she knew or didn't know about Kirk's transgressions. "Did he owe anyone money?"

Janie shook her head. "I doubt it." She looked straight at her. "He made a lot of money. He sold all the wine he made."

"I know," Kally concurred.

"And he paid alimony on time," Janie added.

"Was he depressed that you know of?" Kally asked.

Janie shook her head again. "He was talking about expanding...and this was something he had always talked about...buying property and planting a vineyard on Red Mountain."

Kally knew that to be true, following other winemakers who had become growers. But Red Mountain, in eastern Washington State, was small and practically impossible to get into, whether buying grapes from existing vineyards or buying land.

"Was it a robbery?" Janie blurted.

"I don't know."

"He had library wines. His 95-point ones were stored there," Janie added. Then: "When can I see him?"

Kally hesitated. The funeral home would have to do a miraculous job on the wine stains on his skin.

"I'm not sure. You'll be contacted." *How awkward.* "Do you want me to go with you?"

Kally glanced again at Emma. Her big blue eyes stared up at her.

"Yes, that would be wonderful if you would," Janie answered.

"Of course I will. Have you contacted his parents?" Kally asked.

"It's just his mother and sister. They're on their way."

"I'll have to talk to them at some point," Kally said.

"What did you notice when you went in there?" Janie asked. "Was there anything out of the ordinary?"

Kally thought for a moment, because these were questions she would be asking herself over the next several days. Of course, she wouldn't be telling Janie exactly what she had seen.

"I noticed that the place had been cleaned up from the harvest party last night."

"What about Mark?" Janie asked.

"Mark Manning? He was there. And distraught...very affected. He...um"—*remember Emma*—"found him."

Back in her SUV, Kally took in Janie standing in the doorway again.

*I must be her only friend right now.*

Uncomfortable as it felt, she waved and drove away.

The Woodinville Police Department was tucked away off a main road in the middle of Western Washington's "wine country." Housed within city hall, it was a small department with exactly one major crimes detective—Robert Riggs, the man presently on vacation. But the reason the police team was small wasn't because it needed to hire more people.

It was because *nothing happened* in their Woodinville community. If it weren't for traffic violations, high school pranks, lost pets—including horses—and the occasional domestic dispute, they'd all be out of a job.

Nothing but wine happened here.

Kally turned a corner and heard her phone. Thinking it surely must be her boss, Dale, she hit speaker.

"You're in the car at this hour, on a Saturday?"

It was not Dale. It was her friend and attorney, Samantha—aka Sam—Cutler, the one who kept her out of courtrooms. She decided not to mention Kirk's death.

"Work beckons, as always," Kally answered.

Sam hesitated. "You don't sound good."

"I'll tell you why later."

"Okay. I want to talk to you about a certain name you want to use for your wine, the one you asked me about last week," Sam started in.

"Right: 'M&M.'"

"You *cannot* use it," Sam admonished. "Have you heard of the Mars family?"

She felt Sam's deep-blue eyes boring into her through the phone. "This is wine, though."

"*No!*" her friend said. "You will be working as a cop for the rest of your life if that name appears on a label. Think of something else."

"I like that one," Kally answered. The name signified the two grapes she planned to use in a future blend: Mourvedre and Malbec, a slight deviation in her southern Rhône strategy using the Bordeaux variety Malbec.

"No one's doing it," Kally added.

"It doesn't matter. How about just a big 'M' on the label?" Sam suggested.

Kally was surprised at that. "I'll think about it, actually."

"Please do. You'll be at the party tonight?" Sam asked suddenly.

*Oh my God!* The party for Bud, a wedding shower of sorts with lots of wine, at friend Chris Winthrop's lakeside home.

But Bud hadn't mentioned it. And she hadn't thought of it.

"I forgot," Kally said.

"You, of all people, have to be there."

"I know."

Sam changed the subject. "Where are you right now?"

Kally relented and told her the news.

"Kirk? This is unbelievable!"

"It is, yes. I got the call this morning." Kally filled her in with as many details as she felt comfortable revealing.

"I won't keep you," Sam said after a time. "Actually, I have another call. I'll see you tonight."

"I'll be there."

Kally stopped at a red light. *How could I forget Bud's party?* It was a gathering to look forward to, engaging with friends in something other than police work, especially a death. The problem, though, was that everyone coming to the party worked in the wine industry, so talk of Kirk would surely dominate the discussion.

She stared into space, feeling tired. She glanced at the clock on her dash: 8:53 a.m. The day had barely begun. And not one thing could be pushed to tomorrow.

The light changed and she moved on, the unnatural image of Kirk bent over a wine bin coming back to her. She envisioned the work ahead of her, filling out the police report, going through the lists Manning had given her, meeting with Dale, and cornering Nakamura before he left for his Seattle office.

Then she thought about the work in her own winery and wondered if Seth and Leah had heard the news about Kirk.

She assumed that they had.

Kally turned right and pulled into the station's parking lot. She found a space and turned off her SUV. And sat there. The Woodinville wine industry had never had a winemaker death, not from a machinery accident, not from $CO_2$ poisoning, not from anything.

The person she had seen this morning was not Kirk. His image stayed with her because something was innately wrong with it.

Kally grabbed her backpack and the pages from Manning, and exited the car. Kirk's death would change the "top gun" status significantly among warehouse vintners. Someone who was just below the big three winemakers here—she didn't include herself among them yet—would most likely move up in wine press coverage.

And who would that person be? More importantly, was he a suspect?

# 10

Kally entered the building and headed directly to the cafeteria where she purchased two of the largest coffees sold. They were ridiculously large, in the thirty-two ounce range: the Big Gulp of the caffeine world.

Fortified, she continued on. Passing her boss's office, she backtracked and stopped in Dale's doorway. He looked up at her. He had shaved and gotten a haircut, a buzz cut, probably to tame his persnickety colic. Somehow he'd found the time this morning.

He mentioned the coffee. "I'm guessing one of those is not for me."

"Oh. Here." She passed him one.

"No, thanks. I don't need it. Did you contact next of kin?" he asked.

"Um...actually, I talked to his ex-wife...*recent* ex-wife. She's talked to her mother-in-law...*ex*-mother-in-law, that is..."

"Good."

"It wasn't easy."

"I'm sure it wasn't."

She felt uncomfortable standing there, the two coffees like beacons, the backpack weighing down her shoulder. She should have planned this brief meeting better. Sometimes she felt uneasy around Dale. He had worked with her father before his untimely death. She herself hadn't been in police work all that long, only a year, since returning from France.

Dale: "The warrants are on your desk."

They were the ones she needed to go through Kirk's things, at his winery and apartment. Which she'd already done, of course.

"Thanks."

Dale stared at the coffees again. "Get settled. And get me your report."

"I will. Is Nakamura still here?" she thought to ask.

"Yes."

She smiled and left.

Kally entered her office and put the pages and coffees down. She took everything out of the backpack, placed the bag on the floor, and turned on her computer.

*What a different day I had imagined for myself.*

She looked for Manning's email and opened one of the files. Then, thinking it would be easier to work with hard copies, she printed the wine club list and the employee roster, and retrieved them from the copier.

Kally now had four piles on her desk along with the fermentation logs and the sales receipts. *Is the killer's name in one of them?* She made the assumption that it was. She also realized she had assumed Kirk's death was not an accident.

Before looking at any of the lists, Kally turned to her computer and logged on, to Facebook. She found Kirk's photo and clicked on it, seeing hundreds of "friends."

"This will be impossible." Facebook's names and faces begat more names and faces. Kally reached for one of the coffees and removed the lid, feeling the steam warm her face. For now, she would narrow her focus to the harvest party attendees.

She picked up the first list, Kirk's wine club, an exclusive membership of one hundred and the people who had been invited to the party. She quickly read through the names on the top page, recognizing several. They were executives at area businesses: Microsoft, Starbucks, Boeing, Amazon, Costco. Many of these people had not been at the party, she was sure. But they could have passed their invitations on to family and friends.

She put the list down, not ready to give it her full attention and aware of her scattered thinking. Instead, she took out a pad of paper to begin writing questions. But the only question that came to mind was: Who has keys to the winery? Nonetheless, she wrote it down.

What did it mean that his hands were in fists? Was he angry? Was he in pain? Did he know the end was inevitable? Did he know the killer? And what about Manning? Was he involved? She realized that that thought was ridiculous.

Then she thought of something else:

Kirk's arm had rested on top of the fermenting cap of grape skins, his face buried within. He must have been pushed in, since fermentation had just begun and the floating cap of skins was hard. Yeast would eventually break down the skins making the whole lot pliable.

But that wasn't what she'd seen.

Was it remotely possible that Kirk had closed the large garage door the previous night, thinking that he was leaving, then got busy with something and stayed, while $CO_2$ filled the room?

She may never know the answer to that.

Kally stared into space. How would Riggs react to her being put on the case? He was difficult to work with and the first to complain if assigned more cases when any one of them was on vacation. And she and Bud had the distinct impression that Riggs didn't like women. Perhaps it was his third marriage ending in divorce that had brought them to that conclusion. Essentially, he would have been perfect in a big city police force, like the one he'd come from, where his personality would find a home among others of the same ilk.

She glanced at the clock, knowing she needed to see Nakamura. And she needed to work on the report for Dale. And she needed aspirin.

She reached for her backpack and stuck her hand inside and felt something. She pulled it out. It was the invitation for Kirk's harvest party. Kally recognized the watermark behind the words as one of his more edgy works of art: scantily clad warrior women with whips defending a wall of wine barrels from…what? At one release party, he'd actually had women dressed like that. She took one last look at the invitation and placed it in its own pile next to the others.

She groped around for the container of aspirin, finally finding it. Without looking she shook out three pills and swallowed them with coffee. Then she picked up Kirk's fermentation logs and searched for bin number four.

The last entry for the Brix reading—the sugar being consumed by yeast and converted to alcohol—was logged in at 17:50 military time along with the temperature. Off to the right were Manning's initials, since he had taken the reading just before the harvest party.

"Twenty-one Brix," she said. So fermentation really was just getting started and happening fast. As often happened with reds.

Glancing at the clock again, she picked up her pad of paper, the evidence bags containing the gaskets, the beer bottle, and the pill containers—and her coffee—and headed down the hallway to the medical examiner's office.

Nakamura was one of several county medical examiners, and the one the department liked best. Mostly that was because of his vast knowledge and his personage. He was approachable, unlike the others. Or so she'd heard. That was good news for her, since she'd never worked a case like this.

*He must have known my father.*

"There you are again," he said as she entered. "I'm glad I'll be working with you. I'll need your expertise about winemaking to help answer some questions."

"That's fine," she said, a bit flattered. "I have a few questions of my own."

"Like what?"

"I haven't found his phone," Kally began. "Will you look in his clothes, in what he had on?"

"Yes. Personal effects will be bagged."

She continued. "I think it's odd that his face was submerged somewhat. A cap of floating grape skins early in fermentation is hard."

"His head might have been pushed in," Nakamura responded.

"That's what I thought. But he couldn't have drowned."

"He could have suffocated," Nakamura offered.

Kally didn't answer. Then: "Right. Awful."

"I'll know more after the autopsy," Nakamura added. "Was he a gambler, do you know?"

Kally was shocked at that. And amused. *How does that go with winemaking?*

She shook her head. "I don't think so. Why?"

"Because the manner of death has all the makings of organized crime."

Nakamura was too refined to say "mob hit."

"This reminds me of my days in New Jersey," he continued. "The person who runs afoul of the mob is killed, but the manner of death is done with relish, with an exclamation mark. Like our friend Kirk. It sends a message to others who owe the mob money."

*Maybe he's got a point there.* But Janie hadn't indicated anything of the sort.

"Look closely at the subject of money," he said. "A gambler can spend it all."

"I will."

Nakamura picked up his briefcase, then looked at the evidence bags in her hand. "What do you have?"

"I found them at the winery," Kally answered, handing over the bags of gaskets. "I thought you might get something off of them."

"Okay, good," he said. "I'll give them to the crime lab."

She held up the bag holding the empty pill containers. "These I found at his home. In the medicine cabinet."

"You keep those," Nakamura said, reading the labels. Then he nodded back toward the hallway. "You're going to be more pleasant to work with than—"

"We'll have to see how that plays out," Kally interjected. "He hasn't been told yet." She felt oddly at ease with Nakamura, not that she knew him that well.

"You'll do fine." He put his briefcase down again and reached into a breast pocket, pulled out a business card and handed it to her.

"In case you need to contact me. Use the cell phone number."

But she had a question for him before he left. "Will you be able to answer why his hands were clenched in fists?"

Nakamura hesitated. "I hope so. They could point to the manner of death."

B ack at her desk, Kally stared at the four piles, the harvest party invitation and the questions on her pad of paper. Before the case began, she had planned on spending all day at her winery, getting caught up.

Then she thought about Zack and how quickly she had left him this morning. She reached for her phone to call him but sensed someone in her doorway. Looking up, she saw Bud again, Bud whose real name was Rose after her grandmother.

But Bud liked "Bud" better. It was more "cop-like." She had keys in her hand and looked ready to head out somewhere.

"Anything else I can do?"

"Not now," Kally answered. "I'm just starting to go through things."

Bud turned for a moment to answer a question from one of the support staff, and Kally took in her profile. The only time she didn't like her own blonde hair and blue eyes was when she looked at Bud. Part Italian, part Irish, Bud was absolutely beautiful, in an exotic Latin sort of way, odd as that sounded, given her heritage. Kally often wondered why she had chosen to be a cop when she easily could have been a model.

Bud looked back at Kally. "This may be a bad time to bring this up, but…you remember we have the party tonight?"

"I do!" She silently thanked her friend Sam for reminding her.

"Everyone will understand if Chris wants to cancel, being how you all are in the wine business," Bud added.

Kally shook her head. "Chris won't cancel."

"Well, just buy a dish," Bud said, turning to leave. "We have a lot going on today."

"I was planning on that."

"I'll see you later then."

"Okay! Bye!"

Back to work. She put off the phone call to Zack. Instead, she called her winery and listened as the phone rang for an inordinately long time.

*Something needs to be done about that.*

Finally, Seth answered. "Hullo?"

"Seth, it's Kally."

"Oh yeah, hi."

Kally heard loud music in the background, possibly Led Zeppelin. "I need you to answer the phone with the winery's name, Wine Babe Cellars."

"Okay. But it's Saturday."

"Doesn't matter." Kally moved on. "I'm at work. Have you heard about Kirk?"

"Yeah. Someone called Leah. Can't believe it."

"I know. I'm on the case..."

"You are?"

"Yes, so I'll be in later. What...what are you doing right now?"

"I'm racking the whites," Seth answered, referring to the process of moving white wine off its sediment and into a clean tank. Kally felt a wave of relief wash over her.

"That's fabulous. How many tanks so far?"

"Two."

"Okay. Good job."

"I'll top the barrels this afternoon," Seth added. 'Topping off' or adding wine to every barrel was a once-a-month process to keep the barrel full. Wine had a tendency to evaporate slightly and topping off ensured that oxygen, which could spoil the wine, remained far away.

"That will put us ahead." She had a vision of Seth artfully balanced on barrel racks, two stories up in her cold room, a pitcher of red wine in one hand, a cloth rag in the other. He was younger and more agile and handled this work with ease.

"When do you want to do blending trials on the whites?" Seth asked.

"Let's do it Monday night."

"Okay."

"Is Leah there?"

"Yes."

"Did the labels come in?"

"No."

"Put her on, will you?"

After a short time, Leah answered with a simple, "Hi."

Kally started in. "Where are the labels?"

"I don't know."

"Call the company, will you?"

"It's Saturday."

Kally checked her anger, not wanting a sleepless, headache-laden morning to infuse her voice.

"Call anyway." Kally glanced at her watch. "They're probably open. I'll stop by later."

"Okay. I heard about Kirk. Weren't you at the party?" Leah asked.

"I was. And, yes, it's a tragedy." She paused. "Please call the label people and I'll see you this afternoon."

"Okay."

Kally ended the call. She would prefer that her staff made decisions on its own and then followed through instead of waiting for her. She didn't know why Leah wouldn't do that. Afraid to make a mistake, maybe.

With her cell phone still in her hand, it rang. She looked at the name and audibly groaned, then answered.

"Hello, mother."

"And what are you doing on this beautiful day?"

Kally let out a short laugh. "I'm…working."

"That's too bad."

*Yes, it is.* "How are you, mom?"

"I'm fine. Your brother's fine, too."

Her mother knew Kally wouldn't ask about her brother, Phil, the mid-thirties divorcé living at home again. But the mention did remind her of her ex-sister-in-law, Becky, a forensic accountant, whom she liked and worked with on occasion. She wrote Becky's name on her pad of paper.

"That's nice, mom."

"How's Zack?"

"He's okay. Still working." *Unlike Phil.*

"I see. When are you coming to visit?"

Her mother lived in Kirkland, practically next door.

"I'm not sure. I've got a case I'm working and I've got to get to my winery."

"I thought you were going to let the winery go, after that lawsuit."

It was the topic her mother wouldn't let go. "No, that was never an option. It's work I enjoy."

"I wish you would just focus on your police work."

"I am. I'm…*here.*"

"We want you to come for dinner. Can you come tomorrow night?"

Kally looked at her calendar. Evenings were usually spent at the winery. But then she hadn't seen her mother or deadbeat Phil in almost a month. Guilt crept in, taking over.

"Yes. What time?"

"Six thirty?"

"Okay. I'll see you then."

She sat there, dwelling on her mother and then her father who had died leaving a widow with two teenagers. She needed to give her mother some slack.

Then she thought about Dale and the report he wanted before she left. She turned to her computer to begin reconstructing the events of the morning.

K ally pulled into her winery, her three neon signs—*Wine Babe Cellars! Full Berry! Fresh!*—distinctly dark. She thought back to the flack she had gotten from other winemakers when she put up those signs. But that's what her wine was: a full grape berry taste and fresh, meaning light on oak.

That's how Kirk made wine. That's what got him recognized.

She glanced at her watch: four p.m., a much later start than she had planned. She had to be at Chris's for the party at five p.m. and she still had to get to the store. Before going inside, she took out her phone and called Zack. He picked up on the first ring.

"Hey," he said. "Want to do dinner?"

"I can't, Zack. It's been a day already. And I've got Bud's party tonight."

"Oh yeah. I forgot. You sound tired."

"Do I?" She needed to perk up a bit before meeting her talky friends. "Sorry I didn't call you earlier."

"It's okay. How's it going?" he asked.

"It's just starting, really." She remembered seeing Dale as she was leaving, thanking her for the report and asking if she'd be in in the morning.

"I have to be back at the station tomorrow."

"Are you in charge of the investigation?"

"Um…sort of. I'll be working with Riggs."

"That's the guy you don't like."

"Yeah." She looked at her watch. *So much to do.* "Hey, I've gotta go. I just wanted to apologize."

"It's okay. Have a good night."

"I'll call you tomorrow."

Kally put her phone away. She watched groups of people weaving their way among various warehouse wineries, some with bags of purchases, the nice fall weather helping on that score, and the haphazard gathering of this morning now only a memory.

Most wineries would remain open today, regardless of Kirk's death. They had to: winemakers needed the income from people just like these walking among the warehouses. Ninety percent of vintners had full-time jobs, herself included, so weekends were sacred for sales. Most would gladly be full-time if only finances allowed it.

Kally got out of her SUV and walked the short distance to her front door. She unlocked the door and walked inside, the ever-present aroma of wine filling her senses. Her tasting room was dark…empty…quiet.

Normally, she would be here on a Saturday afternoon doling out samples. She wondered if the case would overtake her life. If so, she'd have to make arrangements for temporary help to run the tasting room.

She walked through the rock-'n-roll-themed room, tastefully painted in various shades of purple and cream. Original posters of '60s and '70s rock groups, confiscated from her late father's collection, hung in expensive wooden frames. Everything was as she had left it.

She made her way down the hallway to the working winery in back, the music—yes, it was Led Zeppelin, "Whole Lotta Love"—getting louder as she approached.

For many wineries in the Warehouse District, hers included, music was a key part of winemaking, especially during the harvest crush. Music played everywhere, adding ambiance to winemaking like a perfectly blended G-S-M— or Grenache-Syrah-Mourvedre to the uninitiated.

But not just any music.

No rap nor weepy romance music here. She played the music of her parents: hard rock, *la norme* in Woodinville. There were, of course, older winemakers who preferred softer rock, or "Carpenters' music," as Kally called it.

She opened the door to her production area and walked in. Bright fluorescent lighting streamed down from above. Seth stood in rubber boots, pant legs tucked inside, on a small platform, working a hose around the inside of a six-hundred-liter tank. Yellow grape gunk and dead yeast poured into the drain from the tank's racking port.

Seth saw her and cinched the hose. "Hey!"

He jumped down, turned down the music, then came up to her. "You gotta try the Grenache. It's great!"

"Finally some good news."

Seth turned the water off and Kally followed him into her small kitchen where he retrieved a glass and a wine thief. Then she walked with him to the big door of her cold room. In one swift motion, he hefted it up. And, as she knew he would, he expertly climbed barrels until he came to one on top, six barrels tall, and took out the bung—a cork made of silicone—that plugged the barrel's opening.

He inserted the wine thief, retrieved a sample, and filled the glass half way. Then he put the bung back in and climbed down.

Seth handed the glass to her. "Tell me what you think."

He put one hand on his hip, the front of his long-sleeved shirt splotched with water spots.

Kally swirled the wine and took in its aroma. "Oh!"

She smelled it again, then tasted it, holding the wine in her mouth for a moment. It was one of her favorite grapes. And they had waited for just the right Syrah to accompany it, one with a peppery profile.

Kally swallowed. "Oh my!"

"Yeah!" Seth exclaimed. "Are you picking up that *slight* oak profile?"

"Yes. It's perfect." It was a nod to their use of two-year-old barrels, which imparted less oak, allowing the variety's berry taste to shine through.

Just like she advertised.

Suddenly Kally was aware she was still in uniform and shouldn't be tasting wine, not that her two employees would report her.

*Report her to herself?*

She felt tired again. She handed the glass to Seth, and he repeated the sniffing/tasting routine. Kally watched him, his blonde hair falling over his forehead as he concentrated on the elixir in the glass.

How long would he be with her? He was a good worker, but she knew that he itched to make his own wine, and control the whole process of picking, pressing, pitching, ultimately producing a product. Every cellar rat in Woodinville wanted his or her own winery, and many went on to do just that.

"Too bad we're going to blend this," Kally added.

"You sure you want to?" he asked, looking up at her. "It could stand alone."

Kally shook her head. "I want the southern Rhône," she added, the double entendre known only to herself. "What's the Syrah like?"

"It's good. Smooth. Peppery, like you like. They'll complement one another. But each could stand on its own."

"A blend it is," she reiterated. "And keep Grenache the dominate variety."

"Okay." He finished the wine in one gulp. "I'll top the barrels soon. I got a little behind. When do you want to cold stabilize the whites?"

"Let's do that in two weeks." She paused, thinking through her wine line-up. "Tell you what: since we only have one white to blend, let's do a preliminary trial of the red blend, too, on Monday...see where we're headed with it."

A huge smile crossed his face. He held up his glass to her. "Great!"

"And give me a split of the Grenache to take with me, would you?" she asked of the half bottles known in the trade.

"Sure."

Kally turned, taking in the rest of her production area. "Where's Leah?"

"In your office, I think."

She looked at her watch. "I'll go see her...then I have to leave. Thanks for your work today." Kally hesitated. "I don't think I'll be here tomorrow. I'll see you Monday night."

"Yep."

She watched him shuffle off, the boots not quite a good fit. Kally went to a small locker off the kitchen and quickly changed out of her uniform, standing there for a moment in her underwear. She put on pants, a shirt, and a vest with the Wine Babe Cellars logo prominently displayed on one side, then walked back into the hallway and knocked on a door. She heard someone behind it get up to open it.

Leah's dark hair was pulled back in a ponytail, her normally clear complexion blotched with red marks. Kally could see that she had been crying.

"Got a minute?" Kally asked.

"Yeah."

She stepped in to her very own office, the converted closet, every square inch of her winery used for some function or another. She saw from the computer screen that Leah was on e-mail.

The two stood there in the crowded space.

Kally hesitated, not sure she should inquire about what was upsetting her. Under a time crunch as she was, she forged ahead with a work question instead.

"Did you get ahold of Premier labels?" Kally asked.

"Yeah. They'll be here Monday."

"Great. So, were there any problems?"

Leah shrugged. "Not that I could see."

"They sent a proof?"

She nodded. "It looked good."

Kally noticed that Leah was having a difficult time maintaining eye contact. Leah was nine years her junior at twenty-four years of age. It was only a short time ago that she had started interning at the winery with Seth, after attending the Northwest Wine Academy. Both had been full of enthusiasm and excited about their prospects in the Washington wine industry. Kally had hired both part-time after crush from the previous year.

But lately, Leah's enthusiasm was nowhere to be seen.

"I believe you about the label, but can I see it?" Kally asked.

"Sure." Leah turned and looked through a pile of papers. She took out a sheet and handed it to her.

Kally perused the label for Wine Babe Cellars Pinot Gris/ Riesling blend. It looked like all of her others. Her winery's name was prominently displayed across the front in black italicized lettering against a white background. A wine glass, outlined in gold, sat in the middle, the federally mandated words "white wine" and "Columbia Valley" right below it.

*So boring!*

She'd like to name the wine after a song, but Sam, her attorney, would say no. She was sure of it. As much as she disliked it, it would do for now. Kally handed the proof back to Leah. "Thanks for checking."

Kally saw Leah moving slightly to her right. *To block the computer screen?*

"I'll be working quite a bit on Kirk's case," Kally said.

Leah folded her arms tightly and looked down at the floor. "Yeah. It's...sad."

"It is." Kally flashed on the image of Kirk again. "So...my time here will be limited."

Leah looked up briefly. "Okay."

"We'll do blending trials Monday night, if that works for you."

She nodded.

"Can you help Seth with clean-up today?"

"Sure. I didn't think he needed help."

*One always needs help with clean-up, Leah. You know that.*

"Well, I'll see you Monday, then." Kally walked back down the hallway. Obviously, there was a personal matter going on in Leah's life. Did it have to do with Kirk?

She stopped in her tracks. *Oh my God!* Had Leah been involved with him? She thought about that, the somewhat bookish Leah with man-about-town Kirk.

*Nah.*

She walked on, into her small kitchen, Leah's odd demeanor still on her mind. Maybe the sizzle of the wine industry was wearing off for her. That was something that happened, and not just to interns, as the reality of cleaning tanks and hoses sunk in. Day-to-day grunt work looked more like manual labor, while attending exciting wine events occurred only every so often.

Kally saw the small bottle of Grenache sitting there for her, just as she had asked. Seth had even put a makeshift label on it, a bright-green Post-it Note with the words:

> *Grenache*
> *2018*
> *95 points*
> *A Robert Parker Selection*

She smiled. Maybe he wasn't far off.

*Can I keep Seth forever?*

She grabbed an empty cardboard box, placed it on the floor, and put the small bottle inside. Then she walked to the back of her cold room where she kept cases of wine.

Kally reached for three bottles of last year's Pinot Gris/Riesling blend and three of her Grenache/Syrah blend. She put them in the box then brought the big cold-room door down and, yelling good-bye to her workers, headed out.

# 13

With the exorbitantly expensive pesto dish ensconced on the seat next to her, Kally left the Whole Foods parking lot in downtown Bellevue and headed south on Interstate 405. In the distance, Mount Rainier, pretty in pink muted light from the fall sunset, dominated the southern sky above Seward Park.

She fell in behind a line of cars waiting to exit, then wound her way down to the shores of Lake Washington, to her friend Chris's lodge-style home. Chris had been an early employee at Microsoft, a bit older and wiser than the rest of their group.

And much, much richer.

It was said her original stock allotment from the software company had split eight times. And so, after that eighth stock split, Chris had moved on, a young retiree who liked wine. That was when Kally met her, at the Northwest Wine Academy. They had taken Wines of the World together and had hit it off immediately. There was a fifteen-year difference in their ages, but it didn't matter. Their common denominator was wine.

Chris founded a wine-touring company that took small groups on behind-the-scenes visits to the Warehouse District, complete with in-winery dinners, barrel tastings, and one-on-one talks with busy winemakers. Kally saw her all the time. Chris was successful and happy, and generous in sharing her beautiful home for charity events and get-togethers.

She ran through the others who would be there tonight.

There was Sarah "Somm" Parker, a sommelier at an upscale

restaurant in the Magnolia area of Seattle. She worked with distributors and led wine tastings every morning with the restaurant staff. Kally had taken Wine and Food Pairing classes with her. Sarah was said to have a perfect palate—a rarity in the wine world—identifying the grape, the continent, and the region in blind tastings, which astounded her professors at the school.

Sarah, however, didn't think much of it. She simply liked wine. She tended to be on the serious side, but Kally could get her to laugh. And she had a pulse on what kind of wine people were drinking.

There was Ellie Fishback, married to a Seattle attorney. She was a tasting-room manager in Woodinville for a new cult winery, Red Mountain Productions, or RMP, which had opened in early summer and was an instant hit. Ellie had all the gossip. She was a natural blonde beauty and athlete, and former Seattle Seahawks cheerleader, who guys liked to stand next to, and when they did, they tended to talk to her about everything, including what so and so was doing. Or not doing.

Ellie never disappointed on the gossip.

There was Sam, attorney to both Kally and Chris, and a budding wine lover now that she had friends in the industry.

Kally thought about Sam for a moment. She was right about M&M. She couldn't use it.

She had met Sam during a particularly bad stretch in her own life. First, Kally had encountered a minor problem at the Northwest Wine Academy: wine chemistry. All those ions and electrons. They made no sense to her. She couldn't pass basic chemistry either, a requirement.

But that hadn't keep her from getting into the wine business.

Three years ago, with bulk wine selling at record low prices, she bought two red varieties, blended them, bottled the product, and created her own label for her successful first vintage from Wine Babe Cellars. It was an outrageously good blend of Grenache and Syrah. In short, she got noticed not only in the local press but around the world.

But not because of the wine.

It was because of the label. On it was a microphone tilted at an angle, along with the profile of a not-very-well-disguised, world-renowned rock star: Mick Jagger.

This was where Sam came in. A lawsuit in London, citing brand

protection, brought notoriety of the kind she didn't need. Since she was not able to reclaim the bottles and change the label, as the lawsuit required, she had a settlement to pay. A big one, in the range of $150,000. It was the reason she was still employed in her day job as one of Woodinville's beat cops.

There was a good outcome from the lawsuit, however. She suddenly had people around the globe interested in her small-lot wines. She was one of the very few winemakers in Woodinville with international clientele.

*Imagine that!*

She pulled into Chris's driveway.

One more person would join them tonight and that was soon-to-be-married Bud, who had gone to high school with Ellie and Sarah.

One other woman was also part of their group. But Janie Remick wouldn't be there, of course.

K ally passed a well-tended lawn and perfectly placed boulders and drove around to the back of Chris's house. She saw a twelve-person white van parked nearby, the logo for VinoTours of Woodinville with grapes in a wine glass colorfully marked on its side.

She parked and, grabbing her pesto dish and wine, got out, then kicked the door closed. With her heavy load, she walked up the back stairs to the large covered deck that provided unobstructed views of Lake Washington and the Seattle skyline beyond.

Maneuvering the door to the kitchen open, she went inside. Kally saw that Chris had put out wine glasses and had opened a few reds. A fire was going in the gas fireplace in the sitting area off to one side. In gatherings past, the few stragglers that remained usually made their way to this comfortable corner of Chris's kitchen.

She went to the refrigerator and placed her dish inside.

"Hey!" Chris exclaimed, coming up behind her. "You're here!"

Kally noticed Chris's newly styled hair and highlights.

"Nice. I like it," Kally said, touching a strand.

"Thanks. It's pretend hair. Like I actually sat in the sun." Then the mood changed. "So…" Chris began, "Kirk."

"Yeah, pretty sad."

"I had a tour scheduled there next week," Chris said. "I mean, it's just unbelievable. Have you seen Janie?"

"I have. That's another story."

"You'll have to tell us." Then, abruptly: "As much as you can, of course. Are you…on the case?"

"I am."

"Oh my gosh! Isn't that...you know, difficult?"

"It is, yes."

Kally looked over Chris's shoulder and saw a wrapped box on the counter. She let out an exasperated sigh.

"I don't have a present for Bud."

"Come with me," Chris said.

Kally followed her down a hallway past a living room/dining room combination dominated by a huge fieldstone fireplace. Two-story windows looked out over the lake. They turned right down another hallway to Chris's master bedroom, nicely decorated in a wildflower motif. She went to a dresser and rooted around inside a drawer, finally taking out a small envelop with "Macy's" on the outside.

She handed the gift card to Kally. "Give her this. One-hundred bucks. You can pay me later."

Kally took the envelope. "You just have this lying around?"

"Yes. For occasions just like this," Chris answered. She reached back into the drawer and found a small bow and stuck it on the outside of the envelope.

"There."

As they walked back to the kitchen, they heard car doors closing and voices below, then footsteps coming up the back stairs as the rest of the guests began arriving.

The women greeted one another and placed their dishes in the fridge. They grabbed wine glasses and poured generous servings of Kally's white blend. Then they sat outside, around Chris's spacious patio table, admiring the view and waiting for Bud, who had informed Chris she'd be late.

Chris busied herself firing up propane heaters that rimmed the deck, then placed a wine bucket on the table holding two bottles of Kally's wine. She disappeared into the kitchen, came back with plates of hors d'oeuvres, and settled in next to Ellie. Sam and Sarah sat across from them. Kally held court at the end of the table.

"Cheers everyone," Chris toasted.

"This is nice," Sarah, the sommelier, remarked on Kally's white.

"Thanks."

"Where'd you get the grapes?" Sarah asked.

People were avoiding the obvious discussion about Kirk, which was odd. Were they waiting for a cue from her?

"I got the Riesling from Evergreen and the Pinot Gris from a vineyard in Tonasket called Duet."

"What's the percentage?" Sam, the attorney, asked, taking in the wine's aroma and coming up to speed on her sensory evaluation.

"Mostly Pinot Gris with a splash of Riesling." Kally took in the aroma herself, still liking the essence of it and happy her friends did, too. Suddenly, she felt enormously tired.

"So what I'm identifying…lemon…is that from the Pinot Gris?" Sam inquired, her nose back in her glass.

"Yes."

"What do you sell it for?" Ellie, the tasting-room manager, asked.

"$14.99."

"Not bad. The southern Rhône's are still the faves in our tasting room," Ellie added, referring to Roussanne and Viognier.

Kally flinched at the mention of the French region. "It's hard to get those varieties. And they're expensive." She took another sip of wine. "Although I did bring a red Rhône we'll taste later."

"Good!" Ellie answered.

Kally looked over the rim of her glass, taking in Ellie's California-like summer glow, a hard thing to achieve in the Pacific Northwest in autumn, with its muted light that photographers and artists loved so much.

Perhaps it was her make-up or her hair, so perfect in color and cut. Or her skin, so toned and taut. Plus, Ellie had a way of looking stylish wearing just the right kind of clothing, with just the right amount of breast showing, as she was doing now.

Enough for guys to get talking.

Ellie caught her eye and winked. Kally was too tired to feel embarrassed. Then, as if on cue, Ellie started in. "Hey, I heard some news...about Kirk..."

All eyes shifted to Kally. She put her wine glass down, then picked it up again to keep her hands occupied.

"That he was murdered," Ellie added.

"No *kidding*?" Chris said, looking at Kally.

"We don't know that. We're...just starting the investigation. The medical examiner will make an assessment soon about how he died."

"Who found him?" Sam asked.

Kally hesitated. "Mark Manning." Then she explained who Manning was.

"Where was he?"

Kally hesitated again, not wanting to divulge too much. But she answered anyway. "He was bent over a bin. He was either put there intentionally or...he fell."

"$CO_2$"? Sarah asked.

"Possibly."

"It was, like, on all the news," Sam said. "I tuned in after you told me."

"As it will continue to be, I'm sure," Kally said. "I'm on the investigation…"

"Oh, wow…" Ellie said.

"It's going to be a long couple of weeks," Kally added.

People nodded in agreement. Kally thought she should mention the obvious. And did.

"Have you all contacted Janie?"

No one said anything.

"I know she'd like to hear from you…from us," Kally said. "She's a friend."

"Yes, she is," Sarah said. "I'll call her. I was waiting to hear what you had to say."

All eyes turned again to Kally. "I just saw her. She's not doing well."

"How's Emma?" Ellie asked.

Kally shrugged. "She…looked okay, all things considered."

An awkward silence descended on the group. Kally knew they were aware she couldn't go into detail about the case, yet they waited to hear more. She stared out at the water shimmering in the evening light.

"Did Janie tell you who she's dating?" Ellie asked, breaking the silence.

"No." Kally was surprised by this. "Other than today, I haven't seen her in a while."

"It's Denny Lane," Ellie said, helping herself to more wine.

"Really?" Kally responded, hearing Denny's name for the second time that day. Manning had taken his spot at Kirk's winery.

"Well…that's…something. For how long?" Kally asked.

"A while now. From what I've heard," Ellie said.

Ellie would be right. Yet she wondered why in weeks past Janie hadn't mentioned it.

"I didn't see that coming," Kally said. How odd to date your ex-husband's right-hand man. Or maybe I'm—as my mother would say—old fashioned. Nonetheless, she tucked the information away in case she needed to revisit it—or Denny himself—an excuse to travel to Walla Walla. But first she'd ask Janie when the time was right.

"Well, I have other news," Ellie said.

"What's that," Kally asked, relieved by the change of topic.

"Jim and Jon are switching to inserts."

"*Really?* Now that's a change."

Jim and Jon Spencer were first cousins who each owned a winery in the Warehouse District. They'd been around for years and were some of the first winemakers, self-taught, to convert a warehouse to a winery.

"What are inserts?" Sam asked.

"Oak alternatives," Kally and Sarah said at the same time, then laughed.

Kally continued: "They're used in stainless-steel tanks to give wine an oak 'presence.'"

She went on to explain how the use of oak alternatives cut down on a winery's costs, as the winemakers could forgo buying barrels.

"I use them sometimes," Kally added. They also allowed her to sell her wine at a lower cost.

"Three of Cups will also use inserts," Ellie said.

"Wait a minute!" Kally said. Now this *was* news. Three of Cups' owner, Mike Metheny, was another visionary winemaker. If he began using inserts, others would surely follow.

"He said he doesn't see a difference in taste," Ellie continued. "No one can pick out which wine was aged in barrel or which was aged with inserts or chips."

"That's what I always thought," Kally added.

"They'll keep the barrels for the winery look," Ellie explained.

The women paused to load up on more appetizers. Chris had outdone herself on the pre-dinner treats, with crab dip and crackers, home-made guacamole, a selection of cheeses and bread, and a large antipasto plate.

"I wonder what's keeping Bud?" Sam asked, pouring more wine and passing the bottle around.

"It's okay," Chris said. "I'm not going anywhere. Is anyone else?"

"Nope," they all said in unison, mindfully settled in and enjoying the setting as well as one another's company.

For a moment, Kally took herself out of the conversation and watched her friends. Chris and Ellie leaned in and discussed Woodinville tasting rooms: who was moving where, who was opening a second location, which Walla Walla wineries were coming into town and driving up competition.

Sarah and Sam discussed a legal matter. Sam, Kally noticed, wore new azure-colored glasses that enhanced her deep-blue eyes. Some women liked shoes. With Sam it was eyeglasses. *She should stick with this color.*

And Sarah had highlighted her hair recently, the red blending in nicely with her natural brown. Sarah, the tallest of their group, reminded Kally of a professor or a CEO. She had that demeanor.

Suddenly, Chris stood up, reached across the table for a bottle of red wine, and sat back down, the motion ballet-like in its fluidness. And so soothing. Kally felt her eyelids drooping.

That was her own Grenache/Syrah blend Chris had reached for. And she would make it again, her own take on a southern Rhône, the kind she loved. That love of Rhône wines was sparked with her introduction to them by Guillaume Tablet and on the train with him to southern France.

She had met him in a Paris café, and they had quickly bonded, speaking the language of wine so fluently. He had taken her all over the Rhône, to the vineyards his parents owned, and his "home," a château, where he'd grown up and where she'd gotten hooked on Hermitage and Châteauneuf-du-Pape, not to mention on Guillaume himself.

But that was a year ago and she had moved on.

Sort of.

*I can't think about him.*

She went through her familiar litany to expunge Guillaume from her mind:

*His work is in France. Mine is in Woodinville.*

*He is there. I am here.*

*He is younger by nine months.*

She looked back at Sarah and Sam, who were still engrossed in their conversation. Sarah picked up her glass and swirled the white wine within. Some people did this well and Sarah was one of them.

Kally was mesmerized by the liquid moving in the glass, like a wave...but a round wave...hitting the shore...but not the shore... whitecaps in the glass...moving onto the beach...

Her friends' conversations drifted away, everything quiet...dark.

Kally jolted suddenly. She had fallen asleep.

*Did anyone notice?*

16

Bud was beyond late. Kally, fully awake now, wondered what was taking her so long. Undeterred, the women continued eating, drinking, and talking.

"So, Sarah," Kally began, "what are people drinking these days?"

Kally knew that, while most individuals who frequented Sarah's expensive restaurant were on expense accounts, millennials like themselves flocked there for happy hour. Both Kally and Sarah knew the numbers on their generation and wanted to keep abreast of its likes and dislikes.

"We have a lot of business diners," Sarah said, her mouth full of Brie and cracker. "Interesting that Europeans want Napa," she added, swallowing, "and Americans want Bordeaux. Asians will take either. And people like us want Muscat or Malbec. From anywhere."

Kally nodded in agreement.

Sarah continued: "Now the C and M crowd…"

Kally smiled, knowing she was referring to the only wine that women of a certain age ordered.

"They *still* want Chardonnay and Merlot. And, if you're from Seattle," Sarah added, wiping crumbs from her chin, "you want a Washington red with a heavier mid palate. And that"— she looked directly at Kally—"is because of you and your buddies in Woodinville. That's what we're used to."

"How does all of this bode for Syrah?" Kally asked, about another favorite grape of hers.

"Not well, unless it's a GSM," Sarah answered. Grenache, Syrah, and Mouvedre blends were gaining traction in Washington State. "When are you going back to France?"

The question caught Kally off guard. Had she assumed a pining-for-Guillaume look? "Not sure. Could be awhile."

"I want to go with you," Sarah said, "and check out some châteaux."

"Yeah, and meet that French guy," Ellie said, smiling at her.

*I'm sure you do, Ellie.*

"I know his parents' winery," Sarah added. "Château Tablet isn't it? We carry one of their labels."

"Hmm," Kally responded. She fingered the bottom of her wine glass.

Kally glanced at Chris, who was staring at her but wasn't saying anything. Only Chris knew her private thoughts about Guillaume, which she had blurted out to her friend after their class on southern French wines.

"Speaking of wine…" Kally got up and retrieved the split of Grenache, now as good a time as any to try it. She helped herself to Chris's red wine-glasses and, standing at a sideboard on the porch, began pouring small tastes into five glasses, including one for Bud but none for herself.

"I want you to try this," Kally said, passing around the glasses.

"What is it?" Chris asked.

"Grenache."

"People ask for that," Ellie said.

"This will be in a blend," Kally explained. "I'm also thinking of making a Malbec-Mourvedre blend." She glanced at Sam.

"Interesting," Sarah replied.

"Have you tried one?" Kally asked.

"No," Sarah responded. "Our age group might like it. But, generally, we like our Malbec straight up."

"Tastes evolve," Ellie said. "The palate changes. And that's an unusual blend."

"True," Sarah answered. Then she asked Kally: "Why don't you give me something I can sell at the restaurant?"

"Like what?" Kally responded, not sure of the question.

"Well…" Sarah took a whiff of the Grenache. "Something like

this," she answered, taking in the aroma a second time. "Don't be offended," she continued, "but the expense account crowd isn't going to buy Wine Babe Cellars. Why don't you put your name—first name—on a label in script with nice edging and sell it for sixty to eighty dollars. We'll push it."

"Thanks, Sarah." *That's not me* was what she wanted to say. "I'll stick with Wine Babe."

Sarah shrugged. "Okay."

"Yum!" Sam exclaimed after tasting the wine.

"Agreed," said Chris as Ellie nodded her approval. Only Sarah, Kally observed, took her time with the wine. She lifted the glass to the light to look at the color and clarity, then lowered it to look at the rim, a thin band encircling the wine in the glass, indicating its youth. Thinner band, older wine.

This one had a rim perfectly delineated from the wine itself yet was ready to drink.

Sarah swirled the wine slightly, sniffed again, then swirled and sniffed again. Four sniffs in all. Finally, she tasted it.

"You've got more than a bulk wine here," Sarah said.

"I know."

"It's got depth. Unusual for Washington Grenache. It is Washington, right?"

"Yes. But I want another layer. I think it's one-dimensional without Syrah."

"I don't know about that." Sarah tasted it again. "Tell you what… you could bottle this, slap a nice label on it…"

They were interrupted by Bud coming up the back stairs.

"Hey, party girl!" Ellie said, jumping up and giving her friend a hug.

"I'm *so* sorry I'm late," Bud said, joining the women at the table.

"No problem," Chris said. "You know this group: we start right in!"

Bud helped herself to a glass of Kally's white wine. Chris passed her a plate of appetizers.

"So tell us about the wedding," Chris prodded.

Between bites, Bud described what she and A-Rod were planning. "We wanted it at Chateau Ste. Michelle," she said, bringing up the well-known Woodinville winery. "But they're booked. So we're having it at DeLille."

"Another beautiful setting," Chris said.

"It'll be great," Ellie added, and Sarah agreed, both wedding attendants.

"The honeymoon will come later," Bud added, "probably Jamaica, since neither one of us has been there."

"Go in February when it's really gray here," Sam chimed in.

"So tell me again how you met Mr. A-Rod?" Ellie asked.

A huge smile crossed Bud's face. Kally already knew this story. Bud hadn't dated that much, which surprised her. She'd met A-Rod on the job, and they had become fast friends. In fact, they were inseparable. Bud kept insisting to people that they were just buddies, until one Monday morning when Bud came to work and Kally knew instinctively that everything had changed. Bud had fallen in love.

"Okay, who's hungry?" Chris asked, changing the subject.

All agreed and Chris got up. "Kally, will you help me in here?"

Kally followed her friend into the kitchen, coming up behind Chris as she opened the oven door and took out a steaming, chicken enchilada concoction.

"You okay?" Chris asked.

"Yeah. It's just been a day."

"I didn't mean that."

"I know what you mean. I'm fine."

"Have you heard from him?"

Kally looked away briefly, her defenses down. "No. It's okay."

"Really?"

Kally nodded. "Yeah."

Chris took a long time taking in her friend's countenance. "All right, then. Will you bring out the reds, the ones over there on the table?"

"Sure."

They ate and talked and drank all of the wine Chris had opened, as well as most of what Kally had brought. Kally herself had stopped drinking, thinking of the drive home. When they were finished with dinner, Chris served coffee and dessert while Bud opened her presents.

Kally sat with a cup of coffee, ruminating on her friends, the setting, and how grateful she was that the gathering allowed her to put the concerns and worries of her police job and winery on hold, if only for a short time.

Before leaving, Sarah picked up her empty wine glass—the one that had held Grenache—and smelled it. Kally knew what she was doing.

To anyone else, it looked like Sarah was taking in phantom aromas. But Kally knew the aromas were real.

Wine, and the oak it had been aged in, stayed in the glass long after the wine was gone. Sarah was merely performing her "somm" duty: investigating scents she might have missed the first time.

Sarah appeared deep in thought as she took long sniffs. She had removed her contact lenses sometime during the evening and was wearing glasses, looking even more professorial.

She looked up and saw Kally watching her. "It's really nice," she said.

Kally sat on the couch in her living room cradling a small glass of red wine. The lights were low, and she looked up at a few stars through her skylight.

What a long, sad day.

In this mood—and in his honor—she had opened one of Kirk's wines, his own take on a southern Rhône. The images of Kirk, and then of Janie standing in her doorway, came back to her.

Two people. So much to offer.

She took a sip of the wine, heavier on Mourvedre—'ved—than most GSM blends, which also gave it its heft—the weight or mid palate—just like Sarah said. The Rhône grapes made her think of Guillaume again, so she went through her routine to get him out of her mind.

Ironically, tired as she was, she focused on Zack. Why couldn't she take the next step with him? He was, as her mother would say, "a *fine* young man." They even liked the same things.

She leaned her head back. She knew very well why. Guillaume stood between them. That and the train from Paris, their first night together in a first-class compartment...

*She wore his big white shirt...they were drinking Hermitage straight from the bottle...she was pinned against the wall and he was kissing her madly...and she was kissing him back...*

They never slept. And they finished two bottles of wine.

Kally felt an ache in her heart. She had promised him she would come back to France.

But she hadn't. She had a settlement to pay, she'd committed to being a cop, her winery needed her...

Kally stared up at one particularly bright star. She envisioned the neat piles on her desk and the endless chores at her winery. The images of Guillaume and Hermitage floated away. With all that needed to be done, she vowed to get an early start in the morning. She closed her eyes and, after a few moments, fell fast asleep.

K ally reached for the first list on her desk, the employee list, and came upon a Kendall Mahoney, a nice Irish girl, and the only Kendall employed at Kirk Remick Cellars. She saw that she was a tasting-room pourer, hired recently.

As far as she knew, Kendall was Kirk's last paramour. She noted the address in Redmond, the next town over, and wrote it down.

Then she quickly read through the rest of the employee names, eleven in all, including Kirk. Justine and Manning were on it, and others she knew only in passing—literally, from passing them in the parking lot. They included: Paula Sampson, office manager; Caitlin Farling, marketing/sales manager; Suri Lakosha, tasting-room manager; and four other names she didn't recognize, possibly interns. She made a mental note to ask Manning about these four.

Kally picked up the wine club list again, vowing to get through at least half of the list this morning. She knew Kirk kept his wine club small intentionally. Word was, the list was full before the public even knew about it. She turned the page and saw executives' names, people who could easily afford the two-thousand-dollar-a-year minimum wine club purchase. There were out-of-state addresses as well, dominated by New York and California, and a few international ones.

In reality, anyone on the list was a suspect, a daunting possibility. And any one of the invited people could have passed along their invitation to someone else, which added more unknowns.

She picked up the copies of the sales receipts, all fifty of them, and put them in alphabetical order to compare them to the wine club list.

But before doing so, she thumbed through them, tallying how much wine had been sold.

Wow! Thirty-nine-thousand dollars so far. In five hours! And it hadn't even been a release party.

Kirk was amazing. Most winemakers were too consumed with getting grapes processed to think about having a party during crush, and most had wine club obligations coming up before the holidays, so time was always at a premium.

She knew Kirk didn't have regular tasting-room hours and people who came to his wine events usually bought wine, using their wine club discount of 15 percent. On forty-five to eighty-dollar wines, that discount added up. People—these people—bought cases at a time. She looked down the sales list, and sure enough, most of the individuals had bought a case or two.

*I mean…really? Are these people suspects? Executives? People with money? People without money who love wine?*

Nonetheless, she knew what was required. Kally dug in with the first name on the wine club list: Riley Anderson. She looked at the sales receipts. Riley Anderson had not been at the party. She put a line through his name on the wine club list.

She moved on to name number two, Joshua Arnaugh, then quickly read the sales list. Yes, he had been there! A suspect! He bought two cases, a cash outlay of $1,083.63. She noted his address in Redmond. She would visit him today, at home and unannounced.

Kally continued comparing names on the two lists, stopping only for a bathroom break. After two hours, she had gotten halfway through the wine club list. Thirty-one people on the list, so far, had come to the event and bought wine. Most of them lived in Seattle and Bellevue. Four lived in Redmond, and those names were now on her legal pad.

Tired of this chore, she picked up Kirk's wine logs to determine how his wine for the year was progressing. Importantly, the logs established timelines for the employees in the winery.

Kally counted the pages. Kirk had fourteen wines in production, so fourteen logs. She read through them quickly, seeing Brix, temperatures, times, and initials of individuals taking the readings. The majority of the logs, each corresponding to a half-ton bin or a stainless-steel tank, were of red varieties. Two logs detailed work on a Chardonnay, his only white wine.

She came to the last page, the name stating only "B" and "tank one" and "tank two." Odd that two vessels were listed and there was no identifying variety. She read down the log, seeing the progression of Brix dropping to near dryness in both tanks, meaning all the sugar in the wine had been consumed by yeast. These were essentially finished, and malolactic fermentation, or "ML," could begin. She assumed they were red wine. She'd ask Manning about this, too.

Thinking of the people she wanted to talk to, she picked up her keys and headed out.

Kally parked in front of the large, two-story condominium complex in Redmond, not far from the Microsoft campus. It was a warm fall day with not a cloud in the sky, a day people in the Pacific Northwest took advantage of.

A passel of kids, both boys and girls, played football on the broad expanse of lawn in front of the building. Kally got out, locked the door, and walked up the long sidewalk to a covered entryway with mailboxes on either side. Looking beyond the entryway, she saw a courtyard dominated by a swimming pool in the middle. No one was in it, but people sat around it, at tables with nice striped umbrellas or stretched out on lawn chairs reading the Sunday paper, something she herself would like to be doing.

She went to a door, found Kendall's name, and, picking up a phone, pressed the button for her condo. After a few rings, a woman answered. Kally started to introduce herself—

"Oh. You're a winemaker," Kendall said.

"Yes. And, as you may know, a police officer in Woodinville."

No response.

"I'd like to ask you a couple of questions."

"About Kirk?"

"Yes. It won't take long."

Kally didn't hear an answer. Then:

"I'm on the second floor."

Kally hung up and put her hand on the doorknob. Hearing the buzzer she walked into a hallway with sage green painted walls and maroon carpet and then up the stairs to the second floor.

Kendall—she presumed it was her, as she was the only person in sight at the end of the hallway—had on a pair of sweatpants and a tight-fitting tee shirt. Kally came up to her and stuck out her hand, and Kendall took it, a limp handshake. She guessed her age at twenty-five, twenty-six. Her long blonde hair was pulled back in a ponytail, and even without makeup, Kally had to admit that Kendall was quite attractive.

"I'm sorry about Kirk."

Kendall nodded and looked away. "Come in."

Kally followed her inside. They passed a small kitchen on the left. To the right was a large bedroom with an unmade canopied bed. Walking farther inside, she saw a bathroom and another smaller bedroom.

She added it up: two-bedroom condo in an expensive area of Redmond. Age: mid twenties. Job: tasting-room pourer.

Kendall plopped down in a corner of a white couch in the living room and tucked her legs up under her, scrunched up within herself. The condo, with its western exposure, was a bit dark, not yet warmed by the afternoon sun.

Kendall said nothing, leaving Kally standing in the middle of the room, which she noted was tastefully decorated in white with glass tables, and book shelves situated in several places. Kendall was young enough not to have the manners of a slightly more mature person, and so Kally, without invitation, sat down at the other end of the couch.

"You were with Kirk the evening he died," Kally began, crossing her legs to look a bit more casual to put Kendall at ease. She refrained from taking out her legal pad. She thought of Kendall as a fawn caught in the meadow where its mother had told it not to go.

Finally, Kendall nodded. "At the winery, yes."

"And later?"

"Are you wearing a wire?" Kendall asked, suddenly.

Kally checked herself from laughing. "No…that's only on TV. No wire."

"Okay. Kirk never showed up."

"He was supposed to then?"

Kendall nodded.

"Did he call?"

"No."

"Did you call him?"

Kendall hesitated. "No."

"Why not?"

"Because I was mad at him! I mean, he didn't even call!" she answered, choking up. "And then I thought...later"—Kendall emphasized the word, drawing it out: *lay der*— "if I had called he might still be alive!"

Kendall started crying softly.

Kally wanted to comfort her somehow. But she was too far away on the couch to touch her. She shifted position, leaning forward. Resting her arms on her knees, she turned again to Kendall, to console her.

"You can't think that," Kally said with authority.

Kendall looked at her with watery eyes.

"You are not responsible. I know that."

"You do?" Kendall asked.

"Yes. I do." Kally paused a beat before continuing. "How long were you at the party?"

"I left before the end."

"Do you remember the time?" Kally asked.

"Um...I think about eight thirty or nine p.m." She dabbed at her eyes with the edge of her shirt, revealing a flat midsection.

Kally remembered seeing her with Kirk, near one of the tanks, at about that time. His hand was on her back side, pulling her close. Kendall had whispered something, and he'd smiled. Then she'd walked away, Kirk following her with his eyes.

Kally remembered all of this because Zack had said something to her and she had checked her watch.

"What did you whisper to him?" Kally asked.

Kendall looked surprised.

"I'm sorry," Kally said. "I was standing with my date and I saw you two."

"I told him I'd see him later. And I said something...personal."

Kally nodded. "And then you left the winery for the evening?"

"Yes."

"How long had you been seeing Kirk?"

"About two weeks, dating," she answered. "We saw each other every day at work, but..." Kendall shrugged.

"But what?"

"Well, we noticed one another and...we tried to keep it discreet."

"Why's that?" Kally asked.

Kendall looked at her with big eyes. "Because he was seeing someone."

*Of course.*

"Did he hire you?" Kally asked.

"He had final say."

"So, I have to ask you this...did Kirk stay here?"

She nodded.

"How often?"

"Like...every night."

Kally nodded again, thinking this was becoming a waste of time. She keyed in on her to-do list: three more people to see. She saw sunlight streaming in through the sliding glass door. It was after noon. She needed to get going.

"Did you see anything out of the ordinary at the winery that night or hear anything...strange?"

Kendall shook her head.

"Did anyone dislike Kirk?"

"I don't think so. He was nice."

"Right. Did he say he was waiting for someone or that he might be late getting here?"

"No."

"When you left, did you leave with anyone?"

Kendall shook her head again.

"Did you come right here?"

"No. I went to the store."

"And then home?"

Kendall nodded.

"So you were here the whole night?"

She nodded again.

"How did you hear about Kirk's death?"

Kendall looked down and played with a thread on the bottom of her sweatpants. "Paula called. She told me not to come in. Obviously."

"Paula is Kirk's...office manager?" Kally asked, remembering Paula on the employee list.

"Yes."

Kally got up. She took out a business card and handed it to Kendall.

"Do you know what happened to him?" Kendall asked, taking the card.

"I don't yet. The ME is trying to figure that out."

"What's 'ME'?" she asked.

"Sorry," Kally said. "Medical examiner."

"Oh. Do you know when the funeral is?"

"I don't," Kally replied. "I would stay in touch with Paula. We're trying to solve this as quickly as possible." Kally pointed to her card. "Call me if you think of anything. Even if you don't think it's important."

"Okay."

She turned to leave, but then turned back. "One other thing: Do you know what 'B' stands for at Kirk's winery?"

"'B' as in 'boy'?" Kendall asked.

Kally nodded. "It's a wine, apparently. It was listed in his logs."

"Oh, that. We didn't know anything about it."

A few minutes later, Kally sat in her car, thinking. If she thought Janie was alone, this girl was really alone. Friends and associates in the wine trade knew Janie and would comfort her, at least initially. But Kendall? No chance.

She entered the next address in her iPhone for Joshua Arnaugh, the man who bought two cases of Kirk's wine.

# 20

Arnaugh's Cape Cod-style home was in an even nicer section of Redmond, an area with expansive manicured lawns and mature trees, all befitting a man who could plop down a cool $1,000-plus for wine. Kally drove up the long driveway, stopping half way. Farther on was a three-car garage with a loft above.

She got out and walked up a cobblestone path, her backpack slung over one shoulder. Kally rang the bell and heard a soothing sound emanate within.

The door opened. Joshua Jr., perhaps, stared back at her.

Kally looked down at him. "Hi. Is your dad here."

"Uh-huh." Then: "*Dad!*"

Kally smiled. And waited. Soon, a man in jeans and a long-sleeved blue Seattle Mariners tee shirt appeared, barefoot. Kally did a five-second assessment: Tussled hair, nice looking. In shape. Late thirties, early forties. Tan. Wealthy.

Someone she might have dated once. Or wanted to.

"You are Joshua Arnaugh?"

"Yes."

Kally introduced herself.

"Oh," he said through the screen door, smiling. And perfect dentition. "What did I do?"

"You may have heard about Kirk Remick's death?"

"Oh, man," he said shaking his head. "Yes."

"You were at the harvest party Friday night," she said.

"I was. Here," he said, opening the screen door. "Come in."

And nice manners.

Kally stepped into the slate-floored entryway of the spacious home. Stairs to her left led to the second floor. A kitchen-to-die-for lay beyond the hallway.

"Come in here," Arnaugh said, gesturing toward the living room and another white couch. He sat in a leather chair and motioned her toward the couch.

Kally took in the room. Expensively framed abstract art hung on the walls. Other than the couch and chairs, the other furniture looked to be antique: the large desk against one wall and the stained-glass lamp sitting on it; the coffee table in front of her; the low-slung table in front of the picture window, holding a plant in a cloisonné container.

And then there was the carpeting: plush. Of everything in the room, only the carpeting, possibly, was in her price range.

Arnaugh crossed his legs. Kally noticed that the portion of leg she could see was also tan. Since he didn't appear to be the type to take in a tanning booth, perhaps he/they had been on a recent beach vacation.

"I'm here as part of the investigation into Mr. Remick's death," Kally began, and Arnaugh nodded. "May I ask you a few questions?"

"Sure."

"What time did you arrive for the party?"

Arnaugh rested his arms on the arms of the chair. He sat ramrod straight. He cocked his right elbow and rested his chin on his hand.

*I wonder what his wife looks like.*

"It was after work. I would say I got there around…seven thirty to seven forty-five. "

"And where do you work?" It was not a question that made a difference to the investigation. She just wanted to know.

"Microsoft."

She nodded. "Did you go alone to the party?"

"Yes."

"Did you know anyone there?"

"I did. Couple of work buddies. And a guy I play golf with."

"What are their names?" Kally asked, taking out her legal pad and a pen.

"Jimmy Monroe…actually James. I call him Jimmy to rile him."
Arnaugh smiled. "He's a 'James' sort of guy."

Kally smiled, too. James Monroe was on the wine club list.

"There were some other programmers. And a guy from accounting."

"All from Microsoft?"

"Yes."

"How long did you stay at the party?"

"Maybe…forty-five minutes."

"And you bought wine."

Arnaugh smiled brightly. "Oh yeah!"

"Did you talk to Kirk at all?"

He shook his head.

"Did you see him?"

"I did. He was standing near the big tanks."

"Was anyone talking to him?"

"Yeah…maybe three guys…"

"Did you know them?"

"No."

"What did they look like?"

"Um…" Arnaugh took his time answering. "Well, quite honestly,
they didn't look like people in his wine club."

"And you say that…why?"

"Because of what they were wearing. They had on dirty jeans. I
think one guy was wearing a sweatshirt with the sleeves pushed up. And
from the way they were standing, kind of slouching."

Kally knew exactly who they were: the three winemakers—Larry,
Bob, and Paul—from the Warehouse District who had stopped by to say
hello and try his wine. Winemakers don't normally dress up for work.

"Anyone else?" she asked.

"Some women."

"Did you know them?"

"No."

"What did they look like?"

He smiled again. "Nice-looking women."

"Anyone in particular?"

"One was blonde, young."

*Kendall.*

"When did you see her?"

"It was right before I left. I passed her and Kirk as I was heading out to the front to buy my wine."

"Right." If his estimation were correct, he would have left the winery at about eight thirty, the time she had seen Kendall with Kirk.

She put her legal pad down on the antique coffee table, carefully.

"So how did it happen?" he asked, suddenly.

She took in Arnaugh's finely chiseled features. *You are going to be a very attractive older man,* not sure why that particular thought had popped into her head at that moment. Perhaps she was thinking a bit too much about Mr. Arnaugh.

"We don't know. The...medical examiner is doing an autopsy, and hopefully we'll know something soon."

"I just can't believe it. He had everything going for him." He paused. "I wish I had talked to him."

"I know." She started to ask another question but saw someone coming down the stairs, a woman carrying a toddler. Her quick assessment of the wife: slender, fashionably cut long black hair. Short-sleeved tee shirt, tight jeans. Same age range as her husband. Also barefoot. Also tan.

"Hi," Kally said.

"Hi."

Arnaugh got up as she entered and introduced her. "This is my wife, Angela. This is Kally O'Keefe with the Woodinville Police Department. She's asking me some questions."

"Oh?" Angela exclaimed, taking the other leather chair. She put the toddler down and handed him a toy.

"About Kirk Remick," Arnaugh explained.

"Oh yes. So sad."

"Your husband is not a suspect," Kally explained. "I'm trying to piece together the events of the evening." She refrained from saying that she, too, had been at the party. Or that she was a winemaker. They apparently didn't recognize her.

"Before I go," Kally said, "was there anything you noticed while you were there or when you were leaving that stood out to you?"

Arnaugh seemed to be thinking that through.

"Anything unusual?" she prodded.

"Only that the music was getting louder," he answered, smiling.

Yes, that usually happened. "Any other people you noticed?"

He put his head back and looked at the ceiling, then looked back at her. "Yeah. There was a group of, I don't know, two or three men and a woman, mid to late thirties, a nice-looking woman...long blonde hair"—he glanced at his wife—"they were standing together."

"Where were they?

"In the hallway, near the bathroom. I passed them going out."

"And...what was unusual about them?"

"Well...they weren't drinking. Nobody held a wine-glass. You don't go to Kirk's place and not drink his wine. Know what I mean?"

"Yes," Kally said. "That is interesting."

Kally backed down the driveway and drove a block, then pulled over to dictate notes. She tried to remember the group of two or three men and the woman Arnaugh had mentioned. The problem with people in a group at a party is that they don't often stay in a group. Maybe they came together. Maybe they came separately and met there.

That evening, when people had entered Remick Cellars, they were each given a wine glass. So the group Arnaugh had been referring to had declined their glasses. Or maybe they'd gotten them earlier, set them down, and were leaving.

She mentioned all this in her dictation and "starred" the group, to come back to them later. Then she thought about the time frame when Arnaugh must have left the winery. It was roughly the same time she and Zack and Kendall had all left. But she didn't remember him.

Because he had gone to the front to purchase his wine? Most likely. Had she seen him, she would have remembered him. She was sure of it.

Kally took out her phone and called Nakamura to ask him about his findings so far.

"I put through an expedited request for toxicity results for Mr. Remick," he answered. "I'm hoping to have them in a few days. You know, even if we have values of nothing, that indicates something."

"I know."

He continued: "All of Mr. Remick's body systems looked to be in good working order. I didn't find any organic matter in the lungs. The brain and heart were unremarkable, and the liver was as you would expect for a forty-two-year old man.

"And, I didn't find anything that points to foul play, like a blow to the head or bruising or stab wounds anywhere on the body. You know that this simply could be an accident."

Kally hesitated. "Yes."

"You don't think it's an accident," Nakamura said.

"I...don't."

"Why not?"

She hesitated again, not sure her reasons would hold sway with one of the best in the business. "Just a gut reaction. And from the way he looked."

"Well, we have to wait for the 'tox' report. That should tell us everything. And Kally...don't let go of that 'gut reaction.' It helps solve crimes."

"I won't. Thanks."

"By the way, I didn't find his phone. And the crime lab didn't find anything on those gaskets except traces of a cleaning agent. The beer bottle results will come back with the tox report. And the juice sample from the bin isn't back yet."

"Okay," she answered, committing his words to memory. *Odd about the phone.* "I've been thinking about your comment...about money. I'll check into it."

"Good. By the way, I've released the body to the funeral home."

For some reason, that comment hit hard. "Okay."

"Good luck with your investigation. My report will be online with the photos. I'll call you with results as soon as I have them."

Kally sat there a few moments. If the toxicity report showed nothing other than a reasonable amount of alcohol and $CO_2$ in his system, then the case would be closed. She would be faced with a Herculean job then to prove her "gut reaction." Kally looked at her phone for the next address, then drove off.

After driving around two more peacefully wooded, nicely manicured areas of Redmond—but not quite to the scale of Mr. Arnaugh's—Kally struck out. No one home. She wrote "Mon," for Monday next to the two names on her list, fully aware that time from the moment of Kirk's death was slipping away.

She glanced at her watch. It was mid-afternoon, and so she headed back to Woodinville, to look around Kirk's winery again.

## 21

Kally walked under the yellow crime-scene tape to the front door of Remick Cellars and tried several keys until the door opened. She entered the darkened tasting room, the smell of wine omnipresent, and turned on a light, seeing again how clean the place was.

And who had done all that cleaning? Manning? Possibly. Justine? Too distraught. Not Kendall, she knew.

Kally proceeded down the hallway to Kirk's office, the sound of her footsteps clicking again on the floor. *Imagine being big enough, wealthy enough, from sales of your wine to have administrative people.*

She tried the ring of keys again until one opened Kirk's office door, and she entered. She turned on a light and moved behind Kirk's desk and sat down in his chair.

*How odd to be sitting here.*

Kally thumbed through the stack of envelopes she had seen previously. There were more bills: electrical, gas, water, sewer, and garbage, all for the winery.

She opened the water bill. Wineries used *a lot* of water. She wasn't sure, again, what she was looking for but Nakamura's comment about money stuck in her head.

The current bill was for $464.96. The last bill, for $393.21, had been paid. She stuck the bills in an evidence bag in her backpack, making a mental note to make an appointment with Paula, Kirk's office manager.

Kally opened the middle drawer of his desk. And saw a mess of paperwork. She pulled everything out. Invoices from vineyards. Well-known ones.

Kally saw the bill from Klipsun Vineyards on Red Mountain for its esteemed Cabernet Sauvignon and Petit Verdot grapes. *Well, it pays to have a vineyard!* Five thousand dollars a half ton? No wonder he charged so much for his wine. It was standing room only to get this vineyard's grapes.

Who would get Kirk's allotment now?

Then she remembered something Janie had said about Kirk's library wines. She picked up the keys and walked into the hallway and stood in front of another door. She'd never been in this room. She tried a few keys until the door opened. Cold air greeted her. She turned on a light and was met with a wall of wine, with names and years on tags on bottles.

Kally remembered a picture on the internet of a Nazi officer's wine collection and the amount he had amassed in his cellar, all taken from the French, the French who had worked so hard to produce that wine, now that she knew just how much work it took.

Would she ever have library wines like these? In France, the wines would be in a cave, lying there for decades undisturbed. Guillaume came to mind again and the time he had taken her through his family's cave, walking hand in hand past barrels and dusty bottles. They had remained in the cave for some time...

She let the thought go and crouched down to the bottom shelf where four bottles were missing, from the 2011 vintage.

Possibly the ones he had served at his party. Certainly not enough to qualify as a robbery.

Kally stood up and walked out, locking the door behind her. Library wines...she could aspire to it.

Kally put the keys in her pocket and looked up. Suddenly a figure appeared in front of her. She let out a surprised yell.

"Oh my God! I thought I was the only one here!"

"You must have come in the front door," Manning said.

"I did," Kally answered, her heart still pounding. "What are you doing?"

"I just finished the punch downs."

"Okay. So...what are you doing now?"

"I'm done."

"Let's go back in the winery," Kally said, recovering somewhat. "I want to ask you something."

Manning retraced his steps as Kally followed, passing barrels on their left as well as the half-ton bin—bin four—where Kirk had been found, still crisscrossed in yellow crime-scene tape. They walked into the middle of the room where the rest of the fermenting bins sat. Against the walls on each side of the room were the stainless-steel tanks. Nothing appeared to have been moved from yesterday.

Manning put his hands in the back pockets of his jeans and stared at her. She noted that he hadn't shaved in several days, but he looked better than he had yesterday.

"How are you?" she thought to ask first.

He shrugged. "Okay. Not sure what will happen now, with the winery."

"You'll stay on, though? Until things are settled?"

That meant getting the wine surrounding them blended and into bottles or barrels, and ready to be sold. Kirk's last vintage.

"Yeah, I was planning on it."

"Good. Great, actually. I know it's not my place to ask but...well... it's something we could do for him."

Then she started in. "On Kirk's employee list, there are four names I'm not familiar with."

"Who?" Manning asked, and Kally named them.

"Oh...they're interns, not really employees."

"That's what I thought. How often do they come in?"

"During crush, every day. But they haven't been here...since..."

"Right."

"But they'll be here tomorrow night to help press some of the reds," Manning added.

"I'll come back and talk to them." Somehow she would fit it in between her day job and her winery's blending trials. "Did you have a beer the night of the party?"

He looked surprised. "No. Why?"

"Nothing. Just wondering." Kally looked around at the large tanks, each with blue painter's tape on the front detailing work from must to wine. One tank at the far end on the left side had no blue tape on it.

"Let's walk over here a minute," Kally said, approaching the tank. Manning followed her.

"I noticed in the logs that one wine, actually two tanks, is listed as 'B.' Is this 'B'?"

"Yes."

"Where's the other one?"

"They were blended."

"What is it?"

Manning hesitated.

Kally waited.

"It's a new red," Manning answered finally. "We're calling it Blitzen. It'll come out at Christmas."

"Clever." *How does he get away with using the name of a copyrighted reindeer?* It was so Kirk, skirting the edges of legality. She could have taken lessons from him.

"It's our first vintage," Manning added. "No one knows about it. Kirk called it his quick wine: whole berry fermentation, like Beaujolais. Make it. Bottle it. Get it out the door."

"What's the blend?" she asked.

Manning hesitated again.

"Come on," she prodded, giving him a look that said she wouldn't be stealing the idea.

"It's Syrah with some Petite Sirah thrown in."

"How much?"

"Twelve percent. Like the twelve days of Christmas."

"It'll have heft, then."

"Yeah. Like Kirk likes to make it."

Present tense, she noted. And then Manning said something Kally would remember for the rest of her days.

"Kirk said any name with a 'Z' in it sells wine."

She thought about that. "Really?" Then: "How soon will you bottle it?"

"Next week. Well…that was the plan."

"Still plan on it," Kally offered.

Kally turned and walked into the small kitchen area and grabbed a glass. She walked to the tank holding Blitzen.

"May I?" she asked.

"Sure."

Kally put the glass under the sample tap. Dark ruby-colored wine, no doubt from the Petite Sirah, flowed forth. She put the glass to her nose, aware that she had stepped out of police mode.

"I'm interested in this because it's Kirk's last wine," she explained. "Not sure it will help the investigation, but I am curious about it."

"Okay."

She held the glass up—*Nice color*—then sniffed again, instantly taking in Syrah berry aroma and a slight whiff of chocolate, dark chocolate.

She looked at Manning. "Inserts?"

He nodded.

"Dark toast?" she asked, referring to the burn on the wood. Dark toast added dark chocolate to red wine. A medium toast imparted a vanilla flavor.

Manning nodded again.

She took a sip. The underlying Petite Sirah was undetectable. But the wine, as Manning said, had heft.

And it was as clean and pure as a mountain stream. And fresh as the fruit it came from, a Kirk hallmark. She turned away from Manning and spat the wine into the drain in the floor and added the contents of her glass.

"What will you sell it for?"

"Twenty-five dollars."

They were interrupted by Kally's phone ringing. "Excuse me." She took her phone out and looked at the name, then answered.

"Hi, Janie."

"Will you go to the funeral home with me?"

"Sure. When?"

"Now?"

# 22

The three of them—Kally, Janie, and Emma—stood twenty feet from the casket, which, for Kally, was close enough. They were in the room where the viewing would be held, the larger of the funeral home's two rooms, to account for Kirk's popularity.

She noted that the lighting was surprisingly bright. Harsh, even. Perhaps the funeral home thought people were more comfortable with death in a light-of-day atmosphere.

And there was a scent that surrounded them. Kally's sensory self took over for a moment. It was a pleasant flower-shop aroma, roses possibly. She saw Janie staring at the flowers.

"They're nice. All the flowers," Kally said, trying to break the silence.

"Yes." It was a soft response, barely audible.

Kally looked at Kirk's profile. He'd been cleaned up well. Oddly, he had on a suit and tie, and these were not clothes she had seen at his condo.

The three of them continued standing there, not saying anything.

"Whose clothes are those?" Kally asked, finally.

Janie looked at her strangely. "The funeral home's. They have a whole store for people to choose from. Kirk never wore a suit."

*So why now?* People won't remember him like this. And it must have cost a fortune coming from here.

"It's not like he couldn't afford it," Janie added, seemingly reading Kally's mind. "I want him to look nice. For his mother."

Kally nodded. "And when is she arriving?"

"Tonight. I'm picking her and Kirk's sister up at the airport," Janie answered. Then: "Thank you for coming here."

"Of course," Kally answered.

"I wanted to see Kirk first without his mother," Janie added. "So I wasn't surprised."

Janie walked up to the casket while Kally remained behind with Emma. Kally saw Janie put her hand out to touch Kirk's hair. Then her hand went up to her mouth, and her shoulders sagged. Kally looked down at the floor, sure that she didn't need to be part of this private moment. And just where was Denny, she wondered, Janie's alleged new guy. Why wasn't he here in this role?

Then Kally, with Emma clutching her hand, walked up to Janie and put her arm around her, hoping to offer some comfort. As she did so, she looked down at Kirk. The funeral home had applied makeup to cover the red stain on the side of his face. And his arms were at his sides, like he was standing at attention but lying down, his hands covered by the half-closed portion of the casket.

She wondered if someone had tried to pry open his fists. Not that it mattered now.

Suddenly, Janie bent down and picked up Emma, then turned so Emma had a view of her father.

"See, Emma…daddy is sleeping. He will be sleeping now forever."

Kally didn't know if this moment was in the Handbook on Children that she was sure every parent referred to. Not being a parent, she couldn't fault Janie. But showing Emma her dead father like this wouldn't have been her choice.

Emma reached out toward the casket. And then, just as abruptly, Janie turned and walked away, leaving Kally standing there alone.

Kally joined them at the back of the room.

"Why would someone kill him?" Janie asked.

"We…don't know that yet," Kally said, uncomfortable as she was and wanting to be anywhere but here. She refrained from looking at her watch. She should have been at her mother's for dinner by now. "The funeral is, when?"

"Tuesday."

"I'll be there," Kally said. She realized she would be the only one working at the solemn event. But she couldn't let the opportunity pass to talk to people, in an appropriate, understated way, of course.

"Kirk brought attention to Washington winemakers," Janie said.

Kally knew that to be true. "Did he have a gambling problem?"

The question came out of the blue, another non-sequitur Kally immediately regretted. At least here, in front of the body.

"A...what?" Janie asked, looking at her in disbelief, in the same incredulous voice Kally had used with Nakamura.

"Maybe money is involved somehow," Kally quickly explained. "The medical examiner asked me this very question, actually."

Janie looked back at Kirk. "No. He never gambled. He never even bought a lottery ticket."

"I see." An awkward silence engulfed them. Kally took one last look at Kirk, his former assistant winemaker, Denny Lane, still on her mind.

"Can I ask you something?" Kally inquired.

Janie, still holding Emma, waited for her to continue. Kally took in her red-rimmed eyes, the crow's feet surrounding them more pronounced. Then she looked at Emma.

"Never mind."

"**M**other, I'm coming! I got held up," Kally barked into her mother's voice mail as she zipped around corners in her old neighborhood. Finally, she came to a stop in front of a 1950s-era rambler with large trees and newer landscaping that lessened the need for cutting the grass. All because her mother didn't cut grass and her brother, Phil, she knew, would never offer.

She reached into a box on the floor behind her and grabbed a bottle of the Grenache/Syrah blend. Then she looked at her watch. She was forty minutes late. Not too bad.

Kally got out and walked to the front door and into the foyer. And stopped dead in her tracks, hit as she was with the most foreign of sounds: country music.

"*Oh my God!* It's Patsy Cline singing 'Crazy.'"

"Yes!" her mother, Maureen, exclaimed, coming up behind her and giving her a hug. "Isn't it something?"

Kally noticed that her mother was dying her hair now, and she had to admit she looked pretty good.

"I just discovered them," Maureen added, taking the wine from Kally's hands.

"Who?"

"All of them: Johnny…Willie…Patsy. They were there all along. I feel like I owe them."

"Owe them what, mother?" Kally asked, taking in her sparkling green eyes.

"My attention." Maureen walked away, signaling Kally to follow her.

But Kally remained rooted in place. She had read somewhere that people who take on a new interest do so because of a change in medication or, possibly, because of something much, much worse, like a terminal condition.

Her mother's interest in country music was an example of this, knowing how her parents had worshipped rock music.

"Come say hi to your brother!" Maureen yelled.

Kally proceeded to the kitchen where aromas of an Italian dish made her forget all about "Crazy."

"Hey!" Phil exclaimed, getting up from the kitchen table and hugging her. "How's it going?"

"Good!" she answered, hugging him back. "How are you?"

"Not too bad."

Kally thought Phil had lost weight. And she noticed his hair was combed. And he had on a pressed shirt. All on a Sunday.

Something was going on in this house.

Kally stood next to her mother and searched in a drawer for a corkscrew. Finding it, she opened the wine.

"We'll eat in here. Much less formal," her mother said.

"Great." Kally took out three wine glasses. "What're we having?"

"Lasagna," Maureen answered. "Phil made it."

Kally turned toward her brother. "Wow."

"Yeah," Phil said. "And no wine for me."

Kally turned toward him again. "Really?"

"Yeah, I'm...not drinking."

"But you can pour me some of that," her mother said, pointing to the bottle.

Kally handed her mother a glass and took her own to the table and sat down.

*How long has it been since I've been here?*

*Has it been a month? Yes, it has.*

*My own family has changed and I never saw it.*

"We don't see you much," Maureen said, taking a sip of wine. "This is good. What is it?"

"A Grenache-Syrah blend. Do you want a taste, Phil?" Kally offered.

"No, thanks."

"Good for you."

Her brother seemed more down to earth, older. The word "responsible" came to mind for the first time. Perhaps he was coming to terms with being thirty-five-years old, divorced, no job, and living with his mother. Two, three, five years could pass, and the scenario might still be the same.

Things hadn't turned out as well for him as they had for her, her lawsuit notwithstanding.

"How's the music?" Kally asked him.

Phil shrugged. "I keep a hand in it. You never know what might come along."

Phil had been in a band in high school and college that Kally thought was quite good. But they hadn't been able to make it with their own music like other Seattle bands. Instead, they did passable covers at weddings and other smaller gigs.

Over time, his band mates got married, got day jobs, and moved on. Phil, she thought, remained locked in another era, past the expiration date one is given to make it in the music business. Even if he was an exceptional guitar player.

"I'm going back to school," he added. "Accounting."

"Wow!" Kally said. "Good for you. Where?"

"U Dub," he answered, using the popular moniker for the University of Washington. "In Bothell. How's the wine business?"

Her mother placed a steaming pan of lasagna on hot pads in the middle of the table.

"It's okay." Kally thought of everything that needed to be done at the winery. "We're about to blend the whites. Then we'll bottle."

"And how's the real job?" her mother asked, bringing salad and garlic bread to the table.

"It's fine. I'm on a case, so I'm busy."

"That's good. And Dale? How's he?" Maureen asked, sitting down. She passed the salad, then cut into the lasagna and put pieces on plates.

"Dale's okay," Kally answered.

Dale, Riggs, and Kally's father, Ken, had all worked together at the Seattle Police Department until her father's sudden death. Dale had been supportive of the family after that, stopping by every so often and taking them out to dinner. And he had been supportive of her when she'd made the decision to go into police work and when she had joined him on the Woodinville force.

But her father's death still hung over them all.

"I called Becky," Phil said. His ex-wife, the forensic accountant, had divorced him four years ago. "We're having coffee tomorrow."

"That's great, Phil."

"Dale hasn't stopped by the way he used to," Maureen interjected, passing the bread.

"Yeah, well…he's busy and we've got this case. A new one about Kirk Remick, the winemaker."

"I heard about that," Phil said. "You're working it?"

"Actually, I'm in charge of it," Kally answered, then filled them in with a few points about the investigation.

"You knew him?" her mother asked.

Kally hesitated for a moment. "Yes." She turned to her brother. "I'm calling Becky myself soon. On a work issue."

"Good!" Phil exclaimed.

"What about that young man in France. Do you hear from him?" her mother asked.

Kally flashed back to the scene in Guillaume's family's cave, since she had just been thinking of it, where they'd wandered in after a long hike through the vineyard. They'd stayed in the barrel room to try samples of his Grenache and Syrah, and then remained there a bit longer doing other things.

She let the thought pass. "I haven't heard from him in a while."

"I should have asked you to bring Zack tonight. I haven't seen him."

*Oh my God! I forgot to call Zack!* How do you forget to call someone you're involved with? She'd do so as soon as she got back in the car.

Kally changed the subject. "Mom, what is this sudden interest in country music?"

"I don't know," Maureen answered, swallowing first. "I came across a radio station in the car. And for some reason, I listened to it. Because the song really said something."

Phil shook his head. Kally nodded.

Maureen continued. "I think in life, as you get older, you come to an understanding of music like that. It's infused with so much…how would I say it…longing. But if you listen closely, there's advice in there about the harsher things in life."

Kally turned to Phil. "Do you agree with that?"

"No," he answered.

"Me neither."

After dinner they sat at the table and Kally and her mother finished the bottle of wine. Phil retired to his room and Kally did the dishes while her mother brought her up to date on what the neighbors were doing.

Before leaving, Kally stood outside Phil's door and listened to him playing the guitar, adding his own riffs to the end of The Rolling Stones' "Beast of Burden." Maybe Phil really was getting it together. Their father's death had been particularly hard on him, and their mother, in turn, had stepped in to shelter him.

When he'd died, Kally hadn't done or said anything. Instead, she had watched people around her falling apart and had vowed to keep it together.

She folded her arms and leaned against the wall as Phil moved on to another Stones' song, "Paint it Black." She had the distinct impression that Phil was about to step out and create a life for himself.

She wondered if country music had been the impetus.

# 24

Kally squinted at her computer screen, then enlarged the crime-scene photo of Kirk taken from behind, his body splayed out over the wine bin, his legs straight out behind him. She stared at the image for some time.

*Don't people who lose consciousness fall straight down?*

"This is not that," she said out loud, reaching for her coffee and thinking it through.

"Got a minute?"

Startled, she looked up and saw Dale at her door. Her stomach lurched, knowing what this was about.

"Riggs is in my office," Dale said, confirming it. "We'll keep it short," he promised before walking away.

Kally made a copy of the photo, then closed the site, steeling herself for the encounter with Robert Riggs, which had loomed over her weekend. He would not take kindly to being second-in-command of a homicide case.

*Wait.*

It hadn't yet been determined that Kirk's death was a homicide. Why couldn't she see it any other way? Kally picked up her coffee, notebook, and pen, and the copy she'd just made, and strode out, concentrating on getting her heartbeat down.

What was it about Riggs? She put his age at early fifties, but it wasn't his age. And it wasn't that he didn't know his procedural work. He did. And he did it well. Perhaps it was Riggs's proximity to her father, a link with him she preferred not having.

Kally heard the low murmur of conversation as she approached Dale's office. Then she walked in.

"Here she is," Dale said.

Riggs had taken the first chair in front of Dale's desk, which meant that Kally would have to maneuver past him in the cramped space to take the chair closest to the wall. She stood there for a moment looking down at him, but he didn't move.

"Excuse me," she said.

Riggs moved his legs to the side so she had room. She shuffled past him, sucking in her stomach, her rear end in his face, which might have been his intention. She plopped down in the chair, vowing to let the indiscretion pass.

"We were just talking about San Fran," Dale said to Kally.

"Nice," she responded, putting her coffee on the edge of Dale's desk and organizing the papers on her lap.

"Checking out the Redwoods," Riggs said.

She didn't ask if he'd taken in Napa Sonoma. A quick glance at him from the side showed Riggs to have gotten some sun, however. And she noted graying at the temple in his otherwise blondish-reddish hair. Actually, Riggs looked good, healthy, in his brown suit, white shirt, and brown tie with a pattern she didn't quite recognize. He was always more formally dressed than anyone on the force. She glanced at Riggs's polished shoes, then at her scuffed ones.

"Okay, I'll get right to it," Dale said, rolling up his shirt sleeves. "Kally is taking the lead on the Remick case and you're going to help her."

Riggs nodded slowly.

"She knows the lay of the land, the people, the wineries. Everything," Dale added.

"Okay," Riggs answered.

"I'm hoping we can wrap this up soon," Dale added. "By the way"—he handed Kally a torn piece of paper—"will you deal with these?"

She looked down at the scribbled names: *Wine Spectator, Wine Advocate, Wine Enthusiast, Wine Business Monthly*, and some blogs, and corresponding contacts and numbers to call regarding Kirk's death.

She remembered some of them. They were people who'd written what she thought were assassination pieces about her when her lawsuit had happened.

"Sure," she answered.

Dale turned back to Riggs: "Your role is to help with procedural things."

"Okay," Riggs said again.

Dale sat back. "So, I've filled in Riggs somewhat. But why don't you bring us up to date on where you are."

Kally looked down briefly at her notes, then began. Since Riggs had been out of town she reviewed everything: getting the call from Dale Saturday morning; what she had seen at the winery; going to Kirk's condo with Bud; visiting Janie, the ex-wife; her talk with Nakamura; the lists she had procured; interviewing Kendall and Arnaugh…

"I'm seeing Kirk's interns tonight," she added,

She noted that Riggs was listening intently.

"I have a list of people who might have been at the party, and I'm starting to sift thought those."

Riggs held up his hand. "I'd put that on the back burner. Get to the main people before this gets cold. And it is getting cold."

*How does he know?* She wouldn't let the chair indiscretion pass after all.

Riggs continued: "Who were the core people around…"

"Kirk," Kally said.

"Kirk," he repeated. "Interview them first, then move out, like spokes on a wheel, to the rest. And soon." Riggs hesitated. "I'll help you."

"I started talking to those people yesterday," she said to Dale. Then to Riggs: "I was at the party the night he died."

"Even better. Who are the main people?" Riggs asked. "Men? Women? Both?"

"Both," she said, remembering people waiting, wine glass in hand, to talk to Kirk.

"Do you know them?"

"Some, yes."

"Who are they?"

"Other winemakers.

"They're suspects, you know."

"No. They're not."

"Yes. They are." Riggs looked at her as a parent corrects a child. "He might have been sleeping with one of their wives."

*He's assuming all winemakers are men. Yet I can't refute his comment.*

She went on. "Business people were there, too."

"Get to the wine people first. Who specifically are the wine people?" Riggs asked.

"Well, there is the assistant winemaker, Mark Manning. Other winemakers in Woodinville. And Kirk's other employees."

"Talk to the assistant winemaker," Riggs said.

"I already have. He was the last one at the winery on the night of… the incident…and the first there in the morning. He was the last person, as far as I know, to see Kirk alive."

"Did you look around the place…when you were there?"

*Does he think I'm an idiot?*

"Bud and I did look around, inside and out."

"And?" Riggs pressed.

"Bud found some gaskets inside on the floor, away from where the body was. And outside I found a beer bottle in a garbage can."

Riggs and Dale waited for her to continue.

"I gave them to Nakamura. The crime lab found traces of a cleaning agent on the gaskets, and the DNA on the bottle is being processed."

"The guy…the assistant…is a suspect. You know that, right?" Riggs interjected.

*Perhaps it's just his manner and not a personal thing.*

"Yes. I've talked to him extensively. He said he didn't see anything."

Riggs rested his elbows on the arms of his chair and steepled his fingers together. He stared past Dale, out the window. "What's the timeline?"

Kally relayed what she had seen during the hour she and Zack had been at Kirk's event. "The party started at six p.m. Zack and I—I took him to the party—we got there about seven thirty p.m. and there were a lot of people there already. We came in the back door, which is a large garage door that faces the alley. He had his crush pad going, processing grapes. People were standing around watching that."

Riggs listened intently, not interrupting.

"Zack and I walked through the crowd. I got a table and Zack went to the front where they were pouring wine, and he got us glasses. Then he came back and we stood at the table. And then he got us appetizers."

She looked down for a moment thinking, remembering details.

"Music was playing as it always does at these events. There were a lot of conversations and it was loud. I had to lean in to Zack to hear him.

"I noticed that there were more men than women, and the women were sort of clumped together around several tall tables. I saw Kirk in the corner talking to three other Woodinville winemakers. They were swirling small amounts of wine in their glasses. And taking in the aromas."

Riggs nodded.

"One of them—Bob—looked over at me and smiled and toasted me with his glass. Then Zack said he didn't want to eat all the appetizers and that maybe we should get a pizza and go back to my place and watch a movie. I remembered looking at my watch: it was eight twenty p.m.

"But Zack had just gotten us more wine and I wanted to finish the wine. So we stayed ten minutes longer."

She paused again, remembering Kendall. "I looked at Kirk. His new girlfriend, Kendall, who works at the winery, came up to him and whispered something in his ear. He had his hand on her"—she glanced at Riggs—"backside, and he smiled at what she was saying. Then she gave him a quick kiss and left. And we left pretty soon after that."

"So that was the last time you saw him? The deceased?" Riggs asked.

"No. We were out in the alley about to walk to my winery two doors away and our cars. I looked back inside Kirk's winery through the big garage door. He was standing near his barrels and people were waiting to talk to him."

"That's it?"

She nodded.

"And this was around eight thirty p.m.?"

"Give or take a few minutes," she answered.

"Did Nakamura give an estimated time of death?" he asked.

"He did. About twelve thirty a.m."

Riggs unsteepled his fingers. "So we're missing the hour and a half before you arrived—not important because we know he was still alive—and everything between eight thirty p.m. and twelve thirty a.m. and on through to the next morning when he was found. When was he found?"

"About six a.m. By his assistant winemaker."

Dale listened and twirled a pen, eyes on his desktop.

Kally continued: "Kirk's employees were there late, cleaning up."

Riggs nodded but didn't say anything. If he had thought of something, he wasn't voicing it.

"Tell me again the people you talked to." Riggs wasn't taking notes, she noticed, not that he had to. All of what she was saying was in her report on the department's intranet, or OPI, for our private intranet.

Kally named the individuals she had interviewed earlier.

"Did any of them see anything out of the ordinary...people who looked out of place?" Riggs asked.

"Mr. Arnaugh mentioned three men and a woman."

"What did they look like?"

"Middle-aged. The woman was...very pretty, apparently. And they weren't drinking."

"Is that unusual? Maybe they don't drink."

Kally voiced Arnaugh's refrain: "It would be odd not to drink at Kirk's winery where you're getting free tastes of highly ranked, expensive wines."

"Maybe they had stopped drinking for the evening."

"I thought about that."

"Can you talk to them?"

"I don't know who they are."

"But you were there," Riggs pressed.

"But I don't remember them."

Then Riggs asked the question she wasn't ready to answer. Out loud, anyway.

"Do you think he was murdered?"

Kally hesitated. "Yes."

She saw Dale's eyebrows rise. Then he frowned.

"Why do you think that?" Riggs asked.

"Because of this." She passed the crime-scene photo to Riggs. He took a long time looking at it, then passed it to Dale.

"I think something happened in the corner of the winery where I found the gaskets on the floor. The angle of his legs…I think he was dragged to the bin."

"Maybe the cleaning lady dropped the gaskets."

"There is no cleaning lady. Only interns."

"You're sure of that?"

"I am, yes."

"What's the motive?" Riggs asked. He wasn't in his position for nothing.

"I don't know."

"Couldn't he have slipped?" Dale asked, passing the picture back to her.

"He could have. But I didn't see any water or wine on the floor when I was there."

"Maybe it evaporated," Riggs said.

"Not in a cold winery on a concrete floor," Kally answered. She added: "Nakamura is expediting the tox results."

"How does he get along with his wife?" Riggs asked, ignoring her comment.

"Ex-wife. They're recently divorced."

"Did you talk to her?"

"Yes."

"And?"

"She's distraught."

Riggs resteepled his fingers. "Tell me about the list you mentioned."

"I have four lists, actually. Thirty-one people on the wine club list, so far, went to Kirk's party and bought wine. I have their sales receipts."

"How many receipts in all?" Riggs asked.

"Fifty."

"You have the actual sales receipts?"

"I do."

Riggs continued staring out the window. Then: "Okay. Here's what you need to consider in this case and beyond."

She didn't remember asking.

"One: You can recreate a crime scene without witnesses—something from nothing. I'll show you when we go to your office; Two: A source out of nowhere will come forward with information. Listen carefully. And recognize it for what it is; Three: Consider the impossible. All those people you ruled out? Bring them back in. Everyone is a suspect until proven innocent; Four: Don't take anything at face value. Someone is lying to you. And on the flip side, saying nothing is a sin of omission."

Riggs paused. Although Kally hadn't written down his advice, his words were burned into her mind.

"Good points, Riggs," Dale said. "Really good. This is helpful, no?" He looked at Kally.

Kally nodded.

Riggs continued. "So let's take your case. Why kill a winemaker?"

"To get him out of the way?" Kally answered.

"By whom? Other winemakers? I don't peg them as killers. Was any money taken?"

"I don't believe so."

"Was any wine taken?"

"No."

Riggs went on: "In my opinion, a wine crime"—he enunciated the word, bobbling his head like a doll—"is an industrial accident."

Dale nodded. "Yeah."

Riggs: "But if this is a murder, everyone who was in the winery is a suspect. Tell me some of the names. Who are the business people?"

Kally cleared her throat. "Lots of CEOs you'd know, since this was his A-list wine club," Kally answered, naming top people at Starbucks, Amazon, Costco, and Microsoft. Then she named some banking and real estate people.

"Noel Jacobsen, the Bellevue attorney?" Riggs asked.

"Yes."

"Do these people usually come to wine events?" Riggs asked.

Good question. "No. But this was an unusual event."

"How so?"

"It was a harvest party, not a release party. Kirk was giving his wine club members an inside look at how wine is made right from the beginning. Most winemakers are too busy during harvest to think about a party." She added: "It was very Kirk, being first in this way. I think other winemakers will follow his lead on this."

Riggs nodded. He crossed his arms and turned to look at her. "The deceased. You knew him?"

Kally was taken aback by his question.

She hesitated, uncomfortable. "I've known him since I came into the wine business, so for four years. He was a work associate. And…a friend. Not a *friend* friend," she quickly added, "but a friend. He was supportive when my lawsuit happened."

Riggs didn't acknowledge her revelations. "So people had invitations to this event?"

"Yes. It's possible that wine club members passed along their invitations to others who showed up."

"Couldn't someone have just walked in the door?" Riggs asked.

"No, other than winemakers. You had to have the invite in hand. I'll ask the interns. They were probably the ones collecting the invitations.'"

"Did the invitations have names on them?" Riggs asked.

"No."

Suddenly Riggs slapped his thighs and stood up. "Okay. Here's what I want you to do. On the white board in your office, write two categories, 'Core People' and 'Others,' and start filling in names."

*He's taking over the lead.*

"I have some things to do. We'll meet in your office in an hour."

"Okay," she answered.

"You've never worked a homicide case." Riggs said it as a matter of fact.

Kally hesitated. "No."

Riggs turned to address Dale. "We'll treat this as a homicide until it's proven otherwise."

Dale nodded slowly. "Okay."

Then Riggs looked at Kally. "I don't think he was killed." He said it in a razor sharp tone. "As I said, this looks like an industrial accident."

Kally saw Dale nod again.

"Why kill the guy making all the important wine?" Riggs asked. "How does that make sense?

"And I don't know that the gaskets and beer bottle will lead to anything, quite honestly," Riggs continued. "But it's good that you saw them and got them tested. That's good work."

His tone had a sing-song manner to it. It must have killed him to admit that.

"Are you going to the funeral?" Riggs asked her.

"Yes."

"Take advantage of that. Talk to people there."

"Yes, I'm planning on it."

Riggs glanced at his watch then at Dale.

"Okay," Dale said sitting back. "Thanks for your help on this."

Riggs departed, leaving an awkward silence in the room.

"Sounds like a start," Dale offered. He got up and closed the door, then sat down again. "I know you think he's taking over. He's not. It's just who he is."

"Yeah," she said, looking away, Dale voicing her very thoughts.

"He can be abrasive. I know. I worked with him."

Kally didn't say anything.

"But he knows how to proceed. He gets results." Dale paused. "Remember: you're the lead."

She nodded.

"This case has generated a lot of publicity," Dale said, moving on. "Your other cases…"

He was referring to her domestic violence case, one she'd just begun looking into, as well as several phone calls, all of which needed to be answered but ones Dale put in the category of "silly." An elderly woman wanted her gutters cleaned. Another wanted the neighbor's trees removed.

"Bud will take them for now," he continued. "Put all your time into this one so we can get it done."

"Right." She got up to leave.

"And, Kally…"

She looked back at him.

"You have knowledge in this case no one else here has."

*Yeah, but can I do this?*

Zack picked up on the second ring.

"Zack…I'm really sorry," Kally started in. She'd reached him at work, at a downtown Bellevue financial services company. "I meant to call yesterday. This case…"

"I know about your job," he answered. "Don't worry."

"Want to get a coffee, around four p.m.?" She knew he oftentimes left work early as he arrived by six a.m.

Zack hesitated. "Uh…can't. I have a meeting. How about later?"

"Later when?" she asked.

"Want to have dinner?"

Kally remembered her interviews, seeing the interns, getting her blending trials started…

"I can't tonight," she said, ticking off the reasons why. "I'm really sorry."

"It's okay. What does the rest of your week look like?" Zack asked.

She thought through what was scheduled. "Want to meet me at the winery tomorrow night?"

"Sure. Sounds good."

"And I won't put you to work."

He laughed.

"Okay, then. I'll order pizza," she added. "I'll see you tomorrow."

Kally ended the call and stared at her blank white board. Zack was slipping away. And she wasn't quite ready to let that happen. And why not? She wasn't putting him first. But how could she, with…everything.

She got up and stood in front of her board. *Zack coming to her winery will be good. We'll get back on track. I need to make the effort.*

She reached for a marker and wrote headings for two columns using Riggs's terminology: *Core People* and *Others.* In the first column, under Core People, she put Kendall Mahoney's and Mark Manning's names and added check marks next to them. Grabbing the employee list off her desk, she added the rest of Kirk's employees, including the interns.

She also added the three winemakers—Bob, Larry and Paul—who Arnaugh had mentioned as not-quite-presentable club members and whom she had seen talking with Kirk.

She smiled at Arnaugh's comment. *You have no idea, Mr. Arnaugh, the manual labor involved in winemaking. They're not going to wear business attire.*

Kally reached for the paper-clipped sales receipts and, in alphabetical order, began writing the names under Others, including Arnaugh's. She placed a check mark next to his. After an hour, with Riggs nowhere in sight, she had filled the board with sixty names, writing smaller as she got toward the end.

She stood back and took it all in. *This is pathetic. I've talked to three people?*

Riggs rounded the corner. "Okay, what'da we got?" He put his hands on his hips while he stared at the lists she'd written.

"It's a start." He picked up the eraser and erased all the names under Others.

Kally was so shocked she didn't say anything.

"Gimme the sales receipts and clean off a space on your desk," Riggs demanded.

She handed him the fifty receipts, then moved files to a credenza and backed away, arms folded, silently fuming. Riggs removed the paperclip and tossed it on top of the file cabinet, then read through the receipts.

In the past, only Dale had made her feel uncomfortable in her own office until she had gotten used to the work. And used to him. Now it was Riggs. She would never get used to Riggs.

"Okay," he said, rounding her desk. He laid out ten receipts in a row, like train cars on a track. He put the others on top of the files on her credenza.

Kally moved next to him while he rearranged them.

"These are the last ten people who were in the winery and bought wine, one right after the other. Ten minutes apart, give or take. Maybe they knew one another. Maybe not. Maybe they saw something. Maybe they didn't. But we'll find out."

*Something from nothing.*

He pointed to the first receipt. "That's Noel Jacobsen, the attorney. He was still at the winery at ten forty-two p.m., within two hours of…" Riggs glanced at Kally.

"Kirk's…"

"*Kirk's* death." Riggs pointed to the last receipt. "That's your Mr. Arnaugh, eight thirty-seven p.m."

Riggs gathered the receipts and moved to the white board, and wrote the names in descending order based on the time stamps.

"You have addresses for these people?" he asked, not looking at her.

"Yes." Kally sat at her desk and reached for the wine club list.

"Read them to me."

She started with Jacobsen. "Bellevue."

Riggs wrote a "B" after his name. He pointed to the next name: "Archer."

"Woodinville," Kally said and Riggs wrote a "W" on the board.

They went through all ten names. Four people lived in Bellevue, four in Redmond, one in Woodinville, and one in Seattle.

"We'll visit Bellevue today," Riggs said. Then he pointed to Core People. "You talk to these people on your own. You can do the wine speak with them. We'll do the others together."

Kally nodded. She took in Riggs's exquisite handwriting, made even more noticeable next to hers. She scribbled, Riggs painted the words.

"And put these lists on OPI," he went on.

"I will."

"We'll update the online report after every interview. And we'll put check marks on your board next to those we've talked to. We'll keep going on this until we get the tox report."

Kally nodded again.

But he wasn't finished. He sat in the chair in front of her desk.

"There's a way to interview. So let's work on the questions. You'll probably add your own questions because you know wine. But don't ask many. You don't need them."

She nodded slowly.

"I don't care about wine," he added.

Kally nodded again, feeling more comfortable sitting at her desk. Riggs looked small for some reason now that she was facing him. She pictured him getting smaller and smaller in the chair, his voice rising with his increasing smallness and how powerful she felt talking to a little person.

"Do you?" he asked.

"I'm sorry…what?"

"Do you have a timeline on when you want to get the questioning done?"

"Yes. This week. It will coincide with getting Nakamura's tox results." She hadn't thought of it, actually.

"Good. We will have done our due diligence. Then we can move on."

Move on? *Don't I make that decision?*

"From my experience, these are the questions we need to ask." He pointed to her. "Write these down." Riggs held up a finger to indicate number one. "Did you know the deceased?" Two fingers: "How long did you know him?" Three fingers: "How long were you at the party?" And so on: "Did you come with anyone? Did you talk to the deceased? Who else was he talking to? And, did you notice anything unusual?"

"These sound like the questions I've been asking," she added, not looking up as she wrote.

"Seven questions," he said, ignoring her comment. "That's it." He stuck his thumb over his shoulder at the board behind him. "And with this many people, it's all we have time for.

"Now, some questions may lead to others," he continued. "But you shouldn't spend more than twenty minutes with the person you're questioning." He looked right at her. Another sharp gaze.

"Got it?"

"Yes. Got it."

"And when you put your report online, I want you to flag anything you think is unusual. Here's an example: you mentioned earlier that three or four people at the party weren't drinking. Flag that."

"Okay."

"And about tomorrow…you'll be working that funeral. Like I said."

"I know."

Riggs picked up Jacobsen's receipt from her desk and looked at it. "People spend this much on wine? This is almost two thousand dollars."

"Yes, people spend that much on wine. Because it's Kirk's wine."

"Is it good?"

"Quite good."

He shook his head and put the receipt back on the desk. Then he rose. "I have an errand to run. Let's meet in Bellevue"—he glanced at his watch—"in an hour. Jacobsen's office is downtown. There's a Mexican place in the lobby. We'll have lunch first."

"Okay," she said, relieved she didn't have to ride in a car with him.

Kally watched him leave. Then she created a box in her mind and filled it with words that described Riggs: *abrasive, abrupt, rude, obtuse, know-it-all, angry, mean…*

But then she looked at the lists on her white board, pared from sixty people to twenty.

In short order, Riggs had made sense out of a sea of names.

# 26

Kally stood in front of her board scribbling the credit card receipt people on her pad of paper.

"What're you doing?" Bud asked, coming into her office.

"Riggs and I are working the Remick case."

"Oh, how lucky you are," Bud said sarcastically. "And how's that going?"

"Remains to be seen."

"Don't let him take over," Bud offered.

Kally let out a muffled laugh. "Yeah."

She looked closely at her Core group, which included people she knew and some she didn't. She didn't know personally, for example, Paula Sampson, Kirk's office manager; Caitlin Farling, the sales/marketing manager; or Suri Lakosha, the tasting-room manager. And she didn't know what they could add. But they and others on the board were the closest link to Kirk.

Suddenly, she thought of someone else and added Denny Lane, Kirk's ex-winemaker and Janie's rumored paramour to the list.

Then she looked at Bud. "Sorry…just needed to finish."

"It's okay."

"You're here about the cases." Kally walked back to her desk, then sat down and motioned to the chair for Bud.

"Yup," Bud said, taking the proffered chair. "I read your reports online. Interesting about Mrs. Hatch. This is…what…the fourth, fifth time she's called?"

"Yeah. Riggs took the previous calls."

"So this happened Thursday," Bud said.

Kally nodded as she reached for a file for her notes regarding the domestic violence call. She thought back to that evening. She'd gone to the Hatch home around eleven p.m. in a wealthy area of Woodinville. The Hatchs' big house and horse barn sat on lots of acreage, and the guest house on the property was bigger than the house Kally had grown up in.

"When Mrs. Hatch opened the door," Kally began, "I saw a red welt on her face, near her left eye. I remembered thinking…'a punch to the temple and you might be dead.'"

"And she later reneged on the charge, according to what you wrote on OPI," Bud said.

Kally nodded again and passed the file to Bud. "Dale wants more follow-up. Especially with the number of calls."

"So a CYA visit?"

"I think so. Dale thinks the abuse is escalating."

Bud opened the file and quickly perused Kally's personal notes. "How much more can we do really?"

"Make another visit."

Bud looked up. "And say what?"

"Ask her if she feels safe. If there is a place she can go if it happens again."

"All of which you did."

"Ask it again."

Bud didn't respond.

"We may have to get an advocate," Kally said. "For now, we'll do our due diligence and follow-up," she added, sounding a lot like Riggs.

Kally paused. "I don't know why women like Mrs. Hatch stay in their marriages. I think it's the 'what's next for me' scenario. As in: 'Where do I go?'"

"Right," Bud answered.

Kally went on. "Apparently Mr. Hatch has moved into an apartment. She told me he wants all the horses. But one was a gift and she won't give it up."

"So this could get messy."

"Just document everything."

"Okay." Bud closed the file. "What else?"

Kally reached for two more files. "There's an elderly lady on Crescent. Mrs. Finmore. She wants her gutters cleaned."

Bud smiled. "I'll go see her. What else?"

"A Mrs. Stevens on Eastridge Drive wants the neighbors to cut down two trees because their leaves are falling into her yard. The neighbors refused. So Mrs. Stevens is raking the leaves and throwing them over the fence into her neighbor's yard." Kally shrugged. "She's called twice."

"I'll see her, too." Bud looked at her watch. "I'll probably do these today. Can I take your notes?"

"Sure." Then: "How's the wedding coming along?"

Bud shook her head. "It's overwhelming with so much to do. But A-Rod wants to help, luckily. Some men wouldn't."

Kally nodded, glancing at her board, feeling pressure to get going.

"Well, I'll leave you to it," Bud said rising. "Good luck with the case."

"Thanks. And thanks for taking these on."

"Not a problem," Bud said at the door. "I'll put my reports up later."

27

Kally looked at the time: ten-forty a.m. She picked up the torn sheet of paper listing the names of wine publications and blogs and called the first number for *Wine Spectator*. A Peter Cavalarri answered.

She heard the relief in his voice that she had returned the call. He asked several questions, and Kally detailed the facts as she had laid them out to Riggs.

"Can I call you if I have more questions?" he asked.

"Sure," Kally answered.

She went through the same questions and answers with the other publications and blogs. Thinking of the wine bloggers, she was surprised she hadn't heard from Mindy Peters of *Wine Hound*. Mindy was another Northwest Wine Academy alum who floated around the Warehouse District every week looking for stories.

*Perhaps she will just stop by. That is, if I ever get to my winery.*

It was now ten fifty-five a.m. Kally picked up the phone to call Paula Sampson, Kirk's office manager.

When Paula answered, Kally started in.

"Paula, this is Kally O'Keefe with the Woodinville Police Department. I'm leading the case about Kirk's death. Can I ask you a few questions?"

"Sure." And: "I like your wine."

"Oh." The compliment caught Kally by surprise. "Thank you." Then: "How did Denny Lane and Kirk get along?"

"They got along okay. Denny was here about three years. He learned Kirk's working style, and they…meshed. He just wanted his own thing, I guess."

"Not unusual," Kally added.

"You know everyone who works here takes away Kirk's method of winemaking," Paula offered.

"His winemaking methods aren't a secret, are they?"

"It was more the percentages of the varieties he used that he kept to himself. Anyone who worked here knew what varieties went into his blends. But they didn't know the percentages."

*Interesting that Mark told me the combination for Blitzen,* Kally thought.

"But he was an asshole and a pig," Paula said suddenly.

The comment shocked her, coming from someone she pegged as a professional woman.

"Who are you talking about?" Kally asked.

"Denny! He went after women here like it was open season."

*Oh and his boss didn't?! And just how had Janie found that attractive.* This was a line of questioning she hadn't anticipated.

"I had to talk with him more than once," Paula continued. "Because women were complaining."

"Did Kirk support you in that?"

Paula paused. "Kirk supported me. He was more subtle about his... interests. He knew how to be discreet."

Kally knew that to be true.

"Thankfully Denny's gone," Paula added.

Kally wouldn't ask Paula about Denny and Kirk's ex-wife, Janie. She'd have that discussion with Janie herself.

But Paula wasn't finished.

"You know...women come here to learn winemaking. Especially here."

"Right." Kally waited for Paula to continue. But she didn't. "Did Denny leave on good terms with Kirk?"

"Yeah. But then there was always someone else to become assistant winemaker."

"I imagine so."

"We're all going to the funeral," Paula said, changing the subject. "It will be hard, but we'll be there."

"Yes, right," Kally answered.

"He had a good heart."

Such a simple statement. And true.

"He did, didn't he," Kally said. "Were you at the harvest party? I didn't see you."

"No. My husband and I had other plans."

"What about the other administrative people?" Kally asked.

"They were on vacation," Paula answered.

"Where?"

"Suri went with her family to the Midwest, and Caitlin and her fiancé went to the San Juans."

"Okay, thanks for this," Kally said, quickly scribbling notes. She looked at the clock: six minutes after eleven a.m. She needed to get going.

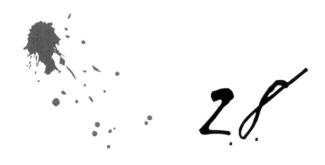

# 28

Kally grabbed her backpack and placed her holstered gun inside. On the way out, she passed her white board without looking at it. *It's not who they are*, she reminded herself, thinking of the Bellevue business people they would be interviewing, *it's what they saw or heard.* She hoped Riggs wouldn't antagonize them.

Kally walked down the hallway, seeing Dale at his desk. She stopped and he looked up but didn't say anything.

"I called the wine journalists," Kally said, from outside his door.

"Great, thanks for doing that."

There was an awkward pause. "I'm meeting Riggs in Bellevue. We're talking to an attorney who was at the winery Friday night. Then we'll go to Microsoft. Then I'll go back to Kirk's winery to talk to people there."

"Okay. Sounds like Riggs is helping."

"He is."

"Any news on the tox report?"

"Not yet."

Dale nodded. "I'll see you tomorrow, then."

Kally walked on. She was doing what Dale had asked, the most basic work in a case like this when you don't yet know if a death is a homicide: seeing people, asking questions, sorting out details. But something gnawed at her. Dale was depending on her. She couldn't screw this up.

And yet…she thought Kirk's death was a murder, even if her two superiors didn't.

Rounding the corner, Kally saw A-Rod coming out of the cafeteria, a coffee in hand. She hadn't seen him since Saturday at the crime scene. And she had only briefly glanced at his report from that morning.

"Hey, A-Rod," she said.

"How's it going?" he replied.

"Not bad."

"Bud said you're working the case."

"It's consuming my time." Kally looked into his bright-blue eyes, thinking what a stunning couple he and Bud made. She caught herself thinking of a certain Frenchman with dark hair and blue eyes and got herself back on track.

"Can I ask you something?" she inquired.

"Sure."

"What time did you get to the Warehouse District on Saturday?"

"Um…I'd have to check my report," A-Rod answered. "But I think it was around six forty…six forty-five a.m."

"And did you go inside the winery?"

"Yeah. As soon as I pulled up in front, a guy unlocked the door."

"A tall, skinny guy with brown hair who looked upset?"

A-Rod nodded. "He said he was the one who called."

"So then what did you do?"

"I followed him to the back. And I saw the body."

"How long were you back there?"

A-Rod shrugged. "Less than a minute. I told him that you had been called and that my role was to be out front keeping people away. And I said Nakamura was coming."

"So then you left…"

A-Rod nodded again. "And I ran into a woman on the way out."

"There was one woman there: Justine." Kally described her.

"Yeah that was her. She was crying."

"Did you notice anything else or anyone else?"

"Um…a crowd was forming. So it's good I got outside." He took a sip of his coffee. Then he stopped. He seemed lost in thought. "There was a woman getting into a car and leaving."

"Really? Where?"

"To the east of the crime scene. In the parking lot."

"What did she look like?"

"I didn't see much of her. Only long blonde hair."

"What kind of car?"

"Black sedan. Newer."

"Was this in your report?"

"No. I just thought of it. I'll add it, though."

"When did this happen?" Kally inquired.

"As soon as I got out there." He paused. "What are you thinking?"

"I'm not sure."

"It was a split-second thing," A-Rod added. "I just happened to see her and the car over someone's shoulder."

"Okay," she said again. "This is good. Thanks."

Kally walked out of the building and got into her SUV. *"A split second thing..."* Everyone there that morning focused on Kirk's winery, the activity going on, the police car, A-Rod himself...

Except one person.

Her train of thought was interrupted by her phone ringing. She looked at the name. It was her friend Chris.

"Hey, Chris," Kally said.

"Can I sit with you at the funeral tomorrow?"

"Sure, that would be great." Kally hadn't thought about the funeral with so much to do.

"Where should I meet you?"

"Out front. I'll be...hanging around out there. Meet me at nine forty-five a.m."

"Okay. So everyone's going, except Sam...she's out of town. But she didn't know Kirk that well."

Chris continued: "Sarah may sit with us if she can get away for the morning. Ellie said she'll be sitting with people from Red Mountain Productions, who are all coming."

"Good to know," Kally responded.

"I wonder if Denny will sit with Janie," Chris added.

"Yeah...I wonder about that, too," Kally said.

"Well, I'll let you go. I'll see you tomorrow."

"Yep. See you then."

She'd have to apologize to her friend about how preoccupied she was. As if Chris couldn't tell. Kally took out her pad of paper and looked at the address again in Bellevue, then drove out.

# 29

Kally got onto Interstate 405 South for the twenty-minute drive to Bellevue to see Noel Jacobsen. Bellevue, to the east of Seattle across Lake Washington, was newer and more conservative in many quarters than its better-known neighbor.

And there was a lot of money here, derived not just from software and tech but also from high-priced professional services—attorney practices, real-estate firms, consulting companies.

Quite a change from strawberry fields...what Bellevue had originally been.

Kally sped up, realizing she might be late. Jacobsen had been the last person to buy wine on Friday night at Kirk's party using a credit card. After interviewing him, she and Riggs would drive to Microsoft in Redmond to interview James Monroe, the man Arnaugh liked to call "Jimmy." Monroe lived in Bellevue but worked in Redmond, thus his name on the Bellevue list. And there were two more people just like him who worked at Microsoft but lived in Bellevue. All were on the time spectrum between Jacobsen and Arnaugh on those credit card receipts.

Kally passed a slow-moving delivery truck, then remained at her passing speed. She didn't have much experience questioning people in a murder investigation. But she remembered from her training that most people—unless they had looked at a watch or glanced at a clock—didn't come close to knowing the exact time they were at a crime scene.

*Which, you know, is an important detail.*

She turned off Interstate 405 and onto Eighth Avenue West and drove into a canyon of gleaming new buildings, the heart of Bellevue's business district. *Mr. Jacobsen's wine purchase at Kirk's was probably a drop in the bucket to him,* she thought. *I bet he has a beautiful wine cellar and many, many bottles of prized Washington State wine.* He probably didn't have Wine Babe Cellars among his holdings yet. But that could change. Even her somm friend Sarah thought so.

Kally spotted the address. Just as she thought, the law practice of Jacobsen Cash Donohue and Forbes, which she'd scoped out on the internet, was in one of the newer downtown high-rises, a firm of 120 attorneys. Big, in other words. Maybe the biggest in town.

She pulled into the building's underground parking and took an elevator to the lobby. Spotting the restaurant Riggs had mentioned, Kally walked in and saw Riggs already at a table, a tray of food in front of him, looking at his phone.

"Hi," she said, walking up to him.

"Get in line before the rush," he answered, without looking up. "My food's getting cold."

Kally went to the counter to order, brushing off Riggs's brusqueness yet again. When she returned, Riggs had already eaten half his food.

She sat down across from him and started in on her taco lunch.

"It's important to see people in their place of business," Riggs said, pushing his phone to the side. He chewed and poked at the chicken and rice on his plate.

"Why's that?"

"Because you get a sense of their personality. At least, the person they *think* they are. For someone like Jacobsen, this is where his power is."

"Hmm."

"I'll tell you what you're gonna see," Riggs continued. "Jacobsen will have a big office, lots of artwork, and a nice view. Minions will stop in and hand him papers. He'll have his own coffee maker and a small refrigerator filled with juices and water."

How did that jive with Dale telling her to go into a crime scene without preconceptions? "Have you been here before?" she asked.

"No. But I know people like Jacobsen. He is of a *type*."

"What type?"

"Above the law." Riggs threw his napkin down and stood up. "Let's go."

Kally looked at her plate, then up at him, her food one-quarter eaten.

Riggs walked away. Kally followed.

They stood in front of a bank of elevators. Men and women in business attire stood with them, looking at their phones.

"He's on thirty-six," Riggs announced after checking the building's directory. He popped a breath mint without offering her one. One of the elevator doors opened, and Riggs and Kally stepped to the side as people exited. When they entered, Kally noted that Jacobsen's office was on the top floor.

Again, she pushed Riggs's shortcomings aside, into that little box she'd prepared for him in her mind so she could get on with her work. She focused instead on Jacobsen's office, as they stopped on floors and people exited. If the office faced west, Jacobsen would have a view over other Bellevue office buildings to Lake Washington, the Seattle skyline, and the Olympic Mountains beyond. If his view was to the east, there would be busy Interstate 405 below, along with expensive car lots, Lake Sammamish, and the foothills of the Cascades.

Either way, floor thirty-six came with a view.

And in Riggs's world, assumptions about power and position.

## 30

The doors opened, and Kally and Riggs stepped into a quiet carpeted lobby.

A receptionist sat thirty feet from them at a low circular desk made from a wood Kally couldn't identify. Beyond her, through glass doors, she saw nothing but sky through office windows. To the right of the desk, several people sat in leather chairs talking on phones or thumbing through magazines.

They approached the receptionist, who smiled up at them. Behind her, the name of the firm appeared in gold lettering against what appeared to be brushed suede wallpaper. Exotic flower arrangements sat on pedestals on either side of the name. The lighting was tastefully dim, just enough to see and read.

Riggs announced them. "We're here to see Mr. Jacobsen." Kally produced her business card and the receptionist took it.

"Do you have an appointment?"

"No," Kally answered.

The receptionist rose and, without saying anything disappeared behind a partition. In less than a minute, she returned and led them down a hallway, everything glass, bright, and sunny. They walked the length of it, passing offices where people worked on their computers or were engaged in conversations.

"You'll be in here, in this conference room," the receptionist said over her shoulder.

*So no chance to size up the man.* Really, she wanted to see if Riggs had been correct.

The receptionist left and they remained standing, taking in the room with its polished wooden conference table, plush cushioned chairs, and a wall of legal books. At opposite ends of the room were two large paintings in bright colors, one a cyclist rounding a corner, the other a soccer player, arms out, ready to score a goal. Perhaps the firm represented sports stars.

"Hello!" Jacobsen entered and closed the door behind him. He came up to Kally and Riggs and shook their hands, his handshake firm. Kally introduced them.

"Please sit!" Jacobsen said.

They sat at the table: Kally and Riggs together at the side, Jacobsen at the head.

Jacobsen pushed his chair back and crossed his legs. Kally did a quick once-over: He was shorter than Riggs at about five feet nine and was balding and wore rim-less glasses. Jacobsen had taken off his suit coat but was wearing a buttoned up vest and an expensive tie. The white shirt still held stiff creases down the sleeves. Cufflinks showed the University of Washington mascot.

Jacobsen placed his hands in his lap.

"You're a Husky?" Riggs asked, noticing the mascot as well.

"Indeed! Are you?"

"No. UC Berkeley."

"Ah."

Riggs went on: "Officer O'Keefe will ask the questions for us."

"What's this about?" Jacobsen addressed Kally.

"We are investigating the death of Kirk Remick," Kally answered taking out her pen and notebook. "You were at the harvest party Friday night?"

"I was, yes. So sad. A great winemaker. Are you a wine connoisseur?"

"I am, actually."

"Then you know how good his wine is."

"Yes. Did you know the deceased?"

"Not personally."

"How long did you know him?"

"Let's see...I've been in his wine club for...nine, ten, years."

Kally scribbled down the numbers. "How long were you at the party?"

Jacobsen thought for a moment. "About an hour and a half. I got there late."

"Did you go with anyone?"

"No."

"Did you talk to the deceased?"

"Only briefly."

"What did you say?"

"'Nice party.'"

"Who else was Mr. Remick talking to?"

"Too many to name."

"Did you notice anything unusual?"

"No."

"What happened to your hand?" Riggs asked.

It was an obvious question, the padded bandage wrapping around the palm on Jacobson's left hand.

Jacobsen held it up and looked at it. "Working with tools. In the garage."

Kally looked down at her notes. Mr. Jacobsen did not appear to be someone who did anything in a garage except park an expensive car.

"So, a wrench...screwdriver?" Riggs asked.

Jacobsen waved it off. "No. Something sharp near the chain. I was changing my granddaughter's tire. On her bike."

"I see," Riggs said.

Kally couldn't think of anything sharp on a bike chain. She closed her notebook.

"That's it?" Jacobsen asked.

"That's it," Kally answered.

"I'm just curious: What's the business of your law firm?" Riggs asked.

*He's breaking his own rules about questioning.*

"Personal injury: car wrecks, medical malpractice, construction accidents."

*That explains the top floor*, Kally thought. "Before we go, is there anything else you want to tell us about the party?"

Jacobsen sat back. "Well, when I got the invitation, I remembered thinking, 'Yeah, I think I'll go.' I never usually go to these things. But it was a chance to see grapes coming in from the vineyard. You never see that."

"And how was that?" Riggs asked.

"It was great. We all had wine glasses, full, of course, and Remick had a big crusher out in back on what he called the 'crush pad.' And there was a guy driving a forklift and lifting a big bin of grapes up in the air and then gradually flipping it so the grapes tumbled out into a tin catchment, and then the grapes moved up a conveyer belt up to the crusher above. And people were standing on either side taking out leaves and twigs as the grapes moved up."

Kally listened intently as Jacobsen explained the evening, so caught up in his recounting that he appeared to be back there, glass in hand, watching the work.

"And his people were coming around filling everyone's glasses with wine. His expensive wine. And Remick was explaining that the grapes *there*—in the crusher—would eventually be *here*, in the glass."

"So it was interesting," Riggs said casually.

"Oh yeah! I hope…"

Jacobsen stopped.

"He does it again?" Riggs asked.

Jacobsen nodded. "What a shame." He continued. "You know, it's hard work. There's machinery. Accidents can happen."

"You mean like a death?" Riggs asked.

Kally glanced at a clock behind Jacobsen.

"I mean accidents that maim," Jacobsen said. "I was thinking of services our firm might render. I didn't mean to defame Mr. Remick."

"You didn't."

"Was his death an accident?" Jacobsen asked.

"We don't know," Kally answered.

Jacobsen rose, and so did Kally and Riggs. Kally took out a business card and handled it to him.

"Please call if you think of anything about the evening, even if it's just a small thing," she said.

"I will."

"Thanks for your time," she added.

The two walked back down the hallway, leaving Jacobsen in the conference room. Suddenly Kally heard her name.

"Kally! Is that you?"

She turned. A thin, fit man walked toward her.

"I thought I recognized you!" he said as he came up to her.

It took a moment, but then Kally realized the man standing in front of her was Jim Fishback, the husband of Ellie, the former Seahawks cheerleader.

Riggs stood to the side as the two carried on.

"Are you working here?" she asked. "I thought you were in Seattle."

"I was. But an opportunity came up, and so here I am."

Kally suddenly remembered Riggs. "I'm sorry. Jim Fishback… Robert Riggs," she said introducing them.

The two shook hands. Then: "You're still in the wine business?" Fishback asked. He folded his arms.

"I am. But right now, we're working the Kirk Remick case."

"Oh yeah. Ellie told me about that." Fishback shook his head. "Too bad."

"It is, yes," Kally answered, at a loss for anything to ask him further. She didn't know Fishback that well, seeing him only at wine events with Ellie.

"Well, I won't keep you. Just wanted to say hi." He turned to Riggs. "Nice meeting you."

Riggs and Kally stood in the parking garage before going to their cars. "What did you think of Jacobsen?" she asked.

"He played to type. I was disappointed we didn't see his office."

"Me, too."

"I'm gonna flag that hand in our report," Riggs said.

"It could be nothing," she offered.

"We won't discount it yet. I'll write it up for OPI." Riggs took out his keys and walked away. "I'll see you at Microsoft," he said over his shoulder.

31

Kally sat in her car, still in the parking garage. She didn't agree with Riggs regarding Jacobsen. Clearly, flagging anything about the man was a waste of time. But Riggs thought otherwise—Riggs, who wasn't very forthcoming about why he thought the way he did.

She wondered about Jim Fishback, though, and his connection to Jacobsen. It was probably all the University of Washington. It was how things worked, really, that college connection. They must have been friends. Or…maybe not; maybe it was just the "U Dub." Fishback had crewed for Washington, she remembered. And he was good. Good enough to compete in the Olympic trials.

Riggs drove past and up the ramp of the parking garage.

Kally continued sitting there. Nakamura and the tox report came to mind. And that thought led to his comment about money. Kally dug out her phone and called Becky O'Keefe, her ex-sister-in-law and a forensic accountant at Bank of America in Seattle.

"Hey! I haven't heard from you," Becky exclaimed when she answered.

"I know, Becks. How are you?"

"Good." She changed the subject. "Your brother called. We're having coffee."

"Yeah, he told me."

"Has he had a religious conversion or something?"

Kally laughed. "He's…making changes. He stopped drinking."

"He mentioned that, too. You know…he has to do that work on his own. I can't…"

"I know," Kally answered.

"So…what are you up to?" Becky asked.

"I'm looking into Kirk Remick's death."

"I heard about that. Really a shame."

"Yeah, the medical examiner mentioned something to me about money, and I can't get it out of my mind. I want to look into his accounts."

"He has one here?" Becky asked.

"Yes. I saw the envelope," Kally said, remembering Kirk's bills in the evidence bag in her office.

"Fax me a warrant, and I'll go through what we have."

"Kirk was very successful," Kally thought to add. "He got into the wine business at the right time. I just can't believe money might be an issue."

"You'd be surprised," Becky said, with not a little bit of sarcasm. "He could have a separate account that I may or may not find. I'll look into it."

"That would be great."

"Send me that warrant and I'll get to work."

"I will. Thanks!"

Kally pulled in next to Riggs in the sprawling Microsoft complex in Redmond where they would see three people unannounced. They walked together toward a building on campus, neither saying anything. It was said Microsoft never hired anyone who came for an interview dressed in a business suit. Best to arrive casual—not tee-shirt casual like the two guys standing outside the entrance vaping, but not far from it.

She wondered how Riggs would do here, a world he wasn't familiar with. But then, neither was she.

A guard sitting at a table looked up when they entered. She watched him as he took in her uniform and badge.

"Woodinville," he said finally.

"Yes. I'm here to talk to several employees," Kally said.

"Okay…who?"

"James Monroe. Jeffrey Bangs. Samuel Lee."

"Do you have an appointment?" he asked.

"No."

"I don't know if they're available," the guard said, picking up his phone.

"We'll wait," Riggs answered.

The guard pointed down a hallway. "There's a conference room on your left. Wait in there."

Riggs and Kally walked down the dark hallway. "What is it with conference rooms today?" she asked.

Riggs ignored her. "He could be a millionaire, that guard."

"Yes. He could."

They turned a corner and entered the room.

"This is the first time I've been at Microsoft." Riggs walked around, taking in the artwork. A floor-to-ceiling window comprised one "wall" and looked out on an overgrown courtyard. For such a large company, the conference room was small, dominated by a long table and chairs.

"I've never been here either," Kally offered. "But I have friends who work here. Or used to." She thought of her friend Chris.

After a time, three men entered, laptops in hand. Two held take-out coffee cups.

"Hi," she said

"Hi," they all replied.

They introduced themselves and shook hands. Kally did a quick assessment of the three men: late twenties-early thirties. Lee and Bangs had on tee shirts and jeans. James Monroe wore a pressed pink Oxford shirt and khaki pants. She saw why Arnaugh referred to Monroe as a "James" sort of guy, not a "Jimmy." In dress and manner, he appeared reserved, studious. His sandy colored hair was cut short and he wore wire-rim glasses.

Lee looked to be in incredible shape. Biceps bulged from his shirt, the front of which read *Don't Mess with Texas*. He wore large black-rimmed glasses and had a modern cut to his dark hair.

Bangs was taller than the other two and had longish blonde hair, a California surfer type. And perhaps he was. His shirt proclaimed *Beer is a Food Group*.

Monroe had moved down the length of the table, away from the rest. He set his laptop down, opened it, then stood still, staring at Kally.

"Please sit," Kally said. Riggs took a chair to her left, Lee and Bangs to her right. Monroe was opposite her at the end of the table.

Kally remained standing. "We are investigating the death of Mr. Kirk Remick, the Woodinville winemaker." She refrained from telling them she herself was a winemaker. "I appreciate your meeting with us today about the case."

"It's okay," Lee said. He sat casually in the chair with one arm draped over the back. Bangs—the 'Surfer'—sat forward, his laptop to the side. Monroe sat ramrod straight, eyes still trained on her.

"All of you were at the harvest party Friday night—"

All heads nodded in agreement.

"Was he murdered?" Lee asked, interrupting. "I always think of a 'case' as a murder. Is it?"

"We don't know," Kally answered. "And, yes, we have cases, but cases are not necessarily murders."

"Interesting. We have projects," Lee thought to add.

Riggs stared at Lee without saying anything. She could only imagine what he was thinking—buttoned-up Riggs in this high-tech/no-tech encounter.

She went on. "Tell me how you all came to be at Remick Cellars last Friday."

Surprisingly, it wasn't Monroe who answered. It was Surfer.

"We all got in early on Kirk Remick's wine club," he said, looking around the table. "We go together to the events."

"Right," Lee agreed.

"Did you know Mr. Remick?" Kally asked, starting in on Riggs's questions.

"Not personally," Lee answered.

"How long were you at the party?" she asked.

The three looked at one another. Lee shrugged. "I'd guess one and a half to two hours."

The other two nodded in agreement.

"Did you notice anything unusual when you were there?"

"Like what?" Lee asked.

"Something that caught your eye—something that made you think 'That's odd' or 'I wonder why he's doing that.'"

Lee and Monroe shook their heads.

"But something did happen," Surfer said. He turned to the others. "Remember when that woman came past really fast and bumped me and almost spilled my wine? And she just kept going, and I said, 'Wow, she's pissed.'"

"Yeah, I remember," Monroe said, finally joining in.

"When was that?" Kally asked.

"I don't know," Surfer replied. "We'd had a few glasses by then. We were talking about finding more appetizers."

"Yeah," Lee agreed, smiling. "It was later. But not real late."

"What did she look like?" Kally asked.

"Blonde hair, long. She came from my right, so I didn't see her full on," Surfer answered. "She bumped my right arm. Looked like she'd had an argument."

"Where were you standing?" Kally asked.

Surfer thought for a moment. "Near the tanks."

There were tanks on both sides of the room. And barrels where the bins usually were. Kally thought for a moment, then moved to a small open area in the conference room.

"Everyone stand up."

Riggs looked at her, questioningly. The three Microsoft men stood.

"I want you to re-enact the evening when you saw the woman. Everyone come over here."

They moved next to her. Only Riggs remained seated, watching.

"Imagine that you are in the winery that night. I will explain what the winery looks like and then I want you to stand where you were"— she looked to Surfer—"when the woman bumped you."

"Okay," they all said.

Kally pointed behind them. "In that direction is the door leaving the production area that goes to the tasting room. That's where you got your wine glasses."

They all nodded.

She pointed to her right out the floor-to-ceiling window, and then to her left. "There were tanks on both sides of the room."

Kally pointed behind her. "The large garage door is back there where they were processing grapes."

"Got it," Lee said.

Each took their places. Monroe and Lee stood across from Surfer. Lee held up his hand as if holding a glass.

"I was talking to you," Surfer said, nodding to Lee.

"Yeah," Lee agreed. "We were talking about whether we were going to meet the deadline for the beta version."

"And I was about to answer that," Surfer said, "when—*bam!*—she hit my arm. And she never said anything. Lucky the wine didn't spill."

"So you were close to the barrels, too," Kally prodded.

Surfer thought for a moment. "Yeah, there were barrels."

Kally surmised that they were within ten feet of where Kirk's body was found.

"Anything else?" she asked.

"After that, a woman came by with a plate of food, and we devoured almost the whole thing," Surfer said.

"And Remick walked around with bottles of wine," Lee added, "and we had to have some of that!"

"So this was later in the evening?" Kally asked. Had to be, because she wasn't there during the time they were describing.

"Yeah," Surfer answered. "He went up to a group of guys and poured for them and talked to them."

"What did they look like?" Kally asked.

"Sort of older, white, casually dressed," Surfer responded.

"Dressed up for us!" Lee said.

"They were business men, I think," Surfer added.

"Can you describe what they looked like?"

"Two were bald, kinda. And they wore glasses," Lee said.

"They looked like CEOs or lawyers or something," Surfer clarified. "You know how older men try to look relaxed when they take off their tie and jacket and roll up their sleeves?" He seemed to remember that Riggs was in the room and turned to look at him.

Riggs stared back without commenting.

"Okay. This is helpful," Kally said, more interested in the woman with blonde hair than the men drinking Kirk's wine. They all sat again at the table.

"How did he die?" Monroe asked, the only one of the three who didn't appear comfortable reliving the evening.

Kally didn't answer right away, so he answered his own question. "It could have been $CO_2$ poisoning."

"Why do you say that?" Kally asked.

He shrugged. "It's a constant in fermenting wine."

"Are you a winemaker?" Kally asked.

"Just a home winemaker."

"Hmm. You're right about $CO_2$. But Kirk—I mean Mr. Remick—was experienced. Personally, I don't think it's a mistake he would have made."

Riggs tapped his fingers on the table.

"So he was killed?" Lee asked.

Kally paused. "We don't know."

"How many options are there?" Monroe asked.

Kally looked down at her notes, where she'd scribbled descriptions of the men. Then she looked up at Monroe.

"Our options will be narrowed once we have the toxicology report."

## 33

"You know to flag the angry blonde, right?" Riggs asked. He and Kally were by their cars in the Microsoft parking lot.

"I do," Kally answered.

"You did a good job in there with...you know...the reenactment."

She was taken aback by the compliment. "Oh. Thanks." Really, she had no idea what he thought of her. Mostly she thought in negatives when it came to Riggs.

"I think Monroe has more to offer," she added. "He was quiet."

"Then flag him, too. You can talk to him again." He paused. "Get this all on OPI, and then you and I need to go over the timeline again. Let's do that tomorrow morning, first thing."

"All right," she said, noting that he was back to setting the agenda. "There's something else."

"What?"

"This is the third mention of a woman with blonde hair seen around the time of Kirk's—Remick's—death. Arnaugh had also mentioned someone."

"What's the second one?"

"A-Rod remembered a woman getting into a black sedan at Kirk's winery the morning the body was found."

"That wasn't in his report."

"I know. He's amending it."

She saw it immediately: Riggs assumed a look of disgust and shook his head, telling her without telling her how upset he was. As if A-Rod had personally affronted him.

"We need *all* the information to investigate the case," he said, finally, which was probably an edited version.

Riggs left and Kally dictated her report while sitting in her car. She flagged Monroe as quiet and reserved, with possibly more information to provide. If she weren't so pressed for time, she'd talk to him now. And she flagged Banks—Surfer—for his encounter with the woman who had bumped into him.

Then she stopped.

If the woman was angry, who had she been angry with?

Kally envisioned the three men again back in the conference room reliving the evening in Kirk's winery. Monroe and Lee had their backs to the tanks, the barrels, and the woman rushing by.

So it wasn't Monroe she needed to talk to again. It was Surfer. Perhaps he had seen the other person. She added this bit of information to her report.

*Is it even important that Surfer had the encounter with the woman?* she wondered. Maybe this person was angry that her husband or partner or date was drinking too much.

There *was* a lot of wine.

Stumped, she ended the dictation and drove off into an early rush hour.

Kally drove into the back of Remick Cellars, seeing Seth's and Leah's cars behind her own winery. She took out her phone and called Seth. Yes, she could walk fifty feet and talk to him in person. But she didn't want to get caught in her winery while she still had police work to do at Kirk's.

She got voice mail and left a message:

> "Seth, you and Leah start the blending trials. I'll be there as soon as I can."

Then she made another call, to Microsoft and 'Surfer,' getting voice mail again:

> Mr. Banks, this is Kally O'Keefe again with the Woodinville Police Department. One quick question: At Mr. Remick's winery Friday night, when the woman with blonde hair bumped into you…did you see anyone else? Anyone she might have been talking to? Whatever you can add will be appreciated. Thank you.

Kally grabbed her things and got out and walked into Kirk's production area. The winery was in full working mode. Four people to her left had their backs to her and ignored her entrance. Probably the interns. She would talk to them soon enough. Manning and Justine stood near the crime-scene-taped bin discussing something. They looked up at her as she approached.

Justine smiled, her countenance better than what Kally had seen Saturday morning. Manning didn't acknowledge her.

"I want to talk to the interns," Kally said, addressing Manning. "But first...is Paula still here?"

Manning looked at Justine, who shrugged.

"I think so." Justine pointed to her right. "She might still be in her office."

Kally walked past them and Kirk's office to Paula's, who was closing down her computer. She looked up when Kally knocked lightly on the door frame.

"Come in," Paula said, getting up to move folders from a chair in front of her desk.

"I'm Kally—"

"I know who you are." Paula stuck out her hand, and Kally reciprocated. She took in a middle-aged woman, dressed for office work in a deep-yellow-three-quarter-sleeve shirt untucked over black dress pants. Paula was the type of person who kept wineries running smoothly so winemakers could concentrate on their craft.

*If only I could afford a Paula.*

"I have the bills that were in Kirk's office," Kally began. "I'll bring them to you."

"I wondered where those were!" Paula said, relief sweeping across her face.

"I'll have them tomorrow." Then: "Did Kirk ever mention buying property to you?"

"He did," Paula said.

"What did he say?"

"No, what I mean is he *did* buy property. Right before his death."

"On Red Mountain?"

"Yes. At least, that was the last word..." She stopped mid sentence. "Didn't mean it that way."

Kally went on. "Who did he buy it from?"

"I don't know. It's a public document, though. You can access the records."

"I'll do that. Do you know when he was thinking of planting?"

"I don't," Paula answered. "Next year, maybe?"

"Right." *Was his death related to his land purchase?* An awkward silence ensued. "Well, I'll see you at the funeral then." Kally took out a business card. "If you think of anything, please let me know."

She left the office and went back into the production area. The four people she had seen when she'd entered were preparing a large tank for racking. She assumed again that they were the interns because it didn't take four people to rack wine from one tank to another. But interns tended to move as a herd, coming as they did from school where they worked so closely together.

She walked up to Manning, who was putting blue painter's tape on a tank and then writing the words: *Pressed,10/24.*

"Mark, are those the interns?" Kally nodded in the direction of the four.

He glanced over his shoulder then back at her. His distraught look from days earlier was gone but with all the work in getting through harvest it had been replaced with fatigue.

"Yeah," he said finally.

"I'm gonna talk to them."

"Before you do that…" He looked at bin four where Remick's body had been found. "Can we move the bin? I need to get to the tanks behind it."

She hesitated. "I would prefer that you not move it yet."

"Okay."

"I want to hear from the medical examiner first. And that may take a few more days."

"All right." Manning said.

Kally looked again at bin four. "Why do you think the Brix stopped at twenty-one?"

"I don't know. Doesn't make sense," Manning replied.

"Is it defective yeast?" she asked.

"No. I used the same yeast on another variety. And it's finished fermenting."

Kally thought for a moment. "Is it too cold in here?"

"No. Everything else has gone through fermentation. We're done. We're pressing the reds."

Then he added "It's too high to be stuck."

"I know," Kally said. Stuck fermentations, when yeast simply stopped working, often happened in the single digits of Brix.

"Can I ask you something else?"

He shrugged.

"Was anyone else here in the winery last Saturday morning other than you and Justine? Someone who might have left before I got here?"

Manning folded his arms in front of him and looked at the floor. Then he looked back at her.

"No." He hesitated. "I thought I already answered your questions."

"I forgot this one."

"*Why* are you asking?"

Kally was taken aback by his attitude and decided not to divulge A-Rod's recent pronouncement. Plus, it was obvious she was in police mode, since she was still in uniform. Manning was just being a...*Never mind. I'll let the word pass.*

"I'm trying to get a full picture of the morning," she said. "Before I got here."

"Okay."

That seemed to explain it for him, although his obstinance stayed with her. Kally changed the subject. "Will you tell me which intern is which over there?"

"Yeah, sure."

Manning turned his attention to the four. Three held a hose while one clamped it onto the tank.

"The one with the brown hair is Abby. Red hair, Jenny. Jason is clamping the hose. Tony is in the blue sweatshirt."

She looked back at her list and hurriedly wrote their names and notes: *Abby—young, in shape; Jenny—50+; Jason—black, buff; Tony—short, fire plug.*

"Thanks." Kally walked over to them. "Good job."

They looked at her blankly, like the stranger she was to them. And then they took in the uniform, their eyes swooping over her badge and down to the belt, and the gun, ammo, keys, cuffs, walkie-talkie, baton...

"My name is Kally O'Keefe."

She refrained from telling them she was a winemaker. Obviously, they didn't recognize her. "I want to ask you some questions about Friday night. The harvest party."

Jason finished clamping the hose to the racking port and stood up, wiping his hands on his jeans.

"Were you all working the party?"

They all nodded.

"What were your roles that night?"

Jenny—red hair, the oldest of the group, but not too old to be a cellar rat—spoke first. "I took people's invitations at the door and directed them to the table with glasses."

"And the two of us"—Abby signaled with her hand to Tony standing next to her—"passed out the glasses."

"I helped Kirk open wine," Jason added. "Out front."

Kally addressed Abby. "Did anyone refuse a glass?"

Abby looked confused. "No. Why would they come if they weren't going to drink?"

Abby was someone who got right to the point. Kally watched her readjust her ponytail, then put her hands on her hips.

"So this was early in the evening, obviously," Kally said. She remembered seeing none of them because she'd come in through the back door, the large open garage door, as other winemakers did.

"Was there anything unusual about the evening that you remember?"

Jenny shook her head. "We were too busy. I didn't notice anything but empty glasses and people wanting more wine."

"Yeah," the other three agreed.

"Did Kirk talk to you at all?"

Jason nodded. "He passed me and said, 'How's it going?' Then he said to me that he was going to pour some library wines, and for me and Tony to follow him and help open them."

"Did you help pour them?" Kally asked, knowing that would have put them in closer proximity to the guests.

"Yes. But mostly it was Kirk pouring," Jason answered.

"When was that?"

"Late in the evening."

Which also explained why she didn't remember it.

"Did you have any of the wine?" she asked all of them.

"Oh yeah!" Tony exclaimed. "It's awesome!"

Then: "Were other people still here when Kirk was pouring the library wines?"

"A few," Jenny said.

"What did they look like?" Kally asked.

Early in her police academy training, she'd learned that people tended to describe others first by race—as she had done in her notes—then by gender and age and height, then by heaviness or skinniness, then by long or short hair. Or no hair. People also tended to remember light or dark clothing but no other specifics. Except men who might offer that a female wore a plunging neckline.

"They were just people," Abby said, with a hint of annoyance.

"White men, middle-aged," Jenny said, clarifying Abby's answer.

Perhaps Abby disliked authority, Kally thought.

"What about dress?"

"Um...nice pants, nice shirts. No ties," Tony added. "Some were in jeans."

"And the women?"

"Same," Tony said. They laughed in unison.

"Did you happen to see a group of three or four men and one woman together who apparently were not drinking?"

For the first time no one spoke, deep in thought as each seemed to be.

"I saw groups of people. But I don't remember any not drinking," Tony responded.

"When was the last time you saw Kirk?" Kally asked.

Jenny looked away for a moment, then cleared her throat. "He was...um...pouring from one of those library wines." Kally noticed her eyes brimming with tears. "He had a smile on his face. And, he was pouring generously. He was in his element. The men he was pouring for were happy, with their glasses full."

"What did they look like?

"Older white guys," Jason offered.

"Balding, glasses, sleeves rolled up?" Kally prodded.

"Yes! Exactly," Jenny exclaimed.

"How about you, Abby?"

Abby gave Kally a stare like it was beneath her to recall anything. She paused before answering. "I don't remember. I was too busy."

"What were you doing?" Kally pressed.

Another pause. Another stare. "I picked up empty glasses and took them to the kitchen."

*Doesn't like clean-up.*

"How late did you stay? Each of you." Kally stopped writing notes about Abby.

"Well, we cleaned up, ran the dishwasher a couple of times. Then we moved some of the bins out of the cold room and some of the barrels back in. So it was about twelve-twelve-thirty when we left."

They were still here close to the time of Kirk's death, as Manning had indicated. "You all left at the same time?"

The four looked at one another and nodded.

"At that time, were guests still here?"

They all shook their heads.

"Who was here?"

Jason spoke. "All of us and Mark and Kirk."

"So, six of you," Kally replied.

"That would be right," Abby answered, folding her arms in front of her.

"How long will each of you be here?"

"You mean tonight?" Jason asked.

"No, I mean for your internships."

"Through January," Jenny said.

"Okay." Kally paused. "Now, I need your last names."

Kally passed Manning as she left Kirk's winery. His back was to her, so she didn't bother with a good-bye.

In her car again, she dictated her notes. The interns had added nothing, really. They were simply working an event. Abby would cycle through several jobs in the industry and move on. It was her lack of enthusiasm and disdain for authority and clean-up that made her think that.

Just like Leah.

But Manning remained on Kally's mind, his disrespect bothering her. She flagged him in her report.

She looked at her watch: 5:19 p.m. The funeral was tomorrow, and she needed to think through how to approach people there. But first, she had work to do in her winery.

Kally was getting out of her car when her phone rang.

"You haven't sent me that warrant."

"Becks! I haven't been to the office yet. I'll get it to you tomorrow."

"Promise?"

"Promise."

"Okay. Because I have information about Kirk Remick's bank accounts."

Kally waited.

"You can't tell anyone I did this for you without having that warrant."

"I won't."

"All right. Here's what I found: basically, Mr. Remick is a wealthy man."

Not a surprise, Kally thought.

Becky continued: "He usually keeps twenty thousand dollars in his checking account at all times and pays everything—that I know of—from this account each month. He has three other accounts with us."

"Okay," Kally said.

"First is a retirement account, mostly in stocks, with a balance of $462,879. He has a college fund for his daughter at approximately $176,000. And then he has a money market account that until recently had a balance of $675,000. Why he kept so much in cash I don't know."

*The Red Mountain land purchase.*

Becky went on. "He may have other accounts I don't know about."

"Wow," Kally said.

"Did he have any outstanding loans?" Kally asked.

"No, not with us," Becky said, then added: "Janie Remick's name is still on all of his accounts."

"Oh wow."

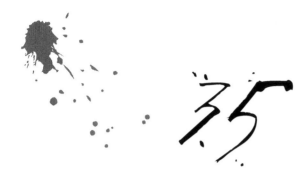

With the warrant request etched into her brain, Kally walked into her own brightly lit winery.

And saw no one.

Music, which was usually blaring from speakers, played softly in the background. She recognized the tune as the Zombies' "She's Not There."

"Hello?"

She walked further in. The place had been cleaned and organized, the floor washed and squeegee-dried. Valves, gaskets, and clamps were lined up in neat rows on the maintenance cart. Stools, hoses, and cleaning tubs had been put back where they belonged.

This was Seth's handiwork.

She heard voices.

"Not everything has to be a fruit bomb!" Leah exclaimed.

"Yes, it does!" Seth countered. "It's what people want."

Kally entered the kitchen. "What's going on?" She saw beakers and glasses filled with wine.

Red wine.

"I'm sure you started with the white?" Kally asked, seeing it nowhere in sight.

"Yes," Seth answered, turning away from Leah for a moment. "And we agreed on the blend: fifty Riesling, fifty Pinot Gris."

He reached for a beaker filled with straw-colored fluid and poured a small taste for Kally.

"I think we're here with this." He passed the glass to her.

"The lemon still comes through," Leah added, not yet recovered from her spirited discussion.

Kally swirled the wine, then sniffed, looking at Leah over the rim of her glass.

Leah was right. The lemon notes were there, probably from both varieties, each grown on a cold site. She swirled again, sniffed again, then tasted. The acidity registered first, then lemon. And a hint of sweetness. The wine was perfectly balanced.

"What's the residual sugar...1.5 percent?"

"Yes," Seth answered. "Exactly."

"Just enough for the American palate. Good job." Kally put the glass on the counter. "Now, what's going on with the red?"

"We don't agree." Leah folded her arms tightly around her.

Kally saw for the first time that her two co-workers really didn't get along.

*How have I not seen this?*

*Perhaps because I'm never here.*

Each had a glass on the counter with a Post-it Note showing the percentages of Grenache and Syrah. She read Seth's: *60/40.* Leah's was *80/20.*

"Let's see what we've got." Kally picked up Leah's glass, which she knew would be a softer wine. She swirled, sniffed, and tasted, taking in fresh berries, light plum, and baking spices.

All of the attributes for Grenache that her friends had tasted at Chris's on Saturday came through here, with Syrah almost imperceptible. With aging, Syrah would add backbone and a bit of depth. But Grenache would definitely remain the star in this blend.

"Not a bad choice, Leah," Kally said.

She picked up Seth's glass, seeing the deeper color imparted by Syrah. She sniffed, getting a much fuller aroma. Fresh berries gave way to dark fruits, slight pepper, and forest floor—she'd had to think about that one when she'd heard it in sensory class as an attribute. But here it was.

Then she tasted it, getting the aroma profile in her mouth along with some evergreen. The full-on Grenache characteristics were gone, yet the blend was superb, so southern Rhône-like in quality and depth. It would be astounding in five years.

Her two assistants had done what she had asked, keeping Grenache the dominant grape. But the differences were striking.

"So, Leah…." Kally put the glasses back on the counter. "I prefer a stronger wine that will stand up to the herbs used in cooking. Think Thanksgiving and the parsley, sage, rosemary, and thyme influence. It's why I prefer Syrah over Pinot Noir."

"Your blend is not wrong," she added, then repeated what her sommelier friend Sarah had stated at Chris's party: "Here, though, we make heavier mid-palate wines. It's what buyers are used to. And what they expect."

Leah shrugged. "Okay."

Seth picked up his choice and sniffed. And nodded in approval.

# 36

Her assistants gone for the evening, Kally sat at her tall table and stared at her to-do board. Seth had crossed out *blending trials whites* and *blending trials reds.* Still on the list: *filter, fine, cold stabilize, bottle, and label.* And she needed to plan a release party for her new wines.

She had no time to think about any release party.

With the two red blends in front of her, she tried Seth's again, confirming it as her wine of choice. She wished she could get a sample to Guillaume in France to get his opinion. She thought back to all the wines they had tried in Provence, sitting in those small cafés, bouncing aroma and taste profiles off one another like they were a team.

He was so easy to be with, so informed, so…

*What is he doing right now?*

*He should be sleeping. Is he alone? Is he with someone?*

*I can't think about that. I can't think about him.*

With great difficulty, she focused on the case. And the funeral. And she needed to read Riggs's online reports before their staff meeting tomorrow.

When would she do that?

Kally drained Seth's blend and started in on Leah's.

She thought about Arnaugh and his comment about the three men and the woman who were not drinking at Kirk's harvest party. She knew from her own tasting room that one or two in a group might not taste wine. But not all of them. Arnaugh was right. And, she hated to admit, so was Abby: Why go to a wine event if you're not going to drink wine?

Unless the four were there for other business.

And that business could be anything, knowing how top-tier winemakers partnered with other winemakers to bring out new labels and blends. Sometimes one only knew about these partnerings when the product was written up in the press.

She reached in her backpack and took out a pad of paper. And wrote down a few questions: Was Kirk involved in other business ventures outside of his own label? She knew about the land purchase. But was there something else?

Was he thinking of moving his winery, as so many were now doing as they got bigger? And Kirk was always getting bigger.

Why did Kirk have so much money in cash? What ailment did he have that required antibiotics six months ago? Was Janie a suspect, since her name was still on all of his bank accounts?

And: What could Kirk possibly see in Kendall, a woman so much younger than himself.

*Come on!*

Kally finished Leah's blend and got up to approximate the wines on her own, pouring rough estimates from the tanks into the two glasses. She walked back to the table, taking a big sip of Leah's blend, feeling it warm her empty stomach.

She wondered if she could get away with labeling a wine like this a GS, instead of the standard GSM, the "M" being Mourvedre, which she didn't have.

Would the general public know what "GS" meant? She didn't think so. She'd have to come up with a name, something catchy. Somehow, in the future, she would find Mourvedre, a hard-to-procure grape, and make her mark with her own GSM.

Paul Storey, whose winery was on the other side of Kirk's, had "P.S." on his back labels: *P.S.: Serve with fish; P.S.: Pour this chilled; P.S.: Pair with chocolate.*

It was a gimmick. One that people remembered. She wanted people to remember her wine.

Wait a minute! She could come out with GPS: Grenache and Petite Sirah, with a compass on the label. Was GPS trademarked? Had someone done this already?

She was sitting there thinking about it when her back door opened and Paul Storey himself walked in.

Kally saw that he was holding a wine thief. But only half of it.

"I broke this," he said, holding it up and walking into her kitchen area. "Can I use yours?"

"Sure," she answered. "How are you?"

"Good." He came up to her and eyed the two glasses. "What do you have here?"

"Two blends. Try them. Tell me which one you like."

She watched him as he tasted each.

"Wow. The one on the right is great."

Kally smiled. "That was my choice. Would you like a glass?"

He shook his head. "I'm heading out. We have a dinner tonight, and I'm late. Again."

Kally took in his chiseled face, gray hair, and in-shape physique. Storey had been one of the first winemakers in Woodinville. When she'd started in the industry she had asked him about winemaking all the time, especially wine chemistry, and he was happy to answer.

But he wasn't open both days on the weekends, and she wondered how he was making it. How he was breaking even, that is.

"Are you in charge of...you know..." He nodded in the direction of Kirk's winery.

"Yeah."

"Isn't it hard? I mean...it's Kirk."

"It is hard," Kally said. "But no one at headquarters knows anything about wine. Or the wineries here."

Then Kally looked around her space. "I haven't had time to think about the fact that he's gone. Or how to get all the work done in here."

"Well, you've got a good worker in Seth," Storey said, following her gaze. "I borrowed him a few times when you weren't here. Don't know if he told you."

"No. But it's okay."

"He helped me move some barrels. Maybe twenty minutes each time."

"Really, it's okay." Then: "You know he won't stay."

"They never do." Storey stretched suddenly, rising to full height. Then he relaxed and crossed his arms. "Offer him a place to make his own wine, and maybe he will."

"I might do that."

"So…is there *anything* you can tell me about Kirk?" Storey prodded.

Kally shook her head. "Not until we get the toxicology report. We just don't know."

"Maybe Manning knows something," he offered.

The comment surprised her. "Why do you say that?"

"I saw him out back with a woman Saturday morning."

This new bit of information took some time to sink in. And, importantly, how had she failed to knock on Storey's door that same morning?

"You were here then," she said finally.

"Yeah. Really early. I was blending."

"Where were they?" Kally inquired.

"In the alley. For a short time," Storey said. "I was outside around my bins. I could see them."

"What did she look like?"

"Her back was to me. But she had long blonde hair, nice body. Shorter than Mark."

"Mark's tall, though," Kally said. "How much shorter?"

"Stand up," Storey asked.

Kally stood up.

"Your height."

"Okay." She sat down, thinking of blonde women her height. "What were they saying?"

Storey shook his head. "I couldn't hear them well."

"How long were they there?"

"Under thirty seconds, I'd guess."

"Did they know you were there?"

"I don't think so."

"What time was this?"

He thought for a moment, then shrugged. "I don't know. Before all the commotion."

Kally was about to ask another question when Storey added more.

"I could see the woman leaving. I saw her pass by through the openings in the bins. She walked back out the alley."

"Going east or west?" Kally asked.

"East."

Storey's winery was on the east side of Kirk's. Someone walking that way around the building to the front parking lot would be able to get in a car without walking past A-Rod. Except that A-Rod had seen someone. She wondered if it were the same person.

*Had to be the same person.*

She now had four references to a woman with blonde hair.

"What did Manning do after you saw the woman leave?" Kally asked.

"He went back inside."

"Did you see him go inside?"

Storey hesitated. "No. I heard the door close."

"Okay. This is helpful."

"Is it? It's not much. Anyway, maybe he can help."

After Storey left, Kally drank the rest of Leah's blend. She looked at her watch: 8:48 p.m. Hungry, she walked into the kitchen and opened her refrigerator. Inside were several bottles of water and two Diet Cokes. She opened the crisper and saw a pear, an apple, and some string cheese.

She took two string cheeses and the apple and closed the door. Then she spotted a large bag of Chex Mix that she served in her tasting room.

Kally got a paper towel and poured some of the mix onto it. She leaned against the counter and ate her dinner, still thinking about Manning.

Kally faxed the warrant to ex-sister-in-law, Becky, and walked back to her office. She had ten minutes before she had to leave for the funeral. She grabbed Kirk's bills, which she would drop off later for Paula, and put them by her pack. Taking a sip of coffee, she looked up and saw Riggs approaching.

She braced for the encounter.

"Okay," he said, starting in. "I read your write-ups. Let's go over the timeline." He glanced at her white board filled with names. "Let's use the conference room. There's a bigger board in there. And bring the credit card receipts!"

Kally followed him to the conference room. *We will do this together.*

Riggs picked up a marker and wrote *What We Know* and *Don't Know* in two columns on the white board that extended the length of the room. A third of the way down the first column, he wrote *12-12:30 a.m. TOD.* A bit farther down in the same column he wrote *6-6:15 a.m. Body found.*

"Let's fill this in, starting at the top." He pointed at her. "When did you get to the party?"

"About seven thirty p.m."

Riggs wrote it down.

"Give me more," he demanded without looking at her.

"Zack and I came in the back door, the large garage door, and walked into the production area."

Riggs wrote, next to *7:30 p.m. K and Z arrive, big door.*

"Keep going. Your impressions…what you saw," Riggs said.

"The party started at six…"

Riggs added *6 p.m.—party begins.*

"So a lot of people were there already. Music was playing. We stood at a table, a barrel with a glass top, against one wall. Zack left to get us glasses from the tasting room in front, where most people entered. He came back with Kirk's Chardonnay. You start with white then move to red."

Riggs didn't say anything. He waited, marker in hand.

"When Zack was gone for those few minutes"—she glanced at the clock above the white board—"I watched people. There were groups of women, three or four standing at tall tables in the middle of the room. Men talked in pairs…"

"Could you identify them?" he asked.

"No. I wasn't paying that much attention." She continued. "A lot of people were near the crusher watching the grapes. We had passed it when we came in. There was a table with appetizers. Zack went to get us some. When he got back, I finished my wine, had some appetizers, and Zack and I talked."

She glanced at the board and its four items.

"Go on," Riggs said.

"The music got louder. Zack went to get us red wine. Kirk stood near tanks opposite me. He was holding a bottle of wine. Zack came back. We ate more appetizers. Had more wine. Then I saw three winemakers come up to Kirk. And he poured them wine. And they stood around talking. One turned to me and toasted me with his glass, and I toasted him back."

"What time is this?" Riggs asked.

"About eight fifteen p.m."

Riggs wrote: *8:15—three WM with D.*

"Then Zack said he wanted to leave, get a pizza, watch a movie. But first, he got us more wine."

"This is a lot of wine," Riggs said.

"They weren't full glasses." She went on. "I stood there waiting for Zack. The music was really loud now. He came back. And then I saw Kendall, the woman Kirk was seeing, walk up to him and whisper something."

"What time?"

"About eight twenty p.m."

Riggs wrote it down.

"Then she left and Kirk watched her leave. And then we left."

"What time was this?"

"About eight thirty p.m."

Riggs added it to the list.

"We walked out the same way we came in, through the big door." She paused. "For some reason, when we were outside, I turned and looked back inside. I saw Kirk near his barrels, and people were waiting to talk to him. That's the last time I saw him alive."

"Can you identify them?" Riggs wrote: *8:31 p.m. last look at D.*

"No."

Riggs stared at the board. Kally stared at the clock.

"Read the names on the credit card receipts," he asked, and she read them aloud. He added all ten names and the times of their wine purchases.

"Tell me when Dale called you."

"About six fifteen a.m. Saturday."

Riggs added it to the growing list.

"Then Dale and A-Rod arrive at the scene," Riggs said. "And Nakamura arrives and you arrive. Nakamura was there before you got there?"

"Yes."

Riggs added them and approximate times. He kept going, adding information from her dictations.

"There's something else," she began.

He turned to look at her.

She declined to mention Manning's obstinance from the previous evening because, in Riggs's world, an incident like that just wouldn't happen. Or be tolerated.

"We have another mention of a blonde woman around Kirk's winery," Kally said.

"In addition to the other three?"

She nodded. Riggs had already added to the list A-Rod's "blonde in black sedan," Surfer's "angry blonde woman," and Arnaugh's "blonde with three men not drinking."

"When is the new one?" Riggs asked.

"A winemaker on the other side of Kirk's winery saw Manning and a woman talking early Saturday morning, in the alley. He said, 'Before all the commotion.'"

"So, before Dale, A-Rod, Nakamura, and you got there."

"Yes."

Riggs wrote *6:10 a.m. Manning and blonde in alley*, then stood back.

Kally perused the list, which now included Kirk's employees and interns. Two things stuck out: the proximity of Kirk's workers leaving his winery to the time of his death. And the mentions of a woman with blonde hair. Everything else was just noise.

She said all this to Riggs, who continued staring at the board.

Not one to let an omission—*omissions*—pass, he pointed to *6:10 a.m. Manning and blonde in alley.*

"Did you question that other winemaker...What's his name?"

"Paul Storey."

"Storey. Did you question him Saturday morning?" he asked without looking at her.

Kally hesitated. "No. I didn't think about it with all that was going on."

Riggs nodded and continued staring at the board.

"Did Manning tell you about this woman, the woman in the alley, when you talked to him?"

"No."

Riggs nodded again. He put the marker down and folded his arms.

She looked up at the clock again and then at Riggs. She had the unsettled feeling that Riggs was about to explode.

K ally arrived at the church and waited outside for Chris, who was running late. People filed past, and she acknowledged them, knowing many of them. But the glaring oversights in her investigation hung over her like a black cloud.

A perfect frame of mind for a funeral.

She thought through the rest of her day: the reception following this, the staff meeting she wasn't prepared for, and Zack stopping by later at her winery.

She took out her phone to check email. Her mother wanted her to come to dinner again.

She put her phone away.

A red Beetle zoomed into a parking place in front of her. Kendall got out, appropriately dressed in a conservative dark outfit, and walked quickly toward her.

"Kendall, hi," Kally said when she came up to her. Then she thought of something. "Can I ask you a question?"

"Sure."

"Do you know anyone who has a black sedan?"

"Is that like a four-door car?"

Kally hesitated. "Yeah, like that."

Kendall seemed to think about it. "No."

"Okay, thanks."

Kendall walked on. Kally wondered where she would sit. Then she sensed someone else walking toward her, someone with quick, determined steps. It was blogger Mindy Peters of *Wine Hound*.

Kally referred to Mindy—in her mind only—as "short stuff." At five feet two, Mindy was a force *not* to be reckoned with. But Kally liked her. She was the only journalist who had treated her with respect when her lawsuit had happened.

"Hey," Mindy said, coming up to her. "Haven't seen you in a while."

"I know. I'm working."

"That's what I thought. Can you give me some information?"

"About Kirk, no doubt."

"Yes."

"I don't have much."

"What do you have?"

"He died."

Mindy stared at her. "I'm going to write a column about his last hours and I want your help. I was out of town and can't *believe* I missed the biggest story *ever*!"

"There isn't much."

Mindy ignored her comment. "Was he killed, do you think?"

"I can't answer that."

"But I want to know what you think."

"I can't have what I think in the press. It has to be facts."

"This is how I'm going to write it, then." Folding her arms, Mindy began: "'There is the possibility that the best winemaker in Woodinville was murdered. Along with accidental death, such as $CO_2$ poisoning, or natural death, such as a heart attack, the homicide piece will be investigated.'"

She unfolded her arms. "See? I'm not attributing it to you."

Kally nodded. She knew how smart Mindy was. No winemaker in Woodinville wanted to be on her bad side. They all needed her good reviews, which were widely read.

Kally looked over Mindy's shoulder and saw Chris exit her car and wave. Mindy remained planted in place, eyes locked on Kally.

Finally, Kally relented. "Come by the winery tonight and we can talk."

"I will! Do you think he died of $CO_2$ poisoning?"

Kally shook her head. "Not Kirk." Then suddenly: "You're not going to use that, are you?"

"No. But I agree with you."

Chris joined them. "Hi, Mindy."

"Hi! How's business?"

"Okay," Chris answered. "Although this is sad."

"It is. Well, I'll leave you two. And I'll see you tonight."

"Okay," Kally answered.

Chris rubbed Kally's arm affectionately. "How're you doing?"

Kally shrugged. "Not sure. This won't be easy."

"I know."

Kally looked out at the parking lot. Suddenly, she thought of something.

"Come with me," she said, walking away from the church.

"Where are we going?" Chris asked, catching up to her.

Kally stopped at edge of the curb and scanned the parking lot. "I need your help."

"With what?"

"I need photos of license plates on every black sedan here."

Chris looked at her watch, then at the parking lot. "You're kidding, right? There's got to be fifty here at a minimum."

"I know. But a black sedan left the Warehouse District Saturday morning with a blonde woman driving. A-Rod saw her."

Chris glanced at her watch again. "I don't think we can do this now."

"It won't start on time," Kally answered, bending down to take a photo of the black sedan in front of her.

"You take that side," Kally added, pointing to her right, then headed off in the opposite direction. "Just two and four doors. No sports cars. No SUVs. I'll meet you back here."

Chris dug in her purse for her phone, then did as Kally had asked.

After ten minutes, they met up where they had started.

"Did you get them?" Kally asked.

"Yeah. About twenty."

"Me, too. You can send them to me later."

# 39

They raced back to the church, then slowed to enter. One row was half empty in back with an obstructed view of the front, and Kally pointed to it, a semi-perfect area to take in guests.

They sat in silence as Kally surveyed what she could see of the crowd. There were winemakers from Walla Walla, Lake Chelan, Horse Heaven Hills, and Red Mountain, all top American Viticultural Areas in Washington State.

Vineyard owners were present, too, vineyards where Kirk got his grapes.

The CEO of Chateau Ste. Michelle entered with his wife, followed by company vice presidents and managers. Then, a contingent of warehouse winemakers filed in dressed in business suits, sans ties, but more dressed up than she had ever seen them. She would have been with them if she weren't working.

She looked for Denny Lane, Kirk's former assistant winemaker, and Mark Manning, the current one, and didn't see either. She didn't, in fact, see any of Kirk's employees. But they had to be here somewhere.

Music began playing at the front. Kally peeked around heads blocking her view for Janie and Emma but couldn't see the front rows.

And then they entered, Janie holding Emma's hand, an older woman, no doubt Kirk's mother, and a fortyish woman, no doubt Kirk's sister, behind them.

They walked to the front and the room hushed.

Once again, Kally felt for Janie. She had taken on a role she had no preparation for nor was expected to be a participant in. Most people in the room knew she and Kirk were no longer together. Janie was doing it all for Emma. And for Kirk's mother.

Kally made a mental note to tell Janie how proud she was of her for being here for Kirk. Kendall would have been inappropriate in the role. And just where was Kendall?

Kally's eyes fell on the closed casket with a photo on top, bringing her back suddenly to the reason she was here. She hoped that Janie had decided on a festive gathering afterward. It was the only way Kirk would have wanted it.

The music stopped and the minister walked to the podium. And the service began. She was aware at one point of Chris taking out a Kleenex and softly blowing her nose, as many people around her were doing.

She herself was too amped up on prodigious amounts of coffee to mourn properly. For her, the reality of Kirk's death had registered when his body was removed Saturday from his winery.

She sat there, half listening, and thought of the timeline on the whiteboard. She thought of Riggs, too, but quickly moved beyond him.

Something had caused Kirk to ball up his hands in fists.

Was he angry at someone? Was $CO_2$ a factor? Was it a heart attack, a brain aneurysm? Was his death caused by another person?

She was brought back to the service as the eulogies began. The CEO of Chateau Ste. Michelle said Kirk and Warehouse District winemakers made Chateau Ste. Michelle strive to be better, and mentioned all the times he had crossed paths with Kirk at wine events around the country.

Two owners from coveted vineyards on Red Mountain—Klipsun and Ciel du Cheval—talked about their associations with Kirk throughout the years. As was common among prestigious winemakers, Kirk had his own marked rows in each of their vineyards, essentially guaranteeing all those highly ranked wines.

"And he didn't even tell us how to grow our grapes!" one of them mentioned to rousing laughter.

Then the executive directors of both the winegrowers association and the wine industry foundation spoke, saying how generous Kirk was in donating wine to the annual auction.

Kally glanced away, spotting Mindy of *Wine Hound* writing furiously.

These speeches were followed by warehouse winemakers sharing personal anecdotes, which added more levity to the sad occasion. Did they really like him as much as they were saying? Out of respect, she was sure, they didn't mention Kirk's *many* paramours.

Then the minister returned to the podium and spoke in spiritual terms about eternity and our short lives on earth. At one point, toward the end of the service, Kally heard him say: "Think of your very best memory of Kirk Remick and hold that close."

She knew exactly what that memory was, the incident occurring only a few weeks ago.

*It was a Friday night, after nine p.m. She was sitting at the tall table in her production area doing accounting work, a sweatshirt wrapped around her shoulders, when her back door opened and Kirk walked in.*

*"Hi!" he yelled out.*

*"Hi!" she yelled back "How come you're still here?"*

*"Ah, work."*

*He walked up to the table, crossed his arms on top of it and put his head down. And stared up at her. She remembered looking into his blue eyes, taking in his dark black hair speckled with gray and his handsome face.*

*For a moment her heart leapt.*

Dammit it, Kirk! I will not let this…that…whatever it is…happen.

*Then, without warning, he straightened up, leaned forward and gave her a quick peck on the cheek. And smiled.*

*It so surprised her she didn't respond. But she knew it wasn't a romantic peck. It was one that said, "We're close. We're buddies."*

*He'd never done that before.*

*Then he got serious. "Do you ever feel alone?"*

*She was surprised at that, too. "I am alone."*

*"No, I mean, do you ever feel really alone? Like it's just you in this business."*

Maybe when you're number one, *she remembered thinking,* you feel that way. Still, it was a rare comment coming from a man most people thought had everything, including all those highly ranked wines and being feted in New York and Las Vegas at over-the-top wine extravaganzas.

*He kept going. "Are you ever lonely?"*

"Yes," she admitted, for reasons not just related to wine. "But I think you have to be a loner to be in this business. It's just you and the wine and all the work that it takes to make it. We're like little islands here, all of us."

Kirk nodded. "I think about getting out."

Another revelation. She couldn't imagine him having this conversation with any of the male winemakers in Woodinville, most of whom emulated him.

"When?" It was all she thought of to ask.

"I don't know! Sometime." He stuffed his hands in his pockets and walked back into her production area.

"Show me what you got in these tanks. What's this?" he asked, walking up to one. He leaned in and read the writing on the blue painter's tape. "Grenache." He turned to her. "Good grape."

Kally walked up to him with two glasses, and he took the one she offered.

"Very popular now," he added.

Kally turned on the sample tap and poured ruby-red liquid into their glasses.

Kirk raised his to look at the color, then stuck it under his nose. And kept it there for some time. "Evergreen. A bit of cinnamon." Then he tasted it, working it around in his mouth. And swallowed.

"Cranberry and a bit of cinnamon on the finish." He poured the rest in the drain in the floor.

"Nice full mid-palate," he said to her nodding.

She smiled.

"What yeast did you use?"

"4028," she answered, citing a strain that enhanced fruity characteristics.

"What's the residual sugar?" he asked.

"1.5."

"It'll be a stand-alone?"

She shook her head. "A blend."

"With what?"

"Syrah."

"You better charge a lot. This is good."

"I will!" She paused. "I have to change my labels, though. Too boring."

"They're not boring."

He was being nice. "I can't stand them!"

He laughed. "Afraid to get burned again?" She knew he was referring to her lawsuit.

*She nodded. "Yeah."*

*"I'm the one who should have been sued," he admitted. "I use actual song titles." Kirk shook his head. "You can't trademark every word on the planet. Nobody could say anything."*

*"That's true," she said.*

*"Let the label reflect you," he added, holding the glass up to her. "But you gotta be out there. You gotta be bold!"*

*She smiled. "I'll remember that."*

*They had walked on and she had poured him more samples from tanks and barrels. They talked about the future—his comment about leaving the industry seemingly forgotten—and the vineyards they used and staff issues and the long hours, and how they couldn't wait to get to November when the rush of crush would be behind them.*

*Winemaker to winemaker.*

*She had felt like an equal to him.*

Kally looked up suddenly, her eyes filled with tears. The service was over. How much time had passed?

# 40

People began filing out. Janie and Emma walked past, Kirk's mother and sister right behind them, looking somber, as would be expected. Kally hadn't caught Janie's eye. But surely Janie had seen her.

Kally and Chris remained seated as all of the rows in front of them emptied. Now Kally could see everyone, winemakers and vineyard owners nodding to her as they walked by.

*Here come the employees*, she thought, including Kendall, looking insignificant. *And there's Manning and Denny together.* She would corner them both later. And she would need to talk to Kirk's mother and sister.

Sarah and her partner, Judith, filed out behind Kirk's employees. So many Washington wine people were present, Kally realized, that if a bomb had gone off the landscape of the state's wine industry would have been forever altered.

Behind Sarah and her partner were Ellie; her husband, Jim; and other men she assumed were with Red Mountain Productions. Ellie was a bit more reserved with the neckline today.

Following them was none other than Noel Jacobsen with a woman she assumed was his wife, his bandage still present. Jacobsen saw her and nodded. Kally returned the gesture.

Kally wondered if Jacobsen knew the RMP people. Then a thought struck her. *Is he an investor in the business?* Not that he'd needed to disclose that to her when she and Riggs had talked to him. Maybe he was a silent partner. She tucked it away for later investigation.

Finally, it was their turn to leave. Kally and Chris stood up and walked out.

People gathered in groups in front of the church, talking. Others headed toward the parking lot. Janie was at the curb near the hearse and signaled Kally to join her and Emma.

"Chris, let's go talk to Janie for a minute."

The two walked up to her, and each gave her a hug. Janie introduced them to Kirk's mother, who was quite drawn, Kally noticed up close, and Kirk's sister, who seemed stern and unfriendly. Emma stared up at them and Kally smiled at her.

"You look very nice, Emma," Kally said, taking in Emma's bright-blue dress, the color matching her eyes, and felt a pang in her heart for Kirk's daughter.

"Thanks," Emma replied.

Then Janie took Kally by the elbow and walked her away from the group.

"We're taking the casket back to the funeral home."

"Not a cemetery?" Kally asked.

Janie shook her head. "We can't come to an agreement on where he should be buried. His mother wants him in Chicago. I want him here. For Emma.

"I see."

"I don't really have a legal say in this anymore. But Emma does. And I'll speak for her." Janie glanced back at Kirk's mother. "If she only knew what his life was like. And mine."

"She has to come around on this and agree with you," Kally whispered.

"I know. You're coming to the reception?"

"I am for a short time." Then she paused. "Everyone in the church knew the role you took on today, and that you didn't have to."

"Yeah, well, the day's not over," Janie said, smiling slightly.

Kally's phone rang. She looked at the caller's name. "Sorry, I have to take this."

"Okay. I'll see you later," Janie said. She kissed her friend on her cheek. "Thanks for your support."

Kally answered her phone, and Nakamura started in. "Do you have a moment?"

"I do," Kally said, walking away from Janie.

"Regarding Mr. Remick's death…I have results for you."
Kally waited.
"Mr. Remick died of asphyxiation from $CO_2$ poisoning."
"*No!!*"

# 41

K ally walked farther into the parking lot to distance herself from people who had turned to look in her direction.

"It can't be!" she said to Nakamura. "He made wine for twenty years. That's twenty harvests, twenty years of fermenting grapes. He would *not* make a mistake like that."

"It's what the toxicology report is showing," Nakamura answered. "And it's significant $CO_2$ inhalation."

Kally shook her head. In the distance, she saw Ellie standing with several men, Jacobsen among them.

Nakamura continued: "Perhaps that night, Mr. Remick closed up shop and left the building. Then he forgot something and walked back in, thinking he would be there less than a minute. And the minutes dragged on."

"I don't think so."

"He had a lot of fermentations going on, did he not?"

"He did."

"And those grapes had just stared fermentation. So a lot of $CO_2$ was being released."

"Yes." She heard a long pause and knew better than to interrupt.

"There is a mathematical model I can use to determine out how much $CO_2$ was in the room. But I need the dimensions of the area, the number of fermenting bins and sizes, and the Brix and temperature readings on each. And the temperature inside the winery."

She knew she could get most of that information. "Okay."

"It will only be an estimation. But I'm betting it will be close. By the way, I've just sent my report to you online."

Which meant that everyone in her office now had access to it. It meant she would have to bring it up at the staff meeting this afternoon. And she still had to read Riggs's online reports from yesterday.

"Okay. Thanks very much. I really appreciate it," Kally said.

"Also...the DNA on the beer bottle is not Mr. Remick's. And the juice sample is only grape juice. Get me those figures and I'll get started."

Nakamura ended the call.

Interesting about the beer bottle. *Who did it belong to?* She wondered if she should go to the reception in light of this new information, or go back to work. Actually, she *was* working.

But her biggest concern was her boss, Dale. After reading Nakamura's report, he most assuredly would close the case. She realized what she needed was an ally to help convince Dale otherwise. And that person was not someone she really wanted to think about at the moment.

But think about him she did. And she would need more than a hunch to convince Riggs to help her.

Kally walked back to join Chris, who was standing by herself now that the hearse had left.

"Everything okay?" Chris asked.

"Sort of," Kally answered.

# 42

Kally parked at the event space in Woodinville that Janie had rented for the occasion, since the winery was still technically a crime scene. She met up with Chris at the door and they walked in.

"I know you're working," Chris began, "so I'm going to mingle, try to drum up some business."

"Okay," Kally said. "I'll catch up with you later."

Kally walked into the crowd, seeing winemakers already at the bar drinking beer, their favorite go-to drink, and preferably a craft brew, which Seattle and Woodinville had plenty of.

She searched faces in the room, spotting two engaged in separate conversations—Kirk's mother and Denny—and each on opposite sides of the room.

She looked at her watch. She had less than 15 minutes before she needed to head back for the staff meeting. She walked toward Janie and Kirk's mother, who were standing to the side of a serving table being filled with giant bowls of salads and pastas, and trays of cheeses and meats. Kirk's daughter, Emma, made her way down the far side of the table, carefully taking in the offerings.

"Hello again," Kally said coming up to the two women.

Janie smiled at her, the first time Kally had seen her friend with a happier look on her face.

"Maria," Janie began, addressing Kirk's mother, "what I didn't tell you is that Kally is a winemaker and knew Kirk."

"Oh?"

Kally nodded, taking in deep lines around Mrs. Remick's sleepless eyes. She couldn't even begin to imagine what her son's death had done to her.

"My winery is two doors down from Kirk's. He"—she paused—"was a friend. I'm going to miss him."

"As we all will," Kirk's sister, Faye, said, coming up to them and handing her mother a glass of white wine. "We need to find the bastard who killed him."

The sister barely acknowledged Kally before looking away.

Kally ignored her and pressed on. "Mrs. Remick, do you mind if I ask you a few questions? About Kirk?"

"I suppose," Mrs. Remick answered taking a sip of wine.

"Is this Kirk's wine?" Faye asked.

Janie shook her head.

"You would think with all these wine people here, you'd serve his high-class wine."

"I would, but I don't have access to it anymore," Janie answered.

*Not since your brother caused our divorce* is what Kally was sure Janie wanted to add. But she didn't. She saw Janie's shoulders sag slightly. Kally wanted to shake some anger into her.

Ignoring her daughter, Maria Remick started in. "I'm only beginning to refer to Kirk in the past tense."

Kally found the comment incredibly sad.

Mrs. Remick continued: "Kirk always did well. He did well in sports. He did well in school. He always had a girlfriend…" She looked at Janie for a moment and smiled.

"Yeah, and after our philandering father left, Kirk looked out for us," Faye added, taking a large sip of her drink. "Until he moved to Seattle."

"Did he have any enemies that you know of?" Kally asked Mrs. Remick.

"That's a preposterous question," the sister said.

"Faye, she's just doing her job," Janie said.

"Do you have information on the cause of death?" the sister asked.

Of course it was the one question everyone in the room wanted answered. And so Kally lied.

"We're…still investigating."

"That's good. Because he didn't make many mistakes in life." Faye drained her wine and walked off to get another.

"I'm sorry for her," Mrs. Remick said, looking after her daughter. "She's quite bitter."

*Goes without saying.*

Mrs. Remick continued: "In his last phone call to me, Kirk mentioned buying property on some place called Red Mountain."

"Yes."

Janie and Kally exchanged a quick glance.

"You knew this?" Janie asked.

"Just recently. From Paula," Kally answered.

"He sounded excited about it," Mrs. Remick went on. "He would have his own grapes. I don't know what will happen now."

*Nor do I*, Kally thought. Across the room, she saw Denny laughing with his former workmates at Kirk's winery. Odd that he wasn't over here standing with Janie. Kally turned her attention back to Kirk's mother.

"Did Kirk ever mention getting out of winemaking?"

Janie didn't say anything. But Kally noted a quizzical look on her face.

Mrs. Remick shook her head. "No, he didn't."

"Were there ever any money problems at any time in his life?"

Mrs. Remick seemed to think about that. "Other than watching our pennies at home…no, I can't say that there were."

"When are you going back to Chicago?" Kally asked.

"In a few days, I think."

"May I contact you if I have additional questions?"

"Yes. Janie has my phone number."

Kally nodded. "I'm sorry for your loss." She was sure the comment came across as hollow as it sounded. "Kirk was…I…I just can't believe he's gone!"

Kally checked herself from crying, her emotion coming on suddenly.

Mrs. Remick reached out her hand, a gesture she thought was incredibly sweet. If anything, Kally should be consoling her.

After another quick glance at Janie, Kally walked off. Composing herself, Kally looked at her watch again. She had eight minutes before she needed to leave. And Manning was nowhere to be seen.

Kally walked up to Denny, now standing by himself and looking like he'd had a few. Seeing her, he began humming Under My Thumb, the Rolling Stones song.

*You really are something.* She fought to keep a professional demeanor.

"How's it going?" Denny asked, smiling slyly.

Denny had that boyish look that women liked: dirty-blonde hair stylishly unkempt; perpetual stubble on his face; a thin, toned physique. And he was a winemaker, always a draw.

"Fine. Nice to see you."

"Too bad about Kirk," he said.

"When was the last time you saw him?"

"'Bout two months ago."

"Here? Or in Walla Walla?"

"Here." He looked at Janie across the room. "I was in town."

"For what?" Kally asked.

He stared at her and didn't say anything. Then: "I see you got your cop face on."

"Yes. It's my job." A job she was finding increasingly difficult to do, mixing it with winemaking. And winemakers.

"I don't know if Janie told you…but we're sort of seeing one another. On and off. Nothing serious".

"What did Kirk think of that?" Kally asked.

"He didn't know."

"I see."

Denny continued: "I saw him to talk about getting a label started. Just the two of us, using Walla Walla and Red Mountain vineyards."

"Did he agree to that?" Kally asked.

"He said he'd think about it. And then…" He shrugged.

Denny reached for a glass of wine on a passing tray.

"You guys got along well," Kally said.

"Yeah. But then we became competitors."

*In more than just wine.* "What do you think Kirk would have thought about your being with Janie?"

Whether Denny thought it was a bold question, she didn't know. But he took his time answering.

"Kirk didn't have it in him to hold a grudge." Denny took a long drink. "He was never going to be with one woman. But I couldn't tell him about me and Janie. That would have hurt."

*How thoughtful.*

"I got to get something to eat," he said.

"Good luck with your winery."

"Thanks."

Denny walked off. The dead man should have been Denny, she thought, for moving in on Janie. That is if Kirk were the vindictive type. Maybe Denny would have been lucky: maybe Kirk would have let the transgression of sleeping with his wife—okay, ex-wife—pass.

*Yeah, right.*

Kally looked around the room. She was now several minutes past her self-imposed exit time. Suddenly, through a throng of winemakers, she saw Manning. He finished a glass of wine and put it on a table. And then he walked outside.

Without thinking, Kally rushed—as much as she could with people in the way—to the door. Seeing Manning's glass on the table, she reached for it and hid it under her jacket.

Then she went outside and looked left and right. But he was gone.

Kally sat in the Woodinville Police Department parking lot, her phone to her ear. She glanced at the time: 1:04 p.m., already late for the 1 p.m. meeting.

Manning wasn't answering his phone. His voice mail began, but she didn't leave a message. She called Kirk's office manager.

"Paula, it's Kally," she said, when she answered.

"Yes, hi."

"Do you know where Mark is?"

"I assume he's at the reception."

"He isn't," Kally said. "He left."

"Then I don't know where he is. Do you want me to leave a message for him?"

"No, thanks. I'll…I'll stop by later. And I'll drop off those bills." She paused. "You weren't at the reception."

"No, I came back here. Someone has to be in the office."

"Right. Okay. Well, thanks."

Kally ended the call and put her phone away. She raced through the parking lot then the hallway to get to the meeting, hearing Dale's voice rise as she got closer.

"Okay, everyone…"

Kally rushed in and took a seat at the back. Dale stood at the front looking out over the assembled staff as remaining stragglers filtered in.

She sat still, trying to slow her heart rate. The last person in closed the door. Everyone was accounted for: Bud, A-Rod, and Riggs, as well as the office's small support staff: Ramone, the HR person/office manager/accountant; Hannah, an intern from the local community college helping Ramone; Kyle, the webmaster/information guy; and Chelsea, filling in part time as the communications specialist.

Only Myrna, who manned the phones, remained out of the room.

Kally took a deep breath and let it out slowly. She looked at Dale and thought he seemed anxious, knowing how he disliked a late start to meetings. Behind him, on the long white board to the left of the timeline, he'd written six items in large black letters, the last being *field reports.*

She glanced up at the clock: 1:07 p.m.

Finally Dale began: "I'll go over a few administrative things and then we'll get your reports."

Riggs sat in a front right seat and turned slightly to look at her, then turned his attention back to Dale.

Kally hadn't had time to read anything Riggs had written on OPI. She hoped he would give the report about their meeting with Jacobsen.

"First," Dale began, "contributions to your 401(k)s will be made this week. If you have questions about any of it, see Ramone.

"Ramone will also need your vacation requests for the holidays soon so don't delay on this. We need people covering the office Thanksgiving and Christmas. And speaking of Christmas, we'll have a caterer here the Friday before. Hannah has a list of places we'll go over later."

Then he went into a discussion—with help from Kyle—about the new computer system that was to be installed next week. All the while Kally sat there trying to get her thoughts in order, needing to convince both Dale and Riggs about giving her more time on the Remick case.

Dale put his hands together. "Questions?"

No one spoke. Dale addressed the support staff.

"Thanks, guys, for coming. You can go now."

They gathered their things and walked out. Kally was startled at hearing her name.

"Kally, we'll get your report last. Bud, want to start?"

"Sure." Bud described how she had put several cases on a "back burner" while she took over three of Kally's. Those "back burner" cases were almost completed: A burglary in a Quik Mart, the teenager caught on tape and detained. A goat that had stuck his head through a fence and mowed down a Master Gardener's flower display; charges pressed against the goat. A bullying incident at the high school; Bud had talked with the young man and his parents, "the uniform and the police car scaring the life out of him." A woman passing a counterfeit fifty dollar bill at a clothing store; that case is pending.

Bud, sitting halfway down the table to Kally's left, turned to face her. "I talked to Mrs. Hatch about the domestic violence call she made. Mrs. Hatch will not press charges against her husband. But there are some red flags that I put in my report."

"Like what?" Dale asked, folding his arms in front of him and leaning back against the whiteboard.

"Well, Mrs. Hatch said her husband had moved out, to an apartment. But his horses are still there. And she said his horses cannot stay there.

"And, she has a special horse—I think the name is Sage—that was a gift. She's afraid that when the horses finally do leave, he'll take that one."

"Did she mention being afraid of her husband?" Dale asked.

"No," Bud answered. She paused for a moment. "But I did detect, well, a great dislike for Mr. Hatch. I had a gut reaction that we may be getting more calls from this person."

Kally saw Dale nod slowly.

"What about the horses?" Riggs asked. "Would she do anything to harm his horses?"

Bud shook her head. "I don't think so. But the horses are in the middle."

Bud changed the subject. "Then I had two more of Kally's cases"—Kally felt a sense of dread at hearing how much Bud was doing, and doing for her—"one about the woman who was throwing leaves coming into her yard back onto her neighbor's property. Remember, she wanted the trees cut down? I did a courtesy call and talked to both neighbors. They've come to a resolution: the one who owns the trees will rake her neighbor's lawn. So that's done."

"Great," Dale said.

"If only life proceeded so simply," Riggs added.

"Then the last case—"

"Yes, and I want to talk to you about this," Dale interrupted.

Bud repositioned herself in her chair. "The woman who wanted us to clean her gutters...she's...elderly. She has a disability. So, well, she has a one-level house, and I cleaned the gutters for her."

People's first response might have been laughter. Instead, everyone waited for Dale's retort.

"Okay," Dale began, standing up straight. "Yes, it was nice of you, Bud. I want to say that up front." He paused. "But don't do it again. Old people have old-people friends. And they talk. And one called here yesterday and wants *her* gutters cleaned. Okay?"

Bud hesitated. "Yes."

Dale moved on. "A-Rod? What'da ya got?"

A-Rod, sitting across the table from Bud, started in. "I've been doing mostly transportation stuff. A couple of lanes were closed last week in town for pothole repair. So I was the car out there."

"Good," Dale said.

"Now there's paving work on 522,"

—a highway heading out of town toward eastern Washington—

"I'll be directing traffic there for the rest of the week."

"Good again. Thanks for doing that." Dale glanced at his watch. "Riggs?"

Riggs sat up and looked around the table as he began.

Kally listened as Riggs described his current cases, listing them in a sing-song manner as he often did: Neighbors complaining about speeding on a side street. A winery with music on weekends and people are complaining about the noise and the traffic. A bank branch saying someone was stealing passwords from its ATM. A lease dispute downtown. An owner wanting a business vacated, but the business won't leave.

"And, I'm helping Kally on the Remick case," Riggs said, locking eyes with her. "My report's on OPI. We briefly interviewed four people"—he gestured toward Kally—"and Kally interviewed two more who had been at the deceased's winery Friday night.

"We have nothing concrete from them. However, Jacobsen, an attorney in Bellevue, has a bandaged hand, which may or may not have something to do with the case."

Riggs continued: "Nakamura indicated that TOD is between twelve midnight and one thirty a.m."

This was news to her, the wider estimation of time of death. But, of course, Riggs had read Nakamura's report and she hadn't.

"But we won't be interviewing anyone else, because cause of death has been established."

That was news, too, not the cause of death but the end of the interviewing. She looked at Dale and wondered why he allowed Riggs to make these decisions when he had, after all, put her in charge of the case.

Riggs extended his hand for Kally to continue.

All eyes in the room were now on her.

Kally crossed her legs and began. "As Riggs mentioned, the ME report is now online, and while I have not read it in its entirety, Nakamura called me this morning and gave me the news about Kirk's"— she paused—"Mr. Remick's cause of death. It is listed as asphyxiation from $CO_2$ poisoning. And he said it's significant $CO_2$."

"So an industrial accident," Dale added.

Riggs nodded.

"But Nakamura has asked for the dimensions of the winery's production area and the number of fermenting bins, plus the Brix readings and temperatures."

"Why?" Riggs asked.

"Because he's going to figure out the amount of $CO_2$ in the room, not just in the body," Kally answered.

Kally saw Dale frowning.

"Again, why?" Riggs asked. "How will his figures change the determination of death?"

Kally felt heat rising on the back of her neck.

"I imagine he wants to *ensure* that the amount of $CO_2$ in the room is consistent with causing death," she answered.

"It's not going to change anything," Riggs said matter-of-factly. He turned to Dale, then back to her. "You're questioning one of the great MEs in the region."

"He asked *me* for the figures!"

"I don't care!" Riggs pressed. "Nothing's going to change!"

"I think he was killed!" There. She had said it to the room. Bud looked down at her hands, the air suddenly thin.

"Kirk wouldn't make a mistake that killed him," she added. "Not in winemaking."

"You know that for a fact," Riggs said coldly.

"I do," Kally answered.

"You need a motive and a murder weapon. You have neither," Riggs retorted.

"The motive was that he was disliked," Kally said.

"I thought he was well liked," Riggs countered.

"People were jealous of him."

"Enough to murder him?"

"I agree that seems extreme," Kally admitted.

"Kally," Dale interjected, "this is Woodinville, not Detroit."

She waited for him to say something else, but then she proceeded, emboldened by Riggs's attack on her.

"I've got license numbers on about fifty black sedans. A-Rod mentioned a black sedan leaving the scene of the crime Saturday morning."

A-Rod nodded. Riggs started to say something, but Kally kept going.

"And we have four references to a woman with blonde hair: two times in the winery that night, one leaving in a black sedan Saturday morning, and one outside Mr. Remick's winery talking to the assistant winemaker that same Saturday morning."

"*Don't do anything* with black sedans," Riggs said.

"The car could lead us to a suspect. Or a witness."

"*Don't do anything* with black sedans," he repeated. "And don't do anymore interviewing."

"We don't have all the answers."

"You *never* have all the answers!" Riggs yelled.

Kally stared at him. His face was turning red. *Why does he dislike me so much?*

She wasn't going to get Riggs on her side. Her only hope now was Dale. But Dale wasn't supporting her either. Not if he was ceding her case to Riggs.

"We need to wrap it up, Kally," Dale said.

"Can we keep the case open until Nakamura does his $CO_2$ study?" she asked.

Riggs shook his head. "I don't get it."

"After you hear from Nakamura, that's it. I want you to take your cases back from Bud so she can do her own work," Dale answered.

"I will."

"When will you hear from him?" Dale asked.

"I don't know."

"Find out. And let me know."

# 44

Kally got in her car and drove out of the headquarters parking lot.

"I feel really alone *now*, Kirk!"

The last thing she wanted to do was work her case. Dale and Riggs had no intention of supporting her. They had made that clear from the start: do the procedural work, wait for the determination of death, then close it down.

That was all she had been asked to do. Not investigate a murder.

But a $CO_2$-related death was not just an industrial accident, in her view. Especially in light of the person who had died.

Kally got onto busy 522 and drove west toward Seattle. In her rearview mirror, she saw the flashing lights of A-Rod's car and him already directing traffic during the paving project.

Her phone rang. She looked at the caller: Jeffrey Banks. *Surfer.* Microsoft. She let the call go to voice mail. After a time, she heard a beep and listened to the message.

> *"Jeffrey Banks here returning your call. You asked if I had seen anyone near the barrels Friday night at the wine party? I did not. Sorry I can't be of more help."*

Well, it was worth a try. She thought again about the funeral and seeing the owners of Red Mountain Productions. RMP was a private company and so she had little information about its owners. She could ask Ellie, of course, its tasting-room manager. But her sommelier friend

Sarah knew the business side of Washington wine. And she'd get a more objective view from her.

Kally drove on, weaving in and out of the before-rush-hour traffic, and soon was near the north end of Seattle's waterfront, near Sarah's upscale restaurant, which sat on Elliott Bay. The view, overlooking a marina, the Seattle skyline, the Space Needle, and cruise ships leaving for Alaska, couldn't be beat.

Plus, the wine list was among the best in the city.

She drove into a large, fairly empty parking lot, got out, and walked up a long flight of steps to the front door. Walking in, Sarah was directing a wine tasting with employees. They stood around a small table filled with wine bottles. Kally noted that the labels were covered.

Kally stood in the back of the restaurant, waiting. Usually, Sarah performed these tastings in the morning. But the funeral had been that morning.

A few employees looked in her direction, eyeing the uniform. Sarah glanced over and smiled. At a bar to Kally's right, a bartender talked to a lone patron. No one else was in the restaurant, in-between the lunch and dinners crowds as it were.

Sarah picked up a wine bottle and poured about two ounces into each person's glass.

People swirled their wine, then sniffed. Then they repeated the gesture, in perfect sommelier-trained style.

"What do you get?" she heard Sarah ask.

"Lemon, other citrus…"

"What kind?" Sarah pressed.

"Lime…"

"Passion fruit…"

"Guava…"

"Grapefruit…"

"I get green apple…"

"Okay. Taste," Sarah said.

All swirled and sniffed again, then took a taste.

Kally knew what they were drinking. She was sure of it.

Most of the employees followed with a second taste. Some spit into spitting glasses.

"What do you have now?" Sarah asked.

"Same as the aroma…"

"Definitely grapefruit…"

"Fresh citrus…"

"Lychee…"

"Mouthfeel?" Sarah asked.

"Steely…"

"Crisp…"

"No oak…"

"Tart…"

"What are we drinking?" Sarah inquired.

"Sauv Blanc…"

"Pinot Gris…"

"Chenin Blanc…"

"DJ, I didn't hear from you," Sarah said. "What do you think this is?"

"Um…" The employee shifted position, uncomfortable about being on the spot. "I'll say unoaked Chardonnay."

Sarah didn't say anything right away. "Did you take Wines of the World at the Northwest Wine Academy?"

"Yeah," DJ answered.

"Take it again."

*That was harsh, Sarah.*

Sarah moved on. "Anyone? What is this?"

"Sauv Blanc."

"Right."

*My guess was correct. I should do blind tastings myself with Sarah, to keep myself sharp.*

She thought back to her time in France, tasting wine with Guillaume. She quickly dispelled the thought.

"In this particular variety, what sensory note is missing that is usually present on the nose?" Sarah asked.

"Cat pee," someone ventured.

Kally was sure the staff would refrain from using that well-known varietal characteristic with their diners.

"Right again. What contributes to it *not* being there?" Sarah pressed.

"The vineyard…"

"Harvest date…"

"Yeast used…"

"Fermentation temps…"

"Very good. You're all correct. And remember, if you are serving a Master Sommelier—and most won't tell you they are one—you may be asked these very questions. The best way to improve your sensory skills is to taste a variety of wines. And taste the same variety from different continents."

"Now, where is this from?" Sarah asked.

"North America."

"Yes. Where?"

"Here."

"Producer?"

No one said anything.

"It's Purple Sky. Woodinville." She removed the covering from the label.

*One of my neighbors.*

"This is a Northwest best. Suggest this one when you're asked for a Sauv Blanc. We'll have another tasting tomorrow morning."

The staff nodded in agreement. Some finished their wine in one gulp. Others poured out their samples.

The group dispersed, and Sarah addressed DJ again. "DJ, if we had been tasting Pinot Gris and you had said unoaked Chardonnay, I would have said that was a pretty good guess," she explained. "But not Sauv Blanc."

"Okay," he said.

"Those classes will help you," Sarah added.

DJ walked away. Sarah came up to Kally and gave her a hug. "I see you're working," she said.

"And you as well."

"I didn't see you at the reception," Sarah said.

"I didn't stay that long," Kally answered. "Can I ask you about RMP?"

"Sure." Sarah directed Kally to a small table near the entrance, and they sat down.

"You don't want to ask Ellie?" Sarah asked.

*A logical question.* "I will eventually. But I want some background first. Who *are* they, do you know?"

"Attorneys, mostly. They're pretty lawyered up. And they have Seattle money."

"Do you know Noel Jacobsen?" Kally asked.

"No. Who's he?" Sarah asked.

"A Bellevue attorney. I saw him talking with RMP people this morning. Could just be the attorney connection,"Kally offered.

"Ellie shouldn't work there," Sarah said. "And you don't want to get involved with them."

"Why not?"

"I'll just be blunt."

*That won't be a surprise, Sarah.*

"They're not…good people. They want to be the largest on Red Mountain, which means knocking off CSM."

"You probably serve RMP wines, though, don't you?" Kally asked. She seemed to have hit a nerve.

"Oh yeah," Sarah answered, a disgusted look on her face. "They want us to *push* their wines. They come in here once a week for lunch— three or four of them—and they say to my staff, 'Bring us *our* wine.' Like the staff is supposed to know who they are."

Sarah went on: "Their wines are good, but they're not outstanding. And they want to be big. You lose something with big. That's why I push the warehouse wineries."

Kally nodded.

"Chateau Ste. Michelle does it right," Sarah added. "Their winemakers make a few small-lot wines, emulating all of you in the warehouses. And CSM casts a big shadow. But it's protective. *Inclusive.* You won't see that with RMP."

"Do you have the names of the owners?"

"I do." Sarah got up and reached for a business card and a pen from a check-in stand near the front door. She sat down again.

She turned the card over and wrote down a name. "From what I can tell, this is the top guy. Then there are these three," she said, writing them down.

Sarah handed Kally the card, and she looked at it. The names meant nothing.

"You can probably find them online, through their law firms."

"All right."

"RMP is building a new winery on Red Mountain. With a hotel," Sarah added.

"A *hotel*?" Kally exclaimed.

Sarah nodded. "You know how much Red Mountain land sells for. RMP is buying up smaller properties out there."

Kally knew there wasn't that much land on Red Mountain to buy. Was land the issue with Kirk? Kirk was so well known, he could do whatever he wanted. And if he wanted to buy land, who would stand in his way? His wines outsold RMP wines by a factor of ten.

"Did you know that Kirk bought acreage on Red Mountain?" Kally asked, fingering the card, sure that Sarah wouldn't divulge this information to anyone else.

Sarah seemed surprised at that. "Hmm. Makes sense. He could certainly afford it. We sell out all of his wines here."

Kally nodded. She paused, not wanting to mention her conversation with Denny and the presumed new label he and Kirk had discussed. She didn't mention it because she couldn't confirm that it was true.

She looked up at a clock above the door, noting the time. "Well, I should get going before traffic gets worse."

With that, they both rose. Thinking back to the funeral, Kally asked Sarah about her partner, Judith. "How are you guys?"

"Eh," Sarah answered. "We've hit a speed bump. But, we're working it out."

"Sorry to hear that," Kally said. She didn't know Judith that well. But she imagined living with Sarah was not the easiest. Their tribulation might also explain Sarah's harsh treatment of her employee.

"And you?" Sarah asked. "You were seeing a guy..."

"Zack."

"Oh yes. Zack."

"He's stopping by the winery tonight." She held up the business card. "Well, thanks for this."

"No problem. Hope you find what you need."

Then Sarah said something that made Kally stop.

"I don't know what's gotten into Ellie. But I know why she stays with RMP."

Kally waited for her to continue.

"There's been talk," Sarah said.

Kally knew exactly what that meant. How could one be Ellie and not have the temptation to stray, with all the attention she got.

Sarah took the card out of Kally's hand and underlined one of the names. Then she handed it back to her.

Kally looked down at it: Richard Fugelson.

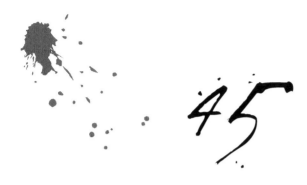

Back at work, Kally did internet searches on the four names Sarah had given her: Greg Sanderson, Elliott Jansen, Phil McDonough, and Richard Fugelson.

She started with Fugelson, whom, she found, was a handsome, mid-forties, senior legal advisor and vice president at a financial services firm in Seattle. And married. With three kids.

He had all the right credentials, having moved up in the company over ten years. Somewhere along the line, he'd been bitten by the wine bug. She quickly checked Facebook and saw photos of Mr. Fugelson with his family.

For a split second—okay, longer than that—she stared at his image and wondered about Ellie. If Kally had read Sarah correctly, then Ellie was involved with him.

And yet Ellie's husband, Jim, who she and Riggs had just seen in Bellevue, seemed perfect for her, a grounding rod as she transitioned from Seahawks cheerleader to the world of wine.

Ellie would be a fool to let him go. But certainly, if you were Ellie, attention came from all directions.

She moved on, doing a quick search on the three other men and finding they were all attorneys at the same upscale Seattle law firm. She'd get into their backgrounds later. She needed to get information to Nakamura so he could do his $CO_2$ study.

She was about to pick up her phone when Bud appeared in her doorway. While she could only speak for herself, Kally thought Bud looked as defeated as she had felt after their staff meeting.

She motioned Bud to a chair inside her office. Kally got up, closed the door, and sat down again.

Without prompting, Bud started in, mentioning the lady with the gutters. And the rebuke from Dale.

"I felt sorry for her," Bud said. "And I don't think I did anything wrong."

"You didn't."

"Would you have done it? Cleaned the gutters?"

Kally paused. "I would have thought about it, sure." She shrugged. "I don't know. Just let it go. You've got plenty to do. And a wedding to plan."

"I don't think I'm in the right line of work," Bud said.

"Yes, you are! Don't think like that."

Bud looked away. But then, just as suddenly, Kally saw a change in her demeanor. Bud set her jaw and looked back at her, her brown eyes deep, dark pools.

"I'd do it again," Bud said defiantly. "I don't care what he says. What are we here for?"

"Right!" Kally said. She paused. She didn't have time to sit here talking to Bud. But it was the least she could do—listen, that is—since Bud had taken on her cases.

"Thanks for doing my work," Kally said.

"It's all right," Bud replied. "Why do you want to keep the Remick case open?"

It was a fair question, and reminded Kally of her long odds in proving her "gut reaction."

"Kirk has no one advocating for him except me and his ex-wife. And she has no power to do anything."

"But you really think he was killed? In Woodinville?" Bud asked.

Kally stared at her, not aware of the intensity of her own gaze.

"Yes, I see that you do," Bud said, answering her question.

"If I had support, it would make my case easier," Kally explained. "But it's not just lack of support. It's the tone. From Riggs."

"Everyone heard it," Bud said.

Kally paused. "I'm only on the case so the department isn't embarrassed not knowing about wine."

"And Dale isn't letting you make the decisions," Bud added.

Kally didn't respond. There was nothing to add.

Finally, Bud rose. "Well...didn't mean to interrupt. Let me know if you need more help."

"I will. And, Bud..."

Bud turned and looked at her.

"We have to be a team, you and me."

For the first time, Bud smiled.

After she left, Kally called Paul Storey to get the dimensions of his winery. His space and Kirk's had the same configuration, and she imagined that he knew the size of it better than she did.

Once Kally had this information, and with the number of bins, the fermentation figures, and the temperatures written in Kirk's logs, she could give everything to Nakamura. The only thing missing would be the temperature in the room on the night of Kirk's death.

"Hey, Paul," Kally began when he answered. "Do you have a moment?"

"Sure."

"The medical examiner's going to determine the amount of $CO_2$ in Kirk's winery at the time of his death. But I need the square footage of his—your—production area. Do you have it somewhere?" Kally asked.

"Yeah...I do. Hang on a second."

While she waited, Kally turned to her computer and opened Nakamura's twenty-two page ME report. On the first page was a summary listing cause of death: *asphyxiation from ambient $CO_2$*; time of death: *12-1:30 a.m.*; manner of death: *industrial accident*; and the ME's one-line summation: *victim died at the scene after losing consciousness from ambient $CO_2$*.

All so neat and tidy. No wonder Dale and Riggs wanted the case closed.

For the first time, she began to think that maybe Kirk did return to his winery—or never left—and was overcome with $CO_2$.

She went on, scrolling through the bulk of Nakamura's notes. She came to the page with an illustration of a man's figure, front and back views, standard in an ME's report. Near the face, he had scribbled *wine stains* and circled the areas on the right side of Kirk's face. Farther down, he had circled the hands and written, simply, *fists*.

Nothing else was noted about anything else on the body.

She kept reading. Pages and pages described the autopsy findings by bodily system. She stopped on the summary of the respiratory system that included toxicology numbers she didn't understand.

*What's taking Storey so long?*

*No liquid or foreign material in lungs*, Nakamura had written. *Significant $CO_2$ present at 2,700 ppm.*

*What would be normal?* She wrote the figure down.

"Here it is," Storey said as he got back on the line. "The size is approximately two thousand square feet. And the height is twenty-five feet, in case he wants that."

"Thanks so much," Kally replied.

"So it was $CO_2$, then?" Storey asked.

Kally hesitated. "Yes. But the ME's going to check further to ensure that the amount in the room was enough to cause death."

"Sounds good," Storey responded. "I mean, it sounds right to check this."

"Yeah."

"Okay," he said. "Well…I'll just see you around."

Kally ended the call with Storey. There would need to be an enormous amount of $CO_2$ generated from the bins to fill a room of that size, she thought. Heavier than air, $CO_2$ falls to the floor then slowly rises as it accumulates, like an invisible pool of water. Was it even possible to fill a two-thousand-square-foot room with $CO_2$? Or fill it high enough so that a man, standing upright, would be overcome?

Kirk could have breathed in $CO_2$ from the bin as he punched down the grape skins. Then he could have fainted over the bin, his legs splaying out behind him, as he breathed more and more of it.

Kally stared at her computer screen. Doubts about how Kirk died crept in. She called Nakamura. When he answered, she gave him Storey's figures and the numbers in Kirk's logs for the fermenting bins.

"I have something else," Kally said. "I have a glass that I'd like to have tested for DNA."

"Send it to me and I'll have it processed," Nakamura responded.

"Would you also have the crime lab compare the DNA on the glass to what was on the beer bottle?" she asked.

"Sure. I'll do that," he answered.

"Great. I've read your report," Kally said. "What does this $CO_2$ number mean?"

"It means Mr. Remick had six times what could be described as normal $CO_2$ in his lungs," Nakamura explained. "Normal $CO_2$ in a room is about three hundred parts per million."

He paused. "Mr. Remick suffocated not because his head was pushed into a vat of wine. He suffocated because $CO_2$ was displacing oxygen in his blood cells. He was losing consciousness. Someone witnessing his death would have seen a man struggling to stay awake."

"But…wouldn't that witness also be struggling to stay awake?" Kally asked.

"That's a very astute observation, Officer O'Keefe. You are correct."
*So people were gone from the room. If they were ever in the room.*

"Did he suffer?" The question popped out before she'd even thought about it.

Nakamura paused. "Let me just say that he was aware of what was happening."

She suddenly felt ill. What had Kirk done to anyone that would cause this to happen? If someone had caused it to happen.

"Could that much $CO_2$ really be in a room?" she asked, thinking of her own winery.

"That's what I'm going to find out," Nakamura answered.

"We use gas in wineries to protect the headspace in tanks from oxygen," she added. "To keep the wine from spoiling."

"That make's sense," Nakamura replied. "Gas is heavier than oxygen. What kind do you use?"

"Argon. But some wineries use nitrogen," Kally answered. "A few might use $CO_2$. But that's rare. Mostly it's used for sparkling wine… to add bubbles."

Kally didn't know what type of gas Kirk used. But she could easily check this. She pictured the tall, heavy gas tank she used sitting on a hand cart in her own winery.

"By the way," Nakamura said, "how's it going over there?"

"Dale and Riggs want the case closed," Kally answered, "especially now that we have cause of death."

"I see."

"How long will it take you to determine the $CO_2$ level in the room?"

"Not long."

"Oh." It wasn't the answer she wanted to hear. He must have heard the disappointment in her voice.

"I'll get you the figure in due time."

# 46

Kally found a parking space at Woodinville Gas and Tank not far from the Warehouse District. She looked at her watch: 5:50 p.m. Ten minutes before closing.

She walked into the industrial green-colored room filled with tanks, valves, and other paraphernalia used in wineries. Mike Overton, the man who filled all the gas needs for the warehouse wineries, stood behind the counter and looked up as Kally entered.

"Haven't seen you in a while," he said, smiling.

She hadn't seen him either, since Seth was bringing her tank in to be filled.

"I know," Kally said, walking up to the counter. Back in high school, Mike was on a short list to become a professional baseball player, good as he was. But he never got out of the minor leagues. So he chose to take over his father's gas business, which was now booming with Woodinville's growth.

After exchanging more pleasantries, Kally got to the point.

"Can you tell me if there were any gas purchases around September 1 and going forward for Kirk Remick's winery?"

"That would be Mark Manning coming in," Overton said, reaching under a counter. He brought out a black three-ring binder and began flipping through pages.

"Shame about Kirk," he said, shaking his head.

"Yeah. It is." Kally paused, not wanting to interrupt him. "I also need to know what type he bought."

"Okay." He continued reading. Then: "Here it is."

He turned the binder so she could read the name and date.

She saw Manning's signature and a date of September 9. And the word "argon" next to it.

"Any other gas purchases by him?" Kally asked, fingering the pages.

Mike shook his head. "Each of these pages represents a week. I went back to late June."

"Okay. Thanks."

Back in the car, Kally was about to pull out when her phone rang. She stopped and looked at the name, surprised at the caller. It was handsome Mr. Arnaugh from Redmond. She wondered if he were standing in his beautiful kitchen. And if he were barefoot.

"I remembered something else about that night at Remick Cellars," he began when she answered. "You got a minute?"

"I do. Go ahead."

"So I was coming out of the restroom…you know, the one in the hallway…"

"Yes."

"…and I was walking into the winery in the back. But as I was passing the barrels—they were on my left—I thought I heard a woman crying."

"Crying," Kally repeated.

"Yeah. Behind the barrels."

*Odd*, Kally thought. "Did you hear any other voices?"

"No. And it didn't sound like any of my business, so I walked on."

"I see."

"I know it's not much, but…I remembered it a couple of days ago and I thought 'Yeah, that was strange…crying at a wine party.' And you said to call if I remembered anything."

"Yes, I did. Do you remember when you heard this?"

"Later during the evening…I had a pretty good buzz on. Probably shouldn't tell *you* that!" He laughed. "And the music had stopped for a minute. That's why I heard her."

"This is helpful, Mr. Arnaugh. Thanks for letting me know."

Kally ended the call. She didn't think much of it as she exited the parking lot and headed toward her winery.

But then she did. And quickly pulled to the side of the road.

She knew what wine events were like, and the number of people attending them. And the *one restroom, one stall* each warehouse winery had.

She quickly called Arnaugh back.

"Mr. Arnaugh. Sorry to bother you, but I thought of something."

"Okay."

"Was there a line waiting to use the restroom when you walked out?"

"Oh yeah, there was!"

"Do you by any chance know who went in after you?"

"Well…it was…Jimmy! That's right! I had been standing in line talking on my phone, to my wife. But I turned and said 'hey' to him."

"Jimmy?" Kally asked. "James Monroe, from Microsoft?"

"Yeah!"

"This is helpful. That's all I need. Thank you."

"That's it?" he asked.

"That's it."

She looked through her phone, found James Monroe's name, and called the number.

He picked up with a simple "Monroe."

"Mr. Monroe, this is Kally O'Keefe from the Woodinville—"

"Yes. Hello," he responded, interrupting her.

"If you have a moment, I'd like to ask you a few questions."

"Sure. Go ahead."

"On the night of Mr. Remick's wine party, there was a point later in the evening when you were standing in line to use the restroom. Is this correct?"

Monroe didn't respond.

"I know this sounds a little strange, but…you were standing behind Mr. Arnaugh. Is that right?"

"Yes, I was."

"So Mr. Arnaugh used the restroom and left. And then you went in."

"Correct."

"What did you do once you left the restroom?"

"I went back to the party. And I stood with the guys from Microsoft. Who you met."

"Right. But before you joined them...did you hear anything near the barrels as you were walking past?"

Monroe paused. Then more time passed. Kally wasn't sure he was still there. Finally, he began.

"I did hear something." He said it like a confession. "I heard a woman. Really angry. She said 'you liar' and 'you'—I'm just going to say the word—'fuck.'"

*And you didn't think to tell me this?*

"Did you hear any other voices?" Kally asked.

"No."

"But she must have been talking to someone if she said '*you* fuck.'"

"Actually the emphasis was on the f-word: 'you *fuck!*' I don't think I would have heard her if the music hadn't stopped."

"So then what did you do?"

"I met up with the guys and stood with them."

Kally pressed on. "And then the angry woman walked out from behind the barrels and bumped into Surf—I mean...Mr. Banks in your group?"

"Yeah. I bet it was the same one."

"Did anyone else walk out from behind the barrels?"

"Not that I saw."

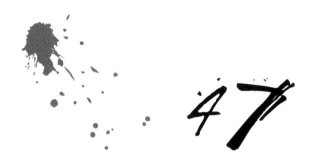

K ally parked in the rear of her winery and sat there for a moment, the aroma of pizza she'd picked up along the way filling her car. With everything on her plate, she thought about cancelling the evening with Zack. But she didn't.

She thought again about Arnaugh and Monroe. When you come out of the restroom in a warehouse winery, you can turn right and go through the tasting room and exit to your car.

Or you can turn left and go back into the production area.

The production area was where the party was, where you're being served expensive 95-point wines.

For free.

And it's Friday.

*Have another.*

Thankfully, Arnaugh and Monroe had chosen to do just that.

She thought of something else: Men don't spend half as much time in a restroom as women do. Even less when there's a line.

From the time Arnaugh left the restroom and passed the barrels to the time Monroe did was probably a minute and a half tops. So the person behind the barrels, perhaps a blonde person, went from whimpering to whiplash in about sixty-plus seconds.

It still didn't tell her who the woman was. But oddly, she felt like she was closing in on her.

She got out of her car, taking Kirk's bills with her but leaving the pizza behind. Instead of going into her own winery, she walked down to Kirk's. The door was open and she went in.

Kally saw two interns high up on barrels, four racks tall in the cold room, topping off. She walked toward them and spoke up to them.

"Is Mark here?" she asked.

One of them looked down at her. He held a pitcher of red topping wine and a funnel. "No. He wasn't here today."

"When will he be in?"

"Tomorrow."

"When?" Kally asked.

They looked at one another and shrugged. "Not sure."

"Tell him I want to talk to him when you see him."

Kally left them and walked to Paula's office. She knocked lightly on the closed door and waited. Nothing. Then she tried the door. Locked. She put the envelope containing Kirk's bills in the plastic container for mail near Paula's door and retraced her steps outside, not bothering with a goodbye to the interns. She needed to pin Manning to a spot and make him talk. Especially about the blonde woman he had talked to Saturday morning.

She went to her car, grabbed the pizza, and headed into her own winery. Kally saw a note from Seth on her table:

> *Leah is leaving. Friday is her last day. Sorry I didn't tell you in person. But you weren't here.*

*Of course I'm not here.*

She put the pizza on the counter in the kitchen.

*Now I'll have to help Seth more often. Which, I should be doing anyway.*

Her back door opened. *Finally, Zack is here.* Kally turned the corner, out of the kitchen.

It wasn't Zack. It was Mindy Peters—*Wine Hound*—making good on the invitation to stop by.

"Hi," Mindy said, coming up to her. She plopped her purse and jacket on Kally's table. "How are you?"

Kally was sure she looked as tired as she felt. "It's been a day."

"Yeah it has. I smell pizza."

"Help yourself. It's in the kitchen."

"I will. Thanks."

Mindy disappeared around the corner, and Kally cleared away the top of her table, moving Mindy's things to a rack of empty barrels.

Mindy reappeared with two pieces of pizza on a paper plate. "You're not eating?"

"Not now. I'm waiting for Zack."

Mindy stopped midbite. "Am I interrupting something?"

"No, no. It's okay," Kally reassured her. "Sit down."

Mindy did and quickly devoured one of her helpings. "What did you think of the funeral?"

Kally thought back to the morning. *Was it really just this morning?* "The industry honored him as they should have. It was nice."

Then she thought of Janie again, taking on the role she did for Emma and Kirk's family. "I think Janie was put in an awkward position."

Mindy nodded. "But what is she going to do? She's got the kid." Then, between bites: "Kirk certainly got around, didn't he? I didn't know his latest."

"She pours wine in his winery," Kally answered. She made a mental note to see Kendall again.

"You know Janie is seeing Kirk's former winemaker," Mindy said.

"So it's common knowledge?" Kally asked.

"From what I hear."

Kally shook her head. "I don't get it. I don't see it."

"Well, here's my take on it," Mindy offered, swallowing first. "There's no accounting for taste. Or attraction."

"Right."

Mindy finished the last of her pizza and pushed the paper plate to the side. "So what can you tell me about Kirk that I don't already know?"

"I'm still working the investigation."

"I figured that," Mindy replied. "When will you get cause of death?"

Kally didn't say anything.

"What will you do if it comes back $CO_2$ poisoning?" Mindy pressed.

Again, Kally didn't respond.

"It already has, hasn't it," Mindy inquired. "You already know."

"I can't confirm that."

"The Warehouse District hasn't had *one* death associated with $CO_2$ poisoning," Mindy said. "Not one."

"I know."

Mindy kept going: "So if what I'm thinking is true, then Kirk's death really is suspicious, in my opinion."

At least they were on the same page.

Mindy wiped her mouth with her napkin and discarded it on the empty plate. "You know…we're a lot alike, you and me."

"How so?" Kally asked, a little surprised at the comparison.

"We uncover things…pay attention to details…go the extra mile," Mindy answered.

There was some truth to that.

"Okay, maybe not a mile," Mindy said. "Maybe ten yards. But ten that make the difference."

"Right."

She took in Mindy's gold bloodhound pin, the dog's head in a sniffing position. Mindy had even adopted a bloodhound puppy, whom she'd named Violet, and put the puppy pics on her blog.

"I think something sinister is happening in our small world," Mindy said, changing her tone. "I've had time to think about this. California is moving in."

"And killing people?" Kally asked, sounding an awful lot like Riggs.

"Kirk's death could be Shakespearean in scope," Mindy explained. "There's a lesson and a message in his passing."

She herself hadn't taken Shakespeare in wine school, so she didn't know what Mindy was referring to. She waited for her to continue, but Mindy changed the subject.

"The warehouse wineries here are like little yapping dogs nipping away at the ankles of the bigs," Mindy continued. "The bigs don't like bites taken out of their wine sales."

Kally nodded in agreement, this pronouncement making sense. Mindy knew the Warehouse District and the Woodinville wine scene better than anyone. Perhaps it was because of that or her exhausted state, or simply because Mindy was so conveniently present, that she broke all the rules in her line of work.

She told Mindy about the investigation, in particular, the three men and a woman standing together in Kirk's winery the evening of his party. Then she mentioned the references to a blonde woman and a black sedan, and Manning talking to someone outside Kirk's winery Saturday morning.

"Manning's not telling me the whole story," Kally said. "I'm sure of it." Then: "You can never mention this."

"I won't."

"He just won't talk. And now he's ignoring me."

"I didn't know he was seeing someone," Mindy said, "if the person at the door was someone he's seeing. I can ask around. See if anyone knows anything."

"That would be helpful."

"You know, you of all people know that Kirk was too smart to die from a stupid mistake," Mindy added.

"I agree."

Kally wondered what was taking Zack so long.

"I'm not writing about Kirk's party now," Mindy said, changing the subject again. "It's past. And the ending is sad. But I need a story. So…you got anything?"

"I have new wines coming out."

"Yeah? Like what?"

"A Grenache/Syrah blend."

"When?"

"At Christmas, maybe." But that wouldn't give the wine time to sit in the bottle. Kally thought about Blitzen, Kirk and Manning's hushed-up wine project, also releasing around Christmas. But she refrained from mentioning it.

Kally got off her stool. She went into the kitchen and grabbed two glasses.

"Come here." Kally walked to the Syrah and Grenache tanks, filled the glasses with a make-shift blend, and handed one to her.

"Taste this."

Mindy swirled the wine carefully then sniffed. "Oh, yes." She sniffed again and looked at the rim.

Kally did the same.

"So, Grenache dominate," Mindy said.

Kally nodded. "I pulled juice off for rose which made the Grenache a little overweighted. For Grenache."

"No one's going to complain about that," she said, then took a sip. "Can I write about this? I really like it."

"Sure."

"What will you call it?" Mindy asked.

Kally hesitated, thinking again of "GS."

"Not sure," Kally said.

"So, Christmas, then?" Mindy asked.

Kally thought about that, too. Now she thought spring would do nicely. She could release her rose and her Pinot Gris/Riesling blend, too. And have a big release party.

"Not sure about that either."

Mindy left and Kally sat at her small table, the hum from the HVAC system the only sound in her winery. She thought through Mindy's comments.

It was true that the warehouse wineries, with their small-lot productions, took sales away from the larger estates, like Chateau Ste. Michelle and E. & J. Gallo, which owned Columbia Winery. But those sales were only a drop in the bucket to them.

Nonetheless, new warehouse wineries were opening all the time. Were they—we—being perceived as a threat? Not according to Sarah, who saw Chateau Ste. Michelle as a gentle giant. But she realized she'd been so focused on the *how* of Kirk's death that she hadn't thought of the *why*.

She looked at the time: 7:45 p.m. Zack was forty-five minutes late. And the pizza was cold. She was busying herself reading her wine logs when he finally arrived.

"Hey," she said, smiling, as he walked in the back door. She took in an uncharacteristically serious look on his face as he came up to her table.

She got up and gave him a quick kiss on the lips.

He didn't respond.

"What's up?" she asked.

"I need to talk to you," Zack began.

Kally folded her arms in front of her. "Okay."

"I'm seeing someone. And it's serious."

Kally froze, stunned.

"I should have told you sooner," Zack said.

*When did you have time to form a pretty important relationship?*

"Who is she?" Kally asked.

"We work together." He paused, then shook his head. "You aren't available, Kally."

"Yes, I am!"

"No. You aren't."

She unfolded her arms, still in shock. "What if I made myself available? I mean…more available."

"Is that what you want? Do you really want to be with me?"

Kally stared at him. She had never seen Zack so serious. Fun-loving Zack who never put pressure on her. She continued staring at him without answering. Because she couldn't say yes.

"I didn't think so," Zack said. "There is someone standing between us. And he will always be there."

He touched her lightly on the cheek, then walked away.

Kally watched him open the door and, without looking back, close it behind him.

48

There was something immediately off about the office when Kally walked in the next morning. It was unusually quiet. And she didn't see anyone.

*Am I late? Or early?*

Her head was still swimming from Zack's news of the previous evening, so anything was possible.

She saw Hannah, the intern, sitting at her desk. She walked up to her and saw that she was crying. Then Riggs came around the corner.

"Kally."

How odd hearing him speak her name.

"There's been an accident," he said.

"Where?"

"On 522."

Riggs' words didn't register at first. And then they did.

*A-Rod.*

Without saying anything, Kally turned and rushed out.

She came upon the scene, seeing three police cars already there. And a fire truck. And an ambulance.

Kally parked and ran toward them. She saw Bud kneeling next to A-Rod, holding his hand. He was on his back, on the side of the road near tall grass. One leg was badly mangled. And she could see there was blood underneath it. A lot of blood.

"A-Rod!" Kally knelt next to Bud and looked at him, his eyes only partially open.

Farther away, a car and a truck had parked alongside the road. Dale was talking to one of the occupants of the car, a woman, who had gotten out and was crying uncontrollably.

She saw paramedics running toward them, bringing a stretcher.

Kally looked down. A-Rod held Bud's gaze. Then he said something.

Kally thought he had said "always" to Bud, a look of peace on his face. Suddenly A-Rod's hand went limp.

"No. No!" Bud cried.

Paramedics crowded in around them, separating her from Bud. One of them directed Kally away from the stretcher.

*"Is he alive?"* Kally asked.

No comment.

Kally walked away from the scene, overcome with emotion and shock. And not just for Bud and A-Rod.

For herself.

She reached her car and got in. Crying, she fumbled around in her pack for her phone. Finding it, she scrolled through her list of contacts, barely able to read them.

She found Guillaume Tablet's number in France, her finger ready to press it, her hand shaking.

Kally hesitated, tears streaming down her face. She continued staring at her phone.

She couldn't press the number.

She put the phone on the passenger seat, set her pack on top of it, and drove off.

# 49

Guillaume Tablet poured a customer a taste of his family's newest vintage, a Châteauneuf-du-Pape, 96-point blend of what the wine writers of Europe were calling "pure perfection." A crowd had gathered at La Dernière Goutte, a well-known wine shop on the left bank, and so his sister, Annette, helped with pouring duties at another table in the crowded store. He was confident that they would sell a considerable amount of their current release.

Guillaume looked up as an elderly man walked toward him, wobbling somewhat and steadied by an aide who stood to one side and guided him forward.

"I knew your grandfather," the man said, coming up to Guillaume. "And his brother. You know that they made Château Tablet what it is today."

Guillaume smiled. "Yes, sir, I do know that." He poured two tastes of wine and pushed the glasses forward.

"Do you have any of his '41s?" the man asked. "We tasted them from the barrel."

Guillaume smiled and shook his head. "No, I am sorry. We have none. That is our 'lost vintage.'"

The man nodded slowly, then looked down.

"But there may be some out there," Guillaume added. "You could try Germany."

"Ah. Germany." The man seemed lost in thought for a moment. Then he picked up his glass, took in the aroma, and closed his eyes. He tasted the wine, and nodded slowly. "Yes, this is Château Tablet. If I may, I would like a case delivered to my home."

"We will arrange that for you, sir," Guillaume said.

"He is right around the corner," the aide said. He handed Guillaume a calling card, and he read the name: *M. Pierre S. Ducat*, noting the address in the sixth arrondissement.

"Thank you. I'll ensure that this is taken care of." He was interrupted by his phone vibrating on the table next to him. Guillaume looked down at it, staring at the name for a moment without moving.

"*Pardon,*" he said to the two men. He picked up his phone and turned away from the counter.

"*Bon jour?*" Then in English: "Hello?"

No one responded.

He walked farther away. "Hello?" he said again.

Guillaume waited. Then he whispered, "Kally."

He waited some more, looked at the phone, then put it in a breast pocket and walked back to his spot at the table.

---

They were back in the conference room, the whole staff, minus Bud, who had gone to the hospital with A-Rod. Kally sat where she usually sat, at the back of the room, a sea of open chairs between herself and Dale, who stood at the front.

She needed to let her friends—and Bud's friends—know what had happened. Then she remembered that, as she was driving away, she'd seen a news truck approaching.

So people would know soon enough.

But they needed to hear it from her.

Dale waited a few moments and then began.

"Paramedics stabilized A-Rod before taking him to the hospital. Here's what we know: A woman in a late-model Toyota Corolla looked down for a moment while driving east on Route 522. When she looked up, she could not swerve out of the way of A-Rod, who had walked into the middle of the road to stop traffic."

Dale's words tumbled out in an oddly professional manner, as if the person who had been injured were "just the victim" and the words "just for the record."

"A-Rod's family has been contacted, and Bud will be gone for a while. On more practical matters, we'll be short-staffed now, obviously. You, Kally, will take your work back that Bud had taken on. And we'll split up the rest of Bud's work among the three of us," he said, indicating Riggs as well.

Dale paused. Kally imagined he didn't want the meeting to end on a cold, procedural note. And so he started what was always a difficult conversation.

"A-Rod is touch-and-go. There is no guarantee that he will make it. Or that he will ever be able to work again. I was the first one there, and I saw how badly injured he was." He paused again. "As is usual in a small office, we all got close to him."

Kally saw Ramone of HR look away.

"We need to send a prayer his way. But we also need to help Bud," Dale said. "Kally, what do you think we should do, individually or collectively, for Bud?"

The question caught her off guard. "Um...I'll call her. I...don't have an answer for you right now."

"Okay. Keep us informed."

"I will."

Then Dale took up his procedural tone again. "Any questions?"

T he rest of the day was a blur with nothing getting done. The office
       remained uncharacteristically quiet as people went about their
work without interacting with one another.

Kally stayed in her office and read Bud's reports on OPI about her
own cases. Bud had detailed everything perfectly, but Kally realized
she herself wasn't retaining the information.

With Bud away, Kally would take on two of Bud's cases: the
bullying teenager—visiting him again to ensure he wasn't bullying—
and the other teen case, the Quik Mart robbery. Kally would take Bud's
place in court.

*How am I going to do all of this?*

She read again Bud's notes on Mrs. Hatch and the husband and
the horses. One thing she sensed was the importance Dale placed on
the case. Mrs. Hatch, she read, had indeed reneged on the charge of
domestic violence. Perhaps it was time now to contact the DV advocate.

Thinking of Bud, Kally picked up her phone and called her. No
answer.

Needing to get out of the office, Kally grabbed her keys and left.

She turned off the main road near the Hollywood Schoolhouse section
of Woodinville and its many wine tasting rooms. The tree-lined road
she was on now would take her into Woodinville horse country and
the estate of Lewis and Sandra Hatch.

Kally drove for several miles, seeing large front lawns and houses
as well as horse barns and exercise tracks. Several well-groomed horses

trotted around as she passed, and a few people looked in her direction, unusual as it was to have a police car coming through the neighborhood when private-security services were the norm.

After several miles, she turned off the road and onto the Hatch driveway, which wound its way up to the main residence. Like many of its neighbors, the Hatch estate sat back from the road behind strategically placed trees and shrubs. She entered a brick circular drive with an Italianate fountain in the middle.

Kally drove by the fountain and parked off to the side, seeing a curtain move in one of the front windows. She walked to the front door of the large Colonial home, the kind of home most people could only dream of, and rang the bell.

The door opened immediately.

"Where is the other officer?" Mrs. Hatch asked before Kally began.

"I'm afraid there was an accident, on 522. One of our police officers—"

"I heard that on the news!"

"It was Officer Rodriguez who…is Officer Milano's fiancé. She's the officer who came to see you."

"I'm sorry about that. So, what can I do for you?"

"I'm paying a courtesy call to see how things are. And if you're okay."

"I'm fine," Mrs. Hatch said, folding her arms. "Mr. Hatch moved out, so I'm fine."

Kally noticed that the red welt near Mrs. Hatch's left eye had resolved.

"Have there been any other disturbances?"

"No."

"How are the horses?" Kally asked.

"They're still here."

"And that's okay?" Kally inquired, remembering Bud's report.

"Yes. Unless I change my mind. Mr. Hatch can be very manipulative."

"I see," Kally answered, wondering how the two Hatchs had ever gotten along. She reached inside a pocket and pulled out her business card and gave it to Mrs. Hatch.

"You gave me one already," Mrs. Hatch said, returning it. "I still have it."

"Okay," Kally said, putting the card in her pocket. "You'll call if you feel threatened in any way?"

"I will. Thank you."

"Then I'll be on my way." Kally bid her good-bye and was walking to her car when Mrs. Hatch yelled to her: "Woodinville Police is certainly doing a good job!"

Kally retraced her route and drove into the parking area for Matthews Winery, now closed for the day.

She stopped and dictated notes about her visit with Mrs. Hatch, adding at the end: "We need to keep a watch on the Hatch property and on Mrs. Hatch herself. I don't believe that the husband's moving out has really solved anything."

When she finished, she sat there staring at two large stainless-steel tanks sitting alongside the winery's parking lot reflecting the last rays of the sun. Then she saw a worker appear with a forklift to retrieve them.

Aware of her inability to concentrate any longer, Kally pulled out and headed to her own winery.

51

She sat at her high table, the reality of A-Rod's near-death accident settling in. Kally felt numb and tired. And very sad for Bud. She tried to focus on winery work instead.

She read the list of items they would tackle on Saturday, which was going to be a very long day. First was finishing barrel maintenance. They'd open each empty barrel and spray it with $SO_2$ to keep bacteria from growing. They did this procedure once a month.

Then they would filter Grenache and Syrah before combining both in a bigger tank. This involved a two-step filtering process of moving the wine through a porous, upright filter and then changing the filter to smaller porosity and moving the wine back through it to the original tank. Each "pass" in the filtering process took out more and more impurities and ensured that the wine wouldn't clog the sterile 0.45 micron nominal filter on the bottling line, a filter so "tight" it removed microscopic bacteria in addition to any remaining yeast cells.

Moving to whites, they would go through the same filtering steps. For whites especially, the more passes through a filter, the clearer the wine became—brilliant, even—a term used in wine judging. She'd do the same with her rose.

She looked around at her tanks. Moving wine always took time. And a lot of cleaning.

Kally got up and added "buy new filters" and "line up bottling" to the list. Then she added the word "labels."

She sat down again. What was she going to do about her labels? She absolutely hated them. Wine was nothing without a smart label, and hers were…she couldn't even put a word to them.

Kally decided right there to bottle the wines without labels, called "shiners" in the trade, until she could figure out what to do. Meanwhile, the labels sat on a palette in a corner of her winery. And would be thrown away.

She looked at her watch, then called Bud again, but the call went to voice mail so she hung up. No surprise. Kally imagined being Bud right now, whose life had been upended on a surprisingly sunny morning on a busy Washington highway. What would she have said to Bud if she had answered?

Her back door opened, and three winemaker friends—Bob, Larry, and Paul—entered. She now realized these men always moved as a group: at Kirk's harvest party; at the funeral; standing around wherever. But she hadn't yet spoken to them about Kirk's death.

"Hey," she said as they came up to her table.

"Listen…" Larry began, always a bad beginning to a conversation. She waited.

"How much longer will the crime scene tape be in front of Kirk's winery?"

She hesitated before answering, taking in their countenances, serious all. "We're still investigating."

"Well…it's scaring away business. We'd like it gone," Larry said. "And soon."

"I don't imagine it will be much longer." She looked at each of them, seemingly processing her brief explanation.

"Understand we're not *blaming* you," Paul added.

"No, I get it. I understand," Kally responded. *Now is as good a time as any.* "Since you're here…where did you go after you left Kirk's harvest party?"

They seemed surprised at the change in direction.

Larry spoke first. "I went back to my winery, closed up, and went home."

The other two nodded in agreement.

"Did you see anything, anything unusual, around Kirk's winery as you were leaving?" she asked.

All shook their heads. "We all left early, so there were still a lot of people out in the alley watching the destemmer," Larry said.

"I didn't see anything," Paul said.

"When did you all come back to your wineries?"

"I came back early Saturday morning to do punch downs," Bob said. "And that's when I saw all the people and the press and—he looked right at her—the police."

"Right." She paused. "How early? And did you see anyone around Kirk's winery?"

Bob thought for a moment. "It was around seven."

*Not early enough.*

"And I didn't see anything. But then, I wasn't looking," Bob added.

"Right," the other two said in unison.

"I'm asking because—" But she was interrupted.

"We know why you're asking," Bob said.

There was an awkward pause. She had nothing else to ask. Or add.

"Well, we'll watch for the tape to come down. And we'll see you around," Larry said.

The three turned and left. She looked after them as her back door closed. Then she heard car doors closing out in the alley and motors starting up.

She sat there, staring at the top of her table, not sure how to process the encounter. There was a time, not long ago, when she'd felt connected to these three.

"*...one of the guys...*"

But not now.

*The four had been on a panel discussion with Kirk during Taste Washington, the state's pre-eminent weekend celebration of wine. The topic: Cult Wineries: Is Smaller the Future? The classroom was packed, standing room only. People stood in the hallway straining to hear the five winemakers.*

*Kally sat next to Kirk. Larry was on the other side of her.*

*The room exploded in laughter. Kirk had just compared winemaking to childbirth.*

*"You get through the crush, and you say you're never gonna do it again: all those sleepless nights, worrying about what might happen. And then...bam! The next vintage arrives! How did that happen?"*

*More laughter.*

*"Well, babies aside," the moderator, a wine writer from New York, said, "let's taste this wine."*

*Eight samples were lined up in front of people lucky enough to have seats. The winemakers had brought their best wines for the audience to try. The moderator led them through the tasting, with comments added from the winemakers.*

*Halfway through the tasting, someone from the audience asked a question: "What is the thinking about whole-berry fermentation, and how much whole berry do you use?"*

*Kirk grabbed the microphone. "So the reasoning here is that using whole berry—and that also means using some of the stems—makes the wine fresher, fruitier, more complex. If you have a high-acid wine, the stems can round out the acidity. And with global warming, stems are riper so we're not seeing the "green" attributes they sometimes give a wine. Normally, you don't use a hundred percent whole berry. The percentage then is winemaker choice."*

*Larry added his two cents: "And you want to do a pump over rather than a punch down to avoid lacerating the stems. Because then you could get too much green in the mix."*

*Then a reporter queried Kally. "Do you use it? Whole berry?"*

*"I do not. I'm pretty much old school: crush and destem."*

*The same reporter asked another question of Kally: "It's not hard to notice that you are the only female winemaker on the panel. Have you ever felt ostracized because of your gender?"*

*Kally thought for a moment, then reached for the microphone. But Kirk grabbed it first.*

*"She's one of the guys."*

*The other three nodded in agreement.*

She looked at the time: nine p.m. She needed to go home.

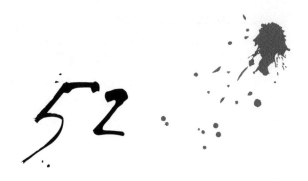

# 52

Kally closed up her winery and left. Standing in the alley, she looked toward Kirk's back door, a security floodlight illuminating it.

All was quiet. She walked the few yards to Kirk's door and turned the handle.

Locked.

Kally reached inside her pack for the key and opened the door. And stepped inside.

Muted light shone down on bin four, still covered in crime-scene tape. But it was alone now on the floor like a character on a stage.

She walked further in. The place was eerily quiet, a winery without a soul.

Kally went to a table, a wine barrel with a glass top, the one she and Zack had stood at the night of Kirk's harvest party. She stood there now and visualized that evening.

Two-dimensional people moved around the room just as she had seen real people doing that night. The music was turned up, the hard rock Kirk always played. Zack was standing next to her now and said he'd go get appetizers. And so he left and she stood there, watching, sipping, the place filling with people.

She glanced at her watch: 8:15 p.m.

She looked to her right. Kirk was talking to the three warehouse winemakers: Bob, Larry, and Paul. They were tasting his wine. And laughing. Everyone in good spirits.

Bob turned toward her and smiled. He raised his glass to her and she did the same.

*Nice to be in familiar company*, she had thought at the time.

Zack returned and brought two more glasses of wine.

A short time passed; it was almost eight thirty now.

She saw Kendall walk by and come up to Kirk. He put his arm around her waist and drew her in. She whispered something to him and he smiled. She kissed him lightly on the cheek and walked away, Kirk following her with his gaze.

Back in the present, she left the wine-barrel/table and stood in the middle of the floor, near the bin.

She pushed the evening forward to nine o'clock or so the night of the party. She, of course, hadn't been there. But she remembered what the Microsoft guys and Arnaugh and Jacobsen had told her.

The Microsoft programmers were in front of her, standing in a circle, talking, drinking. Monroe came up and joined them, having just used the restroom.

Suddenly, a woman appeared from the right and bumped into Surfer and kept going.

Kally looked closely at the woman passing by. She couldn't make out the face. Because she didn't know the face.

The Microsoft guys—startled at first—laughed and resumed their conversation.

Kally looked toward the barrels where the woman had come from. She thought she saw another person emerge. She couldn't make out who it was. Not even the gender. It was just a shadow.

She moved into the hallway that led to the tasting room. Envisioning the evening again, this area was crowded. There was a line for the restroom. Three men and a blonde woman stood in the middle of the floor, deep in conversation, none of them drinking. Again, no faces.

Kally walked on.

In real time again, she stood in the darkened tasting room. Only a night-light gave off some glow. She visualized ten people from that evening buying their wine, cases being filled. There was Jacobsen. And Arnaugh. And more people from the credit card receipts on her desk.

She walked back toward the production area. This time she stopped near the three men and the woman in the hallway. They were still talking among themselves, the words not audible.

Kally turned to the woman: "Did you bump into Surfer? Were you here Saturday morning? Do you drive a black car?"

The woman turned slowly toward her, her face only a shadow. But Kally thought she detected a smile.

Kally backed up suddenly. *"This is creepy!"*

She quickened her pace back to the production area. And looked over her shoulder.

The hallway was empty.

Kally stood there a bit longer, getting her bearings. She saw the bin and walked up to it, then moved slowly around it, looking at the shriveled grape skins just below the yellow crime-scene tape.

She bent down and smelled the must, then quickly rose up.

The fruit was rotting. It couldn't be used.

Five thousand dollars down the drain. Literally.

Kirk would be rolling over in his grave—if he were in one — knowing that Klipsun fruit was rotting away.

In his own winery!

She put her hands on the sides of the bin and looked into the must, thinking.

"Kirk...give me something."

She looked up, spying a forklift in the corner. She looked down at the bin again, then back to the forklift.

*Oh my God...*

She walked quickly to the large garage door, unlocked it and hefted it up in one motion to give her more room. Then she hopped on the forklift and started it, maneuvering it halfway out the big door, then forward toward the bin.

Kally eased the forks under the half-ton container and raised it slightly. And backed up.

She hopped off and walked to the place where the bin had been.

Nestled among dust particles and a few dried grape skins was a phone.

S he arrived early to work the next morning and stood in Riggs's doorway. He turned toward her.

"Got something?" he asked. "About Bud? Nakamura?"

Kally shook her head and walked in. "I need your help."

He sat back and folded his arms. And waited.

"I found something," she began.

"What?"

"Kirk's phone."

He seemed to think about that. "Okay. So...you've got some phone calls...pictures..."

"No," she interrupted. "A recording. It's from that night."

Riggs seemed genuinely interested in that. He kicked a chair out toward her.

"Sit down."

She sat down.

"How many voices are there?"

"Hard to say. At least two. But maybe more."

"How long is it?"

"About three minutes. His battery must have died." She paused. "I think one of the voices might be Mark Manning's. But he told me he hadn't been there."

Riggs was quiet for a moment. He sat forward, a serious look on his face. Then he addressed her again.

"Where's the phone now?"

"In my pocket. In an evidence bag."

She reached into her coat and brought it out. And placed it on the edge of his desk.

Riggs stared at it. Then he sat back. "Here's what I want you to do. Call this guy Manning *on your own phone.* Get voice mail if you can. Tell him you have important information about the deceased that you want to discuss with him. But let his call go to your voice mail. We'll line up his voice with what's on the phone. If it's a match...well, then he's in *incredibly* deep shit. *And* if it is, he can save us trouble and tell us who else was there."

"You think he'll tell us?" she asked, something she had been hoping for all along.

"Oh yeah!" Riggs said, suddenly animated. "He has one other option, and jail time probably doesn't suit winemakers."

But then Kally saw Riggs's countenance change. "Now that I think of it, the phone has to go to the Seattle lab. This could take some time."

Kally shook her head. "I know who can help."

"Who?"

"My brother. He's a musician and has a friend with a recording studio. A really good one."

Riggs didn't say anything.

"I've already talked to him. He said they'll copy the recording. Then we can send the phone to Seattle."

She paused. "We can go there now."

The Tiger Creek recording studio, north of Woodinville, was hidden off a dirt road in a rural part of town. The studio had a growing clientele among recording artists in Seattle and the world who came to its comfortable state-of-the-art facilities year-round.

The fact that one of its owners had played in her brother Phil's high school band was an added plus, and Phil occasionally filled in at Tiger Creek as a studio musician. Following her brother's directions, Kally found the turn-off and drove in, parking near a barn. She saw Phil's car nearby.

Kally and passenger Riggs, sitting silently next to her, got out and walked into the barn.

"Hey, Kal!" her brother said, coming over to greet them.

Kally took in the large recording studio encased in glass.

Phil introduced them to co-owner Travis.

"Long time, Kally!" Travis said, coming up to her and giving her a hug. Kally noticed that he'd aged, and by that, she meant he'd gained quite a bit of weight. Probably a consequence of his sedentary day-job.

"This is Detective Riggs," Kally said, introducing him.

They all shook hands, then Travis turned back to Kally. "How's the wine business?"

"Good. It's good." She reached in her pocket and brought out the bag with the phone inside.

"Ah, the phone!" Travis took it from her.

"It's evidence," Riggs warned.

"We want you to wear gloves," Kally explained and reached in her other pocket.

"Sure." Travis took the pair she offered him.

"C'mon up here." Travis lead them inside the enclosed space and then up a few steps to a raised room that looked out over the recording studio. He closed the door of the soundproof room.

Kally took in a massive console that extended the whole of the room's width, along with six large computer screens.

"So I'll start by copying the recording," Travis began, sitting down in front of one of the screens. He put on the gloves, then took out a charger cord and plugged the phone into the console.

Kally put on her own pair of gloves and moved behind him. "Let me show you what we're interested in." She took the phone from him and scrolled through it. "It's this one."

Travis nodded and pressed the arrow on the phone.

The recording started, and Kally heard again the muffled voices and unrecognizable sounds of that evening.

"It's about three minutes long," Kally said.

"What's the time stamp on it?" Riggs asked.

"Twelve twenty-six a.m.," Travis answered.

"Right in the realm of death. Do you recognize any of the voices?" Riggs asked Kally.

Kally shook her head. "They're too faint."

Travis worked on the computer, and they waited while a blue line on the screen scrolled across the bottom. It took about thirty seconds to copy the recording.

Travis unplugged the phone and gave it back to Kally.

"Let's see what we've got."

"It's important for us to know how many voices there are and, obviously, what they're saying," Riggs interjected.

Travis nodded again as he worked the buttons and dials on his sophisticated system. Soon four wavy lines appeared on the screen in front of him.

"Okay, looks like you have four people." Travis pushed a lever, bringing the volume up.

"What's that sound?" Riggs asked.

"The HVAC," Kally answered.

"I'll take it out."

She watched Travis work quickly on his keyboard. Then he turned to her.

"The lines you see are voice signatures. If you send me voice recordings, I'll see if we can match them."

"Okay," Kally said. "Great."

"In the meantime, I'll clean up everything so that it's cleaner, clearer, louder. This will take a little time. I can also isolate each voice. Or you can listen to all of them as the event happened."

"We may need both," Riggs said.

"So let's look at one of these right now." Travis highlighted the top signature line and copied it. A split image appeared on his computer screen with the copied line on the right.

Travis pushed a lever, pressed a button, and sat back.

The words spilled forth as clear as day:

*"You betrayed me."*

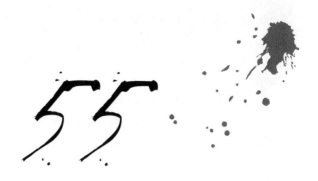

# 55

K ally sat at her desk, back in her office. Finally, she had a break in the case. Or so she hoped.

She thought about the three words they had all heard at the studio. Who had said them? And to whom? And what was the speaker referring to?

She thought again about finding the phone. Who knew what was on anyone's phone? It's a private world in there. But it had given her something.

Before picking it up last night, she'd put on gloves. And then she had reached down for it. She remembered her heart beating rapidly. First, she'd taken fingerprints off the screen, and those were now being analyzed in Seattle.

Then she'd tried to turn the phone on. But the battery was dead. So she'd placed it in an evidence bag and had taken it home.

After sanitizing her kitchen counter top several times, she'd charged the phone. When it was ready, she'd turned it on.

But it required a password.

*What the hell!*

She'd sat down, thinking. *Six letters. Or numbers. Or a combination. What would he use?*

She'd started with the obvious: Remick.

It didn't work.

She'd thought of women's names: Kendall. Too long.

Janie. Too short.

Then she'd thought of another one: Emma. But what else? Emma12? 12Emma?

She'd tried them both. Nothing.

What was Emma's age? She was five. She'd tried 05Emma. And Emma05.

Again, nothing.

Then she'd tried myEmma.

The phone opened. A wave of relief passed over her.

Kally had checked Kirk's recent phone calls and saw calls to his mother and Kendall and to other numbers that didn't have names. Then she'd opened his photos, steeling herself for nude pictures of Kendall. Instead, what she found were vineyard photos. Vineyards that had his labels on posts. And there were barrel pictures. Close-ups of the names of the barrels that also showed the toasting level: *M, M+, M+TH*. All of them were taken recently.

Then there was another photo of some sort.

No, it was a recording.

*The* recording. With a time stamp of 12:26 a.m.

Kally had clicked on the arrow, and it had started to play, with muffled sounds and no video image. In fact, the screen was dark except for a line of light at the bottom.

She presumed that Kirk had put his phone under the bin. And why hadn't she moved the bin? It had never occurred to her that something would be under it. They were looking at what was *on* it (Kirk) and *in* it (nothing but grapes).

And one did not want to disturb a crime scene any more than necessary.

She still had to go through the rest of his phone calls. But she wouldn't do that until she got the phone back from Seattle—in a few days, she'd been promised. And now Riggs was on her side.

*Imagine that!*

A figure darkened her doorway, and Kally looked up. It was Nakamura. She sat still, not saying anything. Never had King County's lead medical examiner stood in her doorway.

"Can I come in?" he asked.

"Of course!" Kally said, still shocked at his presence.

He stepped inside and sat down.

*He's got something.*

"I did the $CO_2$ compilations based on the figures you gave me," Nakamura began. "This is how they work out..."

He proceeded with the math, repeating figures she had given him then adding the volume of oxygen of air in a room and how $CO_2$ displaces it, and adding in the square footage of the winery and...

It all went over her head. She knew nothing of what he was talking about.

"I'll skip to the finding," he said, graciously. "The $CO_2$ in the room was three hundred eighty-nine parts per million."

Kally didn't know what that meant either. But this figure was lower than the one in his initial report.

"Mr. Remick did die of $CO_2$ poisoning," he continued.

Her heart sank.

"But not from what was in the room. That amount would not have killed him."

Kally's mouth dropped open. Then her eyes teared up. She reached across the desk and held Nakamura's hands.

"Officer O'Keefe...you have a murder to solve. Oh, and by the way, the DNA on the wine-glass matches the DNA on the beer bottle."

K ally sat there, still holding Nakamura's hands. She was shocked yet relieved at all he had told her.

She had been right.

And the wine-glass revelation? Her reservations about Manning were proving true. He had lied. But why?

Nakamura sat back. He reached into his briefcase and pulled out a sheet of paper and handed it to her. She saw that a line was highlighted in yellow.

"I've amended my report online," he said. "And no doubt there will be more amendments as you solve this."

*Nice to have an ally.*

She read Nakamura's highlighted sentence. Under cause of death was written: $CO_2$ *poisoning.* Just two words.

"Let me ask you something," he continued. "Do you ever have an occasion to use dry ice in your winery?"

"No," Kally answered.

"Dry ice is solid $CO_2$," Nakamura explained. "Did Mr. Remick ever use it, do you know?"

She thought back to his release party a few years back with scantily dressed women holding whips and protecting wine barrels. Yes, there had been dry ice.

"He did. About two years ago," she answered.

"No, that's too long ago. I'm trying to determine other emitters of $CO_2$ beyond fermenting grapes. Is your HVAC system checked regularly?"

"Yes. Building maintenance does it."

"How about fire extinguishers? Do you have them?"

She nodded.

"Who checks them?"

"Well…we're supposed to."

"Look at the one in Mr. Remick's winery. If he has one. Ensure that it's full."

"I will." She paused. "Was $CO_2$ forced into him?"

Nakamura didn't say anything at first. "It's a possibility. He would have fought it, of course."

*His fists.*

"I understand the body has not been buried," Nakamura said. "I've asked the funeral home to return it."

That surprised her. She thought immediately of Janie. And Kirk's mother.

"Normally, I would need permission from the family. But a presumed murder investigation changes everything."

"Right." She paused. "What will you do to him? I mean, the body?"

"I'll look at the lungs again and other areas in the pulmonary system." He paused. "I also want to open his hands. We…had to break a finger on each hand to get a small scope in. I thought perhaps he might be holding something. He wasn't. But I need to look at them again."

He added: "I'll do this today." He reached for his briefcase, then rose. "You are welcome to be present. You may have questions we can answer there." He paused. "I want you to keep in touch with me as you move through this."

"I will. What time should I be at the…um…"

"Come by at three p.m. And find out what type of gas Mr. Remick used in his winery," Nakamura added.

"I did," she answered. "It's not $CO_2$."

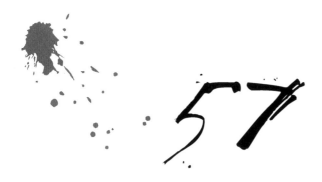

Kally knew that what Nakamura had told her was enough to keep the investigation open.

But she wanted more.

After he left, she did a Google search on Red Mountain land. The area, a recognized American Viticultural Area (AVA) in eastern Washington State, was not really a mountain. And not really red. But it was on a higher elevation than the surrounding hills and got a lot of sunlight and a lot of high heat that fully ripened the most sought-after red varieties like Cabernet Sauvignon, Sangiovese, and Mourvedre.

The earliest plantings went in in the mid-1970s when scientists working at the Hanford nuclear site decided they wanted to be in viticulture instead. So they cleared away the scrub grass and wild sage and planted grape-vines.

What they developed were some of the world's best-known vineyards: Klipsun, Ciel du Cheval, Kiona. Land at the time cost one hundred dollars an acre.

Other vineyards followed. Chateau Ste. Michelle was a late comer. It established Col Solare in 2007 with Antinori from Italy and built a winery on the site with a tall Tuscan tower. Then Red Mountain Productions came in. Both spent significantly more for their land. Today an acre sells for forty to fifty thousand dollars.

The land commanded a high price because Red Mountain was relatively small, roughly four thousand acres compared to eleven million acres in the Columbia Valley AVA. And with its unique setting, small footprint, and celebrity-status wineries and vineyards, Red Mountain property rewarded its owners *very well.*

Kally clicked on the link for the Benton County Assessor's office and then clicked on public records. She was asked to provide a parcel number, which she didn't have.

She picked up the phone and called the assessor's office. A young woman answered.

"This is Kally O'Keefe with the Woodinville Police Department in King County, WA," she began, hoping she wouldn't need pain-in-the-butt paperwork for her request.

"I need information about a purchase on Red Mountain…land that a Mr. Kirk Remick bought."

"Hang on a second."

Kally waited. A man got on the phone.

"Ma'am, I can give you the information over the phone if you fax me a notarized page on your department's stationary."

Small communities, small minds? She didn't want to think that. But sometimes…just sometimes…

"I should tell you," Kally responded, "that we are working a murder investigation."

"The notarized stationery is all I need."

Kally got off the phone, typed a request on police stationary, and hit print. Retrieving the page, she walked through her office, down the steps to the City of Woodinville's offices, and got the page notarized.

She retraced her steps and faxed the page to Benton County. She waited 15 minutes and called again.

The same man answered the phone. "Okay, thank you, Ms—"

"Officer."

"Officer O'Keefe," he corrected. "Mr. Kirk Remick bought the land on October 1 of this year."

*Three weeks ago!*

"How much land?" Kally asked.

"Fifteen acres."

*A pretty big lot in a small area.*

"Who did he buy it from?"

The man paused.

"It's a public document," Kally reminded him.

"I know. I'm looking. Here it is: a Mr. Jack Truitt sold him the land. All of his land."

"How much did he pay for it?"

She heard another pause, then: "Six hundred seventy-five thousand dollars."

Kally thought for a moment. "How much acreage on Red Mountain does Chateau Ste. Michelle own?"

"Um…"

She heard clicks on a keyboard.

"Thirty acres."

"And Red Mountain Productions?" she asked. "It's also known as RMP."

More clicks. "Sixteen acres."

So if RMP had bought Mr. Truitt's fifteen acres, it would have given them a foothold slightly bigger than Chateau Ste. Michelle's. Enough to brag about, she thought, thinking back to her conversation with her friend Sarah.

"So Chateau Ste. Michelle owns the most acreage on Red Mountain?" she asked.

"No. A Canadian company this year bought hundreds of acres."

She seemed to remember that now, for millions and millions.

"Where does Mr. Remick's land sit in relation to Chateau Ste. Michelle and RMP?" Kally asked.

"Let's see…" the man said.

Kally waited.

"Right in-between."

S he didn't have much time to think about Kirk's Red Mountain land purchase. But with the information she had, she walked into Dale's office, where he and Riggs were having a conversation.

The two men, arms folded, listened as Kally explained her findings. She started with Nakamura and the $CO_2$ study.

"Bottom line is Kirk Remick didn't die from $CO_2$ in the atmosphere. But he did die of $CO_2$ poisoning."

"And how does that happen?" Riggs asked.

"From $CO_2$ in a tank, which some wineries use. That's the only thing I can think of at the moment."

She brought up the wine-glass/beer bottle DNA results, which proved Kirk's assistant winemaker, Mark Manning, had lied. And she mentioned her ongoing suspicion that Manning knew more.

Then she told them about Kirk's land purchase near Chateau Ste. Michelle and RMP.

And because Dale hadn't been brought up to date about finding Kirk's phone or going to the Tiger Creek recording studio, she filled him in about that, too.

"The phone information is not yet on OPI. I'll get it up there soon."

Dale nodded in agreement. "This is good, Kally. All of it."

*Sure. Now you're being nice.*

Riggs took off his suit jacket and folded it over a chair. He seemed to be taking his time thinking through what she had just told them. Kally noticed that his hair was a little orangier than the last time she'd seen him. He shouldn't dye it.

Suddenly Riggs caught her eye. "Give me a motive."

"To get Kirk out of the way," she answered.

"Because he bought land?" Dale asked.

Kally hesitated. "Possibly. RMP would have bragging rights with those extra fifteen acres."

"So the real target is Chateau Ste. Michelle," Riggs said. "And Mr. Remick just happened to be in the way."

"He was in the way, but not just because of land. He was a good winemaker," Kally explained. She paused. "RMP is aggressive. They compete with everyone, not just Kirk. But Kirk—I mean Mr. Remick—outsold them."

"It wouldn't be the first time envy or ambition led to murder," Dale added.

"Do you think RMP had a hand in Mr. Remick's death?" Riggs inquired.

"I don't know."

"Do you think they were in the room when he died?" Riggs prodded.

"I don't know that either," Kally answered, thinking of the recording. She hesitated. "RMP has been buying up smaller properties on Red Mountain. They're building a hotel there."

"Is that unusual?" Dale asked.

"Yes. The area is small. You want the land for viticulture. Not buildings."

"What else do we know about Mr. Remick," Riggs pressed, "besides winemaking and buying land?"

*Here it comes. Here's where I divulge his personal, most private...*

"He fooled around," she said.

"Ahh..." Riggs had a sly look on his face. She could only guess what Dale thought.

"Was he seeing anyone in particular?" Riggs asked.

"Yes. A woman who works in his winery."

Riggs turned to Dale's white board and wrote three words: women, winemakers, land.

Reading them, only the land purchase made sense to her.

Kally sat in her car outside of Kendall's condominium. She was here to get a voice recording of Kirk's, because if anyone had one, it would be Kendall.

But there was something else she wanted to ask her.

She got out and walked up to Kendall's building, still thinking about the three words on the whiteboard in Dale's office. She didn't peg Janie or Kendall or warehouse vintners as killers. Nonetheless... they were all part of the mix.

She picked up the complex's phone and called Kendall, hoping she was home.

Finally, someone answered.

"Hello?"

"Kendall?"

"Yes?"

Kally identified herself and asked if she could ask her a few more questions related to Kirk's case.

"Sure," Kendall said, hesitating at first. She buzzed her in.

Kendall was waiting near her door again as Kally rounded the corner from the stairwell. This time, Kendall was dressed in smart casual clothes. Kally wondered if she had caught her coming or going.

"Come in," Kendall said, directing Kally inside.

She pointed to the sofa and Kally sat down. Kendall took her usual seat on the edge of it. She realized she hadn't seen Kendall around the Warehouse District.

"I'm not working at Kirk's anymore," Kendall explained, when Kally asked her about it. "Seems pointless to be there."

"I see."

"I was everywhere with Kirk. Now I don't hear from anyone."

Kally felt sorry for her. "What are you going to do?"

Kendall shrugged. "I'm not sure I'll stay in the industry."

"Sorry to hear that," Kally offered. Then she got to the point of her visit. "I have a couple of things to ask you about Kirk."

Kendall nodded. "Okay."

"You told me earlier that he was seeing someone before he started seeing you."

Kendall nodded.

"Who was she?"

"He didn't tell me."

"You didn't ask?"

Kendall shook her head. "I didn't want to know. And I didn't want him to think of her. Whoever she was."

"Did he say anything about her?"

"Yeah…he said she was someone he had to ext…extra…"

"Extricate?"

"Yes, extricate himself from."

"Why did he say that?"

"Because she got mad when he wouldn't see her. He said she called him all the time."

That might explain the phone number that came up often in Kirk's phone. Kally could check that once she got the phone back from the Seattle lab.

Kendall continued: "Kirk said he wanted to let her down easy, but she wouldn't have it. Then he started getting mad at her."

"And you never saw her?"Kally asked.

"Nope."

"He didn't mention her name?"

"Nope."

"And do you think it was really over?"

"YeP," Kendall said, emphasizing the "p." Then she added: "I don't think she was the brightest bulb to walk into a room."

Mixed metaphor aside, Kally kind of knew what she meant. "Why do you say that?"

"He said they were done," Kendall explained. "And he meant it. She was just embarrassing herself. And him."

Kally nodded and moved on. "I have one more request…do you have a voice mail from Kirk?"

Kendall stared at her without answering.

"I need a recording of his voice," Kally explained, "because we have a break in the case."

"You do?" Kendall asked, surprised.

"Yes."

"I have a lot voice mails from him. I'm not going to erase them." *Thankfully!* "Will you send me one?"

Kendall hesitated. "Is what's on it going to be…you know…public?"

"No. Never."

Kendall got up to retrieve her phone. She sat down again, and Kally watched her look through it, seemingly deciding on a message that would be appropriate.

"Give me your phone number and I'll send it to you," Kendall said without looking up.

Kally gave Kendall her work number, then waited. When Kendall finished, she put her phone down. "Done."

"Let me make sure I got it." Kally took out her phone and called her work number, then checked voice mail. She listened as Kirk's voice came through, startling her, as if he had called her instead of Kendall.

It was an innocuous message about picking up something for dinner before he came home.

*"And then you and I will spend the rest of the night in the bedroom. So get ready!"*

Kally cleared her throat. She wondered if he had been more graphically explicit in other messages. Nonetheless, she nodded and got up to leave.

Kendall walked with her to the door.

Before leaving, Kally turned to her. "Kendall…think twice about leaving the wine business. You have valuable experience now that someone could use."

"I'll think about it."

Kally nodded. "Good."

# 60

Kally parked in the Harborview Medical Center's parking lot but continued sitting there for a few moments. She knew Kendall herself wasn't "the brightest bulb…" but there were a few things Kally did know about her: She was confident in her sexuality. And her hold on Kirk. Those things Kally was sure of.

She opened the door and got out. One thing Kally would never know was if Kirk had been that serious about Kendall.

After signing in at the front desk, Kally took the stairs down to the morgue. Harborview, part of the University of Washington's sprawling medical complex, was the main trauma center for the state. And, it took up an ever-increasing footprint on First Hill overlooking the city of Seattle and Puget Sound.

Kally walked down a brightly lit hallway, her shoes making odd crunching noises on the shiny linoleum. She looked at the numbers above the doors, then stopped and knocked on one. No one answered. She put her hand on the door handle. It was open, so she walked in. A body was on a table in the middle of the room covered in a sheet. Nakamura and an assistant stood on either side of it ready to begin, the bright examination light above illuminating the instruments nearby.

She wondered if Nakamura had put the sheet there for her comfort.

Nakamura introduced Kally to his assistant, Randy. "Stand over there. I put a chair there for you," Nakamura said.

"Okay." Kally walked over to it and stood beside it. She thought she would see a casket in the room, but it wasn't there. She wondered how the body got here. Then she wondered how a funeral home worked in reverse, how a casket once sealed, the air removed, was reopened.

Nakamura put on a spacesuit-like mask and turned toward her. "You can ask questions as we go along."

She nodded. When she had gone through cop school, the class had briefly reviewed what occurs during an autopsy. And she had read a chapter in a textbook about it. But she'd never been present for one. That was Riggs's domain.

Thankfully, the full autopsy had already occurred.

She remained standing and watched the men as they positioned surgical instruments within easy reach. Thinking of the funeral home again, she wondered if a body smelled when it hit air. The only smell here in the room was of a medicinal nature. And sharp to the nose.

She was also aware that she was thinking of anything other than Kirk's body being opened again.

"Does the embalming fluid help control odor?" Kally asked Nakamura.

"It stops decomposition mostly, to get the body through the viewing process," he answered. "There are other chemicals injected, such as disinfectants, that control odor."

He looked over at her. "We don't intend to have the body for long. This afternoon only."

Nakamura continued: "If you start to feel light-headed, crouch down immediately or sit down. I don't want you to pass out and hit your head on the floor."

"All right."

He added: "It is natural to feel light-headed your first time."

"Okay."

"It is your first time?" he asked.

She hesitated. "Yes."

Suddenly, Nakamura pulled the sheet back. And there he was, in repose, just as he was at the funeral home. Except he didn't have clothes on. For a moment, Kally felt like she was violating Kirk's privacy. She tried not to look at his private parts, the pubic hair shaved.

Then she looked at his hands. One was in view to her, his arm alongside his body. His hand was still in a fist, but the little finger extended out at an odd angle.

"We won't redo the tests on the internal organs, except for the lungs." Nakamura adjusted the light above him. "We'll do a thorough examination of his skin and reopen the chest cavity. I'll talk you through this as we proceed. We'll also look at the hands again, as I mentioned."

"What are you looking for exactly?" she asked.

"How $CO_2$ entered the body." He turned slightly toward her. "We'll test the vascular system within one of the lungs. Again."

He had the scalpel in his hand ready to begin. "I want to remind you that this is not the living person you knew."

"Right."

Then he began.

With several clean sweeps of the scalpel, Nakamura opened the Y incision that extended from the shoulder blades all the way down the abdomen. Then he and Randy spread the skin and clamped each side open.

"Doing okay?" Nakamura asked without turning to her.

"Yes. Thanks."

With Randy's help, Nakamura worked on the rib cage, loosening it until it came out in one piece. It had been cut previously, and Kally noticed that the ribs were short. Randy placed it off to the side.

How odd to see his ribs. She was reminded of a grille of a car.

Then Nakamura moved his arms inside the body cavity. He brought out a plastic bag, using both hands to hold it.

"He wasn't a smoker," Nakamura added. "But he lived in a city."

She nodded and looked closer at the bag. Inside was a lung. It was large, like a two-liter bottle. He placed it in a curved dish that Randy held securely for him.

As if reading her mind, Nakamura explained: "The lung is in a bag because the full autopsy already occurred. Organs are put in bags so they don't leak fluids."

"Right," she answered.

"We're only going to test one lung," Nakamura added. "One will suffice. Any questions?"

"Not yet," Kally answered.

"Bring the chisel and come on this side," Nakamura said, addressing Randy.

Randy did as asked. The chisel he held looked like one any home builder or auto mechanic might use. He handed it to Nakamura.

With some difficulty, Nakamura moved Kirk's arm away from the body, then bent down and maneuvered the flat side of the chisel inside Kirk's hand. This took some time, and he struggled with it. Then he rotated the chisel about ninety degrees as best he could.

Nakamura reached for a board and placed it on top of the hand with the chisel still in it.

And then he forced his weight down on the board.

Kally heard a loud crunch.

The next thing she knew, she was looking up at the two men standing over her, one on each side, as she lay on the floor. Nakamura still had on his spacesuit mask but had taken off his gloves. He extended a hand toward her.

Both men hoisted her upright and onto the chair.

"Are you all right?" Nakamura asked.

Kally put her hand on her elbow, then looked at Nakamura.

"I never felt light-headed. It just came on."

"That happens," he answered. The two men seemed to be taking it in stride.

"I saw you fall," Randy offered. "You landed on your right arm."

That explained the sore elbow.

"I did fine with the rib cage and lung," Kally said. "But the crunch of Kirk's hand…. " Kally let the sentence trail off.

"It's hard when you know the person," Randy added.

"I want you to sit here until we're finished," Nakamura said.

61

K ally sat in her car behind her winery, still shaky from her unfortunate fall. Nakamura and Randy had asked her repeatedly if she was okay to drive, and she assured them she was. The worst part of the incident was her embarrassment.

Her phone rang, startling her. She looked at the name and saw that it was her friend Chris with VinoTours of Woodinville.

"Hi, Chris," Kally said, answering.

"How are you?"

"Good." Kally didn't feel the need to explain her fainting mishap.

"You got a nice write-up from Mindy in *Wine Hound*," Chris said.

"I did?"

"Yes. And she wrote about Ellie. She was promoted to vice president at RMP, in charge of three tasting rooms. Did you know that?"

"No. Good for her."

"I took a tour around Woodinville, and we stopped at her place."

"I'll have to see her." Kally realized she hadn't seen her or any of her friends since Kirk's funeral.

"How's Bud?" Chris asked.

"I don't know. I can't reach her. I imagine she's doing as well as can be expected."

"I wonder if the wedding will still go on. It's just awful what happened."

"I know."

There was a pause, and Chris added: "Well, call me when you have time."

"I will. Thanks."

Kally ended the call then brought up Mindy's blog on her phone. The first thing she saw was her label, the one she despised, and the write-up next to it:

> There's a new wine in the works from Wine Babe Cellars, a spectacular southern Rhône blend. This writer tried it from the tank and …wow!…it is something! Release coming soon. Stay tuned.

Mindy also included a blurb on Ellie and her new title at RMP. And she'd included a picture of tan, gorgeous Ellie with that perfectly toned skin.

Kally was about to get out of her car when her phone rang again. She looked at the name and her heart jumped: Mark Manning. She let the message go to voice mail, then sent it to Travis at Tiger Creek.

*"Please let me know if you have a match as soon as possible."*

Only then did she listen to it.

*"Hey, Kally. I'm at the winery. Let me know what you need."*

He was just a hundred feet away!

The message was short.

She hoped it was enough.

Kally turned on the lights in her winery. She came up to her board and read the work Seth had done that day, noting that he had gone ahead and filtered the Syrah and Grenache so that they could take that off their list for Saturday.

She decided then and there to do something for Seth once the case was solved. Maybe allow him to set up his own label in her winery, as Paul Storey had recommended. And introduce him to her grape suppliers.

Then she heard her back door open, and there was Storey himself.

"Kally. I've got something for you."

"What's that?" she responded.

"Malbec."

"Malbec!" she exclaimed, about one of the most sought-after grapes in Washington State.

"I'm not going to sell Malbec this year. I've got enough wine," he explained. "Wanna try it?"

"Sure."

She followed him out, past Kirk's winery with Manning *right inside*.

But she wondered about Storey. Why was he getting rid of Malbec? One didn't just procure this variety. You had to have a contract with a vineyard. And if a contract was broken, someone always stepped up to buy the fruit that very day.

Especially if was Malbec.

It didn't make sense.

Kally walked behind him into his winery. Storey grabbed the wine thief he had borrowed and two glasses and moved to a barrel. He took out the bung and extracted dark purple juice. He squirted wine into each glass and handed her one.

Kally swirled the liquid and put the glass to her nose, taking in the unmistakable aroma of dark fruit and plum. And something else: black truffle. And dirt.

She swirled and sniffed again, then tasted it.

"This is great, Paul," she said. She glanced at the barrel. "How much oak?"

"Thirty-three percent new." He put his hand on the barrel. "This is neutral oak, three years old."

She knew one barrel would give her twenty-four to twenty-five cases to sell.

"How much of this do you have?" she asked, thinking—hoping—he had another barrel of it somewhere.

Three barrels.

*Yes!* "How much are you asking?"

"Let's say…seven hundred per barrel."

"I'll take it."

"It's yours."

"I'll get the forklift," Kally said. "Be right back."

She handed him her glass and turned to go back to her winery. "Will you take a check?" she asked over her shoulder.

"Sure."

On her way out, she saw a tall gas tank just like hers sitting on a hand cart. Out of curiosity, and because it was right next to the door, she read the label: $CO_2$. She stopped. A chill went down her spine.

"Something wrong?" he asked.

She turned toward him, still stunned. And shook her head. "Nope."

Kally walked out, her mind a blur. She'd never thought to ask Storey about the gas he used, just like she'd never thought to knock on his door last Saturday morning.

*How can I make these mistakes!*

Maybe Manning had run out of argon and had borrowed gas from Storey. She needed to think about this before she confronted him.

Her heart was beating so fast, and she was so preoccupied with what she had just seen, that she didn't see Jason, one of Kirk's interns, come out to talk to her. She almost walked into him.

"I'm gonna work with you," he said.

She stopped. "You are?"

He nodded, smiling. "Seth asked if I would. Kirk...I mean Mark... has four interns. He doesn't need that many now with the reds done. And Seth said Leah left."

"Yes. Right. Well...that's great, Jason! Happy to have you."

Seth was running her winery. She'd have to thank him.

"I'll start Saturday. Okay?"

"Perfect. Thanks."

He turned to leave when Kally asked him something. "Is Mark inside?"

"Yes."

She wasn't thinking straight. She needed to wait until she'd heard from Tiger Creek.

"Never mind. I'll catch up with him later."

# 62

Kally balanced the third Malbec barrel on top of the other two on a rack in a corner of her winery. Eventually, she'd move them into her cold room. But right now, she was so focused on the $CO_2$ in Storey's winery that she couldn't think about her good fortune in obtaining his Malbec.

He couldn't possibly be a suspect. He was a friend.

She parked the forklift, closed her winery, and walked out the back door. Kally looked to her left, directly into Storey's open garage door, before getting into her SUV. She thought about the relationship between Storey and Kirk over the years, winemakers working next door to one another. From what she had witnessed, the two of them got along okay. They weren't best of friends. Just work associates.

Kirk was probably too "out there" for the somewhat conservative Storey. She got in her car and drove out. Perhaps that was the reason why she'd never seen him at any of Kirk's events.

Nonetheless, Storey's $CO_2$ was not sitting well.

She stopped at Woodinville Gas and Tank again before going home. This time, she took her time reading through the log's entries, perusing them for someone—anyone—who had purchased $CO_2$. She saw names, dates, and signatures for every winemaker in the Warehouse District.

But only one used $CO_2$: Paul Storey. His tank was filled six weeks before Kirk's death.

There was no question she would have to talk to him. But she'd have to approach this carefully, she thought, walking back to her SUV. Because she respected him.

And he respected her, accepting her completely as a woman in winemaking, a man's world still. He had been nothing but encouraging. How could she question him without him suspecting her of suspecting him? She'd have to think about it.

Kally looked at the time. Since RMP—and Ellie—were close by, she decided to stop in. She turned and headed toward the Woodinville Schoolhouse District.


The RMP tasting room was situated between Trust Cellars and Mark Ryan Winery in a small strip mall. Ellie was finishing with customers, taking empty glasses from them, and thanking them for dropping by, as Kally walked in.

"Hey! Nice to see you," Ellie said, catching Kally's eye.

Ellie looked stunning as always. For the tasting public, Ellie's neckline was appropriately plunged with some cleavage showing, a style Kally used sparingly, if at all.

"Here to taste?" she asked, as Kally sat down.

"I think I will."

"We've got a new white blend. Wanna try it?" Ellie offered.

"Sure."

Ellie brought over two glasses of wine and sat down across from her.

Kally took in Ellie's flowing hair, her face, and her skin. *You really are beautiful. I see why men go crazy. Probably women, too.*

"How's it going?" Ellie asked, knocking Kally out of her trance.

"Um...good. Still working the case. We...don't have much."

Ellie nodded.

"Have you talked to Bud?" Kally asked.

"Yes. I stopped by to see her."

"And?"

"And...she's not in the best of shape, as you would expect. She said she wants to go back to work. To take her mind off things. I was surprised at that."

"Yeah. Me, too." Then she thought of how Bud could help her in her case.

"She's spending most of her time at the hospital," Ellie offered.

"Did she say how A-Rod is doing?"

"About the same."

Kally changed the subject. "Congratulations on your promotion. Chris told me."

Ellie smiled. "Thanks. She was here with a group the other day."

"That's what she said."

There was an awkward pause in their conversation. Kally didn't have that much to say to Ellie. They weren't that close, knowing each other only through the industry. And through Bud.

Kally picked up her glass, finally, taking in the wine's aromatics. Then she tasted it. The wine was fruity with a bit of residual sugar. No oak. Probably all steel fermented. A summer wine that would go well with a Thanksgiving meal. Most people would like it.

"What's the blend?" Kally asked.

"Pinot Gris and Viognier."

"That's a good one. What are you selling it for?"

"Nineteen dollars."

"It'll sell out" Kally added.

"Hope so." Ellie rose suddenly. "I'm going to close up before anyone else comes in."

"Okay."

Kally watched her as she picked up empty glasses from tables and locked the door. "It gets dark so early now," Ellie said. She dimmed the lights a bit.

"Yeah, it's definitely fall in the Northwest."

She took another sip of her wine. Thankfully, she'd thought to change out of her police uniform. Otherwise, she wouldn't be sitting here enjoying this nice beverage.

She looked at her watch: 5:27 p.m. Then she looked around the tasting room, taking in the many tables and chairs. And two gas fireplaces.

"This is a comfortable space," Kally said.

"We try."

"It's bigger than mine," Kally added. "How's business?"

"Great! We're selling out of our reds."

"Wow!" Kally exclaimed. "I was thinking of bringing out my Grenache blend at Christmas. But I'm gonna wait until spring."

"Oh?"

"Needs time in the bottle."

"Speaking of Christmas," Ellie offered, "too bad Kirk won't see Blitzen."

Kally froze mid-sip.

*How does she know about Blitzen?*

*It was Kirk and Mark Manning's hushed-up wine project.*

She looked back at Ellie, who was tallying up money and closing the register. Who told her? Not Kirk. He hadn't told anyone, not even the woman he was seeing. That left just one person.

"I don't know anything about it. Blitzen, I mean," Kally said, mustering a matter-of-fact tone.

"It's a red blend. For the holidays."

63

Kally sat at her small kitchen table at home, a bottle of Château Tablet decanting in front of her. She needed the fortification of a very good wine because the uneasy feeling about Ellie and Blitzen wouldn't dissipate. Nor would the $CO_2$ discovery in Storey's winery.

Why would Manning say something to Ellie about Blitzen?

Was she even sure it was him?

Yes. She was sure.

So if Manning gave Ellie information about Blitzen, what else was he giving her? And what was he getting in return?

Was he seeing Ellie?

She shook her head. Manning was too geeky for head-turner Ellie. So, then…what?

Kally shifted back to Storey and his $CO_2$. She would have to confront him. Should she take Riggs with her? No. She wanted to be less in-your-face than Riggs would be.

She hoped beyond hope that Storey's voice was not on the recording at Tiger Creek. But knowing how she hadn't followed basic police work with him, she would somehow have to prove that.

A chime on her phone announced she had a text. It was Mindy Peters at *Wine Hound*:

*"No one I talked to thinks Mark Manning is seeing anyone."*

Kally texted her back:

*"Thanks. And thanks for the nice write up. I'll get back to you about the release."*

She poured a sample of Guillaume's Château Tablet's southern Rhône blend and swirled the glass on the table. She watched the deep-purple liquid climb the sides, the viscosity, or "legs," slowly dripping back down.

Then she sniffed the wine, smelling France. It was unmistakably Old World, with a bit of horse and leather characteristics—a little Brettanomyces or "Brett,"a spoilage yeast—that were actually positive attributes. In small doses.

This was one of Guillaume's higher-end efforts, and Kally expected a perfectly balanced wine, with a round palate, and a medium-to-long finish. And it would have a more woodsy, flower-pot taste than big-fruit Washington wines. And be lower in alcohol than Woodinville. She squinted at the bottle and read: *Alc 13.5% by volume.*

She put the glass down without tasting it. And folded her arms on the table.

She thought about the man who had made the wine. And their last night together in France.

*They had been inseparable for two weeks, ever since that chance meeting in a Paris café. Unusual that she'd taken to him so quickly. Yet she felt comfortable with Guillaume. They spoke the language of wine so well together.*

*They had traveled to Provence. Guillaume had reserved a room in a picturesque hotel with a view of the water. And he'd brought wine, some of his family's most famous vintages. One was a 1942, so rare he hadn't told his family he'd taken it.*

*She felt honored by that. And sad. She hadn't wanted to admit to herself how much she enjoyed his company and…everything.*

*Kally was looking at him now from inside their hotel room. He was outside sitting on a bench in their private garden. He was opening the '42.*

*Suddenly he started swearing. The cork had broken!*

*She went outside, laughing. Kally stood in front of him, close to him.*

*She had changed for dinner and had on heels and the only dress she had packed: a clingy, low-cut black number that was actually a travel dress you could wash in the sink and hang up to dry.*

*"I see even big wine boys make this mistake," she said, a twinkle in her eye.*

*His eyes moved up her body until they met hers.*

*And then, suddenly, time stopped. And both knew instantly what had just happened.*

*Ever so slowly, Kally crouched down. She placed her hands on his, which hadn't moved since breaking the cork.*

*He looked away then back at her. "Kally, I..."*

*She reached up and lightly touched his lips and said softly in a tone and manner of maturity she hadn't known she possessed: "I know."*

*He didn't respond. So she broke the ice. "How much does this bottle cost?"*

*"About one thousand euros."*

*"Well...let's get the cork out."*

She had promised him she would return. Those were her last words to him at the Paris airport.

And then she hadn't.

Her phone chimed again, a text from her brother Phil:

*"We have a match with Mark Manning's voice."*

Kally's heart beat rapidly. She quickly called him.

"It's slight," Phil said, answering, "but it's just enough."

"It's what I thought all along."

"And there's something else," he added.

"What?"

"Something's going on away from the phone. Travis said it's very weak. He's trying to capture it."

"A voice?" Kally asked.

"Don't know. It's just noise right now."

"So we have four voices still?"

"Yes."

"Okay. I forwarded another voice sample, from the deceased, to Travis," Kally said.

"I'm sure he's working on it," Phil said.

Kally thanked her brother and quickly called Riggs.

"There's a match on the voice recording. Manning was there. I have cause to arrest him."

"Of course you do!" Riggs answered.

"Can you meet me? At the winery?" Kally asked.

Riggs paused. "I've had two."

"Two what?"

"Beers."

"Oh. Well, I can go myself."

"No. Give me the address, and I'll meet you there. But I'll stay in the car."

# 64

Kally pulled into the back of her winery, seeing Manning's car at Kirk's. Off to the side sat Riggs, and she nodded to him. She had to settle her nerves before confronting Manning. What was about to transpire was not going to be pleasant.

Manning had his back to her as she entered Kirk's winery. Two interns were also there. Kally wanted to handle this is in a most understated way and not bring attention to him. Or to herself. But she'd do one other thing first.

She walked into Manning's line of sight, and he started in.

"I called you. Did you get my message?"

Kally nodded slowly. "I need to look at your fire extinguisher."

He paused. "Really?"

She nodded again.

He shrugged. "Okay. It's in the kitchen. I just filled it."

She hesitated. "Was it empty?"

"Only a little. Not much."

*Not much. How much is enough for a murder?*

Kally walked into the kitchen and took the fire extinguisher off the wall. Yes, it was full. Manning had written the date on the outside. The previous date was six months ago. She wouldn't know now just how empty or full it had been.

She put it back and walked into the production area and faced him. "I need you to come with me."

"Why?"

"I'll explain in the car." She paused and then said softly, "I don't want to make a show of this."

Nonetheless, the interns moving pallets of wine near them stopped and turned toward them. So much for not bringing attention.

"Follow me out, please." She turned and retraced her steps out the door.

Soon Manning appeared. "What's this about?"

She motioned for him to move away from the door. And then she read him his Miranda rights.

"You're arresting me?" he asked, dumbfounded. "You can't do that!"

"I can. And I am." Kally walked to her car and opened the back passenger door. "Get in."

Over his shoulder, she saw the interns standing in the doorway watching them.

Manning walked to the police car and got inside.

Riggs backed up and headed for headquarters.

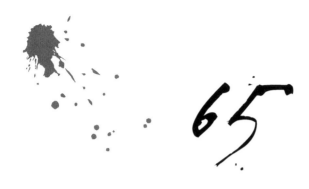

65

The four of them were in the small interrogation room: Dale,
Riggs—no worse the wear from his beer—Kally, and Manning,
who was sitting in a chair in the middle of the room. Dale and Riggs
stood side by side leaning against the wall, arms folded, staring at
Manning.

Riggs walked forward, but Dale put his arm out. He nodded toward
Kally, and she began.

"Mark, we have your voice on a recording that was made the night
of Kirk's death. Your voice has been positively identified."

"What recording?" Manning asked.

"Apparently, Kirk placed his phone under a bin the night he died."

That news seemed to take the wind out of him. He stared at her
without saying anything.

"You were there the night Kirk died."

He looked up at her. Then raised his head defiantly. "Yes."

"How did he die?"

"I don't know."

"What do you mean you don't know!" Riggs barked.

"I don't know!" Manning turned toward Riggs. "He...collapsed.
Just fell over. That was it."

She wasn't sure she believed him. "The medical examiner said he
died of $CO_2$ poisoning."

Manning seemed surprised at that, too. "$CO_2$? The winery was
vented."

"That's the finding. Who else was there?" she asked.

He shook his head. "I want an attorney."

"You'll get one," Riggs answered. "Tell us who else was there."

Kally knew better than to keep pestering, questioning. Nonetheless...

"Who was in the room?" Kally asked again.

She bent down and got close to his face. "There were at least two other people. Maybe more."

Manning seemed to be thinking through his options. "I don't know who they are. They came in the back door."

"After everyone left?" Kally asked.

Manning nodded.

"What did they want?"

"I don't know. Honestly! It wasn't my business."

"What business were they discussing?" Riggs asked impatiently.

Manning paused. "I don't know. I wasn't listening."

Kally: "Who said the words 'you betrayed me.'"

Manning paused again, this time for some time. "I don't know who said it."

Now she was sure he was lying. "Were RMP people there?"

"I didn't know who the people were. Really! I want an attorney!"

Kally glanced at Dale.

"Let me ask you something else." Kally walked around the chair, out of his sight. She did a full circle and came back to face him.

"Why did you tell Ellie about Blitzen?"

Manning didn't look at her. "I didn't."

"You did," Kally pressed.

Dale and Riggs stared at her. She was sure they had no idea what she was talking about.

"Only two people knew about that wine. And Kirk wouldn't tell anyone. Not even the woman he was seeing. Why did you tell her?"

Manning shrugged it off. "I don't know. I just did."

"But she's with Red Mountain Productions. RMP is a competitor. They could use that information."

Manning shifted in his chair. He looked at her, then away.

"Were you giving Ellie information about Kirk's wines?"

Suddenly, Manning turned on her. "You know nothing about him. You think you do. But you don't."

Unrattled, Kally proceeded. "Enlighten me."

Manning didn't say anything.

Kally glanced again at Riggs and Dale. "You are the one who knew the percentages Kirk used in his blends…information that could be helpful to another winery."

He just shook his head. "I'm not saying another word."

Riggs stepped forward. "Tell us who was there the night he died!"

"I want an attorney!"

Kally realized they were pressing their luck. "Were people talking about a land purchase? Land on Red Mountain?"

Again, Manning looked surprised. He shifted in his chair. "Was that on the recording?"

# 66

Manning was taken to the King County jail in Seattle, to be held for seventy-two hours. Kally thought he was a flight risk, if not a risk to himself, and she had convinced Dale of this.

But she didn't think Manning had participated in Kirk's death. If pressed, she didn't know what to think about him. When he spoke, he lied. Otherwise he didn't speak at all.

She stayed behind in the office after Dale and Riggs left, trying to put the pieces together. She walked into Dale's office, turned on the light, and read the whiteboard again:

*women, winemakers, land*

Again, only the land issue made sense.

She looked at the time: 9:20 p.m. Her friend Sarah "Somm" would still be at her restaurant.

Kally parked in *Loading Zone Only* and walked into the noisy, well-lit waterfront restaurant in Magnolia that was busy with a late-dinner crowd.

She saw Sarah emerge from a back room and then approach Kally. "Nice to see you again," Sarah said. She held a bottle of French Chablis and two wine glasses upside down by the stems. "Here to wine? Dine?"

Kally shook her head. For obvious reasons, she didn't speak above the din. "You mentioned that RMP people come in for lunch once a week."

Sarah nodded. "They'll probably be here tomorrow."

"Can you do me a favor?"

Sarah waited.

"When you see them, will you have your phone on record?" Kally asked.

Sarah hesitated for a moment. "This is about Kirk, isn't it?"

Kally nodded.

"Sure. I'll do it."

# 67

The next day threatened rain, but the rain never came. Instead, a heavy cloud cover hung over the Puget Sound region and remained there into the afternoon.

Kally parked in front of Paul Storey's home. The house, a 1920s bungalow, was set back from the street with an expansive lawn in front, a rarity in Seattle as developers built on every open square foot in the city. Storey had had the house painted recently and had put in new landscaping. She wondered if he was planning to sell.

"So let's go over this again," Riggs said, sitting in the passenger seat. Kally turned off the car.

"Gimme what you got," Riggs prodded, getting right to the point.

Kally sat there for a moment. "All I have are suspicions."

"He doesn't need to know that. You're only questioning him. Start at the beginning."

"All right. Storey was at his winery Saturday morning, the day Kirk's body was found."

"Is that unusual?"

"No. It's harvest time and winemakers work all hours."

"And you didn't question him Saturday."

She paused. "I didn't know he was there. And...I didn't think of it."

"I don't have to tell you that that's not good," Riggs said.

"I know."

"What else?" Riggs asked.

"The tank of $CO_2$ in his winery."

"Is that unusual?"

She paused again. "It is not unusual for winemakers to use gas. It is unusual to use $CO_2$."

"Why?"

"It's more expensive. Argon is the usual choice."

"So you're connecting the $CO_2$ found in Storey's winery to the crime," Riggs said.

"Possibly. I mean...he's right next door. And...Storey is getting rid of Malbec."

"Is *that* unusual?"

"*Very.* But I don't think it has anything to do with Kirk's death."

"Let's keep to the crime. Go up and talk to him. It's all you can do at this point."

Kally fidgeted with the keys in the ignition. "So here's where I need help." Riggs would never know how difficult that was for her to say. "How do I start? I know him...I know him well. I don't want him to think..."

"Doesn't *matter* what he thinks!" Riggs interjected. "Doesn't matter. Tell him that you're still working the case. And that every detail helps."

He paused. "Why is this so hard?"

Kally felt her face flush. She looked away out her window. Finally, she answered him. "He was one of the few winemakers who helped me when I was starting out." She looked back at Riggs. "He always answered my questions. I have a lot of questions."

Riggs nodded slightly. "But today you are a cop solving a murder. You are doing your job. Tell me what you're going to ask him."

"I'm going to ask him more about Saturday morning and...why he uses $CO_2$."

"Does he know that $CO_2$ was the cause of death?" Riggs asked.

"Yes. I had a previous conversation with him."

She wasn't sure if that was a good or bad thing. Riggs didn't respond.

"Okay, then. Go do it," Riggs said finally.

Kally took her time walking up the long flagstone sidewalk and up the stairs to the porch and front door. The hardest part of her investigation was thinking about friends or work associates as suspects. It was hard enough with Manning, who really was lying to her. She felt awful about implicating Storey.

She rang the bell.

The door opened.

"Hey!" Storey said. "This is a surprise." He stood there in jeans and a faded tee shirt, his gray hair uncombed, obviously not yet ready for the day. "You're not rethinking the Malbec, are you?"

Kally smiled and shook her head. "No."

Storey looked over her shoulder at Riggs sitting in the car.

"What's up?" Storey asked.

"Can I ask you a few questions? It has to do with the investigation," she said quickly.

Storey folded his arms. "Sure."

"You were at your winery Saturday morning," Kally began.

"Yeah...like I told you."

Kally detected a slightly defensive uptick in his tone. "What time did you get there?"

"You're questioning me," he said immediately. "Why?" Storey's eyes bored into her.

"Because I didn't question you before," Kally answered, holding her ground.

He hesitated but kept Kally's gaze. "I never left the winery. I slept in my van Friday night. So I could get an early start."

*He was there the whole time!* The questions came flooding out.

"Where was your van?

"In front."

Kally groaned. "In front because of the party in back?"

"Yes."

"Did you hear anything?" she inquired.

"When?"

"Late that night. When Kirk died."

"All I heard was his music. He finally turned that off at about midnight. I got in the van a little after midnight and fell right to sleep."

"Did you see anything when you went out to your van?"

"Like what?"

"A car. A person."

"No."

Kally continued. "You are the only one who uses $CO_2$ in the Warehouse District."

"Yes. And you think I have something to do with his death." Storey said it as a statement.

"Where else would the $CO_2$ come from?"

"You're implicating *me*?" Angry now, Storey continued: "I *will* get an attorney."

But Riggs's pep talk had emboldened her. "I have to question you, Paul. I'm doing my job. Don't look at me as a winemaker. I'm a cop investigating a murder."

"You've got a lot of nerve. I helped you."

"I *know* you did. But this is something else. Help me so I can help you." She paused. "Did your tank of $CO_2$ ever leave your winery?"

"This is ludicrous. I'm not answering anymore questions."

Storey stepped back and slammed the door.

Kally stood there for a few moments, a bit shocked and hurt. Then she turned and walked back to the car.

"What'd you get?" Riggs asked when she got in. "I heard the… um…door." He pointed absently at the house.

Kally didn't answer. Instead, she sat there thinking about her line of questioning and Storey's responses and, of course, his shock, anger, and the slammed door. She hadn't even complimented him on his landscaping.

Finally, she turned to Riggs: "He had nothing to do with it."

"Why do you say that?"

Kally took her time answering. "He's not a killer. There's no motive. There's nothing more to ask him."

"What about the $CO_2$?" Riggs asked.

Kally shook her head. "It's not his. We're wasting our time." She reached for the keys in the ignition, but Riggs's next question stopped her.

"Did your father ever talk to you about his work?"

She looked at him. She and Riggs had never discussed personal matters, and especially not anything about her father. She didn't know why he'd brought it up or where this was going.

"No. He never did. He was depressed most of the time." She looked away.

Riggs continued: "Well…I ask because your father went on his gut more than most. And he was usually right. He was one of those rare ones with a real sixth sense."

Kally didn't respond.

"You remind me of him," Riggs added.

It was a weak moment for her, first the confrontation with Storey and now the mention of her father as well as the compliment from Riggs. She fought to keep from tearing up. Instead of doing or saying anything, she just sat there.

Then her phone rang.

Kally looked down at the name—Sarah, at the Magnolia restaurant. Only then did she look at Riggs.

"I have something for you," Sarah said, when Kally answered.

"Can you meet me somewhere?" Kally asked her.

They were back at Tiger Creek, in the recording studio. Kally handed Travis Sarah's phone with the recording from lunch. Riggs stood in a corner, fuming.

She had casually mentioned to him on the drive over that she had asked Sarah to record the RMP people at lunch.

"You can't use anything on that recording!" he had yelled.

*So much for the warm embrace of a compliment.*

"You *will* get in a lot of trouble for asking for it," he had added. "No! Let me rephrase that: you *are* in a lot of trouble! Just because you didn't do it doesn't mean you aren't responsible. I haven't even mentioned the subpoena part."

"I know. But Sarah knows them. She sees them every week. She can identify them. This could be huge."

"Huge and unusable," Riggs had said.

Sarah stood next to Travis, ready to identify the voices. Sitting at the console, Travis plugged the charger into the phone and then into his computer and clicked on the recording. Several voices spilled out, as well as loud background noise from the restaurant. Travis fiddled with the controls and the background noise disappeared.

*"So we're gonna start with our white,"* Kally heard one of the men say on the recording.

"That's Fugelson," Sarah said. She glanced at Kally.

A female voice agreed with Fugelson, saying only, *"Okay."*

"That's me," Sarah explained.

*"Might as well bring the reds at the same time,"* another on the recording said. *"No use running back and forth."*

"That's Greg Sanderson," Sarah said.

Travis stopped the recording and turned to Sarah. "It would help if you drew where the people were sitting."

He handed her a pad of paper and a pen.

Sarah drew a curved line, like a thumbnail, to indicate a round table. "There were four people at the table," she explained. She drew four "X's" to designate where people had sat.

Kally stood to the right of Sarah, listening. She knew the recording could never be used because it was taken without anyone's knowledge. But she had no intention of letting the recording be known. It was just part of her research. It could help in how she approached others, if the voices could be identified. And it appeared that they could.

She watched Sarah write a name above the first "X."

"This is Richard Fugelson," Sarah explained. "Next to him is Greg Sanderson. And the other two are Elliott Jansen and Phil McDonough. Interesting that they always sit in the same places," she added.

"Good," Travis said and began the recording again.

Another man's voice came through clearly. *"So what's the lunch special?"*

"That's McDonough," Sarah said. She pointed to the fourth "X" on her drawing.

Kally heard Sarah's voice spill forth with the specials of the day.

*"We have a beautiful halibut in a mushroom/lemongrass broth with broccolini and mashed potatoes, for thirty-nine dollars, a perfect pairing with your white. We also have a flatiron steak special and an apple-glazed pork tenderloin, both of which will go perfectly with your reds. I'm afraid I don't have the prices on these. The server will be over momentarily to explain all of them in more detail."*

Kally saw Riggs come up behind Travis, his pouty-face gone.

Another voice on the recording. *"So how are sales?"*

"That's Jansen," Sarah said quickly. She pointed to the third X on the drawing. "He always asks."

*"Actually last month was your best month,"* Sarah had answered.

*"No kiddin'!"* Sarah pointed again to Jansen's name.

Travis stopped the recording. "So we've got all four voices."

"Yep," Sarah replied. "And after his reply, I left to get the wine."

Travis worked the console. "Okay, while I have you here, I'm going to see if I can line up one of these voices with a signature on the first recording. And then I want to show you something—"

"You got the voices off that first recording?" Riggs interjected.

"I did, and I'll play it for you," Travis answered without looking up.

They waited in silence while Travis worked on the computer. What Kally saw on Travis's monitor was a split screen again. Four wavy lines filled the right side.

"These are the four voices from your original recording," Travis explained.

A fifth wavy line appeared above the four.

"This is Fugelson's voice from the new recording," Travis said. "Let's see if we have a match."

Everyone stared at the computer monitor. Suddenly, the new wavy line moved down onto the last wavy line on the screen.

"Oh my God!" Kally exclaimed.

"So RMP was in the room," Riggs said.

"I want to show you something else," Travis said. "From your first recording."

As Travis worked the settings, the wavy lines on the screen disappeared. Suddenly a grid appeared, filling the screen with what looked like four plastic board-game people, in four different colors. A person in red lay on its side on the floor in front of a white bin.

"The red person is the deceased," Travis said.

"The man in blue to the left..." Travis looked at some notes "...is Mark Manning."

Kally took in the grid with Manning to the left of Kirk and yellow and green people to Kirk's right.

*How odd to be looking at a replication of the evening.*

Farther away was a purple-plastic person, smaller in size, perhaps not yet identified.

Travis turned in his chair to face them. "Sound has dimension," he began. "And depth. You heard it on the recordings: One voice appears closer than another. With today's technology, we can make these voices three-dimensional, giving them a physical presence, which I've done here."

"We can also walk around the people on the grid," Travis added. He went back to his keyboard, working it so that the grid shifted. They were now behind the bin, and Kirk was no longer visible. Then he brought the grid back to the original setting.

Travis addressed Kally: "That voice mail you forwarded? It lines up with the person who said, 'You betrayed me.'"

"That would be Kirk. I mean, the deceased," Kally said. She wondered who he had been talking to.

"So we've identified three people in the room," Travis continued, "the deceased, Mark Manning, and Mr. Fugelson."

"Fugelson was standing here," Travis said. "He is to the right of the deceased. And I'll bet the person next to Fugelson is on this new recording as well."

They watched in silence as Travis repeated what he had done with Fugelson's voice: moving a new voice above the four voice signatures from the original recording.

Nothing happened until Travis copied the last voice—Jansen's—to the split screen. The voice instantly moved onto one of the original voice signatures.

"There you go," Travis said. "There is your fourth voice."

"So two from RMP were in the winery that night," Kally said, glancing at Riggs. He nodded slightly, still not talking to her.

Travis brought the grid back up on his screen and tapped his finger on the small purple figure in back.

"I'm still working on this one," he said. "I've almost got him."

# 69

Kally and Riggs remained in the recording studio after Sarah left. Finally, Travis would reveal to them what had been said on the first recording.

They stood behind him as he worked again on his computer.

"Okay," he began. "I've cleaned this up as much as I can." He caught Kally's eye. "Listen carefully. There are some surprises." Travis turned up the volume and sat back.

They heard shuffling sounds, then: *"Why do you want it?"*

Kally recognized Kirk's voice.

*"We need it for more plantings."*

*So it is about land*, she thought.

"That's one of your two new voices," Travis interjected. "I'll tell you who later."

Kirk: *"I'm not selling."*

Someone from Red Mountain Productions: *"Yeah? Well people up there are complaining."*

Kirk: *"Complaining about what?"*

RMP: *"That Woodinville's moving in on Red Mountain."*

Kirk: *"I don't think so. I've been working with those growers for years. They know me."*

RMP: *"But they don't want you there."*

Kirk: *"Them? Or you?"*

There was a silence.

Then Kirk continued: *"You're not gonna have the largest holding there. That's been done by a Canadian company..."*

*True,* Kally thought.

Kirk: *"And you'll still be under Ste. Michelle."*

*In acreage,* Kally knew. But he was wrong *if* RMP had gotten the land he had purchased.

RMP: *"We'll pay you double what you just paid."*

Kirk: *"I'm not selling."*

A new voice: *"Why don't you sell to them?"*

*Manning's voice,* Kally thought.

Kirk: *"Don't get involved."*

RMP: *"He is involved."*

Silence. Then Kirk: *"What'd you mean? How are you involved?"*

Kally could only guess at the body movements. In this instance, she was sure Kirk was addressing Manning.

Another silence.

RMP: *"You're dealing with us not him."*

Kally recognized that one of the RMP people was speaking more than the other.

RMP: *"We've gone to the grower who sold you the land. If he agrees, we'll have the contract annulled and we'll pay him double the asking price."*

Kirk: *"You can't do that."*

RMP: *"You forget who we are."*

Silence again.

Then Kirk: *"Did you know about this? Because I wouldn't let you set up shop here?"*

Kirk must have been addressing Manning. So there was Manning's motive for giving away Kirk's winemaking tips. One thing she knew about Kirk: he was smart enough to have figured it out.

Perhaps he just had.

Kirk: *"You betrayed me."*

So the words had been said to Manning.

Travis leaned forward suddenly and turned up the volume, which increased the sounds of scuffling.

Kirk: *"What are you doing here?"*

*Someone else had entered the winery,* Kally realized.

Again, Travis moved a dial. More scuffling. Kally and Riggs leaned forward.

Kirk: *"What the hell!"*
"Why did he say that?" Kally asked.
RMP: *"We gotta get out here!"*
The recording ended.

# 70

Kally and Riggs sat in her SUV in the Tiger Creek parking lot. They had listened to the recording more times than she could count, straining to hear every word. Obviously, something important had happened near the end of it. But they had no more to go on than what they'd heard the first time.

"That's a lot of good information you can't use," Riggs said, sarcastically.

"We need to identify the last person who came into the winery," Kally said, ignoring him. "And Manning saw what happened."

"There's no mention of $CO_2$ on the tape," Riggs added, ignoring her comment as well. "Where does $CO_2$ come in? It's a mystery. Check into that, would you...where does someone get mystery $CO_2$?"

She finally looked at him. "I don't have any intention of confronting RMP with the recording. It's someone else I'm going to talk to. And he won't know a second recording was made."

Riggs shook his head. "Can't use it."

She started the SUV. She and Riggs were talking in tangents, with his anger still very present. She continued anyway. "We're gonna see him right now."

"Shut off the car," Riggs said.

Kally wondered if he was serious. She took in his countenance.
*He's serious.*

She turned off the car.

"Tell me what you're thinking before we start moving," he began.

"We're going to see Mark Manning." Manning, she'd learned, had retained an attorney and had been released from his seventy-two hour jail hold. "I'll tell him we know who was in the room. And I'll name the two RMP people without telling him how I know."

Riggs stared straight ahead, seemingly getting his thoughts in order before responding.

"You could be required, under oath, to divulge how you know that." Riggs remained staring straight ahead, but the edge was gone from his voice. "The only way you know that RMP wanted the land the deceased bought is what you heard on that recording. It is not common knowledge. Correct?"

He turned to face her. "You can *never* say anything about this recording, not the fact that it exists nor the voices you heard. You needed subpoenas, and then you could have gone to *each* person individually, telling *each* that you have a recording and asking *each* permission to listen to it."

"And *each* would have said no," Kally responded. "They're attorneys! They're not going to say yes."

Riggs resumed staring straight ahead. "Here's what we're going to do. We'll go see Mr. Manning. You will not say anything about knowing who was in the room. You will tell Mr. Manning that it is in his best interest—*really* in his best interest—to name anyone who may have been in the winery that night."

Riggs paused. "When you put it that way, he will think you know something. You can add that you can get a subpoena and he will be required under oath to divulge what he knows."

Kally thought about that.

Riggs continued. "He can go to jail for not saying anything if it is found that there were indeed more people in the room. And, of course, we know that there were."

Kally nodded in agreement. What Riggs suggested sounded pretty good.

"Okay."

274

# 71

K ally and Riggs walked up the sidewalk and Kally rang the bell. She felt good about this. She would repeat the words Riggs had suggested to her.

After a bit of a wait, Manning opened the door. He stared at Kally without saying anything.

"I have more questions about the night Kirk died," Kally began.

A figure appeared behind Manning, then came around to the side of him.

"My client isn't saying anything. You get a court order," he demanded. "Otherwise, stay away."

"Who else was in the winery that night!" Kally interjected, ignoring the admonition.

"I'm not taking the fall for this!" Manning said.

The attorney moved front and center, blocking Kally's view. "Direct your questions to me. How can I help you?"

Undeterred, Kally looked around the attorney, catching Manning's eye. "Why aren't you saying anything?"

The attorney put his hand on the doorknob. "That's enough."

"Who are you protecting?" Kally blurted the words, but was speaking to a closed door.

———

Kally dropped Riggs off at headquarters. She watched him head toward his car, get in, and drive away. They had agreed that he would get the subpoena first thing in the morning and they would meet at eight a.m.

In Riggs's black and white world, Manning would talk.

Or he would go to jail.

Kally walked into headquarters, passing Sonny, the janitor, who was engrossed in his work and Myrna, who was manning the call-in lines. Kally startled her as she walked past.

"Oh! Didn't know you were here," Myrna said.

"Just picking up some things. I won't be long."

"Okay. Let me know when you're leaving."

"I will."

She went into her office and, without turning on lights, plopped down in her chair. She leaned her head back and closed her eyes.

*I have information I can't use and connections I can't make.*

For technical and legal reasons, the "evidence" that RMP wanted Kirk's land will remain in the background while a woman with blonde hair is circling the case who cannot be identified.

*Why is this taking so much time? Is it because I'm new at it?* She went over her procedural steps and Riggs's recommendations.

*Have I missed something?*

She thought back to the morning she'd gotten the call from Dale and walked into Kirk's winery and saw his body. Then she talked to Nakamura. She questioned Manning. She found the gaskets.

Then Kirk's body was removed. She and Bud walked around outside. She found the beer bottle. She got Kirk's logs and keys.

Thinking of that, Kally got up and retrieved the binder and flipped through Kirk's logs, seeing pages and pages of Brix readings, pH notations, total acidity figures, and YAN numbers. She read the last entry for bin four, his fermenting Klipsun fruit, the fruit that was now unusable: *21 Brix, 3.7 pH, 6.3 TA, 193 YAN.*

She stared at it for a while, then closed the binder.

*Nothing here.*

Kally sat down again. She had gone to Kirk's condo.

*The condo!*

The empty pill containers. The letters from his mother.

She got up again and looked through a stack on top of her file cabinet. She grabbed the large plastic bag holding the letters and sat down again. And reached for gloves.

Then she took the letters out.

*Read them all? Would that give me anything? How many are there?*

She flipped through them, counting them.

A thin sheet fell out from between two letters and floated to the floor. She put the letters on her desk and reached down for it.

It was a handwritten note.

> *My beloved Kirk,*
>
> *I think about you every moment…how you make love to me, how you touch me, kiss me, taste me.*

Oh my God! It's a love letter.

She kept reading.

> *I have never felt this way with any man. I've never made love to any man the way I have with you, not even my husband.*

Then it got really personal.

> *I love being with you, pleasing you, tasting you, not wanting to stop. And you on me, losing my mind, coming on you over and over again.*
>
> *I want you back.*

Kally sat there, stunned. *Who is this?* There was no name, no date, no envelope. How long ago was it written?

She looked at the dates on the envelopes from Kirk's mother, this letter tucked in-between two of them. One was mailed from Chicago on March 22. The other on April 17.

But Kirk could have stuffed this note between any one of them. It could have been written three weeks ago for all she knew. Obviously, there was an affair going on that was still very much alive.

At least for one person.

Kally read the letter again, the "k" of the last word written with flourish, the tail sweeping out and up like a big "U."

Was it Kendall? No, this woman was married. Was it the woman Kendall didn't want to know about? Was she a blonde woman? Was she the one behind the barrels at Kirk's release and had she bumped into Surfer? If so, then the other person who'd been behind the barrels was no doubt Kirk.

But was she also the woman at the party standing with the three men? And the one at the winery Saturday morning? And the one A-Rod saw drive away?

It was another connection. But she couldn't quite grasp it.

She pocketed her keys, waved good-bye to Myrna, and headed out. She would need to approach the subject of this woman carefully with the person she was about to see.

# 72

Kally pulled into Janie's driveway. She sat there for a few seconds to put in order the things she wanted to say and ask. And hoped Janie realized she was in police mode for all of it.

"Would you like something to drink? Or eat?" Janie asked after they were settled in her living room.

"No. I'm good, thanks."

Kally realized that Emma, Kirk's daughter, was nowhere to be seen. "Where's Emma?"

"She's with Kirk's mother in Chicago. I'm going there Monday to pick her up."

The mention of Kirk's mother reminded Kally of the burial issue discussed at the funeral. She declined to mention Nakamura's recent re-examination of Kirk's body.

"Has anything been decided about where to bury him?"

Janie shook her head. "I'm thinking Colorado. Someplace in-between."

It was the first time Kally had seen Janie smile since…she couldn't remember when.

Janie sat back in her chair. "So…"

The perfect segue word.

"I want you to know something," Kally began. "And I want you to hear it from me and not read it in *Wine Hound* or someplace else."

"Okay." Janie stared at her friend.

"We have evidence that Kirk's death wasn't accidental."

Janie sat perfectly still.

"We have a murder investigation," Kally added, thinking Janie needed more explanation.

Janie hung her head. "Well, I won't be telling his mother *that*. At least not now."

Kally then began the most difficult conversation she had ever had with a friend.

"Can I ask you something?"

"Sure."

"Do you know of anyone Kirk might have been seeing earlier this year?"

Janie didn't miss a beat. "You mean while we were still married?"

"Yes." Kally looked away. "Sorry."

Janie sat up straight and crossed her legs. "I do, actually."

*Good for you, Janie.*

"There was an intern about a year ago," Janie began. "She was twenty three. As far as I know, it ended as soon as it began. But then there was someone else. And I don't know who she was."

Kally hoped her disappointment didn't show. "How long did it last, do you know?"

Janie shook her head. "I don't. But it was because of her that I ended our marriage. She...sent him roses. I saw them in his office. Can you believe it?"

"No. Was there a name on the card?" Kally asked.

Janie shook her head. "Paula saw me looking at them. She said they arrived anonymously, just left at the back door."

"So more than one delivery of flowers?" Kally asked. *I can track this easily enough.*

Janie nodded. "Is this person important?"

"Possibly."

"Well, maybe Mark Manning can help. He might have seen her."

*Manning again.*

Janie continued: "You know that Kirk didn't like him."

"No, I didn't know that. Why not?" She thought back to the recording.

"Kirk thought he was...weak. You know how Kirk liked to be 'out there.'"

Kally nodded. "Did Kirk tell you that?"

Janie hesitated. "No. Denny did."

Denny, the former assistant winemaker.

Janie looked away. "I was seeing Denny. I'm not now. You probably think that's an odd pairing."

Indeed, she did. But she didn't say so.

"Denny was just…I don't know…available," Janie explained. "And I think I was convenient for him."

"That's your business and no one else's," Kally offered. But Janie had hit on her own relationship with Zack. "It's okay. Really." Then: "How are you holding up?"

"I'm all right."

"And Emma?"

Janie paused. "I don't think it has sunk in for her that she will never see her father again."

Kally didn't respond. There was nothing else to say. She kept her focus on her friend, who was smoothing out a crease in her jeans and seemingly lost in thought.

Kally would never know the extent of the pain and embarrassment Kirk had caused Janie. It was for that reason that she didn't bring up Kendall. She was getting all she needed from Kendall anyway. No need to ask Janie about her.

And she'd already determined that Kendall hadn't sent the flowers. She worked at the winery. Why leave them at the back door?

Kally glanced at the clock. Tomorrow they would subpoena Manning. And it loomed large. And she needed to make an appearance at her winery in the morning before meeting Riggs.

But tonight there was one more stop.

Kally sat in front of a flower shop in downtown Woodinville. She took out her phone and called Paula, Kirk's office manager.

"Paula, it's Kally. Do you have a minute?"

"I do."

"Janie Remick mentioned deliveries of flowers to Kirk's winery. I'm trying to find a name associated with them. For questioning."

"There wasn't a name on the cards," Paula said.

"Which flower shop was it?"

Paula confirmed it was the one Kally was already sitting in front of, Art's Floral, the largest in Woodinville.

"How many deliveries?"

"Let's see…maybe three that I know of."

"When were they?"

Paula seemed to think about that. "I'd say over the past three months."

"Okay. This is helpful. Thanks."

Kally showed her badge to the woman at the counter who was adding finishing touches to a floral arrangement.

"Someone ordered flowers for Remick Cellars in Woodinville over the past three months," she began. "Can you look in your records and tell me who bought them?"

The woman moved down the counter to her computer. "You said Remick Cellars?"

"Yes."

The woman took her time as Kally waited. "Here it is. The first was July 27. It was a cash purchase."

Kally's heart sank.

"The second purchase was August 14. And another on September 5. All cash."

"What did the person look like who paid for them?"

The woman shook her head. "The employee who took the orders was Jessica. And Jessica is no longer with us."

Kally needed to find her and talk to her.

"There was a fourth purchase," the woman continued.

"Oh? When?"

"October 24." The woman looked at her over her glasses. "Cash again. The flowers were delivered to the funeral home."

*Right.* "Did Jessica handle that order?"

"She did."

"Where is Jessica now?"

"She moved to New York with her boyfriend."

*Could this be any more difficult?*

"Manhattan?" Kally asked.

"Brooklyn."

Okay, that's helpful. "How long ago?"

"That I don't know."

"What is Jessica's last name?"

"Fellows."

"And the boyfriend?"

"Shawn."

"Shawn what?"

The woman shook her head again. "I don't know. Jessica wasn't with us that long. Maybe six months."

"How long ago did she leave employment here?" Kally asked.

"A few days ago."

So Jessica and Shawn may not even be in Brooklyn yet.

"Do you have a local address for her?"

"Yes. I'll get it for you."

"Before you do that...does anyone else here remember these purchases? I believe the person who bought the flowers is a woman."

"I'm afraid not. We have so many orders. It is unusual to have a cash purchase, though."

The woman disappeared into an office. After a time, she came back and handed Kally a card with a Woodinville address written on the back.

And a phone number. Shawn's phone number.

"Jessica didn't have a phone when she applied here," the woman explained. "She did eventually get one. But we didn't update the files."

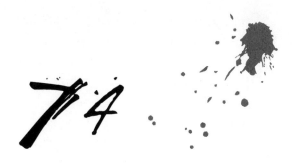

# 74

K ally sat in her car and called Shawn, getting his voice mail.

> *"Shawn, this is Kally O'Keefe with the Woodinville Police Department. I'm trying to reach Jessica Fellows to ask her about someone who bought flowers at Art's Floral and paid cash, and had them delivered to Remick Cellars. And to a funeral home.*
>
> *We are involved in an investigation. Anything she can tell us may be helpful. Please have her call me."*

She drove to the address listed on the card, a new apartment complex off Route 522. Kally walked into the rental office and inquired about Jessica Fellows.

After an extensive search in her files, the woman behind the desk shook her head. "We don't show anyone with that name having rented here."

"How about Shawn?" Kally asked, thinking Jessica lived with Shawn.

"Last name?"

"I don't have it."

Eyebrows raised, the woman stared at Kally. "It will take me *a long while* to look through these files. We organize renters by last name." She paused. "This is a large complex."

"And I appreciate that." Kally laid her card on the desk. "Please call as soon as you find something."

Shawn would have left a forwarding address. She could check with the post office once she had his last name. Plus, Kally had another option. She called Riggs and relayed what she had uncovered so far.

"I need a warrant so I can access phone records for Jessica Fellows."

"Just call the boyfriend," Riggs said.

"I did. And left a message." She went on. "Jessica left employment only a week ago, so I'm assuming she still has her Washington State phone number, don't you think?"

"Probably."

"Do you think I can get a warrant?"

"No."

"Why not?"

"We're getting more like Canada," Riggs explained. "It's almost impossible to get permission to access phone records."

"I just want to talk to her."

"Doesn't matter."

"So I have to wait for Shawn."

"Looks like it."

It was the beginning of another long day. Seth met Kally as she exited her car in the alley behind her winery.

"Did you hear about Storey?" he asked.

"No..." A queasiness grabbed her.

"Go read the sign," Seth said, nodding toward Storey's winery, his garage door closed, odd as that was during harvest season.

Coffee in hand, Kally walked to Storey's door, passing Kirk's winery and workers moving tanks and hoses inside. She didn't see Manning among them. But she'd see him soon enough.

Kally came up to the sign:

> *PS Wines is closing.*

*Oh My God! Did I have something to do with this?* Kally thought.

> *After 15 years in the Warehouse District we are pulling the plug—or cork, as it were. You can find our wines at these locations.*

Storey had listed twenty wine outlets.

> *It's been a wonderful ride. Thank you for your business.*

She was dumbfounded. This explained his getting rid of the Malbec. When had he decided to close? And why?

Oddly, she remembered his landscaping and his newly painted home. He's leaving! But he's not a suspect!

*Did I completely misread him?*

She headed back to her winery and walked into her production area, which was in full operational mode. Seth and Jason, Kirk's ex-intern, were racking Pinot Gris to another tank, passing it first through a tall metal filter sitting in the middle of the floor.

"What do you think?" Seth yelled at Kally above the noise of the pump.

She shook her head. "I don't get it. Storey was established here."

"Could be anything," Seth responded, getting another tank steam-cleaned for racking.

Kally placed her backpack on her table, her thoughts racing.

*I did not misread him. There's another reason he's closing.*

She looked at the time: seven a.m. She had less than an hour before leaving to meet Riggs. She watched Seth roll the six-hundred-liter tank he had just cleaned next to the tank being emptied. It would be another day in which Seth would organize the work.

"What time did you get here?" she asked him, walking up to him.

"'Bout six. I wanted to get the whites underway."

"Thanks for doing that. And, Jason, how are you?"

Jason looked up for a moment. "Good." He was standing on a platform peering over the rim of the Pinot Gris tank. Suddenly, he jumped down and closed the valve on the tank.

"Done here."

Then he moved to the small pump and shut it off.

The atmosphere in the room had changed with the addition of Jason. Kally saw him as someone who actually wanted to be in the wine business and seemed to relish the work. And it appeared he worked well with Seth.

It was a win-win situation: Seth had someone helping to take the load off, and Jason would have a lot more to do here than he did at Kirk's. What a change from Leah. Now...she needed to be able to keep both of them.

Seth removed the hose from the empty tank and attached it to the newly cleaned one. He walked toward the filter, but Kally stopped him.

"I'll do it, Seth."

Jason, meanwhile, turned up the music: Joe Cocker's "Feelin' Alright."

*But I'm not feelin' alright.* Kally got a bucket and positioned it under one of two hoses connected to the filter. Then she crouched down and unscrewed the clamp and gently eased it off the filter housing. Kally put the end of the hose in the bucket. Wine still in the filter and the hose flowed into it.

Kally did the same with the other hose. Then she opened the filter and took out the honeycombed cylinder and took it to the sink in the kitchen. She grabbed a new cylinder with smaller porosity, positioned it inside the filter, and closed the housing unit. Without saying anything to her assistants, Kally reattached the hoses to the filter. They would now move the wine back through the new filter to the clean tank.

Preoccupied with Storey, Kally paced while she watched the wine flowing through the hoses. Then her phone rang. She looked at the name and answered.

Jason turned the music down.

"That thing I mentioned? The noise on the first recording?" her brother, Phil, began.

"Yeah?"

"It's a voice. And it's female."

Kally stopped. *Female?* "I didn't hear a female voice."

"It's weak. Travis finally isolated it," Phil replied.

"Does he know what she said?"

"No. And he's tried everything."

"When does her voice show up?"

"Toward the end."

So had the woman come with the RMP guys? Or on her own? "Did you hear her?" she asked.

"Yes, faintly. I'm doing a gig at Tiger Creek, and Travis asked me to listen to it."

"Could you get anything from it? Any words?"

"No."

"Okay. Well...thanks for this."

Kally ended the call. She stepped up on a small stool to hose down the inside of the empty tank. The morning was proving to be a bit overwhelming in the information department, and, as such, she was having a hard time concentrating on winery work. Yet, she wanted to stay busy and help her two assistants.

Suddenly, Kally stopped and jumped down. "Seth?"

"I know. You have to go."

"How do you know that?" Kally chided.

"You have that 'Seth-I-have-to-go' tone of voice."

# 76

Kally promised her two cellar rats pizza and unlimited beer for all the work they would put in today. But before heading to police headquarters, she called Riggs.

"Something else has been discovered on that first recording," she began when Riggs answered. "There's another voice. And it's female."

Riggs didn't respond, so she continued, telling him about Storey and his winery closing.

Riggs still wasn't saying anything. But then he did. "Is your brother sure the voice is female?"

"That's what he said," Kally answered. "We have even more reason now to subpoena Manning."

"Yes, we do," Riggs said finally. "But let's get to Storey first."

Kally wasn't sure about that. But before she could say anything, Riggs went on. "I'll get another subpoena and meet you at his house."

———

She sat again in front of Storey's home and waited until she saw Riggs's car, which pulled up behind her. She got out and approached it, and he eased his window down.

"Get in and let's talk." He handed her the subpoena for Storey when she was settled in.

Riggs tapped the steering wheel. He seemed unusually anxious.

"What's wrong?" Kally asked.

"Well, up until your call this morning, I thought I had this figured out. The female voice is a puzzle. But it may not add much."

"I don't know about that," Kally countered. Then she told him about finding the letter.

"Boy…your guy was busy!" He paused. "I had a different scenario about how the evening played out. And the new info about Storey plays into it."

"How so?"

Riggs put his hands out in front of him. "Storey was still in his winery that night as people started leaving. He hears the music go off. It's late and he figures everyone's gone. So he brings the tank of $CO_2$ to the deceased's winery."

"At midnight?" Kally interjected.

"You yourself said it's harvest and anything can happen."

Kally didn't remember saying that exactly.

Riggs continued, dropping a bombshell. "I think Storey and Manning worked together in the killing of the deceased."

Kally was so shocked at this pronouncement she didn't answer. She simply stared at him.

Riggs again: "I thought Paul Storey was the noise on the recording that has now been identified as female. But that doesn't mean he *didn't* enter. The recording doesn't tell us *everything*."

"True. But Storey isn't a killer," Kally said.

"But the clues lead to him."

Kally took her time answering. Given the shreds of evidence they had, Riggs's reasoning wasn't completely wrong. Except that she knew the people in the Warehouse District. And none of what he was saying added up.

However, she needed to be careful about how she refuted him. Riggs was on her side now, and she wanted to keep him there.

"The only evidence we have is that Storey was in the Warehouse District that night and that he uses $CO_2$," Kally said, having voiced this once before. "But that doesn't tie him to the murder."

Riggs held her gaze for what seemed like a long time. "You're sure about that?"

This time, Kally didn't hesitate. "Yes. Winemakers aren't killers. They don't have time!"

Riggs threw up his hands. "Okay, then! Don't subpoena him."

Instead of an argument, she had agreement. "Okay."

Riggs changed the subject. "Let's go get Mark Manning."

"Will you give me a minute? There's something I need to know."

"All right."

Kally got out and, with the subpoena still in her hand, walked up to Storey's door.

When he answered, she started in: "Tell me why you're closing your winery."

Storey folded his arms. He looked down.

Kally waited.

"I don't have any money. My retirement accounts are gone. I've used all the equity in the house." He paused. "My wife left. I'm fifty-five and starting over."

Kally couldn't believe what she was hearing. "But...your wines. They sold. And well."

"Not enough to keep up with costs, like barrels and grapes and bottles. And rent and electricity. And..." He shook his head. "The gig's over."

"I can't believe it, Paul. You're one of the best winemakers in the Warehouse District."

"Yeah, well, not everyone makes a living in this business." He paused again. "I shouldn't have quit the day job."

Kally realized she knew him only as a winemaker. "What was your day job?"

He laughed. "Accountant." He saw the paper in her hand. "What's that?"

Kally folded it in half before answering. "It's a subpoena...for you. But you don't have to say anything because I *never believed* you had anything to do with Kirk's death." She looked away. "I'm sorry...for everything."

"You were just doing your job."

"Yeah..."

He put his hand on her shoulder, which surprised her. "Just sell a lot of Malbec."

# 77

Kally walked into the police station and, as a matter of habit, looked for Riggs. They had driven away from Manning's house at the same time—Riggs following her in his car. No one had answered the door, the subpoena of Mark Manning relegated to later in the day.

"Have you seen Riggs?" Kally asked Myrna.

Myrna looked up at her, shook her head, and took another call.

Then Kally saw Bud. "What are you doing here?"

"I'll answer that," Dale said, coming around the corner. "There's been a fire at the Hatch place. Riggs is on his way. You and Bud get out there."

Bud sat in the passenger seat, a place inhabited by Riggs these past few days, and Kally turned to look at her. Bud stared out the window, not saying anything. Her long black hair was pulled back in a ponytail, and she sat ramrod straight, not moving a muscle.

Looking at her in profile, Kally couldn't tell how, physically, she had weathered A-Rod's accident. And she didn't know anything about his condition. Added to all that, they hadn't said one word about the Hatches, odd as that was since they both had worked the case.

"Are you back full time?" Kally asked.

"Yes." Bud turned to face her, and Kally saw then her weary, tired eyes. "A-Rod's going to a transitional care unit for, well, hopefully a short time. He's going to need ongoing care for his leg. For a while."

"Oh," Kally said, at a loss for words.

"But we're not postponing the wedding."

"You're not?" Kally asked, surprised.

Bud shook her head. "One way or another, wheelchair or cane, he's getting to the alter."

Now Bud was smiling.

"That's great, Bud! Really!" Kally reached over and grabbed her coworker's hand. "I'm really happy for you."

"Yeah. It was touch-and-go for a while. Not the wedding. His condition. We'll work through it. There's no need to cancel anything."

"Your wedding will be even more of a celebration," Kally added.

She reached the Hatch driveway, passing two Woodinville firetrucks on their way out. Kally drove up the long incline and pulled in next to the smoky remains of the horse barn, every inch burned beyond recognition. An arson crew walked gingerly through the wreckage, poking at debris, the word "ARSON" prominently displayed in yellow letters on the back of their black coats.

Kally's stomach turned thinking of the animals that may not have escaped.

Bud got out and breathed in deeply. "Only a wood fire," she said, turning to Kally.

"As opposed to…a barbecue?"

"Yep."

That was somewhat reassuring. But when Kally took in the Hatchs' expansive property, she saw no horses. Anywhere. The two walked up to Riggs, who was talking with a distraught Mrs. Hatch and a Hispanic man Kally didn't know.

"I can't find Sage!" Mrs. Hatch wailed. "She's gone!"

"No, no!" the man identified as Jose countered. "No horse bodies. They"—he swept his arm out—"all out."

Kally took that to mean the horses had indeed escaped and were now randomly distributed throughout the neighborhood and possibly making their way toward busy Woodinville proper and the town's many wineries.

"How many horses are we talking about?" Kally asked.

"Five," Mrs. Hatch answered in a little-girl voice. "Where is she?" Mrs. Hatch asked, turning to look at her property. "Where is Sage?"

The four followed Mrs. Hatch's gaze, taking in the compound's several acres. Stands of trees formed a natural barrier to the neighbors and fences made up areas where the trees were absent.

When Kally turned back to face Mrs. Hatch, it wasn't concern she saw. It was a countenance filled with hate and anger.

"He killed her," Mrs. Hatch said. "He knows what she means to me."

Kally realized she had no idea what the horse looked like. It was Jose, looking over Mrs. Hatch's shoulder, who saw her.

"There!" he said, pointing to an area between the house and a wooden fence. A brown horse with a white snout emerged from the shadows. "There's Sage!"

Mrs. Hatch ran to her, sobbing. "Sage! You're all I have."

Riggs turned to Kally and Bud and said under his breath, "So whoever did this unlatched the barn door *first* before burning it down."

"I think we have to question Mr. Hatch. And soon," Kally said.

"Let's see if we have any evidence," Riggs replied. "Why don't you two talk to the Mrs.—try to get a timeline—and I'll see if arson has uncovered anything." But then Riggs stopped. "What do you think about that?" he asked Kally.

"Good idea," she answered. Riggs was asking her opinion for once. It was her case, after all.

Riggs walked toward the smoldering remains while Kally and Bud turned their attention to Mrs. Hatch.

"I know this is distressing," Kally said when they were standing next to her.

"I'll say. And what will be next? The house?" Mrs. Hatch's eyes widened. "Or me?"

"When was the last time you talked to your husband?" Bud inquired.

"That would be yesterday. We were yelling at each other through the front door. He was mad because I changed the locks and he couldn't get in."

"Did he threaten you?" Kally asked.

"Yes. He said 'I'll be back. And you won't like it.' He'd been drinking, as usual."

"Did he say when he would be back?" Kally asked.

"No."

"Why didn't you report this to us yesterday?" Bud asked.

"I've already reported to you, numerous times."

"But this incident is just as important as the others, maybe more so," Kally countered. "We need to fill out a report, the sooner the better."

"Is there somewhere you can stay until we've found the cause of the fire?" Bud asked.

"I'm not leaving my home," Mrs. Hatch answered defiantly. "And I'm not leaving Sage. Can I make another complaint against him?"

Bud and Kally looked at one another.

Kally nodded that she could. "Let's get your report first."

Kally and Bud sat with Mrs. Hatch in her kitchen. Kally jotted notes while Mrs. Hatch put a timeline together, starting with the encounter with Mr. Hatch in the late afternoon of the previous day and then seeing the barn go up in flames around five a.m. She hadn't heard an explosion and hadn't see anyone near the property. She did not suspect Jose or another horse handler who worked with him.

Not much to go on.

Kally and Bud left the house twenty minutes later with a promise from Mrs. Hatch that she would come to the station to file a formal grievance against her husband, the second one in less than a month.

Kally saw Riggs waiting for them.

"Did you get anything?" he asked as they were standing near their cars.

"Very little," Kally replied. "There was an encounter with Mr. Hatch yesterday afternoon and then the fire this morning."

"What encounter?" Riggs asked.

"Apparently, Mr. Hatch came by late afternoon and tried to get into the house. But Mrs. Hatch had changed the locks."

Bud saw an arson investigator crouch down to look at something and walked over to him.

"Mrs. Hatch is going to file another complaint against her husband," Kally added.

Riggs remained quiet and Kally wondered what was churning inside his head.

"Did arson tell you anything?" she asked.

"No." Riggs hesitated. "Not yet." Another pause. "You and I need to keep an open mind about this…this…situation."

"Okay," Kally replied, wondering what he was getting at.

"Domestic disputes are messy," he began. "Sometimes all is not what it seems."

"What do you mean?" Kally asked.

"I mean we need to consider all scenarios and not rule anything out. And question the givens as they're laid out."

Kally watched Riggs as he took a considerable amount of time looking at the Hatch home. "I think we should question Mr. Hatch now."

It wasn't the swiftness with which Hatch opened the door of his upscale townhome that startled the two police officers. It was the look of pure hatred they saw when he took in their badges.

"This better be good," Hatch said.

With Bud in the car watching, Kally and Riggs started in.

"You may or may not know that there was a fire at your property early this morning," Riggs began.

Hatch's countenance changed to one of surprise.

"I didn't know that. How are the horses?" Hatch asked.

"I didn't say it was the barn," Riggs said.

Hatch stared Riggs down.

*You're not going to win this*, Kally thought.

"Right," Hatch offered, looking away. "Well…what burned?"

"The barn," Kally answered. "The horses got out or were let out before the fire."

"Where are they?" Hatch asked with concern.

"Sage is on the property. The others are roaming the neighborhood," Kally answered.

"Those are expensive animals and need to be found," Hatch retorted, as if finding them were the purview of the police.

"I'm sure your horse handlers will take care of it," Riggs said.

Hatch lowered his eyes a moment and took in Kally's name badge.

"Are you Ken's kid?" he asked, catching her eye again.

"I am," Kally responded.

Hatch nodded slowly. If he had anything else to say, he let it go.

`Kally moved on. "Mrs. Hatch said you confronted her yesterday afternoon at her home. You told her you would be back and she wouldn't like it."

"Mrs. Hatch is a liar," Hatch said in an even tone. "I was nowhere near that property yesterday."

Kally and Riggs glanced at one another.

"Okay. Where were you last night and early this morning?" Riggs asked.

"Right here."

"Is there anyone who can corroborate that?" Riggs asked.

"Probably not. I set my alarm for five thirty a.m. and played golf at seven. You can look into that."

"Where did you play?" Kally asked.

"Inglewood," he answered, naming the private club overlooking Lake Washington.

"So you did not go to your house yesterday afternoon and try to get in?" Kally repeated.

Hatch shook his head. "Mrs. Hatch has an agenda. She wants to embarrass me in public, and one way she can do that is by making false statements to the police. Obviously, she's got you on her side."

"We're investigating, not taking sides," Kally responded.

"My family built this town," Hatch continued. "I don't want my name in the paper. I've offered Mrs. Hatch a dollar amount that I think is fair for the divorce she wants. Mrs. Hatch, however, wants to leave town with a lot of cash, and I won't cooperate with that," Hatch added.

"We would advise you to stay away from the property for the time being," Kally said.

"And I won't be following your advice. Because those horses are mine and I need to see that they are taken care of." Hatch paused. "If there is nothing else, I will bid you goodbye."

Dale leaned against the front of his desk, arms folded, listening to Kally explain recent developments in the Hatch case. Riggs stood behind her in the doorway.

"Mrs. Hatch says one thing, and the Mr. refutes it. We don't know what is real."

"What is your gut telling you?" Dale asked.

Kally hesitated, reminded again of Mrs. Hatch's swift change in demeanor just an hour ago. She shot a glance at Riggs. "My gut is confused." Then: "Did Hatch know my father?"

"He did," Dale said. "Your father investigated a few things for him involving his buildings. Actually, he got to know him pretty well. Not that he liked the man. You know the Hatch name goes back a long way in this town."

"He said as much," Kally answered.

"Mr. Hatch is a man with money," Dale added. "But he's a Scrooge."

"Yeah, I picked up on that."

"We're in the middle of a nice domestic argument." Dale walked around the side of his desk and sat down. "I think it's time to get a DV advocate in here. What do you think, Riggs?"

"I think it's a good idea."

"Call the sheriff and ask for a recommendation," Dale said to Kally. "Explain that we have escalation and we don't know if it will get worse. You can say that I think it will. The advocate can work on that side of the case while you work with the fire department."

"Okay."

"Did you tell Hatch to stay away from the property?"

"Yes."

"What did he say?"

"No."

Dale didn't respond, but he seemed to be thinking about something. "Technically, we have no legal right to stop him. He knows that. Only a restraining order would keep him from the property. Mrs. Hatch will have to contact her attorney if she wants one. You said she's coming in here, to file another complaint?"

"That's what she said."

"Okay. Work with her on that. Maybe by the time she comes in, arson will have found something."

"All right." Kally turned to leave as Riggs moved aside. But at the door, she stopped. And addressed Dale: "I…let this case fall through the cracks. I've been busy, and I let this one just sit there. I know how much you wanted me to keep up on it."

"Don't worry about it," Dale countered. "Nothing you did or didn't do would have changed the outcome. We have a mess, and you didn't cause it. And being consumed by a case? That's how this business works, Kally. If you didn't get caught up in your work, then this isn't your line of work."

"Okay." *That was somewhat reassuring.*

Before going to her office, Kally went to see Bud. "Can you do me a favor?"

"Sure." Bud turned from her computer to face her.

"We got Kirk Remick's phone back from the Seattle lab. There are calls on it that aren't identified. Would you look at them…find out who they're from?"

Bud nodded that she would.

"Great. The phone's in the evidence room." Then she headed to the women's restroom.

Kally stood for a while in front of the mirror taking in her reflection, her long hair past due for a cut. She thought about her cases. Dale's words of encouragement notwithstanding, she felt a sense of dread about the Hatch case.

*I don't know which Hatch to believe.*

And then there was Kirk's case and all its unsolvables. And in the background was Mark Manning, who saw everything, knew everything, and wasn't talking. They needed to subpoena him. If they could find him. But today, the Hatch case was mostly on her mind.

She picked up a strand of hair and let it fall through her fingers.

*I don't think I'm suited for police work.*

She took out her phone and made a call.

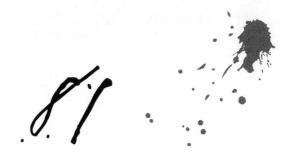

K ally parked in the mall and speed walked to the front door of the salon, seeing as she was being "fit in" to her haircutter's busy day.

And thank goodness for that, she thought, donning a robe and hugging her haircutter when she came out to get her. Kally sat in the chair, taking in her mirror-self, her wet hair the longest she had ever seen it.

"You let it grow!" her haircutter said, picking up a few strands.

"Not on purpose."

"Just a trim today?"

"Yep."

"That will be an inch or more, okay?"

"That's fine," Kally answered and then watched as the cutting commenced. She relaxed and forced herself not to think about her cases. Instead, she eavesdropped on the middle-aged woman's conversation in the chair next to her who was describing her European vacation.

"We had a wonderful little northern Italian wine called Dolcetto," the woman said. "We both thought it was like a heavy Pinot Noir."

*Okay, that's a good comparison.*

*Not all Dolcettos are dark and brooding.*

*But some are.*

"And we had a Barolo that my husband loved."

*So she was in the Piedmont, north of Tuscany.*

Kally watched her haircutter clip off more than an inch on one side, which had the effect of giving her hair some body and bounce.

"Of course we'd go back to Italy in a heartbeat," the woman continued.

*Most people would.*

A salon employee interrupted Kally's eavesdropping by standing between her and the woman next to her.

"Mrs. Nelson, we are ready in the spa anytime you are."

"Okay," the woman replied. "I'll be there just as soon as we're done here."

*What would that be like, having a whole afternoon dedicated to body work?*

"I'm having my second $CO_2$ treatment," the woman said to the person cutting her hair.

Kally bolted from the chair, startling everyone within ten feet of her as her haircutter's scissors flew across the room.

"What did you just say?" Kally demanded.

The woman recoiled before answering. "I was talking about my spa appointment."

"You said '$CO_2$.'"

"Yes. So what?"

"*What* $CO_2$?" Kally demanded.

"It's a skin treatment," the woman answered in a defiant tone.

Kally hurried to the front counter. She reached in her pocket and took out her badge. Covering it slightly with one hand, she caught the eye of a customer representative who came over to her.

"I need to see someone in your spa," Kally said, uncovering her badge as she spoke.

"Sure. Now?" the woman asked.

"Yes."

"Follow me."

Kally followed the woman behind a closed door and into the spa where the lights were dimmed, incense burned, and the walls were painted muted shades of yellow and brown.

Desert colors. Odd for the Northwest.

A handsome, buff young man with stylish hair—she was reminded that her hair was only half cut—emerged and smiled at her, then disappeared.

But nothing here—the quiet, the colors, the eye candy—was calming. Kally rapped her fingers on the counter.

*"A source out of nowhere..."*

Soon enough, a woman came out to greet her and the customer rep left. Kally held her badge in front of her. "I've heard something about a $CO_2$ treatment. Can you tell me what it is and how it works?"

"Of course. You're referring to carboxytherapy…it's given like Botox, as an injection. But instead of a poison, it is $CO_2$ gas."

*This is it! This is what we've been looking for!*

"Who gives the treatment?" Kally asked.

"Only a licensed beautician. Or a physician. It's not a new therapy." The woman reached under the counter and brought out a cellophane-wrapped rectangular box. "It's been used in France since the 1930s." She removed the cellophane. "But it's just getting going here." The woman opened the box, and Kally saw a syringe, protected in its own cellophane wrapping. "Some think it's safer than Botox. But, of course, *we* don't give too much Botox."

"No, of course not," Kally responded.

"It doesn't take much," the woman added, lifting the syringe and passing it to Kally. "Just a few injections of a *small* amount."

"And what does it do?" Kally asked, handling it gently and turning it over.

"It rejuvenates the skin, tightening it slightly. Perfect for wrinkles, acne scars, stretch marks."

The woman put her hand out, then put the syringe back in the box. And closed the lid.

"It dissolves fat cells and opens blood vessels," she said. "But you don't have the side effects—the frozenness, for example—that you have with Botox."

"How many people have had the treatment?

The woman consulted a sign-in book. "Let's see. About twenty so far."

"Can I see your book?" Kally asked.

The woman hesitated. "This is confidential information and—"

"And very important to a murder case," Kally interjected.

Kally held her gaze. Perhaps it was the word "murder" that convinced her

The woman turned the book around. Kally took her time reading through the names of both men and women who'd had had the treatment recently.

She turned the page.

And her heart stopped.

Near the top, on the third line, was Ellie's name, *Ellie Fishback*, the "k" of her last name written with flair, the tail trending upward in an exaggerated "U."

Kally sat in her car in the mall's parking lot. She needed to talk to Riggs. But there was someone else who needed to hear from her first.

Kally hit Nakamura's number and waited, taking in her uneven haircut in her rearview mirror.

"Mr. Nakamura, it's Kally," she said when he answered. "I have something in the Kirk Remick case."

"And I have something for you. But you go first."

Kally proceeded, telling him about the $CO_2$ spa treatment. She refrained from telling him that she knew Ellie Fishback.

"Then what you found and what I found add up," Nakamura said. "We looked at the hands of the deceased a little more carefully. We…um…opened them both flat and scanned them for anything unusual."

Kally felt a queasiness come over her at the thought of Kirk's other hand being broken. She quickly dismissed the image.

"We found a pinprick in the palm of the right hand," Nakamura continued. "It would be consistent with the point of a syringe."

"So Kirk—I mean the deceased—put his hand up to block the syringe," Kally added.

"It makes sense," Nakamura said.

"The woman at the spa told me only a small about of $CO_2$ is needed for a treatment," Kally added.

"Well, the deceased got a lot more than a small amount," Nakamura countered. "But it is not just the amount of $CO_2$ he received. It's *where* it was administered—the hand, which does not have a significant amount of adipose tissue for absorption, meaning the gas entered the blood stream.

"And then, there's the *rate* of administration," Nakamura said. "I'm not an expert on cosmetic techniques, but when you introduce a gas into the body it *must* be done slowly.

He paused. "The injection would have caused gas bubbles, and that is very painful, like the 'bends' in diving. The gas would quickly make its way to the heart, lungs, and brain. He would have experienced a tremendous headache."

"Which explains the closed fists," Kally said.

"Yes. Mr. Remick suffocated from the amount of $CO_2$ in his body. It's not the usual route with $CO_2$, especially in a winery. I have amended my report yet again." Then: "How is it that this woman was able to get a syringe of $CO_2$?"

"That, I still need to determine," Kally answered. But knowing Ellie, anything was possible.

She thanked Nakamura, ended the call, and was about to drive out when her phone rang. She looked at the name: Shawn McCormick.

*Finally!*

"Thank you for calling back, Shawn."

"Not a problem. You're looking for Jessica?"

"Yes."

"She's at her mother's. In Seattle. She's moving here next week."

"What is Jessica's phone number?"

With the new number in her phone, Kally called Jessica Fellows and left a message, the same message she had left Shawn. She knew that Jessica wouldn't have a name of the person who'd bought flowers that had been delivered to Remick Cellars, because that person had paid in cash. But she would have a description, no doubt of a striking blonde woman, a woman she was sure was Ellie Fishback.

Kally entered Riggs's office and sat down in the chair next to his desk. She waited for him to finish on his computer before starting in.

"Whad'ya got?" he asked finally.

"The answer." Kally took out her phone, clicked on a photo, then handed it to him.

Riggs took his time looking at it. "Okay. It's a syringe."

"A syringe of $CO_2$. It's a treatment for softening skin," Kally explained. "It's given as an injection. I have a connection now between the woman who wrote the letter I told you about and a person who had this treatment at the spa. She's...um...someone I know. Someone I know well."

"A friend?" Riggs asked.

Kally hesitated. "We're in the same group of friends."

"And how do you know she's the one?" Riggs asked.

"From her handwriting. The letter I found and the sign-in sheet at the spa match."

Riggs's nodded in understanding, still staring at the photo. "Is this *the* syringe?"

"No. I don't have it."

"You need it, you know. But it would be a longshot to find it. Nobody in their right mind would keep something like this if it is, indeed, a murder weapon."

He paused. "So if I understand you correctly...this woman...this nonfriend...somehow got a syringe of $CO_2$."

"Yes. And I'm hoping to retrieve it."

"Either that or a confession." Riggs handed the phone back. He stared at her hair for a moment. "This is good work, Kally. You really dogged this. And kept to your convictions. So now you've got the murder weapon, so to speak, and the motive. And what is the motive?" he asked, testing her.

"Revenge."

"Exactly!" Riggs smiled.

*Smiled!*

"Have you talked to Nakamura?"

"I did. He found a pinprick in Kirk's—the deceased—right palm that would be consistent with the point of a syringe."

"You're going to question this woman." Riggs didn't pose it as a question.

"I am."

"Don't mention the syringe," he advised. "That's your ace in the hole."

K ally and Bud entered the tasting room for Red Mountain Productions. As it was late in the day, only a few patrons sat inside sipping wine. Others were gathering their things and leaving.

Ellie saw the two officers and came over to them at the tasting bar.

"Hey," Ellie said, putting her hands in her back pockets, which had the effect of spreading her barely buttoned blouse. "Women in uniform. Sexy, that." Then she reached for two glasses.

"We're not here to taste, Ellie," Kally said.

"We'd like you to come with us," Bud added.

"Why?"

"We have to ask you some questions," Kally answered. "We prefer not doing it here. You were seeing Kirk. I know that now."

Ellie put the glasses down. "You don't know that. How would you know that?"

"I found a letter. From you. To him."

Ellie hesitated, stunned. "You went through his things."

"Of course I did," Kally answered. "The handwriting in the letter matches your signature at the Northgate Salon."

Ellie didn't have a retort for that. She stared at the countertop for a moment.

"Handwriting doesn't prove anything," Ellie said without looking up.

She was wrong about that, but Kally let it go. "We have reason to question you. Will you come with us?"

"And if I don't?" Ellie said.

Neither officer answered, leaving the question hanging.

Ellie seemed to be thinking about her options. Then she turned to a pourer at the bar. "Lexi, I have to leave. Will you close up?"

Kally refrained from handcuffing Ellie as she and Bud escorted her out the door. Once outside, Kally looked around the parking lot for Ellie's sports car.

"Where's your car?" Kally asked.

"It's there." She pointed to a black sedan.

"That's not your car," Kally said.

"Mine's in the shop."

Kally stood there for a moment, the image of a black sedan driving away from the Warehouse District Saturday morning as clear as if she'd seen it herself. It was all adding up now. But instead of relief, she felt tremendous sadness.

K ally and Bud directed Ellie into the small conference room at police headquarters. Kally left to get water and ran into Riggs in the hallway.

"You need help with this?" he asked.

Kally shook her head. "I think it best if Bud and I handle it."

"Okay. Give me a sign if you want me to come in."

Back in the conference room, Kally settled in. She wanted to jump immediately to the affair and Kirk's death but she needed to lead up to it. And so she started in on something else.

"Did Manning tell you about Blitzen?"

"Yes," Ellie answered, a confused look on her face.

"Did you know that it was a confidential wine Kirk was bringing out at Christmas?"

Ellie hesitated before answering. "Yes."

"Why did Manning tell you this?"

"Why don't you ask him?"

"I can't reach him. And his attorney has a gag on him." Kally noted that Ellie had buttoned her blouse now that she was in a police setting.

Ellie shrugged. "I don't know why he told me. He just did. Is it a big deal?"

"Did he tell you anything else?" Kally continued, ignoring the question. "Anything about how Kirk made wine?"

"Yes."

"And you passed that information to RMP."

3 1 4

"RMP was looking for winemaking tips, and I provided them," Ellie answered.

"How long did the affair last?"

*Perhaps that was too abrupt.*

Ellie took a long sip of water and stared at the far wall. Then she looked at her high school friend, Bud, who was sitting next to Kally.

"It never ended. At least not for me."

"Were you involved in his death?" Kally asked.

"No," Ellie said calmly.

"Was Mark Manning involved in Kirk's death?" Kally inquired.

"You know you're asking a lot of questions about Mark, and I can't answer for him. And now I'm thinking I need an attorney."

"Were you at Kirk's release party Friday night?" Kally asked, moving on.

Bud put her hand on Kallie's arm. Kally knew she should stop, but she couldn't.

"Yes. For a short time," Ellie answered.

"How short?" Kally asked.

Ellie shrugged. "I don't know…maybe an hour."

"Did you come by yourself?"

"Yes."

"Did you meet people there?"

"I saw people there I knew."

"RMP people?" Kally asked.

"Yes."

"Did you talk to Kirk?"

"Yes."

"Where?"

"What do you mean 'where'?"

"Where in the winery did you talk to him?" Kally pressed.

"We have to stop," Bud said.

"You have my name on a spa sign-in sheet, nothing else," Ellie retorted.

"You have a right to an attorney, Ellie," Bud interjected. "Your husband would know one. Why don't you call him."

Ellie looked away and said softly, "Yeah, I'll do that."

Kally watched Ellie walk out of the police station with her lawyer, who was explaining something as they got into a car.

She knew she had no evidence to hold Ellie other than the letter and the aforementioned sign-in sheet. Not enough to prove murder. Not at the moment, anyway.

She walked into Riggs's office, feeling dejected.

"I'm so close," she said. "But I can't put it together."

"Do you know for certain that this woman…this nonfriend…*had* a syringe?" he asked.

"I don't." But his question made her think of something. "I'll be right back."

"Where are you going?"

Kally walked into the Northgate Salon and headed directly to the spa's double doors, passing her hairdresser along the way.

"We have to finish your hair!"

"I know," Kally said over her shoulder. "Another time."

Kally saw the woman she had talked to previously standing at the spa's front desk. Avoiding pleasantries, Kally started in.

"I need to talk to a young man who works here."

"Okay…there are several young men who work here. Who in particular?"

"I don't know his name. But I can describe him." And she did.

"Oh. You mean Andy." The woman smiled. "Yes...he allows women to dream...I'll get him." She glanced at three people waiting in the reception area. "You can talk in my office."

Kally followed her down a hallway then sat at the woman's desk. Handsome Andy came in and plopped down in a chair. Kally thought he winked at her. She placed her badge in front of him and explained that she was working a murder investigation.

From the look on his face, that jolted him into some seriousness.

"I want to ask you one question. And I want it answered honestly."

He nodded in agreement.

"Did you give Ellie Fishback a syringe of $CO_2$?"

Andy stared at her as if she had asked him to describe in one sentence the atmosphere of Jupiter.

Kally continued: "Ellie Fishback is a very busy woman who runs three tasting rooms and might not have time to come to a spa for her $CO_2$ treatment."

"I could lose my job," Andy said finally.

"Yes, you could. And you could help solve a murder."

"Is it enough to arrest her?" Kally asked Riggs when she was back in his office and explained that she had gotten a confession.

"You went by yourself to talk to this guy?" Riggs asked instead.

"Bud was busy."

"He could refute it."

"No. He can't." Kally reached in her pocket and took out a piece of paper and unfolded it. "I asked him to write it down, and he signed the page. He's worried about being arrested."

Riggs pointed at her. "Very good. Let's get a search warrant for the house."

"It is enough, though?" she asked again, following him out of his office. She thought of the dead ends and the connections she couldn't make in the case.

"Be patient," Riggs said.

Kally ignored the comment. "Do we *have* enough?"

"Depends on what we find! Get Bud!"

With the warrant in hand, they pulled in front of Ellie's home in a wealthy neighborhood of Bellevue. Walking to the door, Kally realized she'd never been here before. She rang the bell and waited while Riggs and Bud took their time joining her on the front porch. They'd also called for backup, from the Bellevue Police to help in the search.

"Whad'ya think? About four to five mil?" Riggs asked about the home's value.

"I don't know. He's done well," Kally answered.

"We met him, right?" Riggs asked.

"Yeah. At Jacobsen's law firm." She was reminded again of Jacobsen's bandaged hand.

She hoped that Jim Fishback wouldn't be here. How to explain searching his nice suburban home for a murder weapon? And did he know about Ellie and Kirk's affair?

The door opened finally, and there he was—Jim Fishback. He looked surprised.

"Kally." He took in Riggs and Bud, then stuck out his hand. And Kally reciprocated.

"Jim, this is Robert Riggs, whom you met a few days ago. And Officer Milano."

More shaking of hands.

"Is Ellie here?" Kally asked.

"Yes." He hesitated. "Is there a reason you want to see her?" Fishback looked at the three of them. "All of you?"

"We have a warrant to search your house," Riggs said.

Fishback seemed to think about that as he stared at Kally. But he said nothing. Then he moved to the side and the group entered.

They walked into a two-story entryway. A blue-hued Chihuly glass chandelier hung from the ceiling.

*This is odd and uncomfortable*, Kally thought, hoping she didn't have to explain the case they were working to Fishback. They followed him down the hallway and into a spacious kitchen and an adjoining family room. The room, with floor-to-ceiling windows, looked out over a covered deck and an expansive manicured lawn.

Ellie was sitting on a couch, her back to them, watching television. She turned toward them when they entered, a blank expression on her face. Then she stood up.

"Kally! Bud!" she said, smiling.

*As if the police questioning earlier had never happened.*

"What are you doing here?" Ellie asked, coming around to talk to them.

"We need to talk to you," Kally said, introducing her to Riggs. He took the warrant out of his pocket.

"Don't worry," Fishback said, addressing his wife. "I don't know what they're doing here. Just work with them. And call your attorney."

"Will you stay?" Ellie asked him.

"I will," Fishback answered.

"Why don't you sit while we proceed," Riggs said, offering Ellie a seat back on the couch. "Bud will sit with you."

Ellie turned to address Kally. "Is this how it works? You look through my things and I just sit here?"

"That's about the gist of it," Riggs answered for her. Then: "Let's go back out front and wait."

K ally and Riggs walked back through the entryway to wait for Bellevue Police.

At the front door she turned and took in the *House Beautiful* living room with its red walls and white-trimmed molding. Striped chairs and a floral couch sat in front of a white marble fireplace. A large mirror in a gilded frame hung above the mantel, dominating the room.

*Yes, it's pretty. But probably not used much.*

Riggs entered the dining room to their right, and Kally followed. He glanced at his watch. Neither said anything.

She had already decided that the two of them would take the upstairs once Bellevue Police had arrived. Bud would remain with Ellie and her husband, as uncomfortable as that might be.

They passed an antique wood table with eight fabric chairs under two identical stained-glass chandeliers. Cabinets surrounded them, filled with china, crystal, and overly large wine glasses.

They entered a hallway with several rooms leading off of it. To the left was a den with a wet bar. Riggs walked in. *Now this is a comfortable space*, she thought, following him. She'd live in this room and the family room that looked out on that manicured lawn in back.

They circled the room, taking in the huge flat-screen TV in one corner and the pool table in the other. Two wine refrigerators sat on either side of a sink, below a counter. Kally opened one and pulled out a random bottle. It was Guardian Cellars' Gun Metal. One of her favorites. She put it back.

There were two more rooms past the den and they entered one.

Pennants and a University of Washington flag hung on the wall, as well as a framed Washington Crew sleeveless jersey. She walked up to the jersey and read a small plaque: *First Place, J. A. Fishback. Windermere Regatta, May 2000.*

The rest of the space was taken up by heavy wooden furniture and bookshelves. She walked around the desk, noting the laptop closed on top of it. Pens, papers, and folders also sat atop, neatly arranged. She saw a business card holder. Kally took one of the cards, read Jim Fishback's name and phone numbers, and put it in her pocket.

She looked out windows at a flower bed beyond.

*Another comfortable space.*

They entered the last room off the hallway—Ellie's office, she presumed. Everything here was minimalist in glass and chrome. A deep-pink couch sat against one wall, the pinks of the abstract painting above it complimenting it nicely. Situated in front of a fireplace, a few chairs surrounded a low, round glass coffee table. The room was comfortable in its own way. Her own style leaned more toward Fishback's.

Kally looked at Riggs, who was staring at the painting. Neither made eye contact. She wondered if he had picked up on anything.

So far, nothing seemed out of place.

Kally walked behind Ellie's desk. The laptop on her desk was open. A dark screen. She bumped the desk with her hip the way one bumps a pinball machine, and the screen saver popped on, a close-up of wine glasses hanging from a rack.

The doorbell rang.

Kally and Riggs looked at one another, then walked back to the front to greet Bellevue Police, passing windows on their right. Five police cars were now parked in front of the house. Yet not one person stood in a doorway nor on the street taking in the Fishback residence.

After brief instructions, the four Bellevue police officers fanned out on the first floor. Kally and Riggs walked upstairs, passing oil paintings and pen-and-ink drawings on the walls.

"You doing all right?" Riggs asked, taking in the four bedrooms and several bathrooms when they reached the second-floor landing.

"Not sure."

"It gets easier," he said, "eventually. Which way?"

"I think the master bedroom is there," Kally said, pointing toward it and heading in that direction.

"Why do you think what we're looking for is up here?" Riggs asked, donning a pair of gloves, and she did the same.

"It's cosmetic. It's probably in the bathroom."

The two walked into a spacious master bedroom with plenty of room for the king-size bed.

*Was Kirk ever here?*

"I'll start with the dressers if you want to do the bathroom," Riggs said.

Kally entered the elaborate room off the bedroom with four sinks—*four?*—a pebbled shower with several shower heads, and a hot tub. Behind two doors, she was sure, were toilets, his and hers.

She stood in the middle of the room and looked in the mirror, which extended the length of the wall. She noted her hair, an inch shorter on one side. Then she moved to her left and opened a mirrored medicine cabinet above one sink.

*This one is his.* She took in shaving paraphernalia, boxes of condoms,

Band-Aids, pill containers, and cough medicine. She put her hand under the mirror at the second sink and opened the cabinet.

Empty.

Kally tried the cabinet above the third sink. Also empty.

She heard Riggs opening and closing dresser drawers in the bedroom, neither saying anything. She thought about the walk-through in Kirk's condo, seeing nothing out of place.

Kally opened the medicine cabinet above the fourth sink. Here were Ellie's things, including her own box of Band-Aids—*strange*—and a pregnancy test kit.

But no syringe.

She heard Ellie's voice downstairs, talking to someone. *Her attorney?*

Next, Kally tried the cabinets underneath the sinks. All were filled with toilet paper, towels, wash cloths, and cleaning utensils. Or they were empty.

Then she began opening drawers, beginning with the one closest to Ellie's sink. First drawer: hairbrushes, a comb. Second drawer: a roll of lint remover, a box of Q-Tips.

Third drawer: wash cloths. *Odd that these are here.*

She lifted them out. And stopped.

*There it was.*

A rectangular box like the one she'd been shown at the salon. She grabbed it and put it on the counter. She hesitated then opened it. The syringe, its protective wrapping gone, was nestled inside.

Kally teared up. The tip could be tested for Kirk's DNA.

She looked toward the doorway. Riggs stood there, staring at her, not saying anything.

Kally and Riggs went back downstairs. Kally held an evidence bag with the box and syringe inside. They came up to Ellie, who was standing with her husband and a woman she assumed was her attorney.

Ellie took one look at the bag but said nothing. Riggs handcuffed her while Kally recited her Miranda rights as Ellie, her husband, and the attorney stared silently at her until she finished.

Then they walked outside. Bellevue police officers were getting in their cars and driving away. Bud remained with Kally. Still no one said anything. Not even Riggs.

Kally and Riggs led Ellie to their car for the trip to King County jail. Ellie's husband and her attorney got into their own cars and followed them.

It was as if everything were moving according to script. People knew their places and acted accordingly.

*How odd is this?*

At the King County jail, Ellie was booked for investigation of homicide, a precipitous fall for a former Seattle Seahawks cheerleader and tasting-room manager. When all was said and done, Riggs walked out to the car. But Kally stayed behind and watched as Ellie was led down a hallway, hand cuffed and shackled. She kept watching until they turned a corner, out of sight.

Back at her desk, she began the difficult task of writing her report on OPI. Once finished, it would close the case. How much easier it would be if she hadn't known the players.

She was interrupted by a figure in her doorway: Riggs. He held a small paper cup and took a few sips from it.

"Yes?" she asked.

"This is a classic case about a spurned woman and revenge."

Kally nodded in agreement.

"Do you want my further opinion?"

*When had he ever asked?* She sat back. "Sure."

"That syringe shouldn't have been there. That was too easy."

Riggs voiced her very thoughts. "You think we were supposed to find it?"

"Possibly. It's hard to interpret the mind of the guilty." He finished whatever he was drinking in one gulp. "We have the motive, the method, and the murderer, so technically, we're done here." He paused, then in one motion crushed the cup in his hand.

Kally stared at his hand, balled up in *a fist*.

"Just think about it," he added.

# 90

And think about it she did, all the previous evening and now all morning long. Before coming to work, Kally had run a few errands for her winery, dropping off supplies for Seth and Jason who were continuing the filtering process. Kally had thanked them profusely, promising to help them as soon as she could.

Now she sat at her desk again. Only she, Bud, and Myrna were in the office. Dale and Riggs were taking the day off. The place was quiet, with the support staff gone and the phones silent. The rain, which had started early, continued, hitting the windows in short, quick bursts.

She picked up a wine cork that sat nearby, a reminder of her other job, and fiddled with it, thinking through what Riggs had said. Then she went through the case one more time: there was Kirk splayed over a bin, an unnatural ending to a respected winemaker; there was ex-wife, Janie, and daughter, Emma, neither of whom would ever be the same; there was his assistant winemaker, Mark Manning, who saw everything and revealed nothing; there was Kirk's last love, Kendall, distraught and tossed out now from the insular world of Woodinville winemaking; and there was Ellie and her silent, surreal walk to the police car and jail.

And then there was RMP and its attempts to be a player in the Washington wine industry.

But it was Ellie who stayed with her: the questioning at police headquarters, the fabricated surprise at her and Bud appearing at her home, the sad realization of secrets held close. Kally decided never again to compare herself to someone she thought had more: more beauty, more money, more house.

She bounced the cork on her desk, catching it in midair. Ellie, by her own admission, thought she was still with Kirk. But Kirk had moved on. Manning, Kally surmised, was in a lot of like with Ellie, the most beautiful woman he would never have. And he must have known that Ellie was seeing Kirk and then saw how Kirk treated her.

Janie said Kirk didn't like Manning.

Maybe Manning didn't like Kirk.

Kally flicked the wine cork up in the air. It flew sideways, hit a chair, and landed on the floor.

She left it where it lay.

Manning, for revenge, could put a big hurt on Kirk by giving away his winemaking techniques and keeping Ellie in his orbit at the same time. So Manning gives Ellie information. Then Ellie starts seeing an RMP guy. Maybe Manning knew this, maybe he didn't. RMP gains by having coveted winemaking tips provided by Ellie. Ellie gets a promotion. And then Kirk buys property out from under RMP.

Ellie, conveniently or not, is involved with all of these people. And while they all had reason to see Kirk gone...

Ellie isn't going to kill the man she loves when she's having help undermining him instead. Manning is a weenie, too cerebral to kill. And RMP has too much at stake in its battle to outdo Chateau Ste. Michelle.

So what was going on?

She folded her arms. There was one question she still couldn't answer: If Ellie was the woman at Kirk's winery Saturday morning, the one Storey heard talking to Manning...*why was she there?*

*Put it together, Kally.*

She looked up at the clock as it ticked past eleven a.m. The rain increased, painting the windows with a solid spray of water. The copier near Myrna's desk started up.

And then it came to her...

Her reaction immediate...

A sudden inhalation of air...

Her hand to her chest...

"*Oh my God!*"

She stood up suddenly, her thoughts racing. And ran to Bud's office.

She wasn't there.

She hurried to Myrna, who was just finishing a call.

"Where's Bud?" Kally demanded.

"She just left," Myrna said, pointing behind her.

Kally ran down the hallway. She didn't see her. She looked through the glass doors leading to the parking lot.

Bud was there, walking to her car.

Kally ran outside in the rain.

"*Bud!*"

She stopped.

Kally came up to her, the words tumbling out. "Did you look at the calls, the numbers, on Kirk's phone?"

"Yes. I don't have anything yet."

"Were there voicemails?"

"No. Just numbers."

"Did you call any of them?"

"Yes. All of them. I left messages to call back."

"Did you get calls back?"

"No."

"Did you call the phone company?"

"No. I don't have the warrant yet."

"Where's the phone?"

"In the evidence room."

Kally ran back inside. She hurried to the room and tried the door. Locked.

She ran to Dale's office, opened a drawer, grabbed a key, and ran back to the room. She unlocked the door and went inside. Kally found the evidence box for the case, signed for it, and took it to a table. Opening the lid, she rummaged around for the phone.

Finding it, she took it out of its plastic bag. And turned it on. It was still charged.

Kally scrolled through the calls:

*Kendall…*

Scroll, scroll…

*Kendall…*

*Kendall…*

*Manning...*

*An unknown phone number...*

She found a piece of paper and a pen and wrote the number down. Then continued.

*Janie...*

*Chicago...*

*RMP —the company or Ellie? —*

*Kendall...*

*RMP...*

*RMP...*

*An unknown phone number...*

She wrote this number down and kept going.

*Kendall...*

*Kendall...*

*Kendall...*

*Maybe he did love her,* she thought.

*Another phone number...*

Kally stopped. There was something about this number.

Slowly, she set the phone down, trying to make the connection.

Then she reached into her pocket and took out a business card. One she had picked up yesterday. She set it alongside the phone.

The numbers matched.

For James Alan Fishback, attorney at law.

Kally looked at the date of the call.

It was the night of Kirk's death.

91

She met Riggs in front of the Fishback residence in Bellevue. Riggs had been skeptical, but then he'd gradually come around to her line of thinking when she described her reasoning.

"Didn't I tell you domestic disputes are messy?" he said.

Kally knocked on the door again.

No answer.

"Did his office say he was leaving town?" he asked.

"They said he had a personal matter and wouldn't be in for several days."

"Well, he's definitely not here." Riggs stood back and looked up at the second story, staring at it for some time, seemingly oblivious to the steadily falling rain. Then he looked at her.

Kally gazed at the street, lost in thought.

They came to the same conclusion at the same time.

"He's fleeing!" Riggs said. "Come on!"

Riggs speed walked to his car with Kally hurrying behind.

"Get in! Let's talk this through."

Kally sat, slamming the passenger door. "Is he on a plane? Train?"

"No. Too many IDs."

"Auto?"

"No. And no rental. Again, IDs."

They stared at one another, trying to predict Fishback's reasoning.

"He's on a ferry!"Kally blurted out.

"Yes!" Riggs answered. "Call Myrna. Get a BOLO out."

Kally flicked the police radio off her belt.

Riggs grabbed her arm. "Tell me what you're going to say!"

"Be on the lookout for a middle-aged white male, short cropped hair, brownish gray—he may wear a ball cap—sunglasses..."

Riggs: "More! Physique!"

"Thin, athletic." The words tumbled out. "Like a runner, wiry..."

"Good."

"Probably dressed casually..."

"What's he carrying?"

She paused. "A suitcase. No, a duffle bag..."

"Why do you say that?"

"I don't know! Because he crewed! A duffle bag!"

"Okay!"

"And a laptop."

"Good." Then Riggs paused. She watched him, deep in thought.

"He'll go to Canada," he said, finally. "Through Victoria. Tell Myrna to get extra people on the Port Angeles ferry. I'll call Dale to call Canadian officials."

"You know this for sure?" Kally asked, hitting the number for Myrna at the call-in desk.

"I don't. It's a needle in a haystack. But we have to do something."

Riggs stopped again, holding his phone. He waited until she was done with her call to Myrna. "He'll take the Clipper, from Seattle. We'll take the Clipper! *Get the schedule!*"

"Right!"

Riggs called Dale, requesting state police in Victoria, BC, to meet all inbound ferries and the Victoria Clipper, the high-speed catamaran popular with tourists.

Riggs started his engine. "Get in your car and follow me!"

# 92

They got onto Interstate 405 and sped to the exit for Interstate 90 and the bridge over Lake Washington to Seattle. They stayed on I-90 for ten minutes then drove into Chinatown—the International District—on the southern edge of the city.

She assumed Riggs had called Seattle Police to let them know they were coming into their jurisdiction. If it were necessary, that is. But really, she had no idea what he was doing.

They parked at the curb in front of a Chinese restaurant. Riggs got out and, without waiting for her, walked in. She came up to him inside as he shook hands with a man she presumed was the owner. The man gave her a once-over.

*The uniform.*

"Bao, this is Ken's daughter, Kally. She's with me, with Woodinville Police."

Kally detected a recognition of sorts: a softening of features, a slight nod. Then Bao turned back to Riggs.

"We need a favor," Riggs began. "We have a suspect fleeing. We think he's going to Canada. He won't use his own passport."

Those brief words explained it all. They followed Bao to a hallway away from customers. Bao said something to Riggs and took out a card. Riggs took it, then shook Bao's hand.

"Come on," Riggs said, walking out.

Instead of getting into his car, he walked up an inclined sidewalk to another establishment and a door alongside it. Kally followed behind.

They entered and went up a flight of stairs. Riggs took the card out of his breast pocket and checked numbers above doors.

"What are we looking for?" she asked.

"This." He opened a door and they walked in. Riggs handed the card to a man at a desk.

The man hesitated, looking at Kally.

"She's good," Riggs said.

The man gestured that they come with him and they did, following him behind the desk, into a room, out a door, down a different flight of stairs, then another to the basement.

Kally took in the smell of the century-old building—rotting wood, damp cardboard, mold. The man reached up and pulled a chain and a lightbulb went on. In the back was a desk, a lamp, a file cabinet, and boxes everywhere. He turned on the desk lamp and sat down.

Riggs and Kally stood in front of him.

"Name?"

"James Alan Fishback," Riggs answered.

He took a ledger from the center drawer and opened it. And ran his finger down a list.

She glanced at Riggs, knowing what this was.

The man got up and went to a file cabinet. He opened the top drawer and thumbed through files, then retrieved one and opened it. He came back to the desk and addressed Riggs, turning the file and the passport photo of Fishback so they both could see it.

"He is Ryan Michael Palmer."

93

"You got it, right? You got the inside joke?" Kally asked. They stood on the sidewalk while she called Myrna with Fishback's new identity.

"What are you talking about?" Riggs asked.

"His initials! It's 'RMP'! He must have been working with them. And it's a big 'fuck you' to Woodinville police." She turned away to talk to Myrna. Then she addressed Riggs again.

"We have another problem."

"What."

"There is one Clipper to Victoria, and it left at 8 a.m. He's already gone."

"*Shit!*" Riggs slapped his suit coat away and shoved his hand onto his hip. "We'll never catch him." He walked toward the street.

Kally moved back against the building to let people pass. Then Riggs took out his phone and she joined him to hear the conversation.

"Dale," Riggs said. "See if Ryan Michael Palmer came through Victoria. It's Fishback's new identity." He listened as Dale explained something. "Okay."

He ended the call and looked at Kally. "If he entered the country, they'll have the name in their system." He paused. "James Alan Fishback, under his real name, did not enter Canada. They now have Ryan Michael Palmer. All we can do is wait."

Since they were in the International District, Riggs suggested getting something to eat at a nearby restaurant. They sat at a table fronting a window that looked out over the street. Kally stared at the passing cars, saying nothing. The rain had stopped but puddles remained. Cars hit them, sending up a spray of water and a rainbow of colors reflected in the afternoon sun.

Riggs passed her a plate with three dumplings from a cart that had stopped at their table. She took it and set it down in front of her. She wasn't sure about spending time again with Riggs at another meal. Oddly, he seemed relaxed and at ease.

Unlike herself.

And there were other things that hung over her.

"What?" Riggs asked.

She shook her head. "I don't know…I'm not very hungry. I'm too anxious about all this."

"If he goes through Victoria, he won't get far."

"How do you know that? He could go anywhere."

Riggs swallowed a bite of dumpling, then answered. "Canada, like the US, will ask what his plans are, where he's going, how long he intends to stay. That info will go into their system."

She didn't say anything as Riggs picked up another dumpling with chopsticks.

"Figure it this way," he said. "He'll get a place to stay and then he'll get dinner. He doesn't strike me as someone who settles for ferry food. And he's not gonna sleep on a bench. *He'll play to type.* Remember…I met him."

"Do you always size up people when you first meet them?" she asked.

Riggs didn't hesitate. "Of course. And we're one up on him…Mr. Fishback/Palmer."

She went on: "All those names that man had in his book…they were people who got illegal passports."

"Is that what's bothering you?"

"Why don't we arrest him?"

"He's not ours to arrest," Riggs answered. "That's for the feds. And Seattle." He paused. "Sometimes in our—your—line of work, you let the small fish go so you can reel in the whales."

"You're talking about drug dealers," she said

"And human traffickers and terrorists. And lawyers who kill winemakers." He looked at her and held her gaze. "I'm not suggesting illegal passports are a small thing. The feds will crack down on it. They always do. They'll clean it up."

"But it'll start again," she said.

He paused. "Yes."

"So that's why you talked to Bao. Because, today, you didn't know who or where."

He paused again. "Correct."

"Do you know why my father took his life?"

Riggs looked away suddenly. He set his chopsticks down and sat back. And stared out the window.

She regretted asking it. "You don't have to answer that."

"He felt trapped in his marriage," he said, finally.

This wasn't news to her.

Riggs went on. "He wanted a marriage that worked. He was willing to stay in one that didn't because of you and your brother. And, he had some bad cases in Seattle that he couldn't shake." She thought of Kirk lying over the bin. "They were young women, mostly. I know how that goes. I had some in San Fran."

Kally nodded, feeling uncomfortable now getting so personal with Riggs.

"They never left him," he added.

Riggs's phone rang. He looked at the name and answered, saying only: "Yeah." Then he nodded and put his phone down.

"They got him."

# 94

Kally, Riggs, and Dale waited while Fishback, with his attorney at his side, was booked into King County jail for investigation of homicide. He remained as silent during the proceedings as his wife had. Kally thought of them as the silent couple. Perhaps that was the problem in their marriage.

Fishback had been arrested without incident by Royal Canadian Mounted Police while having dinner at the upscale Empress Hotel in Victoria, British Columbia, where he was also staying. His dinner reservation was for a party of one, for Ryan Michael Palmer. Following appetizers, but before the main course, Fishback had been escorted from the restaurant, then taken into custody by Washington State Police and driven back to Seattle.

Ellie's attorney was also present during Fishback's proceedings. But Ellie wouldn't be released just yet. She'd been an accessory to a crime by not naming the person who had killed Kirk Remick.

And there was the minor issue of Ellie having a syringe of $CO_2$.

Not because it was a controlled substance, which it wasn't.

It was because she wasn't licensed to administer it.

Before heading home, Kally made one quick stop. She pulled into a subdivision in Woodinville and parked at the curb. After two knocks, Mark Manning opened his door.

"You're here." She didn't wait for a response. "I want you to know we arrested Ellie. And her husband."

Manning stared at her. She could have said anything, and flat-affect Manning wouldn't have shown one chink in his demeanor.

"I want to hear from you what you saw the night Kirk died," Kally added." But before you do that, let me tell you how *I* think the evening unfolded:

"First, you saw everything. You saw Ellie at the harvest party. You saw her standing with the RMP guys. You saw her leave after confronting Kirk behind the barrels. You knew Ellie and Kirk had had an affair. But you didn't like the way Kirk treated her because you would never hurt Ellie. Deep down, you really loved her."

Manning stood there motionless. Then he looked away.

Kally continued: "I know now that Ellie came back to Kirk's winery that night. We have her voice on the phone's recording."

*We haven't yet identified the voice. But it helps my story to say so.*

"But Ellie didn't come back to see Kirk. And it wasn't to see you. It was to stop her husband who had found out about her affair, taken her syringe of $CO_2$ and killed him.

"And it was a full syringe. Too much $CO_2$ for the body to handle. Kirk suffered. It was painful."

She let that sink in. And kept going.

"Ellie was the woman who came to see you Saturday morning because she wanted one more favor from you beyond all those wine tips you so freely offered. She asked you not to name the person who killed Kirk, didn't she."

Finally, Manning met her gaze. "I have to live with this for the rest of my life."

She let him hang there for a moment. Then she asked one more question: "Why did you lie to me about the beer bottle?"

He looked surprised. "What do you mean?"

"You know what I mean. The bottle I found in the trash at Kirk's belonged to you. It has your DNA on it."

He shook his head, then shrugged.

Kally knew the beer bottle was incidental to the case. But she wanted to say something about it. Most people don't like being caught in a lie.

She turned and walked away. She didn't need to hear anything from him, confident as she was in how she had pieced everything together. And knowing Manning as she did, he really would live with Kirk's death for the rest of his life, beating himself up about it every day.

Forever.

# 95

The two met the next morning in Dale's office to hash through the case. Dale had come around the front of his desk and was half sitting on the edge of it. Riggs sat in a chair, one leg stretched out in front of him. Kally leaned against the door, arms folded. She glanced at Dale's white board and the words "women, winemakers, land" still on it, most of the whiteboards in the office used for her one case.

"Congratulations, both of you," Dale said. "And Kally? Good job! Your first homicide case."

"Except that I still had questions this morning," she said, looking at Riggs. "I went back to the recording from the night of Kirk's death. We thought Kirk said the words: 'What are you doing here?' to a person who entered his winery. But it wasn't Kirk. It was one of the RMP guys who we now know was addressing Fishback. So that tells me that Fishback *was* working with RMP."

"That makes sense," Riggs said. "Do you know what kind of law he practices?"

Kally shook her head.

"Land use," Riggs replied.

*Of course.* Now it was coming together. "So Ellie must have hooked him up with the RMP attorneys," she said, wondering if Fishback knew of Ellie's alleged dalliance with the company's Richard Furlong. She guessed not.

"Or Jacobsen hooked them up," Riggs added, "since Fishback was new to his firm. It makes me think Jacobsen is getting into land-use law with all the growth in Bellevue."

"Interesting you bring up that name." Dale reached for a folded newspaper on his desk. He handed it to Riggs, who opened it, read something, and passed it to Kally.

On the front page of the *Woodinville Times* was a photo of Jacobsen—no hand bandaged—crouched down near a young girl identified as his granddaughter. The girl smiled broadly and held a blue ribbon for best-decorated bicycle in the Woodinville fall parade.

Riggs sat forward, arms on thighs. "So was Jacobsen involved with RMP?"

"I thought about that, too," Kally answered, remembering Kirk's funeral and seeing the Bellevue attorney standing in the parking lot with Ellie and two men. "But I don't know. He *is* a wine guy. And wine guys like to be close to the action." She thought for a moment. "I think Jacobsen knew the RMP attorneys. And maybe it was just the attorney connection."

"So…Fishback gets rid of the winemaker for being with his wife and for buying the land," Dale said.

"Double motive," Kally said.

"You only need one to convict," Riggs said. Then: "What about that female voice on the recording?"

"The only answer I have is that it was Ellie Fishback," Kally answered. "She went back to the winery that night to stop her husband from killing Kirk, because he had found out about their affair. She failed, of course, and watched Kirk die, which must have been awful."

"Hmm," Riggs said.

"And someone else watched, too," Kally added. "Mark Manning. The next morning, Ellie went to the winery again to ask Manning not to say anything about the person who killed Kirk. Manning must have thought that, with Kirk out of the way, he stood a chance with Ellie. Truthfully…I don't know what he thought.

"But there's one more thing," Kally said. "Ellie knew enough about winemaking to know that $CO_2$ would be found as the cause of death. But she didn't expect us to dig deeper into the *method*."

A silence enveloped them, everyone lost in their own thoughts. It was Dale who spoke next.

"What will happen to the land?"

Kally thought of it instantly. *Janie!* "It'll pass to his heirs."

"He's divorced, though," Riggs said.

"But he never changed the paperwork."

"Oh!" Dale exclaimed and shook his head.

"So his ex-wife and daughter are the owners." She had a good feeling about that. Janie had gotten the last word. "She could sell the land. And sell to RMP for double the price. Then RMP will have those bragging rights that seem so important to them."

"How so?" Dale asked.

"RMP will be one acre bigger than Chateau Ste. Michelle, on ever-important Red Mountain," Kally explained. "But RMP won't necessarily be better."

She was about to bring up something else when Bud stuck her head in, interrupting them. "Do you have a minute?"

"You're working?" Kally asked, ignoring the question. "Your wedding's soon."

"I know. I'm leaving. Really, you two have to come out here."

Sensing the urgency, Kally walked into the main sitting area with Riggs and saw Mrs. Hatch, who started in without any formal hello.

"Mr. Hatch and I have come to an understanding. I am moving back to Virginia and he is taking the house. The arson people told us the fire was caused by spontaneous combustion from fertilizer bags stored in a corner of the barn."

"Oh yes," Riggs said. He glanced at Kally.

"So there will be no filing of a complaint, then?" Kally asked.

"No complaint. We're done with complaints," Mrs. Hatch answered.

But Kally couldn't let it go. "Your husband doesn't seem like the type who would let a pile of bags sit in his barn, or tolerate that from a worker."

Mrs. Hatch hesitated before answering. "We all got what we wanted." And: "Sage is coming with me."

"So that's that," Kally said, at a loss for a more appropriate response.

"It is," Mrs. Hatch answered. As she was leaving, Mrs. Hatch addressed Kally and Riggs one last time. "I will continue to think highly of the Woodinville Police Department."

"So...you believe him?" Kally asked Riggs, who stood in her office as she continued with paperwork on the Hatch and Remick cases.

"Who?"

"Hatch. The man."

Riggs stirred his coffee, seemingly deep in thought. "The person who really knew him was your father." He glanced at her then looked away. "He could have given us some insight here. We'll never know, really."

But Kally kept going. "Was Hatch *not* at the house? The wife was so convincing."

"Liars lie well," Riggs answered. "The good thing is we can take it off our radar."

He put his coffee on the edge of her desk and picked up the eraser near her whiteboard and swiped at the names still on the board. Then he stopped, eraser in midair.

"Is this okay?" he asked, still facing the board.

Kally smiled a smile he wouldn't see. "Yeah. Go ahead." She returned to her paperwork, scribbling notes from the most recent Hatch conversation. But a question she hadn't voiced in Dale's office came back to her.

She put her pen down. "There's something else I can't figure out. Why would someone take the fall for another person committing murder?"

"You're talking about your nonfriend..."

"Yes, Ellie."

"Guilt," he answered. "The girl wanted to protect her husband."

"Why?" she asked.

"Well, she harmed him in a big way. I guess it was an unspoken understanding," Riggs added.

"Yeah, no kidding." She paused. "Have you ever seen this before?"

Riggs stopped for a moment. "No. Usually it's the other way around: pinning a murder on someone."

"But Ellie's husband was going to *let* her take the blame," Kally added. "See…that's what I don't get."

"He was done with her," Riggs added.

She shook her head. "What an odd couple."

Riggs finished erasing the names and picked up his coffee. And stirred it. And looked around her office. She had a feeling something was up.

"Now that we're done here," he began, "I need your help with something."

"Okay."

"Will you come to my apartment?"

Kally couldn't mask her surprise. "Sure."

It was the first thing she saw when she entered Riggs's two-bedroom apartment on a quiet street in Bellevue. Kally noticed it because it dominated the space.

And it took her breath away.

It was a painting above the couch of a path in the forest, the Redwoods she presumed, because the trees were so large. And so lifelike.

"This is really something..." she said, coming up to it. She leaned in to examine it. "The detail..."

"Thanks."

Kally turned to him. "*You* did this?"

"I did. It's what I do when I'm not trying to find grape killers."

"You're a painter!"

"Yes." Riggs put his keys on the dining room table and walked into the kitchen. "It helps me get away from things. "

Kally turned back to the painting. The trees were illuminated by rays of sunlight, which turned the brown bark copper. There were no people in the painting. Yet it was warm somehow. And soothing.

She heard him opening a bottle.

"Can I get you a beer?" he asked from the kitchen.

"Um...yes."

Riggs walked back into the room and handed one to her. He looked at the painting while he described his hobby.

"I started taking classes in San Francisco after an especially difficult case. After my divorce...my first divorce...the class went to the Redwoods to paint. And I kept going there."

"Why don't you bring some of these to work?" Kally asked, taking in other paintings surrounding them.

Riggs paused for a moment. "Because it's my private world. Like your wine."

"Okay. I get that."

Kally also noticed that Riggs's apartment was spotless, tidied up. Like the man himself.

She walked around to view the smaller paintings. They were of San Francisco street scenes: cars and buildings, mostly. All of them had that light. But none of them had any people.

"You don't have any people in your paintings."

"People are hard to do," Riggs answered. "I find that I want to paint people in an abstract manner, which doesn't go well with representational art."

"I see." But Kally didn't think he had invited her up to see his—

"So…you know I'm a beer guy," Riggs said, starting in.

"Yeah…"

"I need your help. With wine."

"Oh?"

"Come over here. And sit down."

He directed her to the dining room table, then walked back into the kitchen. Kally watched him through an opening between the two rooms as he took wine bottles out of a rack and brought them to the table.

There were four bottles in all. And a box of crackers tucked under one arm. Then he got two glasses, big Riedel glasses for red wine.

That surprised her—the wineglasses—him being a beer guy.

"I want you to walk me through wine." He sat down and folded his hands. "A woman I'm…" He hesitated.

Kally waited. "Seeing?"

"Seeing!" He nodded. "She likes wine. Will you give me some tips?"

"Sure." Kally turned each bottle to look at the label. "You've got some nice ones here."

"The guy at Pete's recommended these," Riggs said.

She knew that, indeed, Pete's, a well-known Bellevue wine store, would steer him in the right direction.

"I need to know everything…how to taste, sniff, talk…by Saturday," Riggs said.

Kally's eyebrows went up.

"For Bud's wedding."

"Oh! Okay. Well, let's get started."

They moved their half-finished beers to the side.

Riggs handed her a cork screw.

Kally perused the four bottles again: a French 2017 Clos des Papes, a Châteauneuf-du-Pape; a Kirk Remick—*imagine that!*—2017 Syrah called The Traveler; a Long Shadows 2017 Cabernet Sauvignon called Feather; and a Mark Ryan 2017 Merlot-dominate blend called Long Haul, the last three wines from Woodinville producers.

She grabbed the southern Rhône Clos des Papes, pushed her chair back, and placed the wine between her legs. After several deft motions with the corkscrew, she had the foil and the cork removed.

"You've done this before," Riggs said.

"Many times." Then she explained to Riggs why she had picked the French wine.

"We'll start with this because it's softer than the other three. That doesn't mean this wine, which is a blend of Grenache, Syrah, and Mourvedre, is light. Some can be quite hefty."

"Okay," Riggs answered.

"Normally, we would decant these. But for now, we'll just pour from the bottle." Then she stopped. "The most important thing about wine is what *you* like. Not what someone tells you to like."

"No wine snobbery, then," Riggs said.

"Exactly."

She picked up a glass, looked at it for dust, smelled it for off aromas, then poured a two-ounce taste. She pushed the glass toward Riggs, then poured herself some.

"The first thing you want to do is look at the wine."

"It's red," Riggs said.

Kally smiled. "Yes. What you don't want is orange or brown."

"Next we'll swirl. This is where you'll look like an insider." She put two fingers on either side of the stem on the base of the glass. "You do this," Kally instructed.

Riggs did as he was told.

"Now, using a bit of pressure with your fingers, move the glass in a circle counterclockwise. The wine will swirl itself."

She watched as Riggs's swirled his wine, the liquid barely moving.

"You can go a little faster. Some people swirl vigorously," Kally added. "You don't have to do that. Do just enough to get the aromas going. But not with a full glass. You'll spray everyone at the table."

Kally picked up her glass. "Now, pick up the glass and sniff. What aromas do you recognize?"

"Red wine," Riggs answered.

"Yes, but do you smell any spices, like mint or oregano, or fruits like plums, cherries, or strawberries? Do you get any oak? Oak can impart vanilla, butter, or, if its darker, burnt toast."

"Well now that you mention it…I do smell a little wood."

"Okay, good. Now put the glass down, swirl again, sniff again, then take a small taste. Hold the wine in your mouth. See what flavors you get. Try to pick up two when you sniff and two when you taste. They can be the same."

She watched Riggs do as he was told. He held the taste in his mouth, a blank look on his face.

"Swallow," Kally said. "You'll get some back-end tastes after the wine is gone."

Riggs nodded.

"Anything?" she asked.

He shook his head. He swallowed again. "Tell me what you…*get*."

Kally put one arm over the back of her chair and swirled her wine, concentrating. She picked up the glass and sniffed with one nostril, repeating the steps she'd told Riggs. Then she tasted the wine, moving it around in her mouth as Riggs watched. Then she swallowed.

"Okay," she began. "On the nose—that's what wine writers say after sniffing—I detect dark plum and light wood. You were right about the wood…"

Riggs sat back, pleased.

"The wood comes to the front because the wine isn't fully integrated yet. That's because it's relatively young. On the aftertaste—the back end—I detect slight evergreen, pine. On the full taste, I get dark fruit, more evergreen, and some sage."

"Wow! You picked up all that?"

"You will, too. In time. Now, let's try Mr. Remick's Syrah."

Kally opened the bottle with the same quick motions she'd used previously. But before pouring, she revisited another topic.

"Can I ask you one more question about the Hatch case?"

"We're done with it," Riggs answered. "You have to learn to let them go."

"Just one."

Riggs waited.

"Do you think he started the fire?" Kally asked.

"I think he had cause to see it happen."

"So that means you think he did it."

Riggs paused for a long time. "Yes. I think he did it. He's used to getting his way."

Kally shook her head. "He was so believable. Like the Mrs."

"You'll learn not to take things at face value."

"Now, let me ask you a question," Riggs said.

"Okay," she said.

"Why aren't you with someone?"

It was a surprisingly personal question from a man who valued his privacy.

"Well, I...was. He...decided he wanted to be with someone else."

"Oh. There's no one else then?"

This time Kally hesitated. "Yes. But he's in France."

"France!"

She nodded. "After I finished at the academy, I went to France for two weeks, by myself. To visit the Rhône." She touched the bottle of French wine, her fingernails clicking on the glass. "And I met somebody. Actually, I met him in Paris."

Riggs waited, his eyes boring into her.

"But we have separate lives." She was letting her guard down about Guillaume. Then she recovered, somewhat.

"He comes from a large wine family in the southern Rhône. It's beautiful there. They have a château."

"Any chance you'll move there?" Riggs asked.

She shook her head. "No."

"Relationships are difficult," Riggs said.

"Yes. They are," she said.

Somehow this wasn't the conversation she thought she would ever have with Mr. Riggs.

She poured two tastes of the Syrah and they moved on.

This wine was darker in color than the French wine and had a bluish tinge in the light, typical of Syrah. She already knew what this wine would taste like and what qualities it would express. She wanted to see if Riggs could identify them.

They repeated their swirls and sniffs, then each took a taste.

"Tell me what you think about this wine," Kally inquired, folding her arms on the table.

"Um…it's good. This is our dead guy's wine."

"It is, yes."

Riggs didn't say anything else, and she could see that he was struggling. It wasn't lost on her that Riggs was the student now and she the instructor.

"I can tell there's a difference," he began, "but I don't know how to say it."

"Do you think this wine is bigger? Heavier than the previous one?" Kally asked.

"Yes! Heavier in taste."

"Good!" she exclaimed. "Now, what else. What aromas?"

"I smell…grapes. Dark grapes."

"All right. What do you get on the palate?"

He took another taste.

"Any…spices, grasses, flowers?" Kally asked.

He stared at her over the rim of his glass.

Kally continued. "Anything earthy? Like…dirt, forest floor?"

It happened so quickly Riggs couldn't have hidden his response if he'd wanted to. She herself had never experienced an "aha" moment during a sensory evaluation. But seeing the expression on Riggs's face, she knew he had gotten it.

Profoundly.

He sniffed the glass again. "It's a path in the Redwoods! I don't believe it!"

Kally smiled. "Great! You're on your way."

"To where?"

"Wine appreciation!"

They tasted through the remaining wines, and Kally noticed that Riggs seemed to be getting more comfortable voicing the attributes he was sniffing and tasting.

She decided then and there that this student would get an A in sensory eval.

With the Kirk Remick case solved and the Hatches moving on, clarity came back into Kally's life.

She got up hours before the wedding and spent time cleaning her apartment, ridding herself of Zack things she still had lying around: UW sweatshirts, tee shirts, sweatpants.

Moving to the kitchen, she opened the refrigerator and took out microbrews only Zack liked. This being the Northwest, she emptied the bottles, rinsed them responsibly, and recycled them.

Now, sitting in her living room with a last cup of coffee, she deleted every reference to Zack on her phone, a process that took fifteen seconds. Then she sat there.

*He's gone.*

She had been comfortable with him. Yet she couldn't deny his assertion about Guillaume.

Kally took a long drink of tepid coffee and thought again about the man she'd left behind in France. Speaking about him with Riggs, Guillaume was very much on her mind.

Yes, we had a great time. It was, in fact, idyllic. If one had said to oneself, *I am going to France to find a wine man,* then what she experienced with Guillaume would be a perfect one hundred.

But it was not what she had sought. She had gone to get away, the death of her father still hanging over her. And she wanted to see the vineyards of France. The fact that she'd met someone had complicated things. *Everything I have is here,* she reminded herself, *and everything here is working: my work, my wine, my life.*

*But I don't have Guillaume. And I won't have him if I stay here. Yet I must stay here.*

*Right?*

Kally pulled into the parking lot at DeLille Cellars where Bud and A-Rod were to be married. DeLille, sitting on rolling hills just south of the Woodinville wine tasting rooms, had a French château-like appearance. And was the perfect setting for a wedding.

Plus, the weather was holding on this late fall day, the sky a beautiful blue.

Kally parked, got out, and walked toward the two-story building. She didn't remember the last time she'd been here, but a former student in her wine production class had become assistant winemaker at this venerable place. Both DeLille and Chateau Ste. Michelle had put Washington State on the international wine map years ago. She remembered drinking a DeLille 2004 Chaleur Estate red and thinking she had gone to heaven.

She walked up the stone steps to the patio. White chairs had been set up on the lawn, and she chose one near the back. Up front, Bud's sisters tied pink flower arrangements to an arbor. To the right, caterers snapped table cloths across bare table tops where dinner would be served under a tent. Another rolled a cart of wineglasses to a bar, the glasses clinking on the stone walkway. Behind her, band members tuned guitars and the keyboardist played the first four chords of "Here Comes the Bride."

She looked at her watch. She was twenty minutes early. Thoughts drifted back to Kirk and his death.

Why had Ellie kept the murder weapon? Who did that? Was it to frame her husband eventually? Did he even know it was in the house?

Wait a minute. *He's* the one who used it. So *he's* the one who brought it back home. She must not have known it was there.

Or maybe she did and left it there.

She shook her head.

*You never have all the answers.*

Kally thought about the love letter she'd found, a document of passion. Ellie was not in love with her husband. Maybe it was easier for

Ellie to have Woodinville Police find the syringe than to say, *He did it.*
Yet Ellie was willing to take the fall for a murder she didn't commit.

Perhaps with the love of her life gone, nothing else mattered.

More early birds drifted in and took seats. Dale and his wife, and
Riggs and a woman she didn't know, entered and sat close to the front.
Kally leaned forward to scope out the woman sitting next to Riggs,
wondering what she was like and how she'd ever picked a man like
Riggs to be with.

*You have no idea what she's like!* She appears to be fine. Normal, even.
And she probably liked his quirks. If he were allowing them to be known.

Then she thought about her own relationship with Riggs and how it
had evolved. Riggs had made every bit of his displeasure known about
working with a rookie. Now that seemed like a distant memory. With
her case solved, would she work with him again? She wouldn't mind
that. There was more to know about feisty Mr. Riggs.

A figure—actually two figures—stopped by her chair and Kally
looked up: her friend Chris and attorney Sam.

Sam, she noted, had switched eyeglasses again, opting for a horn-
rimmed pair that made her look more lawyerly. *She should have stuck
with the blue ones.*

"Saving seats?" Chris asked.

"Just for you," Kally replied, moving sideways so they could
maneuver in.

"Isn't this a beautiful place?" Chris asked, settling in. "I always bring
my high-end clients here. When they taste from the barrel, they feel an
obligation to buy."

"I'll remember that."

Bud's sisters finished at the front and disappeared. More people filed
in. The band started up with light music she didn't recognize.

How different this different this day could have been if A-Rod
hadn't pulled through.

The ceremony was beautiful. A-Rod walked in using a cane, and
everyone cheered. At the front, he turned and smiled and the guests
started clapping. Truly, the day would be about both of them, not just
the bride.

After the ceremony and before dinner, Kally, Chris, and Sam sat at a table on the patio sipping a DeLille Chaleur Estate white, a blend in perfect unison of Sauvignon Blanc and Sémillion. In the distance, Kally saw a short figure with quick steps walking toward them: Mindy with *Wine Hound.*

"Hey!" Mindy exclaimed, coming up to the group and taking the last seat at their table. Kally made introductions, then Mindy turned back to Kally.

"Good work, you. But a surprise, no?"

"You're referring to Kirk."

"Of course! The biggest wine story of the year. We know he fooled around. But her? And then you throw in the husband? You only read this in novels!"

Kally nodded. "Yeah. I know."

The previous day, Dale had entered Kally's office, closed the door, and grilled her for an hour about the case, especially how the accused had obtained a syringe.

Kally had answered: "That's easy. Ellie worked her ways on a cute young beautician's assistant. She asked for a syringe to take home. Because busy Ellie had no time for spa appointments. And I'm sure she paid him for that convenience, in whatever manner he asked for."

Actually, she hadn't said that last thing to her boss.

Dale then addressed the press, thanking both Kally and Riggs for their work. All the Seattle news stations, trade journals, and *Wine Hound* picked up the story, and the *Seattle Times* ran photos of Kirk and Ellie on the front page.

She had wondered at the time what Janie thought about that, seeing those two linked together.

But titillation sells.

"Woodinville won't be the same without him," Mindy added. "Who will take his place?"

"I don't know," Kally answered.

Sarah "Somm" and her partner, Judith, came up to their group, and a server appeared behind them with more wine.

"That was a nice ceremony. And nice to see you, Mindy," Sarah said, introducing Judith to her. Then she addressed Kally. "Have you thought again about rebranding your wine...putting your name on the label?"

"I have. But that's too formal for me," Kally answered.

"You know...formal sells," Sarah countered, taking a proffered glass and immediately sniffing the wine. "Formal means you can charge more."

Coming from Sarah, that pronouncement held weight. Of course she was right. And serving her wine at Sarah's restaurant could really boost sales.

"Yeah, but it's not who I am," Kally answered, echoing Kirk's very words to her.

As a bridesmaid, Sarah was sitting at the head table, so her partner, Judith, joined Kally and her group at dinner. She saw Riggs and his date sitting with Dale and his wife. Riggs had a glass of wine in front of him and he swirled it slightly, and then took a sniff.

He turned and smiled at her. And Kally couldn't refrain from smiling back.

After dinner, dancing began. People walked to the front to dance with Bud, who had never looked more stunning, if that were possible. Even Sarah asked Bud to dance.

Kally looked around at guests sitting at tables and huddled in twos and fours at the wine bar. It was a beautiful fall night. Bud and A-Rod were radiant. And she herself was among friends. It didn't even bother her that she was alone.

Before leaving, she hugged the bride and groom and wished them all good things newly married couples are wished, adding that she would see them when they returned to work, with A-Rod assuming desk duty

99

Kally pulled in to the back of her winery. She got out and unlocked the door. Still in her black dress and heels, and feeling a bit tipsy, she stepped inside and turned on a light, which illuminated a row of tanks along one wall. She walked past them, touching them lightly, feeling the cold on her fingertips, which was appropriately thirty-eight degrees for the whites.

In a corner, where Seth had neatly arranged them, a stack of half-ton bins waited for next year's harvest. Empty cases on palettes waited for bottling.

"Soon enough," she said to the bottles.

She set her purse and keys on her table, aware of how quiet it was. Through these thin walls one often heard the laughter and chatter of a neighbor's release party as well as the music. Tonight she heard only a *drip, drip, drip* in her kitchen. Walking in, she repositioned the faucet to the other side of the sink, then grabbed a glass and went back to one of the tanks. She allowed herself a big pour of white wine, then stood there swirling it gently.

She sniffed.

This was her Pinot Gris. She sniffed again, picking up lemon notes, the temperature preventing other flavors from emerging. She tasted it, feeling the cold on her teeth. It would sit at this temperature until two days before bottling, the low temp a barrier to bacterial contamination.

Kally went to her table across from the whiteboard and sat down. Feeling chilled, she reached for her sweatshirt and put it on, zipping it up over her dress. She swirled the wine again, noting its clarity, its brilliance.

She took a big sip. And nodded.

She liked this wine. She liked it a lot. And she thought other people would, too.

*She* could serve this wine at a wedding, with guests clamoring for more.

*She* just needed to ensure it had the right exposure in the marketplace, something that really made it pop. How to do that?

Sarah's question about rebranding came back to her. Maybe Sarah was right. She needed to think bigger, globally.

"*Globally,*" she said out loud, the syllables rattling around in her mouth, silenced only by another sip.

Why not follow Sarah's advice? Now was the time.

But she couldn't do it the way Sarah wanted.

She thought about how Kirk had branded his wines and how well they sold. What was it he had told her?

*Be bold!*

"Yeah! He's right!"

*I can have what he had: the limos, the sports stars, the high-end wine club, a designated charity.*

*I just have to* brand *properly.*

Kally kicked off her heels and stepped into her L.L. Bean boots. She finished her wine and went to get another. Standing in front of the Pinot Gris tank, she read the lettering again on the blue painter's tape: *Pinot Gris.*

She turned on the sample tap and gave herself a small pour.

"What would Kirk call this?"

She held the wine up to the light, then drained her glass without thinking about sensory elements.

"This is crazy good!"

A song came to mind, and Kally swayed back and forth to it. She sashayed back to her table and picked up a magic marker as the Patsy Cline song gained momentum in her head. Then, she slow-danced back to the tank. She drew a jagged line through Pinot Gris and wrote *CRAZY.* And drew cowboy boots below it, singing out loud now:

*"Crazy for trying and crazy for crying..."*

"In honor of you, Mom!"

She moved to the tank holding her Grenache/Syrah blend. She thought of her father. He'd be proud of her and all that she'd aspired to and done. And not just because she was in his line of work.

How could she honor him?

She poured herself some of this wine and held up the glass. "You are so *purple!*"

Another song came to mind. She crossed out "GS" and wrote the name of his favorite song: *PURPLE HAZE*. She pictured the label: a white guitar broken in half on a dark purple background...

And clouds above the guitar...

"'*Scuse me while I kiss the sky...*"

Onto the next tank. This one held her white blend of Pinot Gris and Riesling.

Very tasty. Very summery.

She poured a big glass of this wine and imagined sipping it in an outdoor café. Then suddenly, she was in that outdoor café. She had sunglasses on. She saw Nicole Kidman walk by. Then Cate Blanchett. Then more Australians.

"Wait! In Woodinville?"

*No!*

Where was she?

She was in LA, Hollywood.

Doing *what*?

Star gazing!

"*Wayfarers on, baby...*"

She crossed out *PG/R* and wrote *STAR GAZING*. She'd have sunglasses on the label!

Kally moved on to the barrels holding Malbec.

"And what to call *you*! *Globally!*" She liked the feel of the word in her mouth.

Kally thought of a song she'd heard growing up, her mother playing it over and over while vacuuming: ground control something.

That's it. She'd call it ground control. With a space helmet reflecting grape vines on the label. Kally stopped. There had to be something else.

She added the words *Rezerve Malbec*.

"*You've really made the grade...*"

She did not take a sip of this wine. Too difficult to manage the wine thief; plus, Storey still had her wine thief.

Kally moved to another tank, her rosé saigneed from Grenache and Syrah. Another song came to mind. This one reflected how she approached life. And work. And of course, wine.

"Gypsy."

She wrote *GYPZY* on the front. She'd have a microphone in rainbow colors on the label...

*"You see your Gypsy..."*

Kally danced to the song, glass in hand.

She danced past the tanks and the newly branded wines, ready to burst forth into bottles. She danced past the Malbec and tapped the barrels. She realized she was happy. She had a direction.

"Thank you, Kirk!"

But something interrupted her. Her back door opened. Then closed.

A figure walked toward her. She didn't recognize who it was.

He came closer, out of the shadows.

It was Guillaume.

Guillaume drove them home. If they had discussed anything, Kally didn't remember it, knowing, later, that she had been too incapacitated to think clearly. But she did remember how happy she had been sitting next to him, as if this—him driving them home—were something they did in the course of their everyday lives.

They entered her condo and Guillaume closed the door. Then he pinned her against the wall and kissed her, a long, deep kiss that brought her back to France.

She felt heady, delirious for him. And from the wine she'd consumed.

He pulled back suddenly. "You called me."

`She was surprised at that. "I didn't." Kally smiled. "But here you are!" She kissed him.

"It was a week ago," he said, pulling back again.

She knew for certain that she hadn't called him. Then she smiled. "You are making this *up!*"

Guillaume took her by the hand and led her to the couch. She still had on her sweatshirt and boots. They sat, and he put his arm around her shoulders. She laid her head back and stared at him.

"You never came back," he said.

"No. Not…yet."

"Did France mean anything to you? Did I?"

That knocked some clarity into her. Did he really doubt it? "Yes. It all meant something. More than you know."

"I want you to come back with me," he said.

Kally felt dizzy from the angle of her head. And she was tired. Even though Guillaume sat right next to her, she was suddenly very tired.

"Can we talk about this in the morning?"

Guillaume stood in the doorway of her bedroom, a towel around his waist, his dark hair wet from the shower. He walked toward her, a coffee cup in each hand, and sat on the edge of the bed, the towel slipping away.

Kally opened her eyes, everything a blur. But the sight of him woke her fully.

"You *are* here," she said, smiling, and sitting up carefully, as much as her overindulged state would allow. She felt a pounding in her head.

He handed her a cup, then rearranged the towel over his lap. "You celebrated yesterday."

"I did." She sipped her coffee, letting the steam warm her cheeks as she took in the exquisite body in front of her. "At a friend's wedding. You could have come with me."

"Hmm." He looked away, then back.

An awkward space arose between them. She hadn't been with him since that night in Provence. Kally wondered if he had been with anyone else. Of course he was handsome and women would make advances. And he worked in a cherished field in France. So what had he been doing? Where had he been? And with whom?

"You have been busy," he said, breaking the silence.

Kally nodded. "And you?"

He shrugged. "Just wine. All the time."

She supposed that was true. "I was put on a case, recently, a death." She realized she hadn't talked about the case openly with anyone, other than bits and pieces with Mindy of *Wine Hound*. And she needed to explain to him why she hadn't returned to France.

"The man who died was a friend. A mentor. A winemaker. A well-known one."

She took another sip of coffee, aware of Guillaume's stare.

"I worked on it with someone...someone who wasn't happy working with me, a rookie."

"And so you fought?" Guillaume asked.

"Early on, yes. But now..." She thought for a moment. "Now I believe he respects me."

"As he should."

*Is Guillaume really this mature? I don't remember him like this in France. Why is this so awkward!*

The timer on the oven beeped. "Are you hungry?" he asked.

They sat in her dining room. Before serving the clafouti he'd made, Guillaume put on a white shirt and jeans, his choice of clothing not lost on her. Then he asked more about her case and how she solved it and what was next in her line of work. And then he asked her about her wine.

"Why don't you just make wine?" he inquired. "Why do you also work?"

"Because I don't have sales to support me."

"Why not?"

"There are a lot of wineries here," she explained.

"There are a lot in France."

"But you are established."

"But you are good!" He smiled.

Kally hesitated. *He doesn't know that. He's just saying that.*

"There is another reason why I work in my job: I'm paying off a fine. But I'm working on my brand. I'm going to keep my name but rename my wines. You'll see them!"

Kally was excited again thinking about it all. But Guillaume focused on something else.

"What kind of fine?" he asked.

"Um…I didn't tell you this in France. Several years ago, I had an artist friend do a label for me of a rock singer. Not an *actual* picture, just an *interpretation* of this person singing. And…well…he was recognized. By a law firm. In London.

Guillaume waited.

"The singer is Mick Jagger."

"Oh!" Guillaume laughed.

"So I was sued, asked to confiscate all the bottles, and change the label, which I couldn't do, of course, because I didn't know where they were. And so I'm paying a fine. A big one."

"How much?"

"$150,000."

Guillaume choked on his coffee. "Are you kidding?"

Kally shook her head. "Brand theft doesn't pay. So now you understand why I continue working. Until I get a foothold in the wine business."

Guillaume seemed deep in thought. "A lawsuit doesn't sound like something Mick Jagger would do. He lives in France, you know. He's nice to his neighbors."

"Yeah, well, it is what it is. And here we are."

Breakfast finished, Guillaume took his coffee to her living room and sat down crosslegged in front of a small wine rack.

"Let's see what you've got." He pulled out a bottle. It was a Château Tablet. He held it up.

"Good choice."

Kally joined him on the floor.

Guillaume put his family's wine back in the rack and pulled out another.

"What's this…Dead Horse…"

"That's a good one," Kally explained, "by Mark Ryan. A Washington wine."

"And this Dead Cheval…it sells?"

"Very well…but it's not about a horse really…it's about how long it takes to get grapes over the mountains. To the winery. The trip would kill a horse."

He stared at her, seemingly confused. He put the wine back and pulled out another. And looked at her.

"Gun Metal? Dead chevaux and guns? You Americans…you have no reverence for the grape…"

"Of *course* we do. This is what sells. Your label has to…to…draw the buyer in. We don't have centuries of winemaking and wine houses... châteaux...

"Well...build a château," he said, half kidding.

She laughed. "Silly! People here don't want châteaux . They want *warehouses*."

She wasn't sure he understood, gauging from the look on his face. "Guillaume, you walked into a wine business centuries old. I am creating one."

"At your warehouse."

"Yes."

"I want to see more of your warehouse."

They stood in front of the first tank. Kally drew samples of her Pinot Gris and handed Guillaume a glass.

"Tell me honestly…what do you think?"

Guillaume swirled the wine, sniffed, swirled, sniffed again, then took a taste. And moved it around in his mouth. Then he spat into the drain.

"Good! Citrusy. Alsace-like."

"Yes! I thought so, too."

"And this is the name?" Guillaume pointed to *Crazy* written on the blue painter's tape.

"Yes." Kally smiled. "For 'crazy good'."

He shook his head.

They moved to the Pinot Gris/Riesling tank and tasted the blend.

"What does this remind you of?" she asked. Guillaume went through his swirling and sniffing routine again.

She waited.

He tasted.

Guillaume held her gaze before answering. "Provence. Sunlight. Beautiful flowers. A beautiful woman. A café. No worries."

Kally nodded. "Good." She was aware that the barriers she had constructed to keep France and Guillaume out of her life were crumbling. Of course she wanted his opinion about her wine. But mostly, she realized, she wanted him.

"Come here and taste this." She gave him a sample of Gypzy, the rosé.

He tasted, then spit. And nodded. "This is good. I would say this is made from Rhône grapes."

"Right you are!"

She signaled him to follow her, to the closed door of her cold room. She hefted the door up in one motion and saw the look on Guillaume's face as he took in the barrels.

"Ah! Here we are." He followed her in.

Guillaume stood next to her holding two glasses as she drew samples from the barrel.

Standing with him now, she was reminded of their time together in his family's cave among the barrels, and what had transpired between them. Surely, he remembered.

"This is Syrah. For down the road," she explained.

She waited as he went through his routine again.

He took his time with this wine, holding it in his mouth. Finally, he swallowed rather than spit.

"I am surprised how good this is," he said.

"That is because of our vineyards. They do a wonderful job with reds."

"I think the winemaker had something to do with this," he countered.

Kally flushed, not sure he was being honest. She bent down and opened a box and took out her red blend.

Guillaume moved closer.

When she rose, she was hemmed in by barrels behind and Guillaume in front.

"What is that?" he asked.

"It's my red blend. I want you to try it."

He nodded. "Do you remember our time in the cave?"

Kally's heart beat rapidly. "I do."

He pulled her close. "And how long we stayed there?"

He kissed her, holding her captive, then said, *"Il n'y a personne d'autre pour moi. Personne ne prendra ta place."*

"I'll ask you what you just said later," she said, kissing him back. She fingered his shirt. "Take this off."

"You take it off."

# 104

Neither seemed to mind the temperature of the cold room, nor the tarp on the floor that served as the makeshift bed. But neither wanted to stay there for an extended period.

Guillaume walked out of the room ahead of Kally, a bottle of her red blend in his hand.

Kally followed, her hand on the rope to bring down the large door. But she sensed something inside and turned back to look. For an instant, she thought she saw an image near a corner barrel.

She did see an image.

It was Kirk. He was smiling at her. Then he disappeared.

Instead of showing Guillaume the rest of Woodinville and Seattle, they drove home and went back to bed, making love all afternoon. Then they fell asleep. It was dark when Kally asked if he was hungry.

Back in the living room, he leaned against the wine rack, and she leaned against him. They had finished a dinner of sausage, cheese, bread, and olives. And they had opened his family's wine, a Châteauneuf-du-Pape, and were comparing it to Kally's blend of Grenache and Syrah.

"I'm not leaving until I have an answer from you," Guillaume said. "I want you to come back to France with me. I don't want to be apart from you."

He pushed her gently to the floor and lay near her.

"Everything I have in France will be yours. You will be the *Grande Dame* of the château. You will be a winemaker with me. You can name our wine a dead *cheval*. Will you come with me?"

Kally froze. Barely twenty-four hours had passed since Guillaume had arrived.

Things were happening too quickly.

"I will give you an answer. But first I have things to do. I have to bottle. And have my release party. Will you help me?"

# 105

The next two weeks were a whirlwind. Kally caught up on the smaller cases she had let languish while she'd worked the Kirk Remick case. Guillaume, alone at home, painted the inside of her condo. One day, he came to work with her and she introduced him to her fellow police officers. Riggs was surprisingly polite, asking him about his family's wine business and mentioning that he had been instructed in the nuances of the industry by the woman at his side.

"I am sure she instructed you well," Guillaume said.

Guillaume worked weekends at the winery pouring wine and, in the process, helped sales immensely, explaining to interested young women the differences between French and American wine.

Then bottling commenced, with Seth organizing the volunteers for the day. Everyone pitched in: Guillaume cleaned empty tanks, helped on the bottling line, and stacked cases on pallets.

*He's earning his keep*, Kally thought, watching the activity. Never before had she had such high-priced labor for free.

At the end of the day, all of her wines were bottled and some of those very bottles lined the table outside where Kally fed the volunteers pizza, salad, and as much wine as they wanted. New employee Kendall Mahoney, who had joined Wine Babe Cellars, explained her ideas for marketing the new wines. And doing so now, not waiting until spring.

Then Kally showed the group the new labels, commissioned by the same artist who had designed the Jagger-interpretation label that had gotten her into so much trouble.

The bold designs with the song-infused names were a hit with the group. Guillaume, however, just shook his head.

Kally took a few days to show Guillaume the rest of Woodinville and Seattle. The three winemakers who had asked her to remove the crime-scene tape from Kirk's winery cornered Guillaume in one of their wineries and peppered him with questions about grape growing in France and his family's château.

Then they came to talk to him again at her winery. They stood near the tanks and got tips on barrel fermentation while they tasted through Kally's wines.

She heard them as she came out of her closet/office and saw Seth standing off to the side, watching and listening to the winemakers. Guillaume noticed him, too, and signaled to him to join them. And handed him a glass.

*What a nice gesture*, Kally thought. *But that's who you are, Guillaume.*

One night, after a day at Pike Place Market and a ferry ride to Bainbridge Island, Kally and Guillaume met Bud and A-Rod for dinner at a downtown Seattle restaurant with a view of the waterfront. The evening was superb, with Guillaume entertaining everyone with stories of growing up in France, his life in wine beginning at the age of five in vineyards and barrel rooms.

Listening to him reminded her that he wouldn't be here forever. But there was one more thing he had promised her: to help out at her big release party.

G uillaume stood at the tasting-room counter polishing wineglasses. It was two hours before the release and activity at the winery had ratcheted up. Flowers had been delivered, and Kendall strategically placed them around the winery. Servers were arriving to set up their tables. The Humane Society of Woodinville was there now with a large donation jar and a sign with happy dogs and cats: *Help us raise $10,000 for new crates and beds!*

*Nice. My own charity. Just like I planned.*

"Where do you want these?" Guillaume asked, pointing to the glasses.

"Put them back in the overhead rack, and also on the trays. We'll take from the trays first to serve people."

Guillaume had been so good at boosting sales that she would have him stand behind the counter again, serving. "How many are coming?" he asked.

"One never knows." Kally moved a case of her new red blend off the hand cart and behind the counter. "I imagine several hundred."

"Do you want any of those opened?" Guillaume inquired, nodding toward the case.

Kally laughed. *What a novel idea.* "Of course. Would you open six or seven?"

Kendall came around the corner from the production area. "Do you want flowers on every barrel or just on the tables?"

"Just on the tables."

"Okay," Kendall answered. "I wonder if any international guests will come."

Kally stopped what she was doing. "What do you mean?"

"I sent invitations to everyone, including your international list."

Kally thought about that and smiled. "Good!" Then: "What's Seth doing?"

"He's moving barrels out of the cold room."

"Okay, great."

Kally had timed the party set-up down to the minute. Once everything was ready, she and the rest of her group would disperse to Patterson Cellars to use the shower, the one lone shower in all of the Warehouse District.

Kally and Guillaume were set to do just that in a few minutes.

When the volunteer pourers began arriving, Kally motioned to Guillaume. "Let's go. The pourers will finish that."

Fifteen minutes before the party, Kally stood with Guillaume in the production area. She took in strategically placed tables, barrels with candles on them—not real candles but the ones you get at Costco that are on timers—trays of cheese and fruit and olives, and baskets of crackers. The servers were at their stations readying salmon sliders, mini pork tacos, vegetable lasagna, mac 'n' cheese, and kale salad. Then there was the chocolate table filled with brownies and an assortment of sea salt caramels.

It was looking very put together.

"Do you think you have enough wine out front?" Guillaume asked.

Kally thought about that. "Let's take more red out."

They each carried a case of Kally's red blend to the front and stashed them under the counter. Then Kally walked into the cold room from a side door, an entrance the pourers would use to get more cases of Crazy, Purple Haze, Star Gazing, and Gypzy.

Moving around in the cramped space she caught sight of a pallet of x-ed out boxes in back. It was her "fined wine," the wine she could never sell.

Kally inched her way toward them. She bent down and pulled out a bottle of her old blend, *My Cloud!* She blew dust from the neck of the bottle and took in the unmistakable image of a rock singer on the front.

"Yeah," Kally said. "That's really you."

She wiped more dust from the image, then stopped, remembering a conversation she'd had with Kirk when he'd come into her winery late one night looking for food.

*"Hi," Kirk said, letting the door slam behind him. He headed straight for her kitchen.*

*"Hi." Kally sat at her table, perusing her schedule, obsessing over her winery work.*

*"Don't you worry about lawsuits…with the names of all those songs you use?" she asked, his back to her as he rooted around in her refrigerator.*

*"No." He came out of the kitchen munching a cheese stick and walked up to where she was sitting, two more cheese sticks in hand. "Those artists are happy you're using their titles. They're flattered."*

*"Well, not Mick Jagger," she had answered.*

*"Pfff," Kirk said. "He didn't know anything about that…It was his law firm that sued you. I'll bet he doesn't even know who you are."*

Kally closed the lid on the case. It wasn't that long ago that she'd had that conversation. She stood up, taking a bottle of My Cloud! with her.

⸻

The British Airways flight from London arrived right on time in Seattle. A tall, lanky man with longish hair was the first to exit the plane. He made his way through the airport, an overnight bag in his hand, and some who recognized him stopped to stare.

After a long walk, he exited the terminal and looked for his limo and the driver holding the sign for his name: *Marvin Jenkins.*

⸻

Kally walked into the kitchen dodging servers and pourers as they readied food and wine for the party. She opened the Jagger wine.

"What's that?" Guillaume asked, walking up behind her.

"I want you to try this and tell me if I was on track when I started." She poured him a taste.

Guillaume looked at the color. He swirled the wine, sniffed, then tasted.

His eyebrows went up. "Oh yes!"

He sniffed again. "Southern Rhone. Grenache. Syrah?"

Kally nodded.

Guillaume reached for the bottle. He took in the image on the label, and smiled. "That really is him!"

# 107

E veryone arrived at once. Or so it seemed.
Wine Babe Cellars was packed, ten people deep at the tasting-room bar and at tables in the production area. All of Kally's friends, co-workers—even Riggs and his new lady friend—and the Woodinville wine community attended. As did her mother and brother. And Travis from the Tiger Creek recording studio.

Plus *Wine Hound* was there, posting and tweeting and reaching the world at large.

Seth, in charge of music, ensured that the band hired for the evening played only '60s and '70s songs.

And the band delivered, standing above the crowd from its makeshift stage situated between two tall stacks of barrels, the sounds and the songs getting louder as the evening progressed.

In a rare free moment, Kally cornered Guillaume near the kitchen.

"What did you say to me in French when we were in the cold room that day?"

"I said: 'There is no one else for me. No one will take your place.'"

But Kally didn't answer. A commotion was brewing out front. People in the production area were hurrying to the tasting room, an area she knew couldn't handle them all.

Kally and Guillaume joined them, jostled about until she saw the reason for the rush.

There, in the middle of her tasting-room floor, stood Mick Jagger, holding the sign *Martin Jenkins* in front of him.

"Kally O'Keefe? Pleased to meet you," he said. "Can you guess my name?"

Kally was speechless. Even the band had stopped playing and had joined the throng, which explained the sudden quietness.

Kally stuck out her hand. "I'm so very pleased to meet you!"

"I understand you have a bottle of wine with my likeness on it. Can I see it?"

"Yes! Let me get it."

Someone thoughtfully offered Mr. Jagger a glass of wine as Kally disappeared into her cold room.

"I'm not supposed to sell these," Kally explained as the crowd parted to let her back through.

"How much were you fined by my overzealous legal team?" Jagger asked. He reached for reading glasses from the pocket of a man standing next to him and put them on. Then he reached for the bottle.

Kally answered: "Actually, it was a hundred fifty thousand."

He looked at her, surprised. "We'll have to do something about that." Then he took in the label and laughed. He handed it back to her. "Excellent! Let's open it! Let's open them all!"

Others crowded forward to shake his hand.

"Seth!" Kally yelled. "Bring out more from the cold room!"

People crowded the tasting-room counter to try the wine. And Kally introduced Jagger to the band.

"Speaking of a band, I'm looking for another guitarist for our US tour. Any suggestions?"

Kally's brother, Phil, stood nearby, and Kally signaled him over.

"This man can play every one of your songs by heart."

Jagger put his hand on Phil's shoulder. "Let's try you out. Come on!"

The two moved to the production area and the stage, and Jagger and Phil joined the band that night, with Jagger leading the crowd in rousing renditions of early Stones' songs, including "Get Off of My Cloud!"

*This is not real*, Kally thought, watching them and Mindy with *Wine Hound*, her phone a permanent appendage in her hand as she snapped pictures and took videos for yet another wine story of the year.

108

The next day dawned bright and beautiful, and Kally would remember it for that.

As well as for the phone call.

Guillaume had gotten up early to fix breakfast. They were sitting at her dining room table discussing the party when his phone rang. He answered, then took his time responding, speaking in French.

Kally sipped her coffee and watched him. It was a long conversation, and he glanced at her periodically.

Guillaume had been in Seattle for two and a half weeks, and she had been wrapped up in him for every moment of it, even during mundane tasks like taking out the garbage, shopping for dinner, and getting supplies for the winery.

She'd gotten used to him being at her side.

He ended the call and looked at her. "I must leave."

Kally set her coffee cup down. Her heart raced. "Why?"

"We have a situation. In France. Our 1941 wine has been found."

He looked off into space. She watched him, deep in thought as he appeared to be.

"They are the long lost '41s," he added. "The lost vintage."

"Where were they?"

"In the ground, buried since World War II. They are still digging them out. You could help me there."

"I can't leave now, Guillaume!"

*Does he believe me?* She didn't know what to do.

"But what about France? What about us?" he asked.

381

Kally got up from the table. She folded her arms and walked into the living room.

Guillaume came up behind her. "We are a team. We can make great wine together."

Kally turned to look at him, then looked away, her eyes brimming with tears. "This wasn't supposed to happen."

"What wasn't supposed to happen?"

"*Us!* I was getting settled here when I went to France. I had a path." Her voice rose. She couldn't control it. "But my path is here, and meeting you complicated things. You complicate things." She shook her head. *That didn't come out right.*

"I want you in my life," Guillaume said. "How will we do that?"

Kally took in his beautiful face, taking in the person who had been by her side all these days. *I can't make this decision now.*

"We'll…work it out," was all she answered.

"Work it out," Guillaume repeated. He looked down. When he looked back at her, his face told her he was serious. "You must come to France. I will not come back." He paused. "I'm going to pack."

They walked together into the airport, having said nothing on the ride there. At the bottom of the escalator, Guillaume put his suitcase down and hugged her.

"*Je t'aime mon amour.*" *I love you, my love.*

He pulled her closer, stroking her hair.

Before Kally could respond, he picked up his suitcase and got on the escalator. At the top he paused, looked down at her, and smiled.

Someone bumped her, diverting her attention. When she looked back, Guillaume was gone.

She stood there, focusing on the space where he had been, now filling with others.

Kally swallowed hard and fought back tears.

She hadn't said she loved him.

109

Kally drove out of the airport and onto Interstate 5. She felt surreally numb as if she could bounce off the cars zooming past her, her last moments with Guillaume shrouded in fog.

She looked at her speedometer. She was driving twenty-five miles below the speed limit. She didn't know where she was going. But she knew she couldn't go home. Nor to her winery.

Kally saw a sign for South Seattle College and the Northwest Wine Academy and, without thinking, took the exit. She had been meaning to come here anyway to get answers about Kirk's wine, the one that had stopped fermenting at twenty-one Brix. There hadn't been a reason why the wine had stopped.

She plugged in her phone to charge it and heard a beep for voicemail.

> *"Hey, Kally. I mean Officer O'Keefe…this is Jessica Fellows. You called and asked about flowers at Art's Floral? So…yeah! I do remember the person who bought them because we started talking about football, and I think I mentioned the Seahawks and she said 'Yeah, I know all about the Seattle Seahawks.' And then she told me she'd been a cheerleader…"*

*Click.*
Kally ended the call, her hunch proven correct.
*Thank you, Jessica.*

# 110

She pulled into the Northwest Wine Academy's vast parking lot and found a space in front. And sat there a few moments to get her bearings. She hadn't been here since her humiliating failure in wine chemistry several years before.

But wine chemistry was the very reason she was here. And to get her mind off Guillaume. Even if just temporarily.

She got out and walked into the modern tasting room/classroom/ winery. On this Saturday afternoon, it was surprisingly empty. She looked for Bruce Vanderbruck, the wine chemistry teacher, and found him in his office at the rear of the building. He was reading something on his computer and turned to see who was standing in his doorway.

"Well, Kally O'Keefe. What a surprise!"

"Hi, Bruce."

"How's the wine business?"

"It's good," Kally answered, the numbness still with her.

"You don't look well."

"Oh…I just dropped someone at the airport."

"Come in and sit down."

Kally took a seat in front of his desk.

"What brings you here?"

"Can I ask you some questions? About wine chemistry?"

"Sure."

"You know I've been working the Kirk Remick case."

"Yes. I followed it closely. Such a shame about Kirk."

She nodded, then started in. "Can a dead body change the pH of a wine?"

He seemed to think that through. "You're talking about a body that hasn't yet decomposed?"

"Yes." She didn't want to think about the decomposing part.

"Then no."

"What about total acidity?"

He thought about that, too. "It would depend on secretions and the rate of decomposition. If the body was recently discovered after death, then no."

"Okay. Kirk's fermentation just stopped at twenty-one Brix. Why do you think that happened?"

Bruce sat back, and didn't say anything.

*Perhaps he is thinking of how he can answer in layman's language…very, very basic layman's language.*

"I would say he was fermenting with ambient yeast and the yeast wasn't strong enough," he said, finally. "He probably had high sugars. But, as you know, stopping at that high of a Brix is unusual. It has to be something else."

Kally nodded.

"Did you do a panel on the wine's chemistry?" Bruce asked.

"Yes."

"And?"

"Nothing was wrong."

"Did you try to start it again?"

"No. It was a crime scene. It just sat there."

"You could try."

Kally shook her head. "It's unusable now."

"Then throw it out."

But something wasn't sitting right. Kally didn't know enough about wine chemistry to ask anything further.

Bruce continued: "Let me offer a conjecture, since you appear to be out of options: Kirk's wine died because he died. I don't know what else it could be."

She didn't like the explanation, and was surprised that the top wine chemistry geek in all of Seattle would offer it. Nonetheless, she accepted it.

"Okay. So that's it, then. Death at 21 Brix. Well…" She rose from the chair.

Bruce added something else. "Why don't you come back and retake the course. It's only eleven classes."

"I would," she said, standing now at the door, "but I don't have time." She paused. "It's not the one night a week for class. It's all the other hours I have to spend studying. Because I don't *get* chemistry."

She took in the change in his demeanor, and while she couldn't know what he was thinking, she was sure it went something like this: *How can you not get chemistry? It's orderly. It's mathematical. It's life itself.*

Bruce nodded. "Well, you're making good wine. I read about you in *Wine Hound*."

Somehow, he was the last person she'd thought read *Wine Hound*.

B ack in her car, Kally sat there for a moment, her thoughts only on Guillaume. Then her phone rang.

"She's willing to talk."

Kally didn't recognize the voice at first. *Riggs.* Calling from… somewhere.

"Who?" she asked.

"Your friend"—let me rephrase that—"your nonfriend."

*Ellie.*

"She wants to give a statement and she wants you there." He paused. "I'll meet you downtown."

———

Kally, Riggs, and the county's prosecuting attorney, who had just informed them that they should not interrupt the accused while she spoke, sat on one side of the table in the small interrogation room at King County jail.

Time passed, with no sign of Ellie Fishback or her lawyer. Riggs, out of Kally's view on the other side of the attorney, drummed his fingers on the table, in no particular rhythm. The attorney himself sat ramrod straight, a gold pen poised in his left hand, ready to begin.

Kally took in a highly starched white cuff peeking out from the prosecutor's navy blue suit. Tall, balding, bespectacled, and obviously well educated, he was not an attorney she knew. Nor did Riggs, from the gist of the introductions earlier.

She looked up at the clock. Guillaume would be in the air now. She struggled to remain on-point, and looked down at her hands resting in her lap.

The door opened.

Ellie and her lawyer, the same one who had been at the Fishback home, walked in. Ellie wore an orange jumpsuit, standard issue, and was unshackled. They sat, Ellie directly across from her. Her blonde hair was pulled back, and she wore no makeup. And she looked older, her normally toned skin not quite so smooth now.

Kally met her gaze.

*Unreadable.*

"My client is prepared to give a statement about the evening and the events surrounding the death of Mr. Kirk Remick," Ellie's attorney began. "She will not take any questions."

The prosecuting attorney leaned forward and pushed a button on a tape recorder. He spoke into it, listing the day, place, and time, and identified the five people in the room.

"Please proceed, Mrs. Fishback," he added.

Ellie sat forward and folded her hands, resting one on top of the other. And stared straight at Kally.

"I did not kill him," Ellie began. "But I know who did. I was there when it happened."

*So I was right about her being in the room.*

Ellie hesitated for a moment and looked away, then met Kally's eyes again.

"I don't know the exact time, but I believe it was after midnight. The party was over. There were only a few people left. I was the last person to enter."

She paused. "I came back to Kirk's winery because…I wanted to stop my husband from harming Kirk. I had been seeing Kirk for five years. Jim only recently found out about us."

The surprise must have registered on Kally's face. It meant Kirk was with Ellie for the entire duration of his marriage to Janie.

*How awful. For Janie.*

"Jim took my syringe of $CO_2$ and was going to use it as a weapon." She stopped. "How did you know I had a syringe at home?"

The question threw Kally. She was about to answer, but then remembered their attorney's directive.

Ellie shook her head. "Never mind. When I came back to the winery that night, I was walking behind Jim. But he was too far ahead of me. I called out to him, but he wouldn't stop. We came inside, and I saw Kirk standing near one of his bins." She looked down at the table top for a moment. "Mark Manning was on one side of him, and Richard Fugelson and Elliott Jansen from RMP were on the other. Kirk was talking to Richard. It looked like they were having an argument. But I wasn't really listening."

*How odd to have past and present lovers arguing in front of you.*
*But not about you.*

"I was only aware I wasn't going to stop Jim," Ellie said. "He was too far ahead of me."

Ellie hesitated for a moment, obviously right back at the scene, the silence among the five at the table palpable.

"I heard Richard say, 'What are you doing here?' And then Jim lunged forward. Kirk put his hand up. The syringe went into his palm."

Ellie stopped again. She cleared her throat. "Kirk yelled, 'What the hell!' He started to pull out the syringe, but Mark Manning hit Kirk's arm away and made sure the syringe stayed in his hand."

Kally leaned forward to look at Riggs.

Ellie went on. "I didn't know Mark had that much strength. He and Kirk wrestled backwards away from the bin. Suddenly Kirk went down on one knee. The syringe fell on the floor. And his hands clenched up."

Ellie had clenched her fists and Kally saw that she was crying.

"And then he fell over, face first on the floor. Jim walked up to him. He calmly picked up the syringe and walked out. And RMP followed. And then I left."

Ellie cleared her throat again and looked down at her lap. She strained to keep her voice level. "I never went up to him. I never touched him. I just walked away." She looked up at Kally, her eyes filled with tears. "Jim intended to kill Kirk. But so did Mark Manning."

Ellie's attorney put her hand up and the prosecuting attorney turned off the recorder. Kally glanced again at Riggs who was staring intently at Ellie.

Ellie and her attorney got up and left. It was a few moments before anyone spoke. The prosecuting attorney broke the silence.

"So here's what we know going forward," he began. "The accused has implicated everyone in the room that night. Mrs. Fishback cannot legally testify against her husband. But the other two men she can testify against. They will be served, but it remains to be seen what their attorneys will ask for in exchange for their testimony. For Mr. Fishback, we are looking at premeditation and aggravated murder. For Mr. Manning, second-degree murder." He turned to Kally. "Is any of what the accused said to you a surprise?"

Riggs shot her a glance, no doubt a reminder to not say anything about the recording taken at the restaurant.

"Yes," she answered. "A winemaker involved in the death of another winemaker."

"Do you think she was telling the truth?" he asked.

"Yes," Kally said again.

The attorney nodded. "Let's get our warrants and bring in the rest of the people. *Today.*"

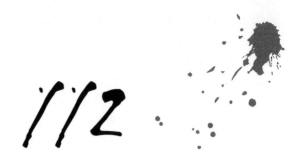

# 112

Kally and Riggs arrested Richard Fugelson and Elliott Jansen as well as Mark Manning. For the second time in as many weeks, Manning was read his Miranda rights and taken to the King County jail.

After bidding good-bye to Riggs, Kally drove home, heading south on Interstate 5 to Interstate 90 and the bridge across Lake Washington. She had been wrong about Manning. He had done more than just witness the crime. He had participated in it.

*How did I miss that?*

She didn't think he had it in him, to kill another human being.

*That's where I made my mistake.*

As the last person in the room, Manning must have dragged Kirk's body to the bin—sweeping off the protective sheet on top of it—placed Kirk over it, and pushed his face into the must. If Kirk had been alive, he wouldn't have remained so for long. But Nakamura's autopsy report showed no liquid nor any particulate matter in the lungs. Kirk Remick had already died. He died on the floor of his winery.

For Jim Fishback and the two attorney-principals in RMP, their legal careers were over, as were any grape expectations about outdoing Chateau Ste. Michelle. She wondered how Fishback and Manning would plead against the charge of murder, each an equal participant in Kirk's death. Would one blame the other for the crime?

And what about Ellie? She would remain in jail but certainly would not receive the severity of the sentence that was sure to hit her husband. Kally didn't know about Ellie or what was to come following all of this.

*Couldn't you have saved Kirk?*

*Couldn't you have called 911?*

She thought back to what Riggs had said to her early on, valuable information about solving a crime:

Something from nothing...

A source out of nowhere...

Everyone is a suspect...

Saying nothing is a sin of omission...

You never have all the answers.

Riggs was especially right about that last one.

*But you can get pretty close.*

Kally unlocked the door to her condo and entered, closing it behind her. It was quiet, empty, just as she thought it would be, magnified by Guillaume's absence.

*Was it just this morning that you were here?*

She looked at the plates from breakfast still on the dining room table. Her unfinished coffee was there, too. She walked into the bedroom. Guillaume had left a tee shirt behind on the unmade bed, the one she had bought him, with a University of Washington husky on the front.

She sat down and picked it up, hugging it to her chest. And began crying all over again.

*What am I going to do?*

K ally stared at the calendar on her phone. In less than twenty-four hours, she had erased three weeks of "have-to-dos," including dinners with friends, wine-pouring events, mother visits, a dental procedure, a play, a concert, etc.

For the time being, Seth and Jason would take over winemaking. Riggs would assume her place in court, at the arraignment of the five involved in the death of Kirk Remick. And Bud would take on the rest of her work.

Again.

Her boss, Dale, had been surprisingly lenient in her request for three weeks off. He gave her two, along with one week without pay.

"You're our wine expert," he had said, making her promise to come back. "We need you, especially in this town."

As soon as she began telling workmates, family, and friends about her plans, she knew she had made the right decision. It wasn't forever, she reminded them. It was a trip for her and Guillaume to determine how they could live their lives together while maintaining residences on separate continents.

Everyone seemed to understand.

She thought back to her wine release party. It had been a huge success. How could it not be with one of the most recognizable rock singers in the world gracing the event. They'd made a sizable dent in the Jagger wine. And sales for her new vintage were off the charts.

She had been especially surprised at Jagger's donation of $150,000 to the Human Society of Woodinville.

And so now, here she was…sitting…waiting…

Someone stopped at her seat and Kally looked up.

"*Bon jour!* Can I offer you a sample of wine before we leave? We have a very nice Bordeaux. Or perhaps something else?"

Kally took in the woman's Air France name tag. "Why, yes, Denise. Do you have a selection from the southern Rhône, preferably a Grenache/Syrah blend with a little 'ved thrown in?"

"We have a Châteauneuf-du-Pape. Will that do?"

"Of course! That is an excellent choice!"

The wine was delicious. It wasn't Château Tablet but it was good nonetheless. Kally finished the two ounce sample, and Denise whisked the glass away.

She turned off her phone and set it on her lap, and felt the plane lurch back from the gate. Kally put her head back and closed her eyes.

She couldn't wait to see the surprised look on Guillaume's face.

They would work everything out.

She was sure of it.

Somewhere over the Arctic Circle, the calls came in and went straight to voicemail:

> *"Miss O'Keefe? This is Samuel Everett at Ashworth Collins Dellmar and Crane in Houston. We are of counsel for the singer/ songwriter Willie Nelson. We have a court order that you cease and desist using the word 'Crazy' on your wine label."*

> *"Miss Kally O'Keefe? This is Sarah von Klingle at Ackman Cline Dougherty and Cross in Los Angeles. We represent the band Fleetwood Mac and have become aware of a wine from your winery titled 'Gypzy.' We would like to discuss an immediate name change with you, as the one used with the microphone on your label may be proprietary. Please call me directly. Thank you."*

*"Miss O'Keefe? This is Henry Bremerton at Argyle Codman Dinwitty and Clayborne in London. We represent the estate of the late Mr. David Bowie. It has come to our attention that a certain wine by the name of 'Ground Control' produced by Wine Babe Cellars in Woodinville, Washington, infringes on the copyright of one of our client's songs...*

*"Haven't we spoken with you before?"*

# THE END

68387930R00241

Made in the USA
Middletown, DE
16 September 2019